Good Karma is the Best Revenge

Bleue Rose

Sequel to The Rogue Tangerine Tablet

Good Karma is the Best Revenge
Bleue Rose

Sequel to The Rogue Tangerine Tablet

ISBN: 978-1-7338194-2-8
ISBN: 978-1-7338194-3-5 (e)

Published by
Bleue Rose
BleueRose.com
BleueRoseNovels IG

Because of the dynamic nature of the Internet, any web addresses or links contained in this book may have changed since publication and may no longer be valid.

Printed by Ingram Spark

Dedication

To Josh and Julia,
May your imagination always run wild.

Art is not what you see,
But what you make others see.
--Edgar Degas

Prologue

The greatness of a man is not how much wealth he acquires,
but in his ability to affect those around him positively.
--Bob Marley

Contents

CHAPTER I

Narrow Escape to Paradise

Carlos Ortiz awoke from an exhaustion-fueled slumber, utterly disoriented. Through eyelid slits, he surveyed his surroundings, trying to assess his whereabouts. His focus rested on a woman in uniform and the continual, tranquilizing hum of an engine in motion. It took him a few seconds to remember he was on an Air France flight from Paris to Nassau, with a brief stopover in Havana.

"Would you like your meal now, sir? I believe you chose option three."

Looking into the hazelnut eyes of the flight attendant, he flinched. Reality was crystallizing. It took him a moment to find his words. His lips were cracked, and his eyes bone dry. He cleared some phlegm, ran his tongue over his lips, and blinked twice before speaking.

"Yes, thank you. May I have a bottle of water too, please?"

"Sure thing. I'll be right back," she assured him.

Carlos pulled out his snack table and the attendant placed the tray in front of him before she disappeared down the aisle again. He was ravenous. His hasty departure for the Paris airport had left him no time for lunch. After he purchased his airline ticket, checked his luggage, cleared security, and executed several urgent business transactions on his laptop, it was close to boarding time. Luckily, the passport check had transpired without a hiccup. Too stressed to feel hunger, Carlos had entered the plane and immediately collapsed in his first-class seat.

Now, more than half way into his flight, his stomach was sending out distress signals. He looked at the *croque monsieur* with field greens and cut a giant-sized bite. Satisfied, he slumped back into his reclined window seat and chewed away with gusto. The oozing premium cheese enhanced with *bechamel* sauce melted in his mouth. He closed his eyes and savored the distinct taste of rich ingredients, thankful the choices weren't limited to vegan fare. Between bites, he popped refreshing grapes into his mouth, relishing their sweet, moist texture. Freedom never tasted so good.

Raising the shade, he peered downward past a sea of intermittent clouds to the vast Atlantic Ocean. The sun began to rise and the glorious scarlet sky morphed into a show-spectacular view. Carlos thought of Helena, wishing he could share this moment with her. Leaving Helena Majewski, the love of his life behind was devastating. The thought of no longer being able to share special moments let alone everyday life with her, seared his heart. However, his unscheduled, urgent departure from their shared Paris apartment was unavoidable. He hoped she would understand his dilemma when she realized he wasn't coming home. Nobody would know how much his heart truly ached for her, except Helena. No one had been privy to their unique relationship.

One of these days, when the news aged and danger passed, he would reach out to her, and to his sister, Hermosa Ortiz in Mexico City. He would arrange for their safe passage back into his life. He paused. Who was he kidding? The danger would never subside for him as long as the Flores family was alive. You don't just decide to leave a Mexican drug smuggling ring and live with abandon.

Once Fernando Flores realized major funds were missing, along with his trusted accountant, his people would be on Carlos's ass in a heartbeat. Carlos would be looking over his shoulder for the rest of his life, unless the Flores brothers and their dangerous cousin, Jose, went to jail. Even then, he had to be mindful of the extended family. No, he would never be entirely free, nor would he ever be able to go back to his native Mexico again. That was his cross, his inevitably chosen fate.

Being raised in a cartel environment had cost him his parents and jeopardized his sister Hermosa, as well as himself. There was never a choice of what his future held. He counted his blessings, he had worked primarily as an accountant for F&S Enterprises. His father recognized his gift for numbers early on and encouraged his education and certification in accounting. He understood that his son, like him, didn't have the stomach for brute work. Splurging on an accounting education for his son had unknowingly been his parting gift, for which Carlos was forever grateful. In turn, Carlos did the same for his sister. Selling family assets, after his father's death, sealed his and Hermosa's future with marketable accounting skills.

Today marked the beginning of his realized dream of cutting loose from the cartel, breaking away and leaving that life behind. He was looking forward to starting fresh with the hard-earned money he'd carefully stashed away over the past decade. His finance skills had served him well and allowed for private, smart investments.

Unexpectedly, his own money was supplemented by cartel money. Emptying Flores's business accounts, money he had been in charge of, had not been part of his original plan, but rather a split-second decision. While he sat at the Paris airport waiting to depart, Carlos made the bold move, transferring additional funds to unmarked accounts. He then emptied them by sending carefully crafted money grams to designated pick up points in the Caribbean.

The French and Spanish governments would have frozen those assets, anyway. It was money already lost to the Flores clan.

Regardless, Carlos seriously doubted Fernando Flores would see it that way. Hopefully, he would never find out first-hand what Fernando really thought. He deserved that money, Carlos rationalized. He had earned it through years of heartbreaking personal loss and the struggle to educate himself and his sister, so they wouldn't have to settle. Skillfully maintaining two sets of books for the Flores family business had been lucrative.

Losing his father as an innocent child and seeing his mother die of heartache, worry and hard labor, had molded him into the man he was. It drove him to change his and his beloved sister's life. One of his airport transactions had included sending a sizable chunk of untraceable money to Hermosa's account. He wouldn't be able to send her monthly checks anymore, but he knew she would understand when she heard the news reports. As these thoughts raced through his mind, he felt sad Hermosa would be worried for him.

Carlos fingered the edge of his new passport in the breast pocket of his starched, white shirt. The passport was an interim document to ensure safe travels and to allow him to secure his funds upon arrival. Another passport, hidden in his carry-on, would provide a permanent identity later on. He was pleased with the new name he had chosen for himself. Casimir Santos had a nice ring to it.

His plan was to retire the Julio Lopez passport as soon as all the funds and money-grams were retrieved. Only then would he transition to the Casimir Santos identity. The passports had cost him dearly, but they were worth every penny to cover his tracks. Thankfully, one had gotten him out of Paris unscathed. So far, his premeditated exit plan was working. He took a deep breath and exhaled a muffled whistle through his teeth. Stress was a killer.

CHAPTER II

Bahamian Trust or Not?

The brief stop in Cuba had gone smoothly. After Europe, the Havana airport was small and impressively red. Castro's favorite color. Since he had time to kill between flights, Carlos popped his head outside and marveled at all the colorful 1950's cars lined up, waiting for fares. Briefly, he imagined himself caught in a time loop from his grandfather's era. He decided to come back one day to explore this contentious island.

When the Air France plane touched down in Nassau, Carlos uttered an abbreviated prayer. Concurrently, with his forefinger, he configured the sign of the cross from his damp forehead to his rapidly beating heart and from shoulder to ripped shoulder. He was here, and he felt like kissing the ground.

Within twenty minutes of his arrival in Nassau, he retrieved his suitcases from the carousel and flagged a cab, instructing the driver to take him to The Cove at the Atlantis Resort. The Paradise Island hotel had looked beautiful online; he couldn't wait to immerse himself. His heart pounded as they drove up to the mammoth structure, his eyes feasting on the grand open-air lobby and its colorful, tropical surroundings. It was more spectacular than he anticipated.

Checking into an ocean-view suite, he threw himself onto the luxurious bed, closing his tired, red-rimmed lids. A few deep meditative breaths calmed him as he reveled in his incredible luck. The fact that he had made it out of Paris without complication or delay, was astounding. His timely research and well-oiled exit plan had saved him from a life behind bars or one chained to the Flores family, both equally intolerable. Every second had been crucial to his escape. However, he couldn't take his success for granted. Now, he needed to work on becoming invisible. He was a hunted man. Changing his name was only step one.

Swinging his legs off the bed, he walked to the wall of windows, and pulled the sliding doors open to admire the postcard view. A gentle ocean breeze caressed his face and cooled his damp body. He could feel his stress dissipate into the sweet ocean air as he took in the layered shades of turquoise, teal and cornflower blue as far as his eyes could travel. White sails and colorful paddle boats dotted the water close to the beach. Closing his eyes for a few seconds, he let the salt dust settle on his taut, shadowed skin. How he had missed that sensation!

He contemplated his next important move. Tomorrow he would go to the bank and open new accounts. It would be wise to disperse funds immediately, but for the rest of the day, he would enjoy what the Atlantis had to offer. His thoughts drifted to Helena. He wished she was here with him. Paradise Island was missing one important component, love.

Carlos locked his valuables into the suite's safe and changed into bathing trunks and a short- sleeved, crisp white linen shirt. He turned on the TV, cranking up the sound, and put on his sunglasses and a baseball cap. Carefully, he closed the door to his suite and hung the 'Do Not Disturb' sign on the handle. Striding through the lobby, he marveled at the generous space interspersed with huge columns. He looked down each hallway that promised to take him on new paths of discovery, but opted for a trip through the gardens. He intended to enjoy his stay here until he decided on his next destination. Walking past the populated pools, he took in the overwhelming sea of sunbathers and headed directly to the beach, grabbing a towel from a waiting pool attendant as he passed.

Dropping his few belongings onto the sand, he fingered the room key in the Velcro-sealed pocket of his bathing trunk and decided it was safest there. He ran straight into the beautiful turquoise surf, keeping one watchful eye on his towel bundle at the waters' edge. The warm water and fading sun's rays stroked his strong body into submission. Relaxing his chiseled muscles, he floated on his back for a long while. How much he had missed beaches like this while living land-locked in Europe.

His thoughts traveled to Mexico and his childhood in Tampico. It made him sad to think of his deceased parents and his displaced sister in Mexico City. He had fond memories of family beach days, of time spent together on a small boat, his father's one material joy. The years had passed so quickly, but at least he had memories to hold on to. They were his to keep and safeguard, which he did, locking them in the deep recesses of his brain where they could no longer hurt him. He let his mind drift to his current surroundings and his more immediate plans. Dwelling on what he left behind on two continents was too unsettling to ponder.

The next morning, Carlos slept in and ate breakfast in his room. Traversing the lobby to the traffic circle, he rented a car and driver for the day and headed straight to the bank. By lunch time he had settled most of his initial financial transactions to his satisfaction. The money grams were all successfully collected and placed into corporate accounts. In due time, he would transfer a portion of the money into additional accounts with different corporate names, once he was established somewhere. He decided to hold onto the Julio Lopez passport instead of shredding it. He opened a safety deposit box and threw it inside with two-hundred-and-fifty- thousand Euro in cash and a few other acquired IDs. Being prepared was key to his survival.

His stomach started to rumble, so he stopped for lunch in town. His inner clock had adapted to Bahamian time rather quickly, particularly when it came to meals. After lunch, he went on a shopping spree for basics. He bought himself two bathing trunks, some lightweight shirts, several trousers, a straw Panama hat, and a waterproof wallet.

When he returned to the hotel, he made a hair appointment for the late afternoon. Dropping his purchases in his room, he headed to the outdoor restaurant with his laptop and ordered an iced coffee. Two young women seated at the table next to him turned to nod and smile. They looked to be around his age, in their early to mid-thirties. Carlos returned the nod and averted his eyes, offering no smile in return.

Paranoia was setting in. He pulled down the front of his baseball cap and hoped they didn't recognize him from the news. Scanning his computer for articles on Fernando and Jose Flores, he was appeased. So far, he hadn't seen anything incriminating about himself in connection to the police raid on F&S Enterprises in Barcelona and Paris. Carlos was thrilled to read that Jose had been arrested on his way to the Barcelona airport. He chuckled when he read, Jose's beloved jewelry, a large Mexican silver and turquoise cross, had tipped off the agent, rather than his picture on the wanted bulletin. Jose's unlikely sentimentality had tripped him up in his flight out of town. How ironic!

Fernando Flores, unfortunately, remained at large. Carlos instantly surmised Fernando must have eluded the European police, much like himself, by executing a quick, pre-planned escape. He was most likely safe, back in Mexico with his family. The Flores family ruled Tampico. Fernando would be lying low somewhere until another case became more urgent. No extradition law would send Fernando back to Barcelona from Tampico. The Mexican police had been bought years ago.

"Damn," he muttered out loud. Carlos closed his laptop and walked to his hair appointment, ignoring the girls' stares.

"Hello, Mr. Santos. My name is Annie. Are you here for a trim or a cut today?"

Carlos took off his baseball cap. The hair stylist undid his ponytail and ran her fingers though his thick, shiny, shoulder-length, black hair.

"I would like to get a stylish cut. I'm in the mood for a change. What do you suggest?"

"Right. Let me show you a few pictures. How brave are you? Are we going short?" Annie smiled.

"Yes," Carlos replied hesitantly. Helena had always loved his long hair. The hair stylist showed him a few pictures and he pointed to a style with razor cut sides and a longish, cropped top.

"This style, please."

"Perhaps we can add a few highlights to give the top some dimension," Annie suggested.

Carlos flinched. That wasn't anything he would normally agree to. After a slight hesitation he replied.

"Ok. Go for it, Annie."

Before too long, Annie had worked her magic. Carlos couldn't believe the transformation, but somehow it worked. He actually liked it, blond highlights and all. Annie had incorporated them sparingly, tips only. The finished product looked tastefully executed.

"Look at how hot you look. The girls at the salon window are giving you their sign of approval." Annie laughed.

Carlos turned his head and noticed the girls from the restaurant, looking at him, thumbs pointed upward. He broke into a rare half smile. His transformation had begun. He would use the nickname Casi, he decided spontaneously.

"Hello, Casi" he said to himself in the mirror.

CHAPTER III

Three is Company....Sometimes

The following morning, while still in bed, Casi checked for additional news articles. As suspected, all F&S Enterprise accounts were frozen and the assets seized. The Paris restaurant he managed was closed as was the Barcelona restaurant Fernando and Jose oversaw. The warehouse in Barcelona that housed their import/export ceramic business was under police control and their ship, the *Corazon de Leones*, had been impounded. Fernando's harbor apartment in Barcelona was most likely lost. Casi was happy he had transferred the deed to his apartment in Paris to Helena, months ago. She must have discovered that by now. He wished he could have done more for her. The deed for the Monaco apartment he had transferred to a corporation owned by Felipe, Fernando's brother and better half. He felt good about that decision. It was his way of saying farewell.

The strain of drugs found on the ship and in the warehouse was identified as the cause of numerous deaths around European cities, including Susanna Svelte, the A list movie star who overdosed at the Berlin Film Festival. Pictures of the Flores brothers and Jose were plastered all over the news, but oddly, Carlos's name wasn't mentioned. "Only a matter of time," Casi thought. He could feel serious tension returning to his gut.

Casi picked up the phone and booked a massage for himself, then got dressed and went down to breakfast. Having skipped dinner the night before, he opted for the buffet. After enjoying a hearty meal, he walked to the beach and secured a chaise. Lying comfortably, he spotted the two women from the previous day. They were soaking up the sun in tiny bikinis. He felt a stir. Flinging his sunglasses onto his beach chair, he ran into the water. He couldn't remember the last time someone, other than Helena, got a rise out of him. Helena had satisfied his every need, and more. In his mind, most women paled next to her. When he came out of the water, the two women were standing at the waters' edge. They waved as he emerged.

"Nice haircut you got yesterday. It looks hot," said the blonde girl in the red floral bikini.

"Thank you. It was time for a change."

"Where are you from?" the brunette asked. Casi casually surveyed her skimpy, sky blue and white polka dot bikini.

"Mexico City," he lied. "How about you?"

"We're from Sweden. This is Alva, and my name is Elin. Are you alone on vacation?"

"Yes. You?"

"We came together. We've been here for a week, and we'll be leaving the day after tomorrow. Do you care to join us for dinner tonight?"

"Sure, why not?" The minute he uttered those words he felt regret. Should he be doing this? He couldn't stop himself, though. He needed some human interaction and these girls were beautiful and nice, not unlike Helena.

"My name is Casi." He extended his strong hand, firmly shaking Elin's, then Alva's.

"Nice to meet you, Casi. Shall we meet in the Cove lobby around 7:30pm?"

"Ok, thanks. I'll see you later." He smiled as he gathered up his few belongings and headed back to his room. He needed to find the hotel's gym to work off some steam.

At 7:30pm sharp, Casi exited the elevator, dressed in his new clothes, casual royal blue slacks and a white linen shirt. He felt like a million bucks, but technically, he was worth a whole lot more. Alva and Elin arrived five minutes later, sporting feminine summer dresses. It appeared they liked what they saw and Casi reciprocated with a genuine smile as he surveyed them.

"You both look very nice tonight."

"Thank you," they replied in unison, returning his smile.

"So, where are we going? Do you have a destination in mind?"

"I made a reservation in one of the hotel restaurants. Follow us." Elin pointed and started walking. Casi studied the girls from behind. They were both pretty, nothing like Helena in terms of sex appeal, but certainly welcome dinner companions. Over dinner and various rum-based drinks, they chatted about travel--life in Europe versus Mexico and the warm hospitality of the Bahamians. A few hours later, Casi paid for their meals, and they left the restaurant together. Outside, he waited patiently while the girls had a brief verbal exchange in Swedish.

"Casi, would you like to come up to our room for a drink?" Elin asked.

"We have a nice bottle of rose' on ice," Alva added.

"Sure. Lead the way." While he had no interest in more drinks, Casi found it hard to say no. "What could possibly be the down side of this invitation," he thought.

"Great. We're in The Cove too. Room 316."

Once in the room, things evolved quickly. Seated in the only armchair, lights dimmed, Casi studied the two girls sprawled on the bed. They were attractive, each in their own way. Elin was a striking brunette with an infectious smile and Alva, a curvy blonde with baby blues, sensuous lips and a ton of reckless freckles. He was pleased to be in their presence, but felt somewhat displaced. Elin handed Casi a glass and probingly ran her finger tips up his muscular arm. Alva poured wine into his glass and touched his hair. He smiled.

"Your new haircut is quite a turn on."

"Thank you. Had I known, I might have cut it sooner." He winked at Alva. She poured some wine into two more glasses and handed one to Elin.

"Cheers," she said as they all clinked glasses.

"*Skal,*" Elin replied, winking back.

Casi took a polite sip and set his glass down on the floor. Usually, he preferred tequila or champagne, but he had to admit, the fruity rose' was refreshing. He waited for their next move, knowing it was coming. Elin drained her wine glass and walked to where Casi was seated. He looked at her in anticipation. She didn't disappoint.

Boldly, she ran her fingers from his cheek, down his neck and along his chest where his shirt parted, traveling down to his crotch. As she leaned in Casi could see her soft, white breasts in the plunging neckline of her flimsy dress. He looked up from her cleavage straight into her eyes, giving his approval with a lazy smile. Leaning back into his chair, resting his head, he spread his legs a little further apart, inviting her into the fold. He felt Alva massage his shoulders and without warning she leaned over from behind and surprised him with a kiss on the lips. It was a soft sensuous kiss and he could feel his body react. He let Elin unzip his pants, revealing his steady rise.

Never taking her eyes off Casi, Elin seductively unbuttoned the front of her dress revealing a lacy, hot pink bra. With his full attention, she let the dress dramatically plummet to the floor, revealing matching bikini panties. Casi's interest, along with other body parts, peaked.

Each woman took one of Casi's hands and nudged him out of his pants and off the armchair toward the bed. While Elin unbuttoned his shirt, Alva peeled off his bulging underwear. He stepped out of the fabric puddle on the floor and reached for Elin. Casi unhooked her bra and guided her onto the bed with him. While he concentrated on Elin's small, perfect breasts, Alva, now completely nude, explored his lower body parts from behind with surprisingly skillful hands. Casi groaned. This was his first threesome and he intended to go with the flow. Usually, he was in charge, but being out-numbered, he didn't know where to turn first, so he let the girls take charge.

Hours later, around four in the morning, totally spent, Casi awoke with a strong need to pee. The girls didn't stir. Picking up his scattered clothes off the floor, he quietly dressed in the suite's bathroom. Once clothed, he opened the door and peered down the empty hallway. The girls didn't notice him slip out. Smiling, Casi walked to the elevator and pressed the up button, basking in the afterglow of a night well spent. So far, he was enjoying his new life.

CHAPTER IV

Springtime in Paris....Ain't No Sunshine, When Love is Lost.

Summer Crenston, her cinematographer, Hope Hoshino and her producer, Ted Braxton were having Sunday brunch in their Airbnb penthouse apartment on rue Malher in Paris. It was a mild, early May morning and Summer reveled in the warm rays flooding through the glass terrace doors into their cozy country kitchen. Ted's potted herb garden was sending fragrant scent darts through the open windows. The fresh spring perfume from blossoming trees mixed remarkably well with the aromatic coffee, warmed French bread, creamed butter, and the strawberry rhubarb jam they were enjoying. The tantalizing mix of fragrances lulled their senses, creating a wonderfully relaxed, lazy mood. Classical music filled the air while light traffic buzzed in the background. Paris in springtime was phenomenal, especially on a rare sunny day.

"Ted, what did the de Fontenays say about letting us extend another month?" Summer stretched long arms over a golden head.

"They weren't thrilled, but they said they would work with us. They don't want to wait a full month, though. We'll pay them directly since the Airbnb will be over."

"No problem. Hope, do you think we can finish shooting in one to two weeks?"

"Absolutely, if we don't have any more rain delays. Even a one or two-week extension could make all the difference, especially if we have to reshoot a scene." Hope looked at the open calendar.

"Maybe we should ask for two weeks to be safe. If we only need one, great. What do you think, guys?"

"We can make it work, Summer, but I don't know if they'll go for that. I'll email them."

"Agreed," Hope voiced, sipping her coffee.

"Tomorrow my mom comes back from visiting my brother in Barcelona. And the following week Jasper is leaving Barcelona for good and coming to stay with Samson for his final week in Europe before he and mom fly back to New York. I want to spend time with them. It'll be great to have both my brothers in Paris, but if we don't finish shooting, I won't be able to enjoy their visit. I pray we don't have any more rain or drama." Summer sighed. "By the way, guys, Helena's boyfriend, Carlos, has disappeared off the face of the earth. She's really in a funk about it, so that could mean a possible delay as well. So far, she's been dependable, despite our constant schedule changes. I hope she can hang in and work through her heartache."

"I doubt that will be a problem, Summer. She's totally professional." Hope offered, sliding her feet into her embroidered Chinese slippers.

"She better be," Ted grimaced.

Summer knew Ted still didn't trust Helena even though she hadn't given him any reason not to. The fact that Summer's film was Helena's first leading role had Ted on his toes, but Summer felt Helena was easy to direct. Her willingness to please made her a pleasure to work with.

"So, what is everyone up to today?" Summer looked around the table.

"I'm meeting Jean-Michel to go see the new exhibit at Beaubourg."

Summer watched a smile spread over Ted's face. Just talking about his French lover made Ted's golden features soften and his tall, lanky frame loosen.

"I'll be looking at recently shot footage, hopefully, with you, Summer, then around 4 pm, I'm out of here. I have a date with that cute guy I met the other night."

"Oh, good. In that case, let's get cracking, Hope. Don't want to impinge on your social progress."

"Good, because I really like this guy."

Summer rolled her eyes. "That's what you always say."

CHAPTER V

Chickens Always Return to the Coup

When Cara Crenston's plane landed in Paris, after a long weekend in Barcelona with her oldest son Jasper, she finally felt at peace. Jasper was coming back to New York with her, following a tumultuous year and a half in Spain. She was thrilled. They had spent the weekend packing and shipping his belongings. The *coup de gras* of the weekend was when Inspector Abello, one of Barcelona's police chiefs, visited Jasper's office at the bank and returned Cara's stolen tangerine tablet. She was simultaneously overjoyed and shocked. She never expected to see her tangerine dream again. It was stolen in a Paris café while she and Jasper had a working breakfast last vacation. Who would have thought the Flores goons would extend their reach that far? To reclaim the tablet in Jasper's office in Barcelona was just mind boggling! To add insult to injury, Fernando Flores had copied and exported her ceramic picture files. The nerve of that crook! She wasn't sure if she should be flattered or outraged although secretly she felt a tad flattered. She vowed to continue to check his website for blatant copies. His ceramic factory was adept at 'borrowing' other artist's designs making only the slightest change. Unethical, but certainly not criminal.

Cara relaxed in the back of the taxi as she rode from the airport to Francois Fereaux's penthouse apartment. She knew Summer was busy working and Cara was dying to see her dreamy French boyfriend as much as possible before she had to return to New York. When Francois opened the door and spread his arms, she swooped right in, snaking her long limbs around his neck.

"I missed you. It feels so good to be back." She leaned her head back and studied his hazel eyes.

"I missed you too, cherie. Let's get you a glass of wine and you can tell me all about your trip."

"Sounds lovely. What smells so terrific?"

"I made us dinner. *Moules marinieres* or, as you would say, mussels in white wine broth. Are you hungry?"

"I am now. That smells heavenly. Can we turn on the news? I want to see if there's anything new regarding the Flores crooks."

"You are such a romantic," Francois teased.

CHAPTER VI

Bittersweet Goodbyes….Even Sangria Can't Remedy

Jasper was glad he decided to stay in Barcelona for an additional week after his mom left. He needed to tie up some loose ends at the Rothchild Bank, his workplace for the past year and a half. It had been a tough decision not to renew his contract, but after his boss, Adriano Aldana, was murdered, Jasper no longer felt comfortable or safe. Overall, his Barcelona experience had been a good one, despite the recent mind-bending events.

A crooked ceramics import/export business, *Corazon de Leon,* linked to a Mexican drug cartel, had been laundering money through Jasper's workplace, his boss being their chosen banker. The Barcelona side of the operation was now in jail, but unfortunately, the mastermind, Fernando Flores, had escaped arrest. Jasper, unwittingly, helped the Flores group make their investments until their business came under investigation by the Barcelona police. Adriano, must have suspected his client's misdoings and as a result was brutally murdered, which left Jasper, his assistant and second in command, in a state of constant jitters, despite being unaware of his boss's findings. The alleged drug dealings had been neatly folded into the thriving ceramics business. Money reaped from this clever operation was laundered through the unsuspecting Rothchild Bank and two lucrative restaurants in Barcelona and Paris.

Fernando Flores had convincingly misrepresented himself as a legitimate businessman, and Jasper was sure Adriano must have, at some point, become suspicious and confronted him. It cost him his life. Jasper had trouble believing that his boss died of a drug overdose when Jasper knew for a fact that Adriano didn't go near drugs. Clearly, the press was not properly informed. The whole scenario was fishy and terrifying, turning Jasper's picture-perfect world and singular foreign work experience inside out and upside down in only a few short months. He was thoroughly spooked and was still working out the residual kinks.

Now that things had calmed down and the crooks were either in jail or on a distant continent, he had resigned his position at the bank. No longer able to work with his respected mentor, the office dynamic had changed dramatically. He felt like he was floundering between various superiors at the bank, with no real anchor. The sadness of losing Adriano, someone he had looked up to, had contributed to his carefully weighed decision.

Jasper was happy to meet his best friend, Enrique, to finally fill him in on what had transpired in recent weeks and bid him farewell. He entered their favorite watering hole, nostalgically looking around. He would miss this place with its beautifully carved wood counters, frosted mirrors behind impressively stocked bar shelves, and its colorful carved glass accents. The place was unique and reminded of glamorous eras past. When he arrived, Enrique was waiting for him, perched on a comfortable leather bar chair at one of the remote high tables.

"Enrique, how are you?"

"*Hola,* Jasper. Good. I took a table so we can talk in private. Come sit down. I already ordered you a sangria."

"Perfect. Thanks. How was your day?"

"The same as every other day. My usual work, nothing exciting. I'm dying to hear about you. What happened at the bank? I heard about Adriano in the news. I couldn't believe it. Poor guy."

"Terrible, right?" Jasper shook his head. "I believe he was set up because he must have stumbled on something he shouldn't have."

"Why didn't you tell me? Or answer my calls?"

"I was in shock, and I didn't want to put you in danger. Until Jose was arrested and Fernando disappeared, I was a nervous wreck. My apartment was broken into, and I felt like I was being watched, even though I knew nothing and did nothing to trigger that. I just executed the usual bank transactions Adriano directed me to do. I had no clue anything this sinister was happening. I might have had a few dark thoughts, but nothing concrete I could base them on. Adriano never clued me in to any suspicions he might have had."

"Good Lord. What a nightmare! When was your apartment broken into and what did they take?"

"A few weeks ago, just before I went to Paris to meet my family. Nothing was missing, but I had all my electronics with me at the time, and I don't keep cash in the apartment. Why would I? I work in a bank. There really was nothing of value to take. It had to be Flores's people. No other apartment was broken into."

"You think they wanted your computer?"

"Yes, to see if Adriano shared his suspicions with me. They tried to steal my tangerine tablet in Paris, but they took my mom's by mistake. She has the same model. Boy, was she upset."

"And you didn't suspect any foul play?"

"By then, I did. I saw huge amounts of cash flowing through their accounts. At first, I figured business was really good, but after a while, I started becoming slightly suspicious. My family and I started piecing things together and the picture wasn't pretty. They were stealing ancient pottery from the Metropolitan Museum of Art and Sotheby's and selling it on the black market. They were also fabricating convincing copies in Mexico and selling them here in Europe."

"Who tipped off the police? Adriano?"

"I still don't know. First, F&S Enterprises was being investigated for stolen merchandise. Then drugs were found in their warehouse, hidden in their pottery shipping crates. Of course, after Adriano died, the police were all over them."

"That's wild. What was Flores like?"

"I never liked the guy. I always felt there was something dangerous and unpredictable about him as if he could blow a fuse at any moment. He had these cold, hunter-green eyes and a super fake smile which incidentally must have cost him a fortune."

"Shocking. So, when are you leaving for Paris? I'm still having trouble processing that you resigned and are leaving. I was hoping you would renew your contract. Any chance you'll reconsider?"

"No. I had every intention of renewing my contract, but then I got unnerved when Adriano was murdered and my apartment ransacked. I no longer felt safe anywhere. Now, I just miss him, and I don't think working there will be as fun. I'm being bounced around between executives, none of who I like that much. I'll be leaving for Paris next weekend."

"Damn, so soon? You must have been super alarmed to move that fast. Can't say I blame you. I would have shit in my pants. I'll miss you, dude."

"We'll stay in touch, Enrique."

"Yeah. For sure, but who am I going to watch soccer with at the bar?"

"All the other patrons?" Jasper laughed. "Seriously, though, I'll miss that too."

"What will you do back in New York? Do you have a job?"

"No. I'll have to rethink my future; another scary prospect."

CHAPTER VII

Friends.......Come and Go but Sometimes Flee.

Waking up late the next morning, Casi blindly grabbed his phone on the nightstand and gasped when he saw it was almost 11am. He reached for his laptop and checked the internet for new articles regarding the Flores family; more of the same. Skimming the headlines, he decided there was nothing urgent enough to warrant his immediate attention. He could glean the details later. More importantly, his name and picture weren't yet in print.

Breakfast was a done deal, ending at eleven. Stomach percolating, he rolled out of bed and stumbled to the shower. He would have to forage in the lobby coffee shop. His body felt tired, used. Facing the warm stream of water, he thought about the previous night and decided he didn't want to see Alva and Elin before they returned to Sweden. He had no intention of exchanging any personal information or keeping in touch, nor did he want a repeat performance. Once was enough. He would make himself scarce today. He thought about Helena as he dressed and felt a stab of guilt. Well, there would be no Helena in the near future, so, he would have to make due. He had needs, after all.

While in the coffee shop, he decided to go sightseeing. He bought a banana and a large coffee and walked outside, pulling his panama hat down over his eyes. Surveying the cars lined up in the circular driveway, he looked around for a suitable driver. He spotted a strongly-built, pleasant-looking, dark skinned man, chatting animatedly with yesterday's driver. He was standing next to a black town car. Casi approached him.

"Is the car with the shaded windows yours?"

"Sure is."

"Can I hire you for the day? What's your rate?"

"How many hours and where do you want to go? Half the day is already done."

Casi laughed as the man tapped his forefinger on the large face of his cheap numerical watch.

"I was thinking of going sightseeing; your suggestions are welcome. We can get back after dinner, maybe? Dinner will be on me." Casi saw the man's eyebrows rise with interest.

"Alright, then. Let's go."

They settled on a flat rate, and Casi hopped into the backseat.

"My name is Peter Cameron. What should I call you?"

"Casi, nice to meet you, Peter. Where should we go first?"

"Shall we start with the Nature Conservancy? It's a special place on the island."

"Sure, but only if you come in with me."

Peter laughed. "Ok, man, I'll introduce you to my niece. She works there. After, I can show you town, Bay Street, the colonial buildings, and we can stop at the Straw Market if you need gifts. Later, we can check out some of the other luxury hotels. The best restaurants are there. They have gambling if you like. The Grand Hyatt and the Crystal Palace Casino are popular."

"It all sounds good except for the gambling. I'm not interested in casinos or gambling, at least not that kind."

"Good for you, Casi. Gambling is for losers. What do you do?"

"Business deals only." Casi laughed, giving Peter a thumbs up, visible in his rearview mirror. The man radiated positive vibes and brute strength, two attributes Casi valued. He felt protected as he glanced out of the car's dark windows. Peter's friendly disposition put Casi at ease, and he could feel his ever-present tension ebb ever so slightly.

At the Nature Conservancy, everyone knew Peter. His niece, Bijou, came out to greet them.

"Hello, Uncle Peter. Are you here for a personal tour, or did you just miss me and want to say hello?"

Casi noticed she teased Peter with an easy smile that made her face glow. Bijou moved gracefully, despite her unfeminine attire, cargo pants, a loose promotional t-shirt, and sneakers.

"Both. Make sure you don't leave anything out of our personal tour," he laughed as he hugged her. "This is Casi, my client. He deserves the best."

"Well, then, let's start behind the scenes first. Have you met our resident parrot?"

"Not Pappy! He's still around? I thought he expired years ago." Peter feigned a shocked expression.

"Well, if you were taking care of him, he might have," Bijou countered with a devious grin.

"Come, Casi. Let me show you around while Peter and Pappy get reacquainted."

"Nice try, Bijou." Peter did a quick-step to catch up to them. "I'm staying with you. Pappy snapped at me last time, the little red devil."

Casi relaxed a little and took in the playful bantering, the amazing tropical colors and the plants and native animals Bijou proudly showed them. His favorite moment was holding an extraordinary, multi-colored parakeet.

"Do you have a phone? I can take your picture with it, Peter offered.

"I got it, Peter. I'll take a selfie." He ignored Peter's outstretched hand and quickly snapped a photo. He didn't want anyone handling his phone. Sadly, Casi realized, he had no one to send his selfie to.

After they left the conservatory, Peter drove around the island, giving Casi a lot of facts and island history.

"Did you know the name Bahamas comes from the Spanish term *baja mar*? Or that the waters around us are uniquely shallow which gives them a beautiful turquoise color? Or that our beaches have beautiful white sand that comes from white calcium carbonate deposits?"

Casi shook his head. "No, tell me more."

"We became a British Crown Colony in 1718 and claimed our independence in 1973. Took a while. Did you know we are one of the richest countries in the world?"

"No."

"Our tourism industry excels, compared to other islands in the Caribbean. Actually, we are not technically in the Caribbean. We are slightly north of it in the Lucayan Archipelago. We have about seven hundred islands, thirty are inhabited. Roughly four-hundred-thousand people live here."

"Do most of them live on New Providence?"

"Yes." Peter nodded. "Do you cave dive, Casi? We have some great caves around the islands."

"No. Never tried it. I prefer to stay above water."

Peter laughed heartily. "Me too. I just fish and snorkel."

Late afternoon, they stopped at a few hotels, and Casi walked around the grounds, surveying the lay out and clientele. He decided he was happy at the Atlantis for now, but he was particularly impressed with the Baha Mar Resort. Its expansive ocean blue and sand tile lobby was inviting, and the outdoor fountains, impressive. While Casi scouted the hotel facilities, Peter waited by the car and chatted with the other drivers. He knew most of them.

"Where shall we go for dinner? Are you hungry yet?" Casi asked when he returned from touring the Baha Mar facilities.

"Sure. I was born hungry. Do you want casual or fancy?"

"Let's live a little. What's nice around here?"

"Luciano's is nice if you like Italian food. It's in a mansion overlooking the water and has a panoramic view of Paradise Island. White tablecloths. People like it. Then there's Virgil's on Casino Drive. They have good barbecued cuisine and it's a little more relaxed, with private booths for dining. There's Café Matisse on Bay Street. It has good French food and a nice outdoor garden."

"They all sound good, but now you got me thinking about barbecued food. I haven't had that in a long time. Italian and French I've eaten recently. You good with that?"

"It's your choice, I'm good with anything. Virgil's is a good choice, for sure; I think you'll like it. Let me call for a reservation."

Before pulling out of the hotel driveway, Peter dialed the restaurant's number on speaker.

"Virgil's. Good Evening."

"Hi, Tessa. Peter here. I have a client who would like a reservation for two, say in a half hour."

"Hi, Peter. Yes, we have you covered. How's Gracie?"

"She's good, thanks. See you soon, babe." He disconnected the call.

"Peter, do you know everyone on this island?" Casi wondered out loud.

"I know all the service people, just about. We're a small island, you know, and I'm almost fifty. Been here all my life."

"Wow. You look more like thirty-nine."

Peter chuckled, clearly pleased. He approached the restaurant parking lot and picked a guest spot. Casi glanced at the outdoor menu, pleased with their choice. It promised to be a good meal. The private booths increased his level of comfort. He needed to be mindful.

"Looks good. Let's check it out. Can you ask Tessa for a booth toward the back?"

"Sure thing." Peter nodded and glanced at Casi, his gaze lingering.

Tessa welcomed Peter with the same familiarity and joy as did his niece, Bijou. Everyone on this island seemed to genuinely like Peter. Casi couldn't imagine what that felt like. He had lived his adult life in the shadows and silently, under the guarded radar of others. Peter inquired about Tessa's family and sent his regards to a slew of family members.

Casi chose the side of the booth that faced the entrance, looking up periodically to examine the customers and staff. Seemingly oblivious, Peter continued to joyously entertain and share island information throughout dinner. He knew everything about everyone, and Casi was a captivated party, soaking up every tidbit and filing it away in his methodical brain.

"Are you aware we have no sales or income tax here? Or that we have the third highest GDP in the west? Or that we are the richest island in the Caribbean region? This is a good island for business, Casi."

"Yes, you mentioned that earlier. I can see that after your tour."

"Since most of our population works in the tourism industry, and we are only fifty miles from Miami, we get many U.S. visitors who spend big money. We also have some grand hotel chains; you visited a few of the best today. Most are owned by large foreign corporations. The *Baha Mar,* for example, is owned by a company from Hong Kong."

"Who is the Atlantis owned by?"

"The Atlantis has a colorful history. The property was sold by Merv Griffin in 1994 to Sol Kerzner who developed the site. It reopened in 1998. The Cove, where you're staying, was built in 2007 after another expansion. Now, the Atlantis is a Marriott owned hotel."

"I'm really enjoying my stay there. The marine tanks and the gardens are spectacular."

"Yeah. Many movies were filmed there. A few of the James Bond movies, for example. Do you watch them, Casi?"

"I do."

"They're my favorite. Pirates of the Caribbean and Flipper were also filmed on our island. The movie list is long. Lots of celebrities bought homes here. Mariah Carey, Nicolas Cage, Diddy, Johnny Depp, Lenny Kravitz, and Eddy Murphy, just to name a few."

"No kidding! I had no idea. What is the local political landscape like? Is it easy to open a business here?"

"Well…that gets a bit more complicated. The big corporations are welcomed since they create jobs for people like me. I've never been unemployed or without income for any length of time. However, off-season can be a bit slow."

Peter truly was a deep well and a wonderful source of island gossip, but Casi suspected that he only spilled what he wanted to. Peter clearly knew what and when to hold back.

CHAPTER VIII

Gems and Stinkers.......Love Hurts Regardless

Summer watched her lead actress, Helena Majewski, arrive on set with a dejected expression, her shoulders slumped. Try as she might, she realized that Helena couldn't get over Carlos's sudden disappearance. Summer had serious difficulty fathoming what Helena saw in him, but then, who can explain love? She thought Helena was an incredibly beautiful woman, inside and out; she felt for her new-found friend. Love lost clearly hurt.

Prior to being the lead actress in Summer's film, Helena had enjoyed a good modeling career. She was popular with her agency's clients, always in demand. More importantly, because she was bright, motivated and had a sunny disposition, she was a pleasure to work with. Under Summer's skilled direction, Helena was becoming a skilled actress. Always receiving attention on set, Helena could have had her pick of boyfriends. More than once, Summer witnessed men tripping over themselves to be near Helena, her brother Jasper included. Yet, she picked Carlos, a sulky, forever frowning, bad boy who rarely socialized and single-handedly succeeded in isolating Helena from all potential friendships. Summer didn't get the attraction, although she had to admit, Carlos had a certain sex appeal when he actually smiled, which was as rare as finding a blue diamond in an alluvial deposit.

Helena was well liked by cast and crew, Ted being the sole exception. Ted didn't trust Helena; he considered her an unskilled novice. Sometimes, Summer wondered if it was because of Carlos that Ted was suspicious. Her sinister boyfriend cast a dark shadow on her sunny orbit. Helena was hard working, easy going, and always came prepared, lines memorized. Summer was stumped. What did Carlos exude that kept Helena loyal and now, perfectly miserable? What was Summer missing?

And now, to make matters worse, it appeared Carlos had disappeared because he was possibly involved in a smuggling and drug distribution ring, the same one that had laundered their funds through Jasper's bank in Barcelona, and the same one whose mastermind shared her mother's passion for well-made ceramics. Her mom had run into the Flores group numerous times at ceramic auctions on both continents, the U.S. and Europe.

Summer was having a hard time wrapping her head around these recent developments, but right now, she was too busy to get involved. Luckily, they were almost done shooting her film. Only a few more days were needed before she wrapped. She prayed the weather, and Helena, would hold out to the bitter end. She would do her best to pamper her leading lady.

"Hi, Helena. Any news from Carlos?"

"No, nothing. It's been a rough few days." Her head hung like a delicate flower pelted by a rainstorm.

Summer put her arm around Helena's sagging shoulders and peered into her saphire blue eyes, concerned. She could see her friend was suffering.

"So sorry. Are you still ok with working today?"

"Of course! This keeps me busy and my mind off Carlos. I love working with you."

"Good. And I with you. You're doing a fabulous job, and we're so close to the end now. Even the weather has been cooperating. I'm so thankful for that. Go get your make-up done while Hope and I finish setting up."

"Yes, thanks." She paused and lingered for a moment. "Summer? You know I knew nothing about Carlos's alleged business, right? I don't even know if what they're saying is true. The police found nothing in our shared apartment. I only know him as a caring and kind man. He was so good to me, and I loved him. I still love him."

"I believe you." Summer smiled reassuringly and watched Helena slunk off to the make-up chair. "She really is a gem," thought Summer. "Even if her choice in men is questionable."

CHAPTER IX

Pillow Talk... But Who is Listening?

Cara woke up late in the guest bedroom on rue Malher. Summer, Hope, and Ted had left early to shoot outdoors in Paris. She was pleased to flounce around the empty apartment, alone. Wrapping herself in a lilac fleece robe, she sashayed through the living room to the kitchen, relishing the quiet. Ted had left her some hot coffee, bless his soul. Summer was lucky to have this thoughtful man on set.

Freshly brewed coffee was just what she needed this morning. She poured herself a cup, adding a generous helping of milk, and sat down at the reclaimed pine table, feeling quite at home in the rustic French country kitchen. It reminded her of her own kitchen and ceramics studio, back home in New York. As she sipped her coffee, she contemplated what to eat. She checked the bread box and discovered a wayward croissant. Bingo. From the refrigerator, she retrieved sweet butter and plum jam.

Samson, her younger son and Summer's twin, was also at work. She was on her own until dinner time. Perhaps she would visit Francois at his gallery? After clearing the breakfast dishes, Cara called him.

"Hello?" He sounded distracted.

"Hi, it's Cara. Are you in the gallery today?"

"Cara, cherie. Yes, come by in the afternoon. I'm busy until after lunch, but we can have dinner together."

"Oh, good. That'll be nice."

"Perfect. See you later. Plan on spending the night with me. I have a plan for you."

"A plan? Now I'll be wondering about that all day."

"Good, keep wondering. *Salut.*" She heard Francois chuckle as he hung up.

Over breakfast she searched her tablet to see if there were any updates on the Flores cartel. Still no mention of Carlos. "How odd," she thought. "Surely, he was complicit. Why else would he have disappeared without a trace?"

CHAPTER X

Cosmetic Renovations: Nip, Tuck, or Rhinoplasty?

C asi spent the fourth morning in paradise on his ocean-view terrace, sipping coffee. Opening his laptop to check the daily news, he gasped when he saw his face staring back at him. The image of him with Fernando and Jose in front of the Barcelona restaurant was featured front and center in one of the latest articles about their illicit dealings. Now, he was publicly considered a person of interest. The picture was taken at the restaurant opening, Fernando insisting he be in it. The police must have supplied the picture from Jose's phone. He was certain Fernando took his electronics with him when he fled. Fernando would have wanted to save his precious company files, none of which were stored in the cloud. Nothing at F&S was ever saved to the cloud, and he and Fernando alone had access to the company's password protected balance sheets, so Casi felt no burning heat there.

At the Paris airport, he had deleted all pertinent company files and spreadsheets from his Carlos Ortiz laptop after transferring funds. He no longer had a need for F&S files; he was starting a new chapter with a clean slate. In the public bathroom, he removed the hard drive and bashed it with a broom handle he found in an unattended maintenance cart conveniently parked outside the door. The attendant was missing in action. When he was done, the hard drive and casing looked like a truck had backed over it. His new Casimir Santos laptop was devoid of all incriminating information.

Glancing at the picture, he wondered what Helena thought about the damning press. Was she shocked? Hurt? Did she hate him now? He could only guess. His thoughts drifted to Hermosa. He hoped she wouldn't suffer for his actions. She must have received his last money transfer from a dummy corporation by now. He was confident, the funds weren't traceable. If nothing else, It confirmed that he was alive and well somewhere in the world. At the right time, he would reach out to her, but right now, he needed to intensify his focus on becoming invisible.

Around noon, he finally left his room so housekeeping could do their thing. Stopping in the hotel store, he bought himself an additional Panama hat. This one was a fancier charcoal version with a black silk ribbon. Hat and sunglasses in place, he spent the rest of the day, researching doctors and making phone calls in a remote garden spot. That night, he had dinner on the terrace in his room, but he barely enjoyed the stunning sunset with its blaze of russet, pink, and gold. Since his face was in print, he felt danger lurking around every corner. He was still sitting on the terrace in stone silence when the charcoal night descended. He needed to dig deep to get through the next phase of his disappearance.

The next day, Peter drove him to the airport for an overnight flight to Brazil with a single stopover in Miami. When his plane touched down in Rio de Janeiro the following morning, Casi took a taxi to the Belmond Copacabana Palace, a traditional Brazilian hotel on the beach.

Doctor Alexandre Monteiro, a renowned plastic surgeon, was happy to make room in his busy schedule for a cash customer. For a generous flat fee, rhinoplasty and a few scar correction treatments could be remedied, pronto.

"Hello, Mr. Santos. I understand you're interested in rhinoplasty. Is that correct?"

"Yes, Doctor. My nose was broken when I was younger, and I always wanted to have it corrected. I would like a narrower, straighter nose and I would love to get rid of this bump." Casi ran his forefinger over the spot on the bridge of his nose as he looked up at the doctor.

"How was your nose broken?"

"In a fight."

"I see. I hope you won," the doctor joked.

"No physical fight is ever a winning proposition. That was the lesson I learned."

"Good lesson to take from a fight."

Casi's finger shot from his nose up to his eyebrow. "I was also wondering if you could do something about the scar on my forehead."

"Let's see. Scar tissue is a little more problematic. Deep scar tissue requires surgery. Surface scars can be lessened with injectable fillers or lasers or chemical peels."

"What do you think mine requires?"

"Let me look. Your scar runs through your eyebrow, but it doesn't appear to be overly deep or long. If we did surgery, you would also need a hair transplant in that area. I think we should try a peel first, then a laser treatment and see how we do. Let surgery be the last option."

"Ok. Let's do it. When can we start with the rhinoplasty?"

"Is tomorrow good?"

"Perfect."

"The first night, we may keep you in the clinic. The surgery takes somewhere between three and five hours. Get excited, Mr. Santos. You'll look fabulous."

CHAPTER XI

Final Cut... and More Goodbyes That Sting

"Cut. It's a wrap," Summer yelled. "Yahoo. Break out the champagne, Ted." She twirled in place. The crew clapped and high fived each other as Summer danced over to Hope.

"We did it, girl. Good work." They smacked hands and cheered, elated.

"Yes, and a week early!" Hope threw a fist pump into the air. "That should leave us a little money and time to celebrate."

"Ted?" Summer turned to her producer.

"Yup, I think so. Good work, girls."

"Hey, good job Helena and Alain, you were right on point today."

"Thanks, Summer." Helena smiled.

Alain, always confident, gestured two thumbs up. His alpha male attitude irked Helena, but Summer used it to her advantage as a director.

"I'm so thrilled we finished before Jasper arrives. Geez, even the weather cooperated," Summer remarked happily.

"Don't get too confident. We still have some post-film clean-up to take care of," Ted smirked.

"Yeah. Who's available to help with that?"

"We all can, Summer," Hope nodded, her black hair flying in the breeze.

Summer was thrilled she could spend the next week relaxing with her mother and older brother before their return to New York. Thankfully, she had time now. All she needed was a good ten-hour rest to combat exhaustion; then she would be ready to party. Ten hours of uninterrupted sleep would do miracles. Ted would have her back. He had things under control.

She, Hope, and Ted had two weeks to pay crew, say their good byes to everyone, and clear out of the rue Malher apartment. Six months had flown by and Summer hadn't regretted a single moment. Her film grant money covered almost everything, thanks to Ted's stringent planning. The only out-of-pocket expenses were for wardrobe and dinners out, not an insignificant number, but manageable. Summer worried about post-production back in New York, but they had allocated a certain amount from the start and hadn't touched it. Hopefully, it would be enough. She was doing much of the final editing herself once the reel was synced by assistant editors. The final edit would be a day-and-night job, but for now, she was going to enjoy her much needed break.

"Don't forget, everyone. We'll have a goodbye dinner next weekend for cast and crew. Check your emails for details. Anyone who can help Hope and Ted with equipment returns, let Ted know. Every set of hands is appreciated. Thank you all for your dedication, long hours and excellent work."

Summer texted Samson. *We wrapped. Call you tonight.*

Summer knew her twin brother would be thrilled for her. He was her biggest cheerleader and staunch supporter. Since he worked for the associated press corps in Paris, he would give her a plug when the timing was right. It was great to have him around every week end. She would miss that when she returned to New York, but she wasn't going to worry about that now. Now, she would enjoy an unencumbered week of spring time in Paris with her entire family. Her next text went to Pascal, the Frenchman who tickled her pink whenever she made time for him.

CHAPTER XII

Love and Life Plans Don't Always Line Up, Do They?

Cara was sitting in a cozy French restaurant, sipping a *kir* and looking into Francois's comforting eyes. She was happy.

"I wanted to talk to you about your one-woman show, Cara. How would a date in late December work for you? We could spend the holidays together."

"It sounds great to me now, but I need to check with my family. We generally try to spend Christmas together. In theory, December should give me enough time to get my pieces done. However, I never know how many holiday orders I'll have and how time-consuming they may be. It certainly would be wonderful if we could all regroup in Paris again, but I can't promise anything right now. I totally love the idea, though. If not, maybe you could come to New York?"

"I understand. I have the same holiday pressures. We could always do the show in the new year."

"Yes, I think that's better. Let me get back to you on that."

"Have you decided what you would like for dinner?"

"Yes, *crudité* and *poulet-au-moutarde*. You?"

"I think I'll have *escargot* and *coc au vin*. Would you like another *kir*, or do you want to switch to wine?"

"*Kir*, please."

"When is Jasper coming?"

"This weekend. Saturday morning."

"You must be thrilled. It'll be nice to have him and Summer back in New York."

"Yes, I am. Did I mention I got my stolen tangerine tablet back, too?"

"Noooo. When? How?" Cara laughed at Francois's genuine surprise.

"Inspector Abello, who investigated the Flores gang in Barcelona, returned it to me when I visited Jasper's office. Of course, the inspector didn't know I would be there. He had a meeting at the bank and was going to have Jasper sign for it. He suspects Flores had it stolen, thinking it was Jasper's tablet, which is the same color as mine. Remember, I told you we were working in the café together the day it was absconded?"

"Of course, I remember. You were beyond upset."

"It's a creepy thought that we were being watched and targeted."

"Mon Dieu! The plot thickens every day. This is better than an *Inspector Clousseau* movie," Francois teased, eyebrows raised. "Did Flores at least add some interesting material to your files?"

Cara giggled. "Haven't discovered anything new yet, but he did copy my ceramic files."

"You're kidding!"

"Nope." Cara shared the surprising details.

It really was a twisted turn of events. Now that Jasper was safe, she could laugh. Only a couple of weeks ago, she had been fearful for his life.

"Unbelievable. Summer should make this story her next script."

"That is exactly what my friend Samantha said. Summer writes comedy, and this story is more like a nail-biting thriller, including grand theft and brutal murders. I'm not sure she would find comedy here."

"True, but a story this good is hard to pass up. Don't the best stories come from real life experiences?" He reached over and patted her hand for emphasis. She smiled warmly. His dimples were too cute, especially when he was directing them at her.

"You may be right there. I'm wondering how this story will end." She leaned over and tenderly kissed him on the lips.

CHAPTER XIII

Pre-Party Confessions and a Budding Romance?

Jasper texted Cara when he arrived at Samson's apartment in Paris. He was elated to be back in town and thrilled to see his family.

Hi, Mom. What are our plans for tonight? I'm here, and Samson is clueless.

Welcome back. I'll text you after I confirm with Ted. He's finalizing party arrangements for the cast and crew. By the way, Helena will be there, too.

She added a smiley emoji sporting popping red heart eyes.

Jasper laughed and showed the message to his younger brother.

"She has your number, Bro."

"Well, you got to admit, Helena is beyond gorgeous and as sweet as the dessert, *belle Helene*."

"And surprise, surprise. it looks like she's single now. Carlos has vaporized into thin air. Lucky for you."

"Aren't you jumping to conclusions, Mr. Investigative Reporter?"

"Call it an educated guess, given the evidence. I would be clear across the world if I was in his shoes. I hear Bora Bora is nice this time of year." Samson smiled, swaying his arms back and forth akin to a palm tree in an ocean breeze.

"Funny, Samson. I'd call that an unsubstantiated hunch and actually I've had enough of the Flores clan to last me a lifetime, thank you very much. I don't want to steal the drug dealer's girlfriend and end up with a third eye in my forehead."

"Well, I can tell you this. If I wasn't dating Natalie, I would be your competition. Helena is a rare gem from where I sit."

"Remind me to buy Natalie dinner and persuade her not to let you go. You're just Mr. Wonderful."

"My girlfriend already knows that. Why do you think she's still around after nine months? Rhetorical question, don't answer. How about a glass of rose' and you fill me in on your last week in Barcelona?"

"Not rose' again. Anything but rose'! How about a beer and a comfortable seat?"

"You got it." Samson pulled two beers out of the fridge and popped the tops. "Let's go into the living room."

"The Flores clan is fodder for spine-chilling stories, even after they disappear into the sunset. Did you know Mom got her tangerine tablet back and that Flores liked her work? He copied all of her ceramics files."

"What? Dude, that's hilarious. How do you know that?"

Jasper took a deliberately long swig of his beer, then recounted recent events.

Later that evening the two brothers arrived at the dinner party. The festivities shook the rear room of the quaint Montmartre restaurant as the brothers arrived amidst roaring laughter. A rowdy, sizable group had assembled. In addition to the Crenston family and Ted, Hope, and Natalie, Jasper estimated there were about twenty-five people. The crew had been invited for a *prix-fixe* dinner without their significant others, as the budget would only stretch so far, but after dinner, anyone with a wallet could show up for drinks. Jasper noticed Helena had not yet arrived.

He greeted everyone, hugged his family, and seated himself next to his mom at one end of the table. A few empty seats remained for stragglers and he secretly hoped Helena would fill one of them with her lovely *derriere*. Jasper watched as Samson wedged a chair beside his twin sister. He always wanted to be near Summer. They had been inseparable as children, and clearly, not much had changed. Natalie sat across from them, looking slightly annoyed to be separated from her boyfriend.

Jasper chatted with his mom and Ted about his final week in Barcelona.

"So, what are your plans when you get back to New York?"

"I don't know, Ted. I guess I'll start updating my resume and get in touch with some of my old contacts. Hope for the best. Actually, I'm looking forward to having a couple of weeks off this summer to go to the beach, have a few frozen drinks, and catch up with friends."

"Sounds reasonable, especially considering your last few weeks. I have nothing lined up, either. I've been so busy here, I haven't had a moment to check what new projects are being posted. Now that we finished early, I'll spend a little time snooping."

"What are you looking for? Another producing job?"

"Of course, that would be ideal, but I'll take anything in the arts that allows for a flexible schedule, so if a film job comes along, I can jump on it. That's how my industry works. Oh look, the glam queen has arrived in full regalia."

Jasper noticed all eyes shifting to Helena, who arrived, looking spectacular in a navy slinky, form- fitting, cut-out-dress. Her brown high-lighted hair framed her face in loose waves, and her barely-there, make-up was ….well, barely there. Soft browns surrounded her eyes and luscious, pale pink accentuated her full lips. Jasper couldn't unglue his eyes. Helena was his idea of classic beauty. Ted's ironic comment was wasted on him. He was a fan.

"Hello, everyone. We did it! I can't believe this is the final good bye. I'm going to miss seeing you all in your 5am attire."

A few cheers, greetings, and groans erupted around the table, then the chatter continued.

"Hello, Cara. Nice to see you again."

"*Bonsoir,* Helena. Come sit here."

Jasper noticed Cara pointing to the seat next to him. There were times he loved his mom's subtlety. He winked at her.

Helena turned to Jasper.

"Hi, Jasper. Can I sit here?"

"Yes, please sit down. It's not often I get to sit next to an award-winning actress. The last one I wanted to sit next to died, before I could ask her on a date, Suzanna Svelte." He laughed at his joke. "Congratulations on finishing the film. I can't wait to see the final cut."

Helena smiled. "Me too. Not sure about the award-winning part, but I definitely had fun playing the leading lady. Your sister is an infinitely patient director. What are you drinking?"

Helena grinned, generously bestowing her glorious smile on him.

"Rose'. Can I pour you some?" Cara answered, reaching for the bottle next to her.

"Yes, thank you. My favorite!"

"Rose'? Mine too." Jasper lied.

"So, I hear you've left Barcelona for good and are moving back to New York. I hope you'll stay in Paris for a bit first."

"I am. My mom and I are leaving next weekend. Is there anything we should do or see in our final week?"

"Oh, yes!" Her smile brightened.

Jasper listened to Helena rattle off a few events around Paris as he studied her mesmerizing face. Did this woman have any flaws? If she did, he couldn't detect a single one. He was dying to pull out his phone and take a close-up picture to have and to hold, but he didn't dare. He knew he could count on his mom to do that for him. She never missed an opportunity to make memories. As the night progressed, a few more people arrived.

By the time the party left the restaurant, it was after 2am and the doors were locked behind them. Jasper and Helena, still deep in conversation, waited until the last heartfelt goodbyes were slurred. He could barely tear himself away from Helena's angelic face to go home with his brother. All fears of the Flores clan had magically subsided …for now.

CHAPTER XIV

Facial Rejuvenation or Damage Control….Is there a Difference?

Casi woke up feeling groggy. The surgery had been successful, but he was sore, swollen, and had bandages across his face beneath two seriously black eyes. As requested, he stayed in the clinic the first night. The second night he moved back to his hotel with a nurse in tow. The extra pillows on his bed propped him up so much, he was practically sitting through the night. In the morning, he woke up crabby with a stiff neck and a parched throat, but nonetheless, he dismissed the nurse, along with the cumbersome nasal packing. He was instructed to stay in Rio for at least two to three weeks to ensure proper healing. Too scared to deal with any complications on the road, he obliged. If it weren't for the highly effective pain killers, sleep would have been elusive those first few nights. He missed his workouts, and he missed Helena. The few times he was sick, she had been caring and sympathetic to his needs. Sleeping alone was particularly depressing when he was feeling so vulnerable. Helena's kind, loving touch would have been welcome. However, he couldn't wallow in self-pity for long.

On the fourth morning post surgery, he grabbed his laptop to read the morning news. The initial post-surgery scare had passed, and he was ready to resume life, despite temporary restrictions. The articles on the Flores cartel had dwindled, but he found one article that gave him a much-needed update. As he suspected, Jose had a high-powered lawyer working for him, courtesy of Fernando Flores. He remained in jail and enjoyed no visitors, besides the paid variety. Casi guessed no one from Mexico dared visit for fear of being held by the Barcelona police. Flores was presumed to be back with his family at an undisclosed location. In reality, he was in hiding and it was doubtful the location was luxurious.

Casi had anticipated as much. He knew Fernando had finalized his exit plan months before trouble arose since they had discussed an emergency strategy in detail. It was an occupational hazard to always be on the run. There was no mention of missing funds, but Casi was certain Fernando and his lawyers had detected that discrepancy by now. Lawyers were always on top of the money aspect. They needed motivation to perform.

Casi could only imagine Fernando's temper tantrum when he realized Carlos, the trusted accountant, hadn't hidden the funds, but permanently disappeared with them. Vengeance was best served cold, and Casi felt chilled at the possibilities.

While working for Fernando, Casi always managed to circumvent his boss's wrath by making few mistakes and letting others report the ones he did uncover. He was most proficient in the less "hands on" portion of the business. Jose had always handled the brute work while Casi tended to the brain work, managing different sets of books, most efficiently. At first, Fernando insisted on Casi accompanying his enforcers, wanting to toughen him up, but when he realized Casi had a tendency to vomit when people were being brutalized, he changed his tactics and focused on his bookkeeper's strengths. Besides, Casi getting nauseous during inopportune moments did not bode well with payback schemes. Word spread quickly when someone presented soft, and Fernando couldn't tolerate that in his camp. His reputation was at stake.

Math and business skills were Casi's talent, and Fernando came to trust him with managing their money. Casi was the only person in the inner circle of the Flores clan, who wasn't family. He was also toast if they ever got their bloody hands on him. He shivered at the mere thought, despite sitting in the scorching Brazil heat.

He finished reading the news, carefully hand-showered, avoiding his face, and dressed to go down to breakfast in the hotel restaurant. He wasn't leaving the premises for long periods, except to go for his follow-up doctor visits, but he still liked a somewhat "normal" routine. Today he would take his first walk on the beach. Shielded by his Panama hat, but minus the sunglasses, he left the hotel before the midday sun hit. He hoped he could resume wearing shades again soon. He felt safer behind their enclosure.

CHAPTER XV

Sunday Brunch or Hang-over?

Cara woke up first Sunday morning. All was quiet on rue Malher. She slid into fuchsia ballet slippers, her midnight-blue leggings, and a white V neck t-shirt, then sauntered toward the kitchen, to brew coffee. She toasted a baguette and prepared scrambled eggs, adding herbs and cut up veggies. The party last night had been a beautiful finale to a successful venture and she was thrilled to have shared the experience with her daughter. To have another short feature under her belt, helped cement Summer's feet in the fickle film world. She could now spend the summer months editing the rough cut. Hopefully, Summer and her editing team could get the film ready in time for the film festival circuit in the fall and winter. They would be working around the clock.

Hope walked into the kitchen as Cara, lost in thought, washed blueberries.

"Morning, Cara. Man, that coffee smells good."

"Morning, Hope. Grab a mug. Wasn't last night a wonderful conclusion for all your hard work? Can't believe you guys are done."

"Yes, it was. I can't believe it either. I'm so not ready to go back to L.A. I like it here. I've had way too much fun."

Cara laughed. "Yes, me too, and I didn't even work on the film. Do you have anything lined up when you get back?"

"Yeah. I have a job that starts right after July 4rth weekend in L.A. I won't have the summer off."

"Oh, good for you. Well you'll just have to make the most of the last few weeks here."

Cara smiled warmly when she heard approaching footsteps. "Morning Ted…and Jean-Michel."

"Hi, Cara. Mmm, that smells really good. I'm so ready for coffee. Jean-Michel?"

"Oui, merci."

Cara turned to Ted. "So, what's the plan for this week? What do you still have to take care of? And more importantly, can I help?"

"We've already returned all the equipment, props, and wardrobe. We also returned the truck. I had lots of help from our crew last week. It was pretty painless, considering the load and how long it took us to assemble everything. We still need to pay some of the crew and do paperwork. That's it in a nutshell, so no, Cara, enjoy your last week. I have it covered."

"Wow, Ted. You really are Mr. Efficient. Good job! Francois has been teasing me with special plans for this week, but he isn't sharing what they are. Anything in particular you want to do before leaving Paris?"

"Don't know. See friends mainly. Catch a show or two. Enjoy the outdoors. I've always wanted to go to Versailles. We haven't made it anywhere we weren't shooting. What do you think, Jean-Michel?"

"Sure. Let's do it." He beamed at Ted.

"What about you, Hope?"

"Haven't had a moment to think about it, Cara. I do have some Chinese friends from my neighborhood visiting, so maybe I'll do the tourist thing with them. What about you, guys? Any family outings?"

"I'm sure we'll come up with something. Then there's packing and shipping, of course. I'll help Summer get her new additions home." Cara rolled her eyes. "More junk in my garage."

"Thanks, Mom," Summer chirped.

"I'll have lots of boxes arriving in New York, but not the kind I'm excited about. Does anyone know if Helena heard from Carlos? He's now been linked to the drug cartel in the news. The police want him for questioning," Cara announced as she glanced at her tablet.

Summer shook her head. "Nope. Not a peep."

CHAPTER XVI

Friends with Benefits

A few days later, packing and shipping completed, Cara was primping for her dinner date with Francois. She decided to abandon her usual pants for the night and pulled a little black dress out of her suitcase. She slipped into black suede pumps from an earlier Paris trip and touched up her make-up. She decided to wear her long brown hair down.

Reflecting on her day with Jasper and Summer, she thought about the wonderful morning at the Rodin museum, her second time visiting. Samson had to work. They had followed it up with a late, but leisurely lunch in a nearby outdoor café, dining *al fresco* in the glorious spring sun. Afterward, they walked through the grand Carre' section of the Tuileries Garden, admiring the stone fountains while gabbing about what needed to be done once back in New York. The sweet sunshine had made the day all the more pleasurable. Looking in the mirror now, she discovered a luminous glow. She was happy for the time she had with her children and smiled, remembering their happy chatter.

"I'm going to have an onion bagel with smoked salmon and the works when I get back to New York."

"Is food all you think about, Jasper?" Summer inquired with a smirk.

"No, I'm also excited about having a good margarita."

"A Mexican concoction? Really?" Summer wrinkled her nose and laughed.

"No connection between the Flores clan and a good margarita in my mind."

"Mine either," Cara chimed in. "Guys, look at these gorgeous plants and sculptures."

"We filmed a scene here near the water basin, Mom."

"Cool. Can't wait to see that."

They had been walking back to rue Malher when Jasper's phone rang. Cara noticed he answered it without checking the screen. He was definitely reverting back to his old, relaxed self. The fact that Jose was ruminating in jail for drug trafficking and alleged murder, lightened Jasper's mood substantially. Fernando Flores was far away in Mexico resuming his trade, without restriction, Jasper no longer on his mind. As she listened to Jasper's half of the conversation, she surmised Helena was calling to invite him to a Friday night party. When Jasper hung up, he could barely contain his smile.

Cara winked at Summer.

"I was wondering when that was going to happen. I think she likes you, Jasper."

"Really? Well, obviously, I couldn't ask her out. She was the star of Summer's film, and she had a very scary boyfriend. That would have been uncomfortable all around. Has she heard from Carlos yet? I hesitated to ask her the other night."

"Not a word. I'm wondering why I didn't get invited to the party?" Summer teased.

"Don't know, but she didn't mention you. So sorry, Sis! I suppose it's not surprising she hasn't heard from Carlos. His hasty departure is an admission of guilt in itself. He must have been involved up to his eyeballs to let her go. Well, his loss, my gain."

Summer laughed and teased him all the way home.

"Where's the party?" Cara wanted to know.

"At a restaurant. It's being thrown by someone from her modeling agency."

"Oh, boy. Samson will be so jealous." Summer giggled. Cara had enjoyed watching them tease each other, just like old times when they were kids. Cara relished those moments.

Summer was sprawled on the daybed in Cara's room watching her get ready for an evening out and still chatting about the pros and cons of Jasper dating Helena.

"Summer, sweetie, you do realize Jasper and I are leaving in a few days and Helena is remaining here in Paris, right? This is just a fun night out for both of them. They've been through a lot. Maybe letting off a little steam together is a good thing."

"Well, look at you and Francois. You're dating long distance."

"I don't know that I would call it 'dating'. Francois and I are more like friends with benefits." Cara waited for the reaction she knew would come. She was baiting her daughter and holding her laughter.

"Ewww. T.M.I. Funny, Mom. Really hilarious! You know Helena will be visiting me in New York, and if I get my film into Sundance, she'll come a few times."

"Be real. One date among friends doesn't mean Helena and Jasper will survive a long- distance romance. Trust me, it's hard, even with added maturity. Besides, Helena is so gorgeous, she'll have men in Paris lining up once they realize she's single."

"I don't know, Mom. She hasn't exactly advertised her relationship with Carlos…. or his departure. Those two always flew under the radar."

"Hmmm, well, he did come across as a bit of a recluse."

"Understatement of the year. I think she reeeally likes Jasper, but she's also exceedingly loyal. I don't know. She never strayed when Carlos was around and believe me, guys swarmed around her on set. She was totally devoted to him. I can't believe she would jump into anything yet. I don't want Jasper to get hurt."

"Maybe she didn't dare? And guess what, Jasper may be smitten, but he isn't stupid."

"I doubt it, Mom. Helena told me on a few occasions, Carlos was very good to her, and she knew nothing about his alleged connections."

"Well, pleading the fifth doesn't necessarily render you innocent. Seriously though, I think she may be a little lonely, and Jasper is a nice, convenient, fill-in for one evening. By the way, I may stay at Francois's apartment tonight. We have a date, and it will be a late night."

"I believe her, Mom. Friends with benefits…ha ha. Wait until I tell Samson."

Cara caught Summer rolling her eyes in the mirror as she applied her magenta lipstick.

Their eyes locked momentarily, and she grinned back at her daughter, winking.

When Cara got to the gallery, Francois waved her over to his desk and greeted her with a soft kiss. She felt her lower belly stir.

She wanted to move closer to him, but his assistant was working nearby.

"Hi, don't you look nice! I need another half hour, then we can leave. Have a seat. Want some coffee or tea?"

Cara nodded and helped herself. Maybe some herbal tea would calm her flutters.

"Here are some new submissions for the gallery. Look through them and tell me what you think." He handed her some photos and stood behind her, rubbing her shoulders.

"Ok." His touch felt so good. She leaned back into his capable hands and purred.

When Francois was ready to leave they stopped at an art opening two doors down, sharing a glass of wine with the artist and Clovis, the owner, while studying the sculptures. Clovis's wispy blond hair fluttered elegantly as he spoke, and his animated, green eyes focused on Cara with interest. He was explaining his fascination with a particular artwork, expecting his audience to concur. The show comprised freestanding, contemporary collages made from repurposed materials. Cara listened with interest, then walked away when the subject changed to business.

The rest of her time was divided between walking around the mixed media art and people watching while Francois continued chatting with Clovis. Cara stole glances at him from afar. She loved his profile and the way he engaged people in conversation. Their faces lit up when they talked to Francois. Clovis was smiling and nodding in agreement. Moments later, Francois signaled her, pointing to the door. Clovis had moved on to a potential client.

"Let's go. I had to say hello, but I don't want to grow roots here. Clovis and I sometimes cover for each other when we travel, so I had to make an appearance."

"He seems like a nice man. How long has he been in business?"

"Longer than me. Over twenty-five years, I think. Here, lets grab this taxi."

"Where are we going, Francois?"

"It's a surprise, I know you'll enjoy. Ready?"

"I think so. I like surprises. Especially yours." Cara beamed at him.

Twenty minutes later they exited the taxi and entered the Paradis Latin, a cabaret with dinner, dancing, and lots of champagne.

"O.M.G., Francois. This is so fun! And touristy. I hate to admit it, but I love it."

Cara leaned into Francois and kissed him gently on the lips, recognizing a flicker of fire in his eyes. This promised to be a memorable night. She reflected on her luck, having met this remarkable man, who sparked her imagination and ignited her passion. Taking a deep breath, she willed herself to concentrate on the starting show.

Before the curtain went up, her thoughts traveled to Jasper. She hoped he was ok with Helena. In the depth of her soul, she wondered about Carlos leaving Helena behind and the possible repercussions.

CHAPTER XVII

Casi's Changing Facial Map

Casi stepped out of the shower and wiped the adjacent mirror with a hand towel. His nose looked better. It still showed slight swelling after two weeks, but he had certainly turned the corner. After a follow-up examination later in the week, Dr. Monteiro gave him permission to move forward on the scar over his eye. Initially, he had wanted Casi to wait three full weeks after rhinoplasty, but now he agreed to shave a few days off. The healing process was progressing nicely. With further consultation, Casi decided to remove landmark moles on his neck and shoulder as well. They had always irritated him, and their removal was easy enough, requiring only minor incisions.

The tattoo removal discussion proved to be more complicated. Surprisingly, tattoo removal threatened to be the most complicated procedure of all. The sheer length of time it would take to laser the skull and rose branding from his arm overwhelmed him. He decided it would have to wait. The cover up makeup he currently used would have to suffice. He would reorder the very effective Tarte Amazonian Clay online.

Casi needed to stay in Rio longer than initially planned, but he was fine with that. It was imperative his transformation be completed, and so far, he was pleased with the progress. Between the hair, nose, scar and mole removal, his appearance was morphing into a positive disguise he could live with. He already looked infinitely more refined. As he studied his reflection in the steamed mirror, he decided his smile would be next on the agenda.

To add to his new look, Casi decided to splurge on new jewelry. He wanted to pick something special to commemorate his transformation and lift his spirits, fueling the hope of seeing his leading ladies again. First on the agenda was the replacement of his trademark 22kt gold hoop with a single solitaire diamond. The hoop earring had been his mother's, and he had worn it since her death, along with her gold cross pendant. Hermosa had the other half of the earring. He stopped at the concierge's desk to get jeweler recommendations. Within minutes, he had an appointment not far from the hotel.

Perusing jewelry showcases in a private suite above a popular shopping area, he selected one carat round, quality diamonds, set in 18kt white gold bezels. Since the diamond earrings came as a pair, he decided to fashion the second diamond into a pendant for Hermosa. He chose a delicate, three-tone gold link chain and waited for it to be soldered to the diamond bezel earring. He would hold it for his sister in anticipation of a reunion. He saw the diamonds as a symbol of unity, an unbreakable bond, joining two precious halves to complete a whole--a *yin and yang* commitment.

With Helena in mind, he picked out multicolored dangling tourmaline earrings set in yellow gold. He would hold them for their meeting one day. He needed to believe, to have that window of hope. She was always on his mind. In fact, not a day went by when she didn't creep into his thoughts. Her carefree laugh, her loving hugs, and her sexy catwalk were imprinted on his brain.

Casi looked at the gold watch showcase and thought about replacing his steel Swiss Army watch. He had been pictured in the news with it. Hadn't Jose's jewelry landed him in jail? However, the more he looked at gold watches, the less they appealed to him. He didn't identify with that flashy, golden color. That was Fernando's style, and he didn't want to be reminded of anything Flores. The memory churned his stomach. After forty minutes of an intense watch education, delivered by a salesperson smelling easy prey, he was stuck between two steel and gold, preowned watches, one, a Rolex and the other, a Cartier watch called the 'Roadster.' The latter was mainly steel and had a tasteful, thin gold strip running through the center of the bracelet and around the white, roman numeral face. The name appealed to him and so did the look of the watch. "I'll take that one," he said, pointing to the 'Roadster'.

When Casi got back to the hotel, he put his new watch and the jewelry gifts into the hotel safe, along with his mother's gold hoop. He decided to continue wearing his Swiss Army watch while still in Brazil, but switched to the diamond stud earring. Admiring himself in the mirror from all angles, he decided it was about time he added a touch of sparkle to his dreary, stressful life. Besides, the picture of Fernando, Jose, and him in the newspaper clearly showed all their jewelry. The gold hoop had to go. When he was ready to leave Rio, he would switch to his new watch, but for now, it was safer in the hotel safe.

For the rest of the day, Casi planned his future itinerary. He was excited to visit a few new cities in South America before deciding where to sprout roots. He wasn't particularly well-traveled. With his family, he had visited a few people around Mexico, and with Fernando, he had seen New York City and the European cities, Barcelona and Paris. None of those areas were in consideration for obvious reasons. He wanted to start fresh in an unexpected location. The brief stopover in Cuba didn't count as foreign travel, but the Bahamas left him with a warm afterglow. His thoughts drifted to Peter. His detailed description of the islands had resonated. The man had left an indelible impression on him. Few men in his life did, with the exception of his father.

Casi enjoyed traveling, and if it took him a few more weeks to figure out the right spot where he felt comfortable, so be it. God only knew, he missed Mexico, but home was out of the question. The Flores clan would weed him out like a stray cocoa bean in the coffee jar--too risky.

He spent the rest of the afternoon mapping out his next destinations, but he didn't book anything. That could wait until his scar treatment was done. He was scheduled for dermabrasion, followed by injections, so taking it easy for a while longer wasn't just a suggestion. When he was ready, Casi would resume his exploration. He was looking forward to visiting Buenos Aires. In the meantime, while he healed, he spent his afternoons researching cities in South America and people watching. Brazilian beach babes were not meant to be ignored.

CHAPTER XVIII

Kiss and Tell

Saturday night was Cara and Jasper's last night in Paris. The plan was to spend it with family and friends over a leisure dinner. Their group included Summer, Samson, Natalie, Francois, and Helena. Ted and Hope had other plans. Jasper's date with Helena on Friday night had been memorable, so Cara wasn't surprised when Jasper asked her if Helena could join them for their final dinner in Paris.

"Of course, she can come! Sounds like you had a good time the other night."

"We totally did," Jasper's face lit up at the memory.

"Well, we're happy to include her. We have a growing extended family, and there's always room for more members."

During dinner, Cara noticed Jasper and Helena's heads stuck together, chatting as if no one else existed. "Interesting, but slightly disconcerting," she thought. Cara sat between Francois and Jasper, yet she couldn't hear a word Jasper and Helena were uttering. After dinner, he whispered in Cara's ear,

"Helena and I are going for a nightcap."

"Make sure you're back in time to go to the airport tomorrow, Jasper. You need to pick me up at 11am on the dot."

"Don't worry, Mom. I'll be there."

Although Cara was happy for Jasper's diversion, Helena's missing boyfriend was on her mind. Hopefully, he was far, far away. Dating a gangster's girlfriend could have frightening repercussions.

Cara vividly remembered the New Year's Eve party Helena invited them to and how closely Carlos had watched her. She also remembered how passionately he had kissed her, announcing his unmistakable status in her life. It was the only time Cara ever saw him smile. They definitely had a close connection. It wouldn't shock her if Carlos magically reappeared in Helena's life one day. She hoped Jasper wouldn't be there when that happened.

Helena resembled a sparkly, precious diamond. One couldn't help but be mesmerized by its radiant beauty, inside and out; it was hard to look away or let it go. Cara imagined, letting Helena slip through one's fingers would be a man's greatest regret in life.

When Jasper picked Cara up the following morning, she sighed with relief.

"Good Morning! Happy to see you made it." She said nothing more, hoping to get details on the long flight home…or not. Jasper rarely shared private information, even with a captive audience.

Cara sat in her ceramics' studio Sunday night perusing her emails. Francois had sent her a heartfelt message, thanking her for a wonderful time.

"I miss you already. I can't wait to come to New York. I wish it was earlier than late summer."

Three months was a long time to wait, but long-distance relationships were costly and tricky.

Cara tried her best to have few expectations.

The next morning, she was up early. After checking world news over a cup of rooibus tea, she walked into her studio, ready for work. As she sorted through her new orders, her best friend and client, Samantha Cadwell, stopped by with delightful pastries from Nero's Neoclassical Bakery, their neighborhood obsession.

"I thought I would invite myself over for breakfast. I missed you! How did the rest of the trip go after I left Paris?"

"Things ended well. Jasper is here, still asleep, and Francois offered me a one-woman show in his gallery. Those are the highlights."

"My goodness, you move fast! Does that mean we're going back to Paris for the opening?"

"It appears so, but not for a while. The dates aren't set yet."

"Now tell me about Jasper. What happened after I left?"

"Let me brew some Columbian. This'll take a while."

CHAPTER XIX

Breaking Tents and Hearts

The prospect of leaving Paris made Summer sad. The last six months had passed in a blur. Filming in Paris was everything she had hoped it would be, despite the usual hurdles, but even those had made her smarter and stronger. She had grown proficient in so many ways. Navigating the challenges of French bureaucracy, dealing with rain delays, equipment malfunctions, illness amongst her crew, power outages, and political unrest, all contributed to unexpected schedule changes and stress, but in the end, team work prevailed. Ted's unflappable disposition and organizational skills, coupled with everyone's dedication and flexibility, helped her persevere. The film footage she and Hope had previewed looked good, and she was itching to start editing it with her team back in New York.

The last week in Paris was devoted to wrapping up paper work, saying good bye and cleaning house for the de Fontenay's return from Southern France. Luckily, Madame Balon, their shared housekeeper, helped tirelessly. She did not, however, part with her famous *coq au vin* or *clafoutis* recipes.

"You'll have to come back and visit. This is my insurance," she uttered in broken English and laughed.

Ted tried begging and bribing, with no luck. Madame Balon's resolve was as resistant as stainless steel cookware when it came to disclosing her recipes. There was no chance of separating the two.

Summer heckled and teased him mercilessly over his failed attempts.

"Ted, there's one thing you haven't offered her yet."

"Yeah, well….I don't swing that way. Maybe she'll consider passing it down in her will if I outlive that tough old bird."

Summer and Hope cackled deviously. "Now, there is a murder mystery worth writing."

As a parting thank you gift, Summer left the de Fontenays two peony teacups from her mother's collection. She propped a thank-you note against the beautifully wrapped box Cara had brought, signed by all of them. She also asked her landlords about possibly renting again in the winter. It didn't hurt to plant the seed early, she thought.

Her family was on board as they all wanted to be there for Cara's art opening, but since the dates were not yet determined; no firm plans could be made just yet. Summer also had her own agenda. She wanted to schedule a movie showing at the theater in Montmartre. The theater and its director, Mimi, had been so instrumental in making her film a success, it would be great to give back to them and her French crew by organizing a private and public screening of her film.

Saying goodbye to the friends they had made was difficult, but Ted, Hope, and Summer would be in touch with everyone as they still had the film's success in common. Summer planned on keeping everyone in the loop regarding her progress. She could sense Helena was particularly sad the filming ended. She had just lost Carlos and now, she was losing her American family as well. Summer felt her emotional distress, but she didn't know how to help.

"I'm so sad you're leaving, Summer. I enjoyed meeting your whole family. You're so lucky to have them."

"I know, Helena, but I promise we'll all be in touch. You're invited to New York, anytime. We'll make a plan, ok?"

"That would be great. Thanks." Helena's eyes teared up as she hugged Summer.

Summer sensed Helena's loneliness, a foghorn in the dark.

CHAPTER XX

Coming Full Circle and Then Some

The next six weeks, Casi traveled around South America, visiting six countries and a few of their nicest coastal cities. He enjoyed the food and music in Buenos Aires, the ferry ride to beautiful Montevideo and its spectacular *rambla* and harbor, the vineyards around Santiago, the fine art museum and the historical sites of Cartagena and finally, the scenic beaches of Tamarindo, Costa Rica. His two favorite stops were the Rosario Islands off Cartagena, and Tamarindo, but the international airport access from Tamarindo was a little too far for Casi's comfort, and Cartagena did not have favorable international banking laws, so that was out of the running too. His soul needed a beautiful coastline, but his head needed to be close to a substantial airport. Being trapped in the middle of nowhere, no matter how beautiful, it was, would make him anxious, claustrophobic. Having a deep-sea harbor nearby was an additional consideration. In a pinch, leaving somewhere by boat was just as comforting as an airplane. It was good to have exit options.

After his whirlwind six country trek, Casi was happy to go from the beauty of South American beaches to the bustling streets of Panama City. While he enjoyed his travels and information gathering immensely, none of the locations he visited jumped out at him as a place to settle in permanently. One thing he was sure about, though, he could never live landlocked again. Paris was and would remain the exception.

He also knew he wanted to eventually buy a pleasure boat somewhere. He loved being on the water, always had. The happiest memories he had with his father, were on the family boat. After his father died, his mother sold it, so the family could survive and Casi could finish his education. It broke his heart, and he vowed to replace it one day, time and money permitting. He never managed to do that before his mother died.

Something about Panama City struck a chord. The city was flourishing with activity and businesses. The harbor bustled with positive energy, and the off-shore banking laws were favorable for Casi's diversification purposes. He immediately got to work, meeting with a financial advisor, and setting up a corporate account. With referrals in hand, he contacted two brokers to look for businesses to buy.

Panama City's location, fifteen minutes from the canal linking the Atlantic to the Pacific Ocean, fascinated Casi. He spent hours at the harbor, checking out the boats. The next day, Casi treated himself to a private tour of the Miraflores Locks, touring the three observation decks, and having lunch at the restaurant onsite. It was mindboggling to watch the Panamax barges threading through the narrow waterway. At night, he walked around his neighborhood. His hotel, the Intercontinental Miramar, was centrally located and allowed him to walk to diverse destinations.

Between meetings with brokers, Casi visited a dentist for a consultation. Now that his face was almost healed, he wanted to find out about capping his teeth. Realizing that the process was somewhat lengthy, he decided to wait until he was settled somewhere, but at least he had the facts. He would take care of tattoo removal and his teeth simultaneously…soon. For now, he would rely on tattoo covering makeup. It had worked well so far.

After looking at several business options, Casi left Panama without making a commitment, but some of his money was invested and working for him. He needed time to think. So far, Panama was the strongest option. Only the weather patterns bothered him. It was a tropical, humid climate, and the sun didn't shine a lot in Panama City.

After a summer on the run, Casi's plane touched down in Nassau. An earlier text to Peter shared his flight information and ensured a familiar face at the airport. With no real home anywhere and no decisions made, Casi was happy to see Peter back in the Bahamas. He had made no friends on his whirlwind tour. Even a loner, with no money worries, needed meaningful human contact sometimes. The joy that Peter radiated, the spectacular weather, the magnificent water views, and Bahamian hospitality, felt like a warm embrace. He was home.

When Casi exited the airport and spotted Peter, he waved. To his surprise, Peter looked right past him with a blank stare as if searching for someone else. He stopped a foot in front of Peter and took his sunglasses off. "Hello, Peter. Thanks for coming. Have you already forgotten what I look like?"

Peter did a double take, but recovered quickly, breaking into a grin.

"Welcome back, man. How are you? You look …different, but good, very rested. Must have been a formidable trip."

Casi grinned. "Yes, it was, but I'm glad to be back. This place is starting to grow on me."

"Oh, good. You back for a while, then?"

"Yes, maybe. What does your day look like tomorrow? Can I hire you?"

"Sure thing, man. I'm going nowhere. Where you staying this time?"

"The Coral at the Atlantis."

"Good choice. Welcome home, Casi."

CHAPTER XXI

New Projects Fueling the Fire

Late summer in New York was a busy time for the Crenston family. Cara was preparing her early fall orders and feverishly working on her personal art for the upcoming one-woman show, which still remained dateless. Summer spent days on end in the lab editing her movie, together with a small, trusted team. As soon as a section was edited and locked, it was color- corrected. The production line was stacked in her favor. It was good to have a dedicated team behind her. Short of setting up a cot there, she had time for little else. She was determined to finish the edit on schedule, and it was a tall order, but considering all the hands on deck, it wasn't impossible. The mid-September deadline for the Sundance Film Festival loomed like an impending thunderstorm. When she wasn't editing, she was eating, sleeping, running, or writing promotional materials with Ted and Jasper. Who knew her brother had marketing talents?

Jasper was networking and setting up interviews for himself, but so far, nothing had panned out. Everyone in banking wanted the inside scoop on what happened in Barcelona at the Rothschild Bank, but they didn't have open positions. Word got around in the banking industry. Jasper kept his involvement on the down-low, remaining totally loyal to Adriano in death and the reputable Rothschild organization.

"I know, whatever you heard in the news and no more," was his standard line, garnering disappointed faces. Cara's, Jasper's, and Summer's paths crossed occasionally over a meal, but everyone was busy. When they did meet, they read through Summer's new script outline, critiquing the content. For the first collaborative dinner, Summer came fully prepared.

"Jasper, if you're ok with it, I would love your help on a script about the Flores family. I wrote a proposal and skeleton outline on the plane, coming home from Paris. Can you take a look?"

"I figured that was coming. I'm only ok with it if you change all names, places and a good portion of the content."

"I agree! I was going to suggest the same," Cara added with fervor. "We don't need any more unwanted attention from the Flores family. Besides, if you write fiction, you can embellish as you please. A documentary requires accountability and total accuracy. That isn't your thing anyway, is it?"

"I guess not. You're right. I'm not a doc filmmaker nor do I want to be."

"No, you aren't. You love to exaggerate. Summer, write the story as if it were fiction. You don't want to get on the Flores's radar. We got off easy the first time."

"I agree with mom. I think using the Flores name may endanger us. I can only give you my ok if you change all names and call it a fictional piece. I can't live in fear again as I did those last few weeks in Barcelona. That was pure hell."

"Alright, alright. Point made. But I have to throw this out there. El Chapo was dying to have a movie made about himself."

"El Chapo is in jail because of his vanity."

"Ok, ok. I hear you. Now, take a look at my script. I need you guys to help me fill in the blanks."

CHAPTER XXII

Home is Where Your Heart Is....or your Money

The next morning, Casi felt the Bahamian sun welcome him as he lazed in bed. The blinds pulled wide open, he looked out over the glorious, sun-kissed ocean, sparkling in the soft morning light. He felt so happy to be back. Something about the Bahamas and its surrounding turquoise waters spoke to him more than any other place he'd been to, even Panama. The people were friendly and welcoming and it had an unmistakable cosmopolitan flair, which he attributed to the large volume of tourists and a thriving expatriate community. People were always coming and going, and that suited him perfectly. He liked Panama City too, but the damp, tropical weather and lack of sunshine was a definite deal breaker. Casi needed to live somewhere warm, sunny, touristy, and by the ocean. He felt that need passionately in his heart and soul.

Having spent the previous night doing research on local businesses, Casi was ready to do some leg work. He called his bank the minute it opened to make an appointment with the financial advisor, Clinton Hughes. By the time Casi was showered and had his morning coffee, Peter was waiting. His phone pinged with Peter's text as he gulped his last sip.

Am downstairs. Come whenever you are ready.

Casi grabbed his wallet, put on his new steel and gold Cartier watch, and scooted out the door.

"Morning, Peter. Today I have a meeting in the financial district in Nassau. Drop me on Bay Street, please."

"Right. Off we go then. Would you like a bottle of water? It's chilled."

"Thanks, Peter. Save it for later. So, what's new on the island?"

"You're lucky you missed most of the rainy season. With September around the corner, we're looking at beautiful weather. Hopefully, we'll dodge the hurricanes this year."

"Are there any new business developments?"

By the time Casi arrived at Bay Street, Peter had him up to speed on island news.

"Ok, here we are. I'll wait on the corner of Bay and Nassau."

"If you come back in an hour, that'll be fine. No need to wait here that long."

"Good, I have an errand to run for Gracie. Never hurts to keep the woman happy." Peter laughed.

Entering the bank, Casi spotted Mr. Hughes waiting. He was a distinguished looking, older, dark-skinned gentleman in a meticulously tailored suit and a blinding white shirt. His name tag gave him away. He greeted Casi warmly.

"Good day, Mr. Santos. Won't you come into my office? How can I be of service?"

"Hello, Mr. Hughes. I wanted to discuss a few things with you."

"Please, sit down. I'm listening."

"I have some corporate accounts in your bank and recently transferred more money here with the intention of possibly investing in a business on the island."

"Which business would that be?"

"That is what I need your help with. I'm looking to buy an existing business and develop it. Are you aware of anyone having or wanting to sell?"

"I see. What type of business? Are you a resident of the Bahamas?"

"Possibly a tourist-based business. I'm not set on anything in particular. I 'm also interested in establishing residency. That was my next question. Can we work on both simultaneously?" Casi watched Clinton Hughes's impassive face as he studied Casi's account summaries on his laptop.

"I believe we can. Let's start on some paperwork, shall we? I'll refer you to the proper office for a resident application, but in the meantime, I can suggest some businesses I know the bank is looking to sell, foreclosures and such. You understand."

"I do. Perfect, just what I had in mind. Thank you."

"You may also want to contact a local commercial broker."

"Yes. I thought I would start here first."

"Of course, Mr. Santos. We have periodic auctions, but in the meantime, I can help with a few suggestions."

When Casi reemerged over an hour later, Peter was there, waiting.

"Listen, Peter. I'm thinking of buying a business and staying a while. Any ideas?"

"Really? Well, the best businesses are tourist-based. We get a lot of visitors with money to burn. We don't have a lot of natural resources. Our beautiful beaches and shallow waters are our main attraction and resource, so a good restaurant close to the beach is a sure bet if you ask me."

"Hmm… that could work."

"If you can take over a restaurant in one of the big hotels, you'll most likely do well. What business were you in before?"

Casi cleared his throat and answered thoughtfully. "I did a few different things, including managing a restaurant."

"No kidding. Well, there you go, man. You just answered your own question. Stay with what you know. Shall I check around and see if anyone is retiring or selling? I know people in almost every service business here."

"Sure, thanks. It never hurts to have an inside advantage. In the meantime, I have a short list of businesses to look at. Here are the addresses, but first, I need to stop by this office to get a resident application." He handed Peter the paper.

"Ok. I'll wait outside. It's literally around the corner.

When Casi returned with his residence and business applications in hand, Peter had the day mapped out.

"These places are a little spread out, so let's do the ones in this area first."

By the end of the day, Casi and Peter had traversed the island, from Cable Beach to Paradise Island, checking out numerous options, ranging from a charter boat business to a snack shack. Casi wasn't sold on any of them. He hadn't found the right business in Panama City, and he was beginning to wonder if he would here. He didn't want to rush into just anything. This would take time, and luckily, he had that luxury. The idea of being on Cable Beach or near the Baha Mar appealed to him. He didn't want to be tethered to the rise and fall of a large hotel. The notion of having hotel executives looking over his shoulder or in his face on a daily basis, didn't sit well with him. Patience and a little more due diligence would surely yield something, eventually.

In the meantime, he got a dentist recommendation and didn't waste time making an appointment to start capping his teeth. He scheduled his first tattoo removal appointment for the same day. He wondered if he would need pain killers.

The following week, Casi met with a lawyer to assist him with a permanent residence permit. Since he entered the country with a substantial net worth and intended to open a business on the island, thus creating new jobs, the lawyer assured him his application would surely be approved. Accelerated consideration was afforded those applications which brought considerable wealth to the Bahamian Islands.

Once the process was completed and successful, Casi looked at residences at the Baha Mar and The Reef at the Atlantis. He liked the idea of living in a place where all the amenities were included and maintained, so he could focus solely on building his business. The transient hotel lifestyle would provide a single man like him with fleeting companionship and revolving, easy entertainment. His immediate social needs would be covered. The large hotel venues would allow him to fade into the crowd. Vacationers were notoriously preoccupied. In the small towns in South America, he would have become everyone's business. In his experience, people in small towns were curious, especially about newcomers. Here, no one cared who came and went.

With residence papers stamped and approved, Casi chose a three-bedroom condo at the Baha Mar Resort. The apartment was in mint condition and minimally furnished. Casi transferred payment for the condo, signed the papers, and unpacked his bags a few weeks later. Peter's wife, Gracie, came to help him get settled, buying him basic groceries and cleaning supplies. She cleaned his cabinets, lined the kitchen shelves and showed him where to shop for additional necessities. With that settled, Casi continued his hunt for an appropriate business. Ironically, a car was last on his purchase list. Peter was readily available and good company as he carted Casi around the island. He also minimized Casi's exposure.

Casi knew he was taking a calculated risk by staying in the Bahamas, but the island just felt right. He was tired of traveling, and he was tired of running. He briefly weighed the hurricane risks, but decided Mexico was no stranger to that threat, either. He was used to hurricane warnings. Besides, he would diversify his assets over time. The first step had been taken. He had a new home and a new friend he hopefully could trust in Peter.

CHAPTER XXIII

Casi's Small Business Dream Takes Shape

By mid-September, Casi found the kind of business lead he was looking for. Making it materialize was a different issue. Peter's inquiries had led him to a restaurant owner who was contemplating selling his business to enjoy his golden years. The man's retirement plans were merely a thought, not a well-organized foray into his future, but Peter managed to sprout and nurse the seed over a few late-night drinks. He convinced the owner to meet with Casi before he made any drastic decisions.

"Listen, Casi. Benny won't sell to just anyone. He doesn't want to sell to a corporation. He would like someone to follow his footprint if you know what I mean."

"Yeah, he poured his heart and soul into the place. He cares."

"Exactly. You got it. I told him he would like your business plan and should lend you his ear over a beer one night this week. It wasn't easy convincing him, but he agreed."

"Thanks, Peter. Let me do a little research on the location. Ask him if we can come Wednesday. You free then?"

"Yeah, I can free myself up. You do have a business plan, right?"

"No, but I will by Wednesday. Pease come. I'll pay you for your time."

"Sure thing."

When Casi and Peter met to view Benny's property, Casi was pumped. He was eager to strike a deal before the parcel of land hit the open market. The fact Benny wasn't in a rush to sell was a challenge to him. He liked what he discovered when he researched the property days earlier and had already driven by a few times. There were few properties like this available on the island and he doubted many changed hands to total strangers. Peter was his most valuable asset.

"I'm telling you, you will love this place. It needs work, but the location can't be beat," Peter insisted.

"Ok, then. Thanks for coming. Let's check it out," Casi answered noncommittally.

They drove into the wide-open parking lot, an expansive ocean front plot overlooking Cable Beach. The lot was merely packed dirt, and the building's placement was off center with the kitchen facing the street. The sturdy, stone and concrete ranch house had large picture windows opening to a spectacular ocean view. The small wood porch, facing the water had bougainvillea vines twirling around the pillars, creeping up to a sad, sagging roof, but the base structure was solid.

Casi noticed the kitchen when they drove up. The back door was wide open. The not so grand entrance faced the larger portion of the parking lot, off to one side. The employee parking was on the opposite, narrower side of the lot, bordering an impressive cluster of stately sea grape trees. The place had clearly seen better times, but Peter was right, the location and potential were singular. Casi instantly fell in love with the property. When he exited the car, a strong tropical flower scent filled his nostrils.

"I like it, Peter. What is that delicious scent?"

"Those are the ylang ylang trees over there. They're sheltered by the sea grape bushes and trees all around. Someone here has a green thumb. These trees need care and pruning to look and smell like that."

"It's intoxicating."

"Coco Chanel thought so too. Ylang oils are used in her perfume, Chanel #5. Ready for business?"

"Yes. Let's see what we can do here." He marveled at the breath of Peter's knowledge. There was nothing that Peter wasn't interested in and his power of observation was keener than a hungry coyote circling a fawn.

"Just move slowly and tread lightly," Peter cautioned, wide-eyed.

"I got this," Casi assured him, although not quite feeling it.

Armed with his calculator and a flexible business plan, he and Peter circled the building before entering through the unassuming front door into a small foyer. He noticed the kitchen, bathrooms, and office were off a long hallway to the right, the bar and dining room to the left, facing a heart-throbbing view. Peter sent Casi a confident smile and flashed him a thumbs up signal behind his back.

"Good luck," he whispered over his shoulder, looking around for Benny. Nervous, Casi nodded and returned a half smile.

Peter spotted Benny and introduced him to Casi. Benny was a short, slim, dark-skinned man, who carried himself with pride. He wore a straw fedora on top of a full head of grey hair and moved with the grace of a jaguar. Benny's demeanor was confident. He knew he was sitting on gold and he wasn't going to sell to the highest bidder. His legacy was more important. Casi observed Benny and guessed he could strike a deal, even if it would require some convincing. He believed his knowledge and flexible business approach would convince Benny to sell his business now, not six months from now.

He hoped he wasn't mistaking cocky for confidence, but he usually read people right.

After a tour of the restaurant, including its antiquated kitchen, the three men settled outdoors over drinks and finger foods to discuss options.

"Thanks for meeting with me, Benny. I know this is an important life decision you're making."

"You got that part right." Benny nodded, eyes glued on Casi, sizing him up.

Casi continued, "I can see you've poured your heart into this place. It shows. It's authentic, beautiful, has character entirely its own, and"--he paused for emphasis-- "Peter tells me you serve great food too. These appetizers are delicious."

Benny cracked a meager smile, which disappeared as quickly as a starfish in the surf. Nonetheless, Casi caught it and was encouraged to continue his sales pitch.

"Peter and I walked around the grounds before entering, and I can tell you this, there's not a lot I would change in terms of the bones of the place. It has a desirable layout, solid stone walls, and the size is perfect."

"Keep talking," Benny said dryly, raising one eyebrow.

"This is a strong Bahamian structure that probably withstood a few storms, so why mess with what's already proven?"

"So, what would you change?" Benny squinted and pushed his Panama hat upward.

"I would update the existing structure, add a new, stronger roof, new double-paned accordion glass pane doors where the windows are and expand the outdoor area." Casi paused, trying to gauge Benny's reaction; he got nothing.

"What else?"

"I would update the kitchen and furniture, paint the walls and add more tables on a stone patio. Yeah, that about covers it at first glance. Do you have any suggestions, Benny?"

"An outdoor barbeque. I always wanted to build one, but never quite got to it."

"That's an excellent idea. I could totally see that. Where did you plan to put it?

"Next to the porch by the outdoor stone bar I never built."

Casi flashed Benny a winning smile. "Perfect spot. Near the terrace. I agree. Look Benny, in essence, I would like to keep the feeling and integrity of a traditional Bahamian villa, marrying the inside and outside elements. I would just infuse a few bucks and give this place a needed face-lift."

Benny's poker face twitched ever so slightly, and a miniscule smile formed in the corner of his lips. His eyes started to glisten.

Listening to Casi but looking at Peter, Benny tapped one arthritic finger on the table to a reggae beat. He winked at Peter.

"Ok, man. I like your ideas. Now, let's talk money." He turned his full attention to Casi.

"Well, what figure did you have in mind, Benny? What would make you happy?"

"I know this place needs updating, but the location is prime. I would like to sell it for this figure here, and I want to be kept on as a consultant, receiving, say fifteen percent of the profits until I die. I'm 74 now." Benny slid a folded piece of paper from his shirt pocket across the table.

Casi unfolded it and whistled through his teeth. Peter broke a sweat.

"That's a big number, Benny. Only a corporation could pay that, and they would turn this land into a concrete block in a heartbeat to get their return quickly. They'll also buy you out with no profit sharing plan, you know that, right? I'm an accountant, so I know how these things go." Casi pulled out a pen and drew a line through Benny's number, then wrote his generous counteroffer and slid the folded paper back to Benny.

"Here's my cash offer, and I'll include the profit-sharing plan you want, although I cannot promise fifteen percent. That isn't feasible."

Negotiations followed after which they agreed on a lower cash price and a five percent profit cut. The final amount was substantially lower than Benny's asking price, but Casi promised him the profits, long term, would more than make up the difference once they got started. The restaurant would have to be gutted and completely renovated, a big initial investment. The building also needed a new roof immediately, Casi pointed out with emphasis. However, given the spectacular location, coupled with the right marketing at all the hotels, Casi believed he could have a booming business Benny would be proud of.

"Trust me, Benny. I am confident I can make this work. You'll stay part of an exciting venture."

"I think I like your offer, Casi. Let me sleep on it." Benny squinted. "Go check out the Blue Sail Restaurant on Sandyport Beach. Good for inspiration."

"Ok, I'll do that. Listen, I doubt you'll get a more generous offer with your specifications. For the record, I'm looking at other businesses on the island, businesses that were foreclosed by the bank, so don't wait too long with your decision. I'm ready to move now. The money is here."

"I hear you. Give me forty-eight hours to discuss this with my family."

The following night Benny asked Casi to come back.

"I like your offer, Casi. We have a deal." They shook on the terms, and within three days, Casi had a lawyer draw up the contract, which they went over with Benny in great detail. Benny was deliriously happy and smiled from Miami to Nassau.

"Good luck, Casi. I hope you'll be as happy here as I was for over thirty-five years."

"I think I will, Benny. I can feel it in my gut."

CHAPTER XXIV

Pen Pal Heaven or Hell?

Summer's film was edited and submitted to the Sundance Film Festival in September. The film's final version was worked on until the last day it was due. A group email went out to her cast and crew, making it available for them to view on line with a protected password. She wanted to hear their comments and critiques. She could always tweak things before the next submission, if absolutely necessary. However, once a film is locked, making changes includes adjusting many moving parts like sound, dialogue, color, and so on. Luckily, the feedback was encouraging.

Her script about the Flores family was also materializing since Jasper had taken an active role in co-writing it. Cara and Samson made their own contributions, making it a true, collaborative venture. Switching gears, Summer began working on a proposal that would be pitch perfect for obtaining future funding. Jasper, still unemployed, was helping her fine tune the winning words. He was now fully invested in the project. Summer had a way of sucking people in before they could yell for help and run.

When Summer sent her film proposal to a few trusted cast and crew members, she was surprised at the swift positive response. Helena answered first.

Dear Summer,
Your film is fabulous! Poignant, funny with beautiful cinematography.
Bravo to you and Hope. I will keep my fingers crossed for Sundance.
Either way, I'm thankful for the experience and opportunity, you
gave me.
Your new film proposal sounds equally excellent. I'm in if you
want me.
I can work on generating interest and raising money here in Paris,
when you are ready.
Let me know.
Hello to Jasper and Cara. I miss you guys. Have to call Samson one
of these days.

Bises, Helena

Summer forwarded Helena's email to her family members, Hope, and Ted, asking for their thoughts. The answers were unanimous. Even Ted agreed on casting Helena again. She replied to Helena.

Dear Helena,
Hope all is well in Paris. How is work with the agency? Have you
heard from Carlos? Talked to Samson?
Thank you for your kind feedback. Now that the skeleton script is
written, I would like to do some research to improve it. I may have
to take a trip to Mexico. I'll keep you posted. Wish you could come.

Hugs, Summer

Helena's reply came almost immediately.

Dear Summer,
I would love to go to Mexico with you. Send me the dates, and I'll make it happen.
No, sadly, I never heard from Carlos again. I tried finding him online, but had no luck.
I don't know if this is helpful for your film research, but Carlos had a sister in Mexico City. Her name is Hermosa Ortiz and she's an accountant, like him. I think she works for a major hotel there, but I don't know which one. She's not online either. I checked.
His parents are deceased. That is all I know about him besides the fact that he is a good man, and I miss him.

'Bises' Helena

Summer digested the information and decided to do some digging. She would call all the major hotels in Mexico City and find Hermosa. Then she would figure out what her next move would be.

CHAPTER XXV

Demolition Across the Board........ House, Teeth and Tattoo

Casi waved papers at Peter as he got into the waiting car.

"Peter, I have a signed contract. Can I count on your help going forward? I need a demolition crew. Five to ten guys would be good. I want to move quickly. I can pay a decent daily rate, two hundred and fifty in cash sound ok?"

"Yeah, man. I'm in. I'll have a crew there whenever you get the legal part squared away. Just give me forty-eight hours' notice."

Casi sighed. He knew Peter was serious and was relieved that his new friend was on board. He needed people he could trust, and he genuinely liked and trusted Peter. The next few months promised to be exhausting, so having competent support was key.

"Great. We have a lot of work ahead of us. I'm counting on you, Peter. I'll check into a good roofing company, an electrician, and a plumber. Any recommendations you have are welcome." Casi could see Peter smiling in the car mirror.

"I'm thinking. Give me a day."

Once the contract was signed, delivered, and the deed transferred, things happened quickly. Work and renovation permits were rushed through the appropriate offices. Since there were no structural changes to the existing building, the process was painless.

Bahamians knew the value of winter profits, so they helped speed the paperwork along. The local government supported new island businesses. The goal was to be open for the holiday season. Casi hired a core demolition crew, assembled by Peter. His resources were impressive. The day the paperwork was completed, Peter had a group of guys ready for work. A core group came daily while others came and went as their other jobs permitted. Peter worked every day, excluding Sundays, managing the crew.

The kitchen and restaurant interior were gutted first. They broke through the wall to the left of the inside bar to add direct kitchen access. Having the kitchen staff share a hallway with incoming guests had been the building's only design flaw. The wood decking was removed, and concrete for the new, expanded stone terrace was poured. Since the compromised roof needed immediate attention, a roofer was hired to start work instantly and materials were ordered.

Casi chose a multiple-panel hip roof with a 30-degree slope to withstand hurricane force winds. A notched frieze was installed along the gutters around the perimeter of the building, and a central shaft was added to relieve wind pressure. As the basic concrete structure was already slightly raised, the risk of flooding would be reduced. Nonetheless, Casi chose textured, sand- colored tile flooring and installed it on a raised layer of poured concrete. When they tackled the roof, he wondered why such a sturdy house with a concrete base would have such a flimsy roof, to begin with. He made a mental note to ask Benny.

Peter's men replaced the drywall before the tile floors were installed. Once all tiling was complete, the walls were spackled and painted. Casi chose a warm off-white for the inside. The raised concrete and stone patio extended far beyond the previous wood one, since the house was a good distance from the beach. The roof was extended to cover part of the patio and strong concrete columns were erected to support it. An impressive stone outdoor bar ran three quarters of the patio between two columns on the front door side of the building with a protective wall behind it, so there was plenty of room for storage and a good barrier between the bar and the parking lot. Opposite the bar, on the other side of the patio, he left a space for an outdoor pizza oven and grill, a spring project. Benny had advised them on the wind currents for placement.

Casi lined up all of Benny's old furniture and appliances in the far corner of the parking lot and allowed local people to come and take whatever they liked or needed. He didn't have to place an advertisement. Word spread quickly, and things disappeared daily. The generous gesture created a buzz amongst the local service industry and their families, generating renewed interest in Benny's old place. Would there be jobs offered? Paid publicity couldn't have worked better.

Portable heat lamps were ordered, and long heavy wooden benches were positioned and cemented in strategic spots around the outdoor perimeter of the terrace, offering priceless vistas for waiting guests. Outside the kitchen, a smaller concrete patio was poured, a small portico erected and an attractive retractable awning was installed to extend over two wood picnic tables for the staff to eat and do dirty work like corn husking. Since guests entered the parking lot on the kitchen side, it also made that side of the building more inviting. Before, it had been a bit of an eyesore.

Over the front entrance, they extended the tile roof in another small portico, this one a semi-circle. A short, curvy stone walkway meandered to the parking lot, so ladies who preferred high heeled shoes didn't have to walk through the dirt. At some point, plants and flower pots would be added to make the entrance shine. On the other side of the building, in the employee parking lot, they built a three-sided concrete garbage area, leaving enough room for a potential vegetable garden in the far corner of the lot where the sun hit in abundance. The low wall for its perimeter was set. Another spring project to look forward to.

Casi ordered beautiful whitewashed, wood tables and chairs for his restaurant. The outdoor chairs were made of bamboo and teak wood and folded, so they could easily be stacked under the tiled roof for safe keeping during stormy weather. He kept the indoor décor simple with whitewashed exposed brick walls, merely adorning them with captive island photography for sale by a local artist, one of Peter's many cousins. Only, the kitchen appliances were top of the line. Casi spared no expense in outfitting the kitchen.

Amidst the outdoor construction, Casi pulled Peter aside one day.

"Listen, Peter. The renovations are close to done; thanks to you and all your family and friends. I was wondering if you would like to make this place a permanent home away from home?" Casi looked at Peter in anticipation. He sincerely hoped Peter would stay.

"What did you have in mind, exactly?"

"I would like to hire you as my general manager. You'll be my front man, field all interactions with customers and staff." He watched a broad smile form on Peter's sweaty face, his joy contagious. How wonderful it would be to work with that positive energy every day. Besides, he was growing extremely fond of Peter. He held his breath, hoping for the right answer.

"Yeah, I was getting a little bored with sitting in a car day after day, and I was feeling it here." Peter gripped a shrinking spare tire around his waist. "What are you paying, man?"

"What are you making now?"

"Around thirty thousand BSD a year for five days work."

"How does sixty-thousand for five days work sound? But they will be long days. Plus, a year-end bonus if business is good, a three-week paid vacation, and extra medical benefits." Peter's smile widened. "That definitely works for me."

"Good, you are officially my first employee. Welcome aboard. You start now, and your first job as a general manager is to hire your staff. I will handle the chefs, the menu, the building, all ordering of supplies, and whatever accounting problems arise. I prefer to work behind the scenes."

"Perfect. I'm not big on computer or paper work."

"I figured as much. It's settled then."

The goal was to open Thanksgiving weekend. In his mind, Casi could visualize people sipping cocktails on the benches around the back terrace, enjoying the sunset and waiting for their dinner table. Now, all he needed was a good chef and support staff. He advertised the position internationally, adding a picture of his state-of-the-art kitchen and the restaurant's location. Sitting with Peter over lunch one day, he brought up hiring staff.

"I can't believe how quickly we're pulling this together. Your crew is incredible. We might just make the Thanksgiving goal if we can get the place staffed and the kitchen operational."

"Even if we still have things to do, we can open with the bare bones if we get the kitchen in working order. Any luck with chef applications?" Peter asked.

"Still working on that. No stand outs yet."

Through the demolition process, Casi managed to see a dentist regularly to improve his smile. He wanted the new veneers intact for his restaurant debut. He was close. The tattoo removal didn't go as well as expected. He started with the skull between the two roses and it was shrinking ever so slowly with the laser procedures, but tattoo removal was proving to be extremely painful, not to mention, skin damaging, so he was seriously considering switching gears. Finally, after one particularly painful session, he decided to abort plan A. Plan B was adding one glorious, blue rose between the two magenta blooms to cover the skull remnants of his cartel past. For now, he kept his tattoo covered, focusing on his smile.

"I can see your smile across the restaurant parking lot, man," Peter told him one day. "You could light up the harbor at night."

"Good. Hopefully, it will attract paying customers." Casi cracked a smile. He laughed more frequently these days. With each step forward, his happiness escalated.

"Good food will take care of that, Casi. Word gets around quickly. What will you be serving?"

"Bahamian food every night, but once in a while, we'll mix it up with international nights, where we serve specials -- Mexican food, Italian, pizza with crazy toppings, tappas, Mediterranean style, South American and Middle Eastern fare."

"Sounds good. I can't wait for opening night to finally get some food in this kitchen. I'm hungry."

"You're always hungry," Casi laughed. "Once the construction work is done, we'll be done with sandwiches. We'll have a working kitchen and hopefully, some kitchen staff. I do have a finished picture in my mind and it definitely includes great food."

CHAPTER XXVI

Good News on All Fronts

Cara was looking forward to Francois's arrival. For now, they were burning up their email accounts, but the joy of an anticipated physical connection could not be overlooked. She missed looking into his eyes, his soft, touching hands, their intimate dinners, and their long, meaningful talks about art and life. In anticipation of his arrival, she gathered up her new art work and strategically placed it on one end of the butcher block table in her studio. She also made a run to Nero's Bakery and to the liquor store for some premium sparkling wine.

When he arrived a couple days later, she was overjoyed. Sitting across from him over a thoughtfully planned welcome dinner, he surprised her with some good news.

"I've decided to make some changes in my life. You're my inspiration."

"Me?" She pointed a finger at her chest and held her breath.

"I'm closing my London office. My partner bought me out. I'll be looking for gallery space in New York."

"Really?" Her eyes widened.

"Yes, really. My daughter will continue to sell my artists' work in her framing store in London so, I don't have to ship anything back. I can use her store as my London base of operations, and she can take a commission for anything she sells. Business has slowed there, and I've been thinking of making a change for a while now. I've done well with my New York artists in Paris, and perhaps, I could do better with my French artists in New York. What do you think about that?"

"Oh my God, Francois. That would be fabulous. I say it's worth a try if you can swing it."

"I plan to start looking for gallery space this trip. Maybe I could share a space to start until I test the market? I don't know. Depends on the rents. I was thinking of Soho."

"Makes sense. I'll help you wherever I can. I can also ask Summer for staff suggestions if you like."

"That would be great. I'll need help. Once I pick a space, the workload will multiply quickly. There's so much to do to launch a new place. I'm also going to look for a studio apartment near the gallery to make things easy."

"Sounds good. Let's toast to your new endeavor. For selfish reasons, I hope it works out."

"Yes, me too." He smiled wistfully.

"I have a surprise as well. Summer, Jasper, and I were planning to spend Thanksgiving in the Caribbean this year. We would like you to join us. Will you be back in New York in late November?"

"That sounds nice. I've never been there. Send me the dates when you decide, and I'll try to plan around them. I'd love to go with you."

"Wonderful! We'll have fun. The weather will be nice that time of year."

The next morning Cara called Summer to chat.

"Francois arrived, and he's thinking of opening a gallery in New York City. He closed his London one. Do you think any of your friends might want to work there? He'll need help setting it up and marketing. He wants to open before Christmas.

"Really, Mom? He plans to live in New York? With you?"

"No, not with me. He'll get a studio near the gallery."

"Oh, so you'll be in the city more then."

"Possibly. Are you going to help or just give me the third degree?" Cara teased.

"Of course, I'll help. Just trying to get the facts straight."

"I see, Sherlock. Any other information you need?"

Twenty-four hours later, Summer called back, saying Ted was interested. He was working freelance jobs, but would prefer something regular, as long as Francois would be flexible regarding film work. Cara checked with Francois.

"Fantastic, yes! Ted will need a back-up, though. If he's out on a film job, he'll need to arrange for someone reliable to cover for him. That will be his responsibility. I can't handle that, if I'm out of the country," Francois responded immediately.

"Knowing Ted, I'm sure he'll have you covered. You can make me number two on the sub list. If my workflow is slow, I can fill in occasionally. I wouldn't mind a little extra cash, and I'm ok with working on weekends," Cara replied.

"Yes. You can definitely be an alternate."

By the end of the week, she and Francois had weeded out two potential gallery spaces. While Cara was working, Francois visited four potential new artists to represent in New York. Two of them looked particularly promising. He was moving fast. The following week, he decided on a shared space on Broome street, around the corner from the Cupping Room Cafe, Cara's favorite brunch spot on West Broadway.

Over the week end, he and Cara met with Ted and Summer. Ted was ready to start work. He wasted no time starting the necessary paperwork to be filed in New York. Francois would assume his half of the gallery sublease in October, but the opening would officially take place in mid-November. The gallery didn't need much work. It was a small space with crisp white brick walls and a functioning bathroom. Francois asked the super to put up shelving in a designated office corner. A few white movable walls on casters were brought in, so he could add exhibit space and section off the tiny office area. They partitioned off a section in the front, just large enough for a desk and a table, using half of one of the two front windows. Francois hated rooms with no view. Ted was in charge of hiring part-time staff and accepting inventory shipments, which began arriving pronto. He also set up the office area with whatever electronics were needed. Once that was done, Francois, Ted, and his helper concentrated on building a mailing list.

Francois moved from Cara's home to a nearby boutique hotel, so he could be close to operations. They were working after hours to get everything done. He also began apartment hunting. Sharing his frustrations with the building's superintendent one day, Francois became aware of an apartment above the gallery becoming available in January. It would be newly renovated. The one-bedroom apartment was a small, third-floor walk-up, facing the street. The super promised brand-new appliances and a fresh paint job. By New York standards, it was a good deal. Overjoyed, Francois rented it. So far, his transition from London to New York was painless. The funds from his London partner's buy out, financed his move and launch in New York. He needed it to be a successful venture.

Francois and Ted decided to open the gallery with a group show. They wanted to show a cross section of art, so they could gauge the market. Cara was invited to submit two or three pieces. She was elated. The thought of having Francois around for weeks at a time was Christmas arriving early. She also enjoyed the opportunity to show her artistic side. Sometimes the stars aligned just right.

CHAPTER XXVII

The Sea Grape Garden Restaurant is Launched

Casi looked up from his laptop in his outdoor office, comprised of a small slatted, collapsible, cedar table, and a director's chair. He was set up under a large canary yellow umbrella at the far corner of the patio. Job interviews, placing orders, and general office communications were conducted from this scenic spot. His indoor office had Wi-fi but no furniture yet.

"Peter, I think I found a chef. He's from Chile. I'm flying him in this weekend to see the kitchen and cook for us. Can you help me judge his cooking?" Casi knew the answer before it was uttered.

"Yeah! Finally, some food at this place. I'll be here, all night if I have to, but where is he going to cook? The kitchen appliances aren't hooked up yet."

"My place." Casi laughed. He smiled a lot now that his new teeth were done. His life was improving immeasurably, and his transformation conveniently coincided with every step forward at the restaurant. The Flores' curtain of oppression was lifting and fading into the Bahamian sunset. He no longer checked daily for news articles about Fernando Flores. There was no news, and there hadn't been any in a long while.

However, Helena and Hermosa were always on his mind, especially when he was alone at night. One day, he would have to hatch a plan to contact them, but first, he needed to establish himself. He wanted to make them proud, share in his success.

The weeks leading up to the grand opening were hectic. The chef from Chile was hired, and much to Casi's surprise, he brought his own support staff and pastry chef, who also happened to be his girlfriend. Matias and Isa were put up in a furnished apartment, one of Peter's friends provided for reasonable rent. It was agreed they would stay there in the interim. The team was hired on an eight-month trial basis. Casi's lawyer was busy getting them the necessary work permits. The sous chef and the relief cook, or roundsman, shared the second bedroom in the apartment. Additional kitchen help and servers were local and had previously worked for Benny. Casi hoped they would all get along. The personalities provided an interesting mix that could either combust or jive. Time would tell.

The Chileans were a lively, territorial bunch, and once they took over, they allowed no one other than kitchen staff onto their turf. They made their position clear from the start by setting non-negotiable boundaries. Casi decided to go with it. He let them set their own work rules, giving Peter and him time to focus on other pressing matters. By day three of assessing the kitchen, they handed Casi a detailed list of demands. They also supplied him with a reasonable industrial kitchen supplier and an excellent wine supplier. He placed all their orders without question. The smug smile on Matias's face was priceless and made Casi laugh. Clearly, Matias was testing the waters. The one thing Casi insisted on was all expenditures and orders be routed through him. He kept a precise balance sheet of all his operational costs. His start-up and building maintenance costs were logged separately.

"You better hope Matias cooks like a champ. It will take serious work to cover these expenses," Peter grumbled one day after being hustled out of the kitchen with a new list.

"I believe in him. It will work," Casi replied confidently.

Peter's gentle, jovial disposition set everyone at ease. Even in the tensest situations, he could diffuse tempers and get people laughing in spite of themselves. On more than one occasion, he smoothed things over between the kitchen posse and his wait staff. Casi knew Peter was worth every penny he paid him. He had no interest or patience to deal with wayward personalities, and Peter didn't seem to shirk them.

When they had their first managerial meeting prior to opening, Casi covered Peter's duties in detail.

"Just to confirm once more, the wait staff will report directly to you, regarding schedules and shift switches. The kitchen staff will be handled by Matias, but he has to keep you informed on any schedule adjustments. You will keep me in the loop on everyone. You can go ahead and interview for an assistant manager, but I want to meet the person you choose before you hire them as I'll have to work directly with them when you aren't here. We might want to hire a PR manager for our launch. That will be a temporary or part-time gig unless they bring enough business to justify an additional salary. That person I want to meet too. Any supply orders or structural problems, I will handle. I'll do all restocking orders for food and liquor, all business expenses, and the payroll. Matias will handle the kitchen, giving me all receipts, but you are in charge of the bar. Also, you are the front man for all customer disputes, party planning, and reservations. I think that covers everything. We'll meet at least once a week, maybe every Monday morning, to make sure we are set for the upcoming week. Sound ok?"

"Yeah, man. I hear you. What do you think of Tessa for PR? Her hostess hours at Virgil's just got cut. She's studying marketing in college and knows staff in all of the hotels. She's also my niece, and I trust her to do a good job."

"Set up an interview. Oh, and Peter, you are on your own with wait staff and kitchen staff meetings. I will pop in and out. Just keep me informed."

"Got it."

"You're going to be a busy man, my friend." Casi laughed and patted him on the back.

"No worries. I got this."

Casi had no reason to doubt that.

The following weeks, Peter finalized his wait staff and put together a tentative schedule that considered everyone's needs as much as possible. He ran his choices past Casi for a final yes. It was a pleasure to work with Peter. Casi liked his staff choices and trusted him implicitly. Peter was fair, but firm when he needed to be. He gave the restaurant an unmistakable island vibe, a warm Bahamian touch unique to the island and to him as an individual.

One day, when Peter was helping with the last of the outdoor set up, his wristwatch took a fatal hit, the dial smashed beyond repair. Peter, usually unflappable, was visibly upset.

"I loved that watch. Gracie bought it for me for our tenth anniversary. Damn."

Without hesitation, Casi took off his Swiss Army watch and offered it to Peter. "Here, take this one."

"I can't take your watch, man. You told me it was your father's."

"Of course, you can. I got myself a new one recently, and I don't need more than one. I want you to have it. Besides, I bought it for my father, and now, I want you to have it. My choice who I give it to."

"I've never had such a cool watch. I love it. And if you tell Gracie I said that, I'll deny it." He grinned as he carefully held the watch to his wrist. Then he put it in his pants pocket and patted it.

"I'm not going to wear it until the heavy work is done around here. This one is a keeper. Thank you, Casi. That's very generous of you."

"Consider it a thank you gift for all you've done so far. Listen, Peter, I could never have pulled all this together in two-and-a-half short months without you and your friends. I really don't have words."

"You're welcome. I like my job change, and I'll like it even more when we are up and running. It feels good to start something new. I'll take the taxi sign off my car shortly."

"Good, because I'm getting a company truck this week. I don't want to keep paying your daily car rates." Casi winked. Peter hadn't charged him in weeks.

"Too bad. I was just going to raise my rate on you." He laughed heartily. "So, what are you going to call your restaurant? We need a name for advertising."

"I agonized over this. However, when we were installing the outdoor benches, it came to me. I decided to call this place Sea Grape Garden Bar and Grill in honor of Benny's beautiful sea grape trees on our beach. I love the way they look, especially at sunset. Maybe we can have an artist paint some sea grape trees on the outside walls in the spring, but we're not going to tackle the outside until next year. Got to earn some money first."

"Sea Grape Garden. Yeah! I like it. I'll have Tessa design some cards for you to consider. Maybe we can also plant a few more of those trees and cross pollinate them?"

"Good idea. Let's do it. I want this place to be visually beautiful, lush. I'm not going to pave the parking lot, either. I like the rustic feel and all the wild plants around us."

"Gracie makes a mean jam from those sea grapes. We can serve that for brunch or maybe even bottle it and sell it here."

"Yeah. You're full of good ideas. Keep them coming."

"Thanks, man. Let's talk to Matias about that fenced-in garden. We should plan ahead what we want to plant before spring. Our employee parking lot is huge. We could plant more trees, lemon, or fig maybe. They tolerate sand and salt."

"Lemon would be great. Matias and the kitchen staff can help maintain the garden and harvest it."

"Gracie can help too. She has a mean green thumb."

"Good. Well, the base wall is there. We'll just add a fence in the spring when we're ready to plant."

"Yes, we'll also need compost and good soil. I love the garden idea. It adds an organic quality to our restaurant."

Casi smiled at Peter's choice of words. It sure sounded like Peter was fully invested in the Sea Grape Garden Bar and Grill.

CHAPTER XXVIII

Dangerous Final Touches at the Sea Grape Garden

"I want to order some colorful accent pottery to go with our white textured dishes. Matias had me order all white dishes to showcase his food arrangements. Everything is white. We need a splash of color, maybe some decorative show pieces for the dining room, to put flowers in and brighten the décor. Any ideas locally?" Casi looked at Peter inquisitively.

"You might want to order that from elsewhere. Not a big selection on the island."

"Ok. By the way, the electrician is coming tomorrow to hook up kitchen appliances. I think we're ready. Matias finalized the kitchen layout with the plumber. Everything is where it's going to stay."

"Good. I'll make sure I'm here for that."

The following morning, while Matias and Peter were working with the electrician, Casi sat in front of his laptop and clicked on Cara Crenston's pottery website. In the last twenty-four hours, he had perused numerous companies, but few compared. He kept navigating back to view her exquisite work. What sold him was her light muddled glazes. They fit his vision perfectly. Pastels fit into the Bahamas landscape like muted sunsets. He moved his favorite items to the virtual shopping cart and typed in Peter's company credit card information, but held off pressing the submit button.

After looking at a few more companies, Casi finally ordered fifteen decorative pitchers with muddled pastel finishes-- a soft lemon yellow, a light mossy green, a sky blue, a muted terra-cotta peach, and a flamingo pink, three in each color. He added an oversized vase with all the same colors for the indoor bar area. It had a faded pastel Mediterranean design that featured citrus fruits, peaches, green grapes, and pears. They would look great against his Navajo white-washed walls and furniture. When he checked out, he received a corporate discount. Casi would now be privy to Cara's blog. In hindsight, it was a bold move, but the pottery was so beautiful and uniquely glazed, he wanted it. On a more irrational level, it gave him a momentary connection to Helena even though it wasn't a connection at all, really.

When Casi looked up, he saw Peter eyeing him with interest. No restaurant order had ever taken him so long, and Casi registered Peter's surprise.

"Are you done with my card?" Peter asked. "I want to pay the workmen."

"Yes."

Peter was extremely intuitive but never nosy. He knew Peter wouldn't comment on his difficulty deciding. Peter rarely asked direct personal questions or questioned Casi's authority or decisions at the restaurant. He was observant and a great listener, when Casi wanted to talk, but Casi rarely did. Peter usually arrived at the truth silently, using his keen sense of observation.

One of Peter's greatest attributes was his ability to be discreet. While he was the recipient of island gossip on a daily basis, Peter could discern what needed to be kept private and what could be passed on without repercussions. Any conversation he had with

Peter was truly private. Peter and Helena were very alike in that respect; they both treaded lightly and instinctively knew when not to push him. Casi appreciated not being challenged or prodded. He did as he pleased, no longer accountable to anyone.

Together with Tessa, Casi opened a restaurant Instagram account but decided to skip all other social media. They would also have a website Tessa would design. Casi studied Cara's Instagram, looking through her lengthy list of followers. Sure enough, he found Summer and Helena. He stopped himself from following them, but now he could access their accounts since neither was private. As he scrolled through Helena's professional modeling pictures, Casi felt a stab in his heart. He had briefly put his longing for her aside as he worked tirelessly on his business, but the fact remained, he yearned for her. He needed to come up with a plan to contact her… soon.

"She's gorgeous, man." Casi didn't realize Peter had approached and was looking over his shoulder.

"Yes, she is, isn't she? I just ordered the pottery, by the way." Casi hoped he kept a poker face.

"Order me one of her, too," Peter joked.

Casi quickly closed the window featuring Helena, revealing pictures of the ordered jugs.

"Here's what I got."

"Nice."

Casi returned to his email. He was glad Peter hadn't asked about Helena. It was getting increasingly difficult to lie to his friend, but he knew he couldn't reveal his past. Technically, he didn't lie; he just withheld all information about his prior life.

Cara's pottery arrived November 12th, shortly before opening night. Casi unwrapped it with great care, placing the pitchers on random off-white shelves sprinkled high along the whitewashed brick wall. It gave the appearance of a beautiful wall border, above the photography display at eye level. He could feel Peter's eyes on him from across the room as he thoughtfully placed the pieces, then rearranged them several times. He unwrapped the large pastel citrus patterned vase with the skilled expertise he learned working for F&S Enterprises years ago, and set it at the end of the indoor bar, near the reception area. He stood back and admired its beauty and placement.

"What do you think, Peter?"

"Splendid. Very classy."

Casi smiled, satisfied with his purchases. "We'll fill this with fresh seasonal flowers every week."

Three nights before their opening, Casi invited Benny, the staff, and the construction crew to dinner. Matias designed the menu and served it with pride, his chef hat standing tall. They sat outside at sunset, enjoying drinks and a wholesome meal. Everyone agreed the food was fantastic and would surely catapult the restaurant to the top of the island's list of places to dine. Casi nervously gave a heartfelt thank you to all for their hard work and issued an inspiring speech about how this restaurant was his dream come true. In conclusion, he thanked Peter and Benny with an added tribute.

"What do you think, Benny?" He asked when he sat down between Peter and him.

"I think I made a fantastic choice, selling to you." Benny's smile was heartwarming.

"Thanks, Benny. Now help spread the word. We'll need a good season to pay for everything."

"I think the word is already out. The place looks spectacular. Good job, good food, good vibe." Benny warbled with misty eyes.

Opening night was sold out. All thirty tables, fifteen inside and fifteen outside, were booked for two seatings. Tessa had advertised in all the big hotels, handing the concierge in each a stack of business cards, flyers, and personal drink vouchers, she designed for their use. Peter told all his cabbie friends to mention the new venue. He promised his cronies free drinks at the bar if they came in on a weeknight after the holidays. It worked like a charm. The restaurant was booked solid every night for the entire week. Although there were minor glitches here and there, the first few days were tremendous. Matias shone in his new chef's gear and Peter burst with pride as he welcomed people into the restaurant in his new white- collar, sea grape embroidered shirt, courtesy of Casi. The wait staff looked equally professional in their logo shirts, black bottoms, and pastel-colored high-performance aprons with faux leather straps. They had all picked their own favorite signature pastel color. Casi observed the night from his office monitor, only occasionally sneaking out to get a first-hand view. He could not have hoped for a bigger splash.

CHAPTER XXIX

Thanksgiving Joys and Jokes

The Crenston family, along with Francois, arrived at the Atlantis resort with overt enthusiasm. The opening of Francois' gallery in Soho had gone well, and everyone was delighted with his success. All hands were on deck for the gallery opening, and although it was a slow start initially, they ended strong with more than a few sales. Their feet were wet in the New York art world.

They arrived the Monday before Thanksgiving, exhausted and ready for a week of sunshine and rest. As usual, Cara had rushed to get extra last-minute orders out before leaving. Fifteen pitchers and a large vase were shipped before the Fereaux Galleries opening. She was dying to see the restaurant in the Bahamas that had placed such a costly order. Francois was certainly extending her client base with his advertising, she thought.

When the Crenston family arrived at the hotel, Samson was there, waiting in the lobby. Cara was overjoyed to see her son. On second glance, she noticed how spent he looked, as if he had taken a punch in the gut. His last-minute decision to join them from Paris had surprised her.

She wondered what had changed his mind.

"Welcome to the Bahamas. So glad you're here, Samson." She hugged her son, then stood back to look at his face. "You ok? You look tired."

"I am. We'll talk over dinner. Just so happy to see you guys. Hey, Jasper."

"Hey." Jasper high fived his little brother and patted him on the back.

"What about me?" Summer wedged her way in for a hug.

"Nice to see you, too."

Summer studied her twin brother. Never mincing words, she spit out what everyone else was thinking, "You look like shit. What's wrong?" She stayed inches from his face.

"I was going to tell everyone later. Natalie and I split up." Samson's expression was pained.

"So, that's why she didn't come. I was wondering about that. So sorry." Summer hugged him again, as Cara looked on, concerned.

"Sorry, Samson. We'll just have to find ways to distract you. I'm really glad you came. What happened, or do you not want to talk about it?" Cara squeezed his hand.

"Later. Hi, Francois. Nice to see you. How did the opening go?"

"Good. A few good sales. Hopefully, the gallery will catch on."

"I'm so glad you came, Samson. I want your opinion on my script. You need to fill in some blanks," Summer interrupted.

"The Flores script?"

"Yes."

"Let's save that for dinner or better yet, over drinks in the room. There might be moles with arrows in the lobby."

"I see your humor has survived the break up."

"Only my black humor."

"Are we checked in, Mom? Let's go see our rooms." Summer was bouncing off the walls with anticipation. The girl couldn't be still in a crowd.

An hour later, everyone assembled for an early dinner at the outdoor restaurant. The muted lighting, tropical beauty, and warm ocean breeze had them on a natural high in no time.

"I'm so hungry I could eat a shark. What looks good on the menu?" Jasper asked.

"The buffet," Cara deadpanned. "I'm going to order us a carafe of rum punch, ok?

"Fine, Mom. Samson, did you see any of my crew in Paris?"

"Speaking of that, I ran into Helena the week before I left. I hadn't seen her since your crew dinner. Didn't see anyone else, but I haven't been out much."

"How is she?" Summer shot him a side glance, putting her menu down.

"She looked ok, but there's still a lingering sadness about her. She's not her usual sparkly self. I totally understand how she feels. She said she's working all the time and not doing too much else. We had coffee together and she asked about you, Jasper."

"I emailed her a few times. She mentioned something about wanting to go to Mexico with Summer." Jasper turned to Summer. "What's that about?"

"What? No way. Summer, you're not going to Mexico. You can't run around asking questions about drug cartels. You'll be signing your own death warrant. What are you thinking?" Cara's face flushed and puckered like a raspberry.

"It was just an idea. I wanted to do some general research and get a feel for the place."

"Hell, no," Cara blasted, slamming her hand on the table. "The U.S. issued a travel advisory for five states in Mexico." She held up one hand, fingers extended, for emphasis. "You could just as well go to Afghanistan or Syria. People are disappearing like dew drops in the sun. Did you know Mexico has one of the highest murder rates in the world?"

"Ok, Mom. I get your concern. Let's change the subject before we end up in a fight on our first night of vacation."

"Fine. There's nothing else to discuss. You are not going to Mexico to research a drug lord. Boys, help me out here." Cara looked to Jasper for help, exasperated.

"Mom is right," Jasper added. "Way too risky."

"Yeah, Summer. I can help you do research from here." Samson patted his sister's extended hand.

"Ok, ok. So, what are we doing tomorrow?" Summer was very adept at changing the topic when things got heated around her. She hated confrontation, but rarely backed down from her views.

"I'm going to lie on the beach and swim in the ocean all day. Cara, you'll join me, I hope?" Francois smiled, trying to diffuse the tension. It worked.

"Yes, totally. One day, not tomorrow, I would like to go to the Botanical gardens. I hear they are special. Should I make a restaurant reservation for tomorrow night at the Sea Grape Garden?"

"Yes, or we'll never hear the end of it. What time do you want to go, Mom?" Jasper laughed.

"Shall we say eight? Sound ok, everyone? Stop rolling your eyes, Summer."

"Do we all have to go?" Summer countered, rebelliously.

"Yes! Everyone is on their own during the day, but I want us to have dinners together. This is a family vacation."

"Sounds good, Mom."

"Thanks, Samson."

"Ok, Mom." Jasper looked at her reassuringly, nodding.

"Summer?"

"All right, Mom. I heard you." Summer looked skyward and back at Samson, making a face.

"It's settled then. Pass the rum punch, please."

CHAPTER XXX

Dark Forces Align…..Almost.

It was a Tuesday night, and Casi was dead tired. He had worked on orders and payroll all day and come home early to go for a mind-clearing run. Post-run, all he wanted was a cocktail and a small supper on his terrace, wearing nothing more than a pair of boxer shorts. As he stepped out of the shower, his phone rang.

"Casi, I hate to ask you this, but can you come back to the restaurant tonight? One of the bartenders called in sick. Jenny is needed for waiting tables, and there's nobody at the front desk. The restaurant is crazy busy."

"Yes. I just got out of the shower. Give me a few minutes to get dressed."

"Thanks, man. I called Chrissy to see if she could hostess tonight, but she hasn't arrived yet. Even if she comes soon, we need an extra set of hands."

"I hear you. No worries. I'll be there shortly."

Casi dressed, pocketed his wallet and grabbed a fist full of nuts. He was starving. He looked nice in his new burgundy linen pants, light blue cotton shirt, and navy leather sneakers. The recent additions to his growing wardrobe were useful, especially the comfortable shoes. He was retiring his cowboy boots for going out only. The restaurant business was a dirty one, requiring a frequent change of shirts and exceptionally comfortable footwear.

As a restaurant owner, he tried to look sharp, even if he hid in his office most of the time. He kept a few clean shirts in his desk, for emergencies. Reaching for his new navy linen jacket, he slammed the front door shut behind him.

On his way to the truck, he noticed the woman from Apt 5G was back. She always left her sandy beach toys outside her door when she was in town—a Frisbee, a float and a sandy, surf boogie board. She owned a one-bedroom apartment at the end of his hallway and flew in from Miami every few weeks. He had seen the airline tags on her luggage, previous trip. From the tags, he knew her first name was Rose. As he walked along the curved path to his truck, he saw her coming back from a day at the beach, sand-covered and sun-kissed. Her lazy rhythmic walk, hips swinging side to side, mesmerized him as he hurried to his truck. He turned to watch her sexy persona from behind. The setting sun illuminated her golden hair like a halo and her tiny bikini under the transparent beach cover-up left little to the imagination. His imagination was definitely heading in the wrong direction for going back to work. Right now, Rose looked incredibly enticing. He watched as she gracefully slung her beach bag over her shoulder and disappeared into their building, trying to recall the last time he had sex.

Minutes later, Rose still on his mind, he pulled into his spot at the restaurant and hurried past a line of people at the front door. Peter greeted him with a sigh of relief.

"Oh, good, you're here. David is sick with the flu or something, so I'll tend bar outside. Can you pretend to be both the manager and the host until Chrissy gets here?"

"I'll try, but I won't be as good as you." Casi said with a serious demeanor.

Peter smirked. "Of course. Your other job choice for tonight is bartender."

"I'll stick with hosting, but you're still the manager. If you mix bad drinks, you'll be the one to hear about it."

"My drinks are memorable. Everyone knows that, just ask Gracie."

"Good to know. Mine are too, but it's usually a hazy memory."

Casi loved to make Peter laugh. He positioned himself at the counter by the front door and greeted the next arriving group, flashing his most winning smile, in spite of his growling stomach. The flow of arrivals was continuous and he could see his staff was working hard. He directed everyone to the outside bar and handed them a starfish-shaped buzzer for notification when their table was ready. Thankfully, there was a slight lull after the 7:30pm seating. A headache threatened to bloom. The constant probing questions, from people on the waiting list, were making him dizzy. He needed food. Within the hour, Chrissy arrived, and he was happy to leave the front-line hot seat.

"Thanks for coming on your day off, Chrissy. It's a madhouse tonight. I've been trying to keep all the new arrivals happy at the bar. Things just slowed down a bit. I haven't eaten in hours. Can you take over while I grab some food?"

"Sure, Casi. Go eat."

He wandered into the bustling kitchen and was ignored by everyone. A well-oiled machine was in motion, and even the slightest ripple could cause an upset.

"What can you spare for a hungry man that is quick and easy?" He directed his question to the sous-chef.

"Would you like some fresh barbequed shrimp and garlic-roasted asparagus? It's one of the specials that's ready for serving."

"Perfect. Thanks."

"You can't eat it here. Go out to the picnic table or eat in your office. You know Matias's rules. No extra bodies in the kitchen."

"I know. I'll take it to the office."

When Casi walked back out to the restaurant floor after wolfing down his food, Chrissy was ruling with poetic grace.

"I'm good here, Casi. See if Peter needs help at the bar."

As he walked to the outside bar, his eyes traveled around the tables. Almost every table was filled and those that weren't were being cleared for the next seating. The outdoor bar was mobbed.

"Hey, Peter. Chrissy is here, manning the front. Do you need anything or can I retire to the office?"

"Yes, sliced limes and another case of *Sancerre*." He placed the empty container on the side bar.

"Ok."

As he perused the tables, his eyes riveted back to one table in particular. Casi choked and stared in horror. His stomach lurched, threatening to send the shrimp back up. Seated in the far corner of the outdoor patio was a table of five. He instantly recognized the Crenston family. His instinct was to run back into the kitchen and hide, but then he remembered he looked different. Would they even recognize him now and here? He broke into a cold sweat. The thought of being exposed was unthinkable. He had worked so hard to start fresh. All his old fears resurfaced. He couldn't risk being discovered, and yet he couldn't take his eyes off their table. Why did they come here, to the Bahamas of all places? He scurried back to the kitchen to think. Instructing one of the dishwashers to take the case of wine to Peter, he stalled for time, cutting the limes himself. In his haste, he sliced his finger. Rummaging for a band aid in the kitchen's first-aid kit, he caught Matias glaring at him.

"Out of my kitchen, now. And send my dishwasher back. Can't you see we're slammed?"

"On my way."

Clutching the plastic container of lime wedges, he headed to the outside bar. Peter looked up and reached for the limes.

"Thanks. You ok? You look like you've seen a ghost."

"Fine. Matias threw me out of the kitchen."

Peter chuckled as he poured some beers from the tap. "What ya do?"

"Cut some limes and bloodied my finger. The table of five in the corner over there. Who's serving them?"

"Jenny, I think. Why?"

"They might need more drinks. I'll tell her."

Casi walked briskly to the kitchen and checked the order tickets. Matias glared. The Crenstons were having all his favorite dishes--conch fritters, grilled lobster, barbequed shrimp, and sweet barbequed chicken. Strangely, he was glad. Casi couldn't figure out why he cared, but now that they were here, he wanted them to enjoy his restaurant. A small measure of success from familiar faces, if nothing else. When Jenny came back to the kitchen to get their order, he told her to send them a free order of Bahamian papaya rum cake, compliments of the chef.

"Sure, Casi. Just them?"

"Yes. It looks like they're celebrating something." Before Jenny could respond, he added, "They'll need more drinks, too." He turned to look at an incoming text.

"Peter needs lemon slices and more mojito mix," he announced. "Who can slice the lemons?"

"Not you," Matias bellowed. "No more blood in my kitchen tonight."

Casi smirked and waited for the lemon wedges and mojito mix, then, reluctantly headed back out, his hands shaking.

The Crenstons were having a lively conversation, definitely celebrating something as their glasses repeatedly chimed. Casi couldn't overhear them over the roar of the bar, but he could see toasts being uttered and faces glowing in the lantern light. He wanted to move closer, but he was terrified someone may recognize him. Ducking behind the shadows of the bar crowd, he couldn't take his eyes off their table. Paralyzed, he observed the Crenstons while keeping one eye on Peter, in case he needed anything else.

"Casi, I need a few more bottles of Myer's dark rum. *Hurricanes* are in demand tonight."

"Coming up."

As Casi exited the kitchen's hall door, loaded with rum bottles, he found himself face to face with Cara Crenston on her way to the ladies room. She briefly glanced at him and continued to the bathroom. Casi's heart nearly stopped. He didn't read recognition on her face, but he remembered her lack of expression from past encounters in Paris. There was no telling what that woman registered. He spied on her as she returned to the table and was relieved to notice that conversation continued as before, no one looking in his direction. He supplied Peter with another delivery, just in time to see the complimentary dessert arrive. He heard them ooh and ahh over his prize-winning cake. It made him smile, ever so fleetingly. He hoped the distraction was enough to detract from their encounter.

A half hour later, they paid and left, instructing the waitress to thank the chef for the incredibly delicious treat. Cara pointed to her pottery as she exited and informed Chrissy she was the person who hand crafted and supplied the ceramics. She inquired if Peter was around. Chrissy told her he was busy tending bar since they were short staffed. Before leaving, utterly content with their dining experience, the Crenstons made another reservation for Saturday night.

Casi looked at the reservation spreadsheet. Generally, entries were made with hotel names if applicable. He wanted to know which hotels were sending him customers. He noticed the Crenstons were staying at The Coral in the Atlantis Resort. He wasn't sure what he would do with this information as he needed time to process the night. He was still in shock. The rest of the evening, Casi was preoccupied with keeping the bar supplied, and trying hard not to chit-chat with clients. He much preferred to manage the behind-the-scenes work, so his operation would run smoothly. In the comfort of his office, manning the cameras, he felt in charge. Maybe one day, that would change, but for now, watching from the shadows of the sidelines, was his preference. He wouldn't risk being stuck as a host again. Tonight, was a stark reminder of how vulnerable he really was. He couldn't afford to forget that.

CHAPTER XXXI

Princess on the Pea

Cara and Francois woke up early the next morning and headed down to breakfast in their swimsuits and cover ups, ready for a day of play. The younger generation slept in.

"Shall we get coffee and a muffin? I'm still stuffed from dinner." Francois patted his stomach.

"Good idea. I think I'll have a yogurt and a fruit cup instead of a muffin."

They walked to the concession stand. The line was short. "Fine. Shall we eat it by the pool?"

"No. Let's go down to the beach. I love having my morning coffee by the ocean. You know, since Summer got into Sundance, we may have to rethink the winter holidays and my Paris show dates." Francois paid for their food, and they walked through the gardens, the sweet tropical blooms wafting up their noses.

"When is the Sundance Film Festival?"

"It starts in mid-January. I'm not sure what Summer has to do to prepare. Let's find out later." They walked through the shady, green pool area and sat down on the low wall by the beach. Looking out at the sparkling turquoise water was therapeutic beyond measure.

"We can have your show in February," Francois suggested, sipping his coffee.

"I hear springtime in Paris is spectacular."

"Your hearing is excellent." Francois winked and cupped his ear.

"Oh, look, Samson and Summer." Cara waved. "Are you guys going jogging on the beach?"

"Yup, I need to burn some calories after that papaya rum cake." Summer adjusted her dark sunglasses.

"Summer dragged me out of bed. Jasper is still out cold. That coffee sure smells good. Why am I running when I could be sitting here drinking coffee and enjoying the view?"

"It's good. I won't lie. Think how much better it will taste after your run. A small reward. Shall we go to the Botanical Gardens tomorrow morning?"

"Maybe. Not too early, though." Summer made a face.

"Ok. Work for you, Francois?"

"Yes, fine."

"Where shall we have dinner tonight?"

"Let's stay in the hotel. The choices are endless. The concierge said Virgil's is popular."

"OK. I'll make a reservation. Have a good run." When the twins left, Cara turned to Francois.

"Something about the restaurant last night keeps ruminating in my brain, but I can't quite put my finger on it. It just opened and yet there is a certain familiarity. I feel like I've been there before."

"Maybe it's the fact your pottery is so beautifully displayed?"

"Thanks, that must be it. Let me lie in the shade and ponder the possibilities. You coming?"

CHAPTER XXXII

Risking Head or Hide?

Casi woke up feeling tired. Half the night, he had tossed and turned, playing out numerous frightening scenarios in his head. They all included him getting caught and ratted out to the police or worse, the Flores family. He decided it would be a stupid idea to approach any of the Crenstons, even though he was longing to get a message to Helena. He couldn't blow his cover and his chance at a happy life, but the thought continued to nag him all day.

If he did approach anyone in the Crenston family, it could only be Summer, who was in direct contact with Helena. He could offer her money for her next film project in exchange for giving Helena a message, thereby ensuring her silence, but was that smart? Was his yearning to contact Helena clouding his judgement? What if Summer said no and notified the authorities? Everything he worked so hard to build would go up in smoke. Poof. No, it was too risky. Threatening or scaring her into silence wasn't his style and it was never a good long term solution anyway. He never had adhered to the Flores method of intimidation. And so his morning went, with him tormenting himself over what action to take if any. Alone at his desk, he checked the extradition laws in the Bahamas.

To calm himself, he went for a morning workout. Still agitated, he called Peter to tell him he was running late. After showering and dressing, he drove to the Cove. Parking his truck, he reached for his Panama hat and sunglasses, then traversed the lobby and pool area. On the boardwalk, he walked back and forth, scanning the beach and pool, but he didn't spot any of the Crenstons. Buying a coffee, he sat down on a bench in the shade and waited. A few minutes later, he saw Summer and her twin brother jog up from the beach. They stopped for coffee and water bottles, then continued into the hotel. Even if he dared approach her, Casi realized he would never catch Summer alone. Someone from her family would always be there or pop up, especially on the hotel premises. He couldn't decide what to do. He threw his half- finished coffee cup in the trash and left the hotel. His heart desperately wanted to get a message out, but his head told him he was thinking like a crazy man.

Back at the restaurant, he hid in his office, pretending to do paperwork, but he couldn't concentrate on anything. Helena and Summer occupied his mind. A part of him didn't want to let this opportunity slip through his fingers, but in reality, he knew he should count his blessings if the Crenstons left the island none the wiser. He was torn beyond measure. His head and his heart weren't in sync, a feeling he was unfamiliar with and had yet to reconcile.

CHAPTER XXXIII

Intuition, Clairvoyance or Hallucinations

Over barbequed chicken and beers, the Crenston family planned their next day in paradise, deciding to appease Cara and visit the botanical gardens in the morning and tour the downtown area after lunch. Figuring out the starting time was tricky, as everyone had a different idea of what was too early. They finally settled on 10am at the taxi line.

After a delightful morning, viewing exquisite plants and birds, they lunched in town and walked around the government buildings on Bay Street. They toured the straw market searching for treasures. With souvenirs in hand, they headed back to Paradise Island.

"What are we doing tonight?" Cara asked as they approached the hotel.

"Shall we go to the Baha Mar Resort for dinner? I hear it's a beautiful resort. I wouldn't mind looking at it while we're here," Francois offered.

"Sounds good to me," Samson agreed.

"Me too. Jasper?" Cara glanced at her son.

"Yeah, let's do it."

"I'll see you all in the lobby at 7:15pm."

Arriving at their destination early, they explored the Baha Mar grounds.

"This is beautiful! Let's walk down to the beach," Cara marveled. They explored the pool area, the flamingo corral and the extensive fountains and gardens. When an employee walked by, Cara asked him, "Are these buildings all part of the hotel?"

"Yes and no, Ma'am. Those over there are the private residences."

"Nice," said Jasper. "Shall we check in for dinner early?"

"Hungry as always. You guys go ahead. Francois and I will look around a bit more. If you get seated early, order us margaritas on the rocks."

While enjoying the surrounding vegetation, Cara recognized the man from the Sea Grape Garden walking toward them. Abruptly, he turned around and sprinted back to a truck in the parking lot as if he forgot something. His gait and mannerisms looked so familiar. Lightning struck. The man reminded her of Carlos Ortiz, Helena's missing Mexican boyfriend, but it couldn't be him. Surely, he was in Mexico with Fernando Flores. Besides, close up, he had looked entirely different. It must be a coincidence. How strange.

Cara decided not to mention her suspicions to her children. If by some remote chance it was Carlos, she didn't want Jasper to get upset and Summer to talk to the man. Summer would do that in a heartbeat. It took Jasper months to stop looking over his shoulder. Bringing back bad memories from Barcelona wouldn't serve anyone. Nonetheless, she was curious and felt the need to investigate. She would google Carlos Ortiz for any articles she might have missed and the Sea Grape Garden restaurant in regard to ownership. She could also check with the hotel's concierge for any information he might have.

Bahamian trusts were legendary, equally private to Swiss banks and as tax friendly as Monaco. Perhaps this was not as far-fetched as she first thought. It actually would be a pretty smart move. Bold, but smart, she thought. Suddenly, the random pottery order didn't seem quite so random. Good, God! Could it be? Did Carlos move his restaurant from Paris to the Bahamas? But she didn't notice any other familiar looking people working at the restaurant. They all looked like locals. Should she even take her family back to the restaurant Saturday night? Did he work there, own it, or was he a guest? The credit card used to pay for the pottery order had the name Peter Cameron on it, she remembered.

That night, after she and Francois made love, Cara's brain was still spinning. She didn't know what to think. Her inquisitive mind couldn't let this mystery rest--she needed to know for sure. Were the drinks she had earlier playing tricks on her psyche?

CHAPTER XXXIV

Sweet Dreams......or Not

Casi drove home from the restaurant around 7pm, extremely tired after barely sleeping the previous night. He was glad it was Peter's turn to lock up. Having the Crenstons on island had knocked the wind out of him. As he walked toward his apartment building, he suddenly became aware of Cara Crenston staring at him. Instinctively, he turned and headed back to the truck, pretending he forgot something. What the hell was she doing here? Was she looking for him?

It dawned on him that many people came to the Baha Mar for dinner or to gamble in the casino. As he sat in the truck he tried to console himself with that thought. His hands were shaking and his insides churned. He never could stomach unpleasant surprises, and this was certainly a shocker. After six months of peace, he had gotten quite used to his predictable lifestyle on the island. Yes, he was busy with the restaurant, but it was a good kind of busy. He enjoyed managing his own business, filled with people he chose to surround himself with, good people. He couldn't go back to a life of constant worry and stress. He decided right then, he wouldn't approach Summer even if the opportunity presented itself. He would have to get a message to Helena a different way. Why had he even considered approaching Summer? It was nuts!

Once the Crenstons left the residence area, he exited the truck and went home. To satisfy his curiosity, he called the Baha Mar restaurant and asked if the Crenston party had arrived. The hostess confirmed with a quick yes. He hung up and exhaled.

The apartment was clean; housekeeping had been there. Somewhat relieved, he opened his bedroom window, letting the ocean breeze caress his face. After lingering through a few deep, meditative breaths, he showered and got ready for bed. He would watch a little TV and make it an early night. He was at peace with his decision to avoid the Crenstons at all costs. It would be foolish to risk his new life. He fell into a deep sleep the minute his head hit the pillow at nine, but nightmares plagued him through the night.

The next morning Casi woke up winded. He went down to the gym at six to clear his head and regulate his anxious breathing. On his way back, he grabbed a coffee and a *guava duff* to eat outside. Sitting on a bench, enjoying the early morning solitude and his sweet treat, he saw the woman from Apt. 5G. As she walked by sipping her coffee, Casi smiled at her and nodded

"Good Morning. Great coffee, right? I live down the hall from you in 5A."

"Oh, hi. Yes, it's good. Worth waking up early for. You just moved in a few months ago, right?

"Yeah. How long have you been here?" Casi squinted up at her.

"Since the resort opened. I live in Miami, but I'm down here a lot."

"My name is Casi. Nice to meet you."

"Rose. Rose Nowak. Perhaps I'll see you later, Casi? Are you going to the beach?"

"No, not today. I have to work."

"Where do you work?"

"The Sea Grape Garden Bar and Grill. Do you know it?"

"Oh, I heard about that place from one of the taxi drivers. I plan on coming one night. Is it good?"

"Very good. If you decide to come, drinks are on me. And by the way, we have great coffee too."

"Thanks, good to know. That's definitely an incentive." Rose laughed.

Casi liked the way her whole face lit up when she smiled. Sunglasses perched on top of her golden locks, he looked into her clear, turquoise eyes. Yes, he liked her. She possessed an unencumbered, exuberance that magnetically attracted him.

"Thanks for the tip. I'll see you soon, I bet." And with that declaration, Rose took off with her luminous hair and 'Mona Lisa' smile. Casi's gaze followed her scrumptious ass as she strode off in her fitted runner's shorts and sports bra. He was pleased with himself for finally taking the initiative. He liked the idea of getting to know her, but realized new contacts were potentially dangerous, especially when they lived in such close proximity. If he wasn't mistaken, Nowak was a Polish name. He chuckled to himself that once again, he was attracted to a Polish girl.

CHAPTER XXXV

Best Laid Plans Backfire...Sometimes

Thanksgiving and the day after were busy at the restaurant. Casi worked long days as lunch and dinner shifts melted into each other. He was filling orders continuously to keep supplies on hand; he was thrilled he was making money. His business had taken off thanks to Tessa, Matias, and Peter. Managing the payroll on a weekly basis, along with all expenditures, let him see his profit margin clearly. It was super encouraging. Of course, he had yet to cover the renovation expenses. That would take a good, long while to recoup.

So far, his staff was working out well. He didn't anticipate anyone leaving before the holiday season was over as healthy tips were being collected. Peter kept everyone in good spirits despite the work load. On occasion, at the end of the last shift, when the restaurant was cleared and set for the next day, the staff would sit around the bar for a nightcap to rehash the day. It brought everyone closer and it was fun for Casi to hear some of the stories they shared. One such night, Jenny mentioned the Crenston family.

"Casi, you know the family you sent the papaya rum cake to the other night? They were celebrating the daughter's film being accepted into the Sundance Film Festival. She must be a pretty good director."

"Really? Good for her. Glad I sent the cake."

"I think they're coming back Saturday night. They confirmed their reservation today. They left a really nice tip too."

Casi frowned. "Peter, do we have a full staff for the week end?"

"Yes. All shifts are confirmed."

"Good. You're in charge. I have tons of paper work and orders to catch up on. We are going through supplies faster than I anticipated. Don't count on me for pitching in."

"No worries. I got us covered."

Saturday afternoon, Casi disappeared into the office. He worked on pending orders and balanced the books. Around dinner time, he briefly resurfaced and ate at the indoor bar. The outdoor bar was crowded for happy hour. The weather was beautiful, so groups of people took their drinks to the beach. Peter had lined up extra portable chairs for that purpose. In addition to the bolted down wood benches, the folding chairs came in handy. People didn't mind waiting as much if they were seated with a drink. Around seven thirty, Casi retreated to his office. He could check the restaurant's activities from multiple screens.

The Crenstons arrived a few minutes after 8pm and were seated inside by the open accordion doors. Casi wasn't thrilled about the location. They were slightly elevated, smack center, and could oversee the whole restaurant from their vantage point. They wouldn't miss a thing. Knowing this, he would be confined to his office until they left-- it wasn't worth tempting fate again. So far, things were under control.

When Peter stuck his head in the door around 9:30pm to tell him that a young, beautiful blonde was asking for him, Casi's heart almost stopped. Did Summer Crenston recognize him?

"What's her name?"

"I don't know. Does it matter? She's hot."

"Where is she? Show me on the screen."

Peter looked and pointed to a woman at the outside bar.

Casi squinted and realized that Peter was pointing to Rose Nowack.

He let out a huge sigh and smiled.

"Peter, can you give her a drink on the house. Tell her I'll be out to say hi in a few minutes."

"Sure thing, man." Peter lingered for a moment, looking at him questioningly as if he was going to say something else, but then, thankfully, changed his mind. Casi was relieved when he left without another word. Perusing the three screens in his office, he noticed the Crenstons were done with their main course. Rose was at the far end of the outside bar. Should he wait until they left? Making Rose wait that long would be rude, especially if the Crenstons had dessert. He reached for his fedora and walked out through the kitchen's back door, circling around the building, through the parking lot to the beach end of the bar. He greeted Rose, turning his back to the Crenstons.

"Good evening, Rose. I'm glad you could make it."

"Hi, Casi. Nice hat. The restaurant is lovely. What a great location! I can't even remember what was here before."

"Thanks. The location is what sold me."

"Casi, this is my friend Taryn. She's here on vacation."

"Hello, Taryn. First time in the Bahamas?"

"Oh, no. I love coming to the island. It's my third visit."

"Nice. Hopefully, you'll make this place a regular stop. Welcome to the Sea Grape Garden."

"Thank you. I'm sure I will. This is quite a special spot. Are you the manager?"

"The owner."

"Wow! Congrats. I think you hit the jackpot. This place is a dream. I love the outdoor bar and the benches overlooking the water."

Casi noticed Rose studying him with renewed interest.

"Thanks. We kept the décor simple and focused on the natural resources, hence the name. In the spring, we want to expand and plant an organic garden over there, to grow some of our own vegetables. Farm to table concept, you know?" He smiled brightly at the thought.

"Awesome. What a great idea. I can't wait to see that," Taryn gushed.

Casi turned and peered over at the Crenstons. They were engrossed in conversation. Reassured, he turned back, chatting with Rose and Taryn for another few minutes.

When he turned around again to check the dining room, the Crenstons were gone. The cause of the assuagement of his anxieties dissipated instantly. Excusing himself, he mumbled something about work and coming back later. He walked back through the dining room and was nearly at his office when the ladies' room door swung open and he found himself face to face with Cara and Summer Crenston. For a split second, the three of them looked at each other.

Casi stepped aside, looking down, so the hat would shield his face. He let them pass in the narrow hallway and hurried into his office, slamming the door. Throwing his hat on the floor, he leaned back against the door, breathing heavily.

"Damn, damn, damn," he muttered, eyes shut. All night, he had been so careful to avoid them, only to end up nose to nose in the hallway. He cursed profusely, in his native Spanish. Did they recognize him?

CHAPTER XXXVI

Eyes…..Windows to the Soul?

Cara's consciousness switched gears to full alert when she exited the ladies' room and looked squarely into the man's eyes. The face was different, but there was no mistaking that shade of chocolate brown and those incredibly long eyelashes. Either Carlos had a brother or a double because this man moved exactly like him. He was light on his feet—a cheetah came to mind. She couldn't quite decide if it was really him or not, and it irked her. The restaurant ownership, which she had googled earlier, was listed as a corporation. She wondered if Summer noticed him, too. Her daughter was usually pretty astute. Cara said nothing on the way home, but her brain was racing.

"The food was delicious. I'm glad we decided to go back there," Jasper observed in the taxi.

"I agree. Tomorrow it's back to French food for me. I'm so glad I came this week. I had a great time, guys." Samson sighed.

"I'm glad you came too, Bro," Jasper echoed.

"Me too. Your help on my script was appreciated."

"One track mind as always," Samson groaned, making Summer laugh.

When they arrived back at The Coral, Francois and Cara dropped Jasper, Samson, and Summer at one of the hotel bars. She and Francois went to their room to sit on the porch and enjoy the lit garden views and the ocean lull. A half bottle of chilled rose' was waiting.

"Let's get out of our clothes and into our robes. I'll get more ice."

"Good idea." Cara took her time washing up, running a cool wash cloth over her face, and changed into her robe. She was still thinking about the man in the restaurant.

"To a wonderful vacation. *Sante'*." Francois handed her a glass and moved closer for a musical toast.

"*Sante'*. To many more. How did you like the restaurant second time around?"

"It was great. I particularly liked the ceramic decoration."

"Oh, right. You get brownie points for that observation."

"What are brownie points?"

"Hmmm, Let me show you when we go inside."

Cara leaned over and kissed Francois. Mid-kiss, she slipped her hand inside his robe.

CHAPTER XXXVII

Dreamers and Schemers

Summer and her brothers were sitting in the bar, chatting.

"What time is your flight tomorrow, Samson?"

"Early. I have to leave after breakfast."

"I'm glad we have one more day, Jasper. I'm not ready to go home yet."

"Yeah, for sure. Going to the men's room. Order me a beer when the waitress comes."

"Ok." Summer turned to Samson. She was dying to tell him she might have seen Carlos Ortiz at the Sea Grape Garden, but she couldn't be sure of his reaction. He was a journalist and might feel compelled to uncover something she wanted to secretly explore in private for her own reasons. She hadn't quite decided what to do, but she was determined to delve further into whether the man was Carlos or not. She would sleep on it and decide her next move in the morning. Besides, Samson was leaving early. He couldn't go back to the restaurant anyway. Should she ask Jasper? He had been so rattled in Barcelona. She knew that probably wasn't a great idea either. He immediately shut her down whenever she talked about traveling to Mexico.

"Samson, are you going to be ok without Natalie?"

"Yeah. I was ok before Natalie, so I guess I'll survive after her. It does hurt, though. We had fun together. I felt so betrayed."

"Cheating will do that. Well, just call or email me when you're feeling down. Do you have any good business trips coming up?"

"No."

"How long are you planning to stay in Paris?"

"No idea. I'll try to come home for either Christmas or Sundance. I can't do both."

"Good. I vote for Sundance. You know, you should call Helena when you get back."

"Jasper will hate that idea."

"Jasper is in New York. Besides, I didn't say, date Helena, did I? Seriously, she gets invited to so many parties, I bet she would be happy to include you. She just lost her boyfriend, too. She'll understand how you feel."

"I guess I could do that. Might be fun."

Summer detected a small smile. "I'll email her."

The waitress came and they ordered a round of drinks just as Jasper returned.

"Now that I have you both here one final time, let's talk about my script." Both men groaned.

"Summer, give it a rest for five minutes."

"Yeah, Summer. Email us, and we'll comment."

"Geez, you guys. Am I that obsessive and transparent?"

"Yes," they both answered in unison, making ugly faces.

The following morning, the conversation over breakfast centered around the next holiday and who was doing what. The Crenston family loved their reunions. It looked like Sundance would be the next reunion as all the men loved skiing. In the lobby, everyone hugged Samson goodbye, offering advice for life after Natalie. Samson smiled bleakly.

Summer, in the interim, was scheming. She had a strong urge to revisit the Sea Grape Garden. She couldn't let this opportunity go since going to Mexico had been vetoed by her entire family. The only question remaining was, should she take Jasper, or go alone? She didn't feel safe going alone, so in the end, she decided to lure him into her web.

"You're awfully quiet this morning, Summer. Sleep ok?"

"Yes, Mom. Just sad to see Samson go."

"Yeah, me too. He looks a lot better than when he arrived, though. Will he be ok?"

"I think so. I told him to call Helena. She has so many model friends and parties going on. They can cheer each other up."

"Hmm, did Jasper agree?"

"Agree with what?"

"Really, Summer. What cloud are you floating on?"

"Sorry, Mom. Samson will be fine. Stop worrying."

Summer inserted herself between her mother and Jasper and whispered,

"Jasper, what are your plans for today?" She leaned in close, directing him away from Cara.

"Hanging out here. Why, what do you have up your sleeve?"

"What makes you think I have anything up my sleeve?"

"That look and the tone in your voice. You are up to something. I know you."

"I was wondering if we could go back to last night's restaurant for a late lunch together, without mom and Francois."

"I think I'd rather just hang here today. Twice was good enough for me."

"Please. I'll buy." She knew she was pleading.

"Why? Any reason? Did you fall in love with the bartender or something?"

"I just really liked the place and I wanted to surprise mom with pictures of her ceramics on site." Summer knew she could melt Jasper with a good deed for their mother.

"Alright. If you're buying, I can be persuaded. The food was pretty good. Are you paying for the taxi too?"

"Yes. Pool or beach now?"

"Beach."

CHAPTER XXXVIII

Personal Boundaries Crushed

At 1:30pm, Summer and Jasper hopped into a taxi and headed to the Sea Grape Garden. Summer was nervous. She had no idea how to approach the man, she thought might be Carlos. If he felt the same way about Helena as Helena did about him, that would be her best angle, her only angle. Hit him in his soft spot. Samson looked like he was really suffering from his break up, and Helena had certainly taken Carlos's departure hard. Perhaps he was hurting too. Summer was banking on matters of the heart.

The restaurant was bright and cheery during the day with a good-sized lunch crowd who looked like they were lingering indefinitely. Most were done with their meals and nursing coffee. The ambiance and setting were so compelling, she didn't blame them for staying. The hostess seated them at the bar.

"I'll have a table cleared shortly. People are paying."

"No worries," Summer answered as her eyes scanned the dining room.

Carlos was nowhere in sight. They ordered a fruity cocktail and moved to one of the benches facing the ocean, their backs to the dining room. After a few minutes, Summer grew restless and sprang up.

"While we're waiting, I'm going to take a few pictures of mom's pottery and go to the ladies room. The lighting is perfect now. The shots will look great on her Instagram and website.

"Ok. I'm good here. Take your time. Mom will definitely be thrilled."

Summer walked into the dining room and took a few pictures. She peeked into the kitchen. No one noticed her; the employees were all working with purpose. She walked past the ladies' room, to the office, and raised her hand to knock. Her heart was racing. After taking a deep breath, she knocked on the door. She leaned in, trying to detect any activity, but all she heard was a radio playing softly in the background. She raised her hand and knocked again, louder.

With no response forthcoming, Summer turned to walk away. The hallway was empty, so on a whim, she turned back and opened the door. The man sitting behind the desk looked at her with a steely expression.

"This area is private. The restroom is down the hall."

Summer stepped in and closed the door behind herself.

"Hi, I'm Summer Crenston. Maybe you remember me?"

He didn't respond, his face statuesque. She decided to take a different approach.

"My family has eaten here twice this vacation week and we really enjoyed our meals. You have my mother's pottery on the shelving in the dining room. I wondered if it's ok for me to take a few informal pictures."

"Suit yourself. The pottery is quite beautiful. You have a talented mother."

Summer waited for his facial expression to change, but he didn't move a muscle.

"Thank you. I'll be sure to tell her." Summer took a deep breath. "You look somewhat familiar. Do you know someone named Helena Majewski from Paris?"

The man shrugged, shaking his head.

Summer observed a twitch around his mouth, but his eyes revealed nothing.

"Are you Carlos Ortiz?" Her voice was a hoarse whisper.

"No, sorry. You're mistaken. That's not my name. If you'll excuse me now, I have work to do."

Summer knew she wasn't mistaken. She remembered his chocolate eyes with those long, unforgettable lashes, a dead giveaway. She also remembered the warm tone of his voice. She knew she had to work quick. He was ready to kick her out. Her adrenalin was pumping.

"Look, I'm not here to cause trouble. I'm very close to Helena, and she's suffering, worried sick about you. She was absolutely crushed when you left. It would mean the world to her, to know you're safe. I have no intention of exposing you, nor does she. I want to see her happy, and getting a message from you would make her very, very happy."

Summer waited for a response, but got nothing. He also didn't ask her to leave, so she continued courageously.

"I know Helena is probably being watched by the police, and that you can't contact her directly or your sister Hermosa either, for that matter, but perhaps I can be of service to you. Can you trust me, Carlos?"

"I'm listening. And stop calling me, Carlos."

"Right. Sorry. Here's what I propose. Helena will be coming to the U.S. in a few months for the Sundance Film Festival. My film, the one she co-starred in, was accepted."

"Congratulations."

"Thank you. Park City, Utah, will be flooded with people, so that would be a good time to arrange a meeting. You will get lost in the crowd. I can also help you get a message to Hermosa."

Helena and I were talking about traveling to Mexico to find you, but my family was dead set against the idea. Helena told me Hermosa is an accountant and works for a large hotel in Mexico City. I found her, but I haven't contacted her yet." Summer held her breath.

"Your family is right. Listen to them. It would be a terrible idea for you to go to Mexico and ask around about things that are none of your business. You wouldn't make it back alive. You also, would endanger Hermosa and she's an innocent in this. I strongly advise you to back off and mind your own business," he growled, standing up. Resting his hands on the desk, he glared at her crossly.

Summer sucked in some air. With an unsteady, emotional voice, she continued,

"Look, my brother is probably wondering what I'm doing in the ladies room this long. Think about what I said. We're having lunch here. Maybe you and I can talk again after lunch?"

"I think you better leave while you can. Do I need to check you for a wire?" He walked toward her.

"What? Heavens, no. I'm not wired up, and for your information, no one in my family recognized you. I swear." Summer lifted her hair and her t-shirt a little exposing her abs. "No wire."

She took a step backwards. He was making her anxious. She wondered if it was wise to tell him all she had, but she felt emboldened by the fact Jasper was close, and she was leaving the next day. The words had just spilled out, unfiltered. She placed her hand on the door handle.

"I'll leave now. Please think about what I said. If I don't hear from you, I'll keep this meeting to myself. I would never break Helena's heart. I care deeply about her. I'm leaving the island tomorrow and you won't have to worry about ever seeing me again. If you don't want to contact her, I'll never reveal that I saw you. Please, believe me. Trust me."

With a trembling hand, Summer opened the door and walked out. Her knees felt like Jell-O. For one brief second, she thought he might shoot her in the back and dump her in the garbage outside.

CHAPTER XXXIX

Do, Die, or Run Like Hell

Casi slumped back into his chair and let the trapped air leave his body via a sigh. He couldn't believe what had just transpired. How had she recognized him? He looked so different. The woman had guts. Or maybe she was ignorant of the danger she was potentially putting herself in. Had this been Mexico, she would have never made it out the door. His mind was racing. He couldn't let her endanger Hermosa by asking around or worse, telling her where to find him on an unsecured phone. What to do next?

There was another knock at the door. Casi's heart skipped a beat. Before he could find his vocal cords, Peter stuck his head in.

"You alright? You look weird, man."

"I'm fine. Just doing book keeping. I'm a little cross-eyed."

"Did I just see that pretty blonde come out of your office?"

"Yes. She introduced herself because her mother runs the company in New York we bought the decorative pottery from. She asked me if she could take pictures."

"And?"

"And what?"

"Did you say yes?"

"I did. She can take pictures of the pottery only. I don't want her taking pictures of the employees. No one poses, ok? Watch her, please."

"Got it. Any special reason?"

"It's a security thing. What did you come in for? Need anything?"

"Yes, we're low on Nassau Royale. Can you order some?"

"Sure. Keep an eye on her, Peter."

"Will do."

When the door closed, Casi turned to his screen. Summer and her brother were sitting outdoors at a table near the edge of the beach, sharing conch fritters and field greens with grilled shrimp. Over fruity drinks, they appeared to be enjoying the day, chit-chatting and laughing as they dipped their fritters in the accompanying sauce. Casi watched them, brooding. He had to do something. Summer could ruin everything with her brazen ignorance.

After a few minutes, he turned to his computer and opened two email accounts under the name CXSX69@hotmail.com and SundialXOX96@hotmail.com He scribbled them on a blank piece of paper, which he folded and put into his pocket, then sat back in his chair. Had Summer not recognized him, he would have never blown his cover, but now, she posed a serious threat. He wondered what she really wanted. Why would she care if Helena and he ever saw each other again? Were she and Helena really that invested in each other? There was more to this than met the eye. He wanted to investigate further, not just to protect his sister or get a message to Helena, but to find out Summer's real motivation. He couldn't fully trust her, could he? Her offer to contact Hermosa was enticing, but he had to stop her from asking around about his sister. Killing two birds with one stone would be a dream. On the flip side, the danger was paralyzing. How dare she contact his sister out of the blue?

Casi grabbed his cell phone and left the office. He seriously regretted ordering the pottery from New York. Maybe they never would have come here, had he refrained from doing so. Had he dug his own grave? He cursed at himself in the foulest language possible. He would have to do damage control and hope it works.

CHAPTER XL

He Who Does Not Trust, Cannot be Trusted -- Lao Tzu

Summer skipped the ladies' room and exited into the bright, soothing sunlight and blinked. She shifted her sunglasses from the top of her head back to the bridge of her nose and looked around for Jasper. She spotted him at a table in the last row by the beach and waved. She was glad to see they had an umbrella. Hoping Jasper wouldn't notice her trembling hands, or how rattled she was, she plopped herself beside him and forced a smile.

"Nice table, Bro. How did you manage this plum location?"

"Pure skill and running shoes. Oh, good, you didn't get kidnapped by the bartender. I was beginning to wonder."

"Sorry. There was a line in the ladies' room. Guess the people leaving dipped into the rum punch over lunch."

"No worries. We will too by the time we leave. I just ordered us another round. Since you are paying and all."

"Right. Thank you for that, I think. I got a few pictures. Mom will love them. What shall we get?"

"I ordered conch fritters and a salad with grilled shrimp. Sound ok?"

"Sounds perfect."

"You're easy today. Where's my sister?"

As Jasper talked mindlessly about the Bahamas, the hotel, and the good time he had, Summer couldn't help but wonder if Carlos would respond to her. Or would he just kill her on the way out? What had she been thinking? Her mind wandered to various dark places until the food arrived. Fear made her hungry. She and Jasper dug in, and Summer let her brother continue his monologue. She placated him with strategic nods and sounds of approval. She wanted him to think she was listening, however, she found it extremely difficult to focus. Samson would have called her out on it, but not Jasper, especially with a plate of delicious food in front of him.

When they finished their lunch and drinks, Summer ordered coffee for Jasper and the bill. Carlos was nowhere in sight. She placed her credit card on the table.

"Here, pay the bill when the coffee comes. I want to take a few more pictures."

Summer walked inside the almost empty restaurant. As she lined up a particularly good angle of the pottery with ocean scenery in the background, Casi walked up from behind and spoke softly over her shoulder.

"Walk with me to the beach."

He gave her a fright, creeping up from behind. She took in his fresh scent and smooth, velvet voice, trying not to panic. Emboldened by the drinks, she nonchalantly took her shot of the pottery and slowly pivoted toward him.

"Sure, but I can't walk far. My brother will follow." Summer waved to Jasper, she would be right back, then followed Casi down to the sand.

Casi stopped at the water's edge and began talking.

"I'll make this quick. I'm not sure what your real motivation for seeking me out is, but I can promise you this; if it's for the wrong reasons, it will backfire for you. I have used this opportunity to start a new life, free from the Flores family. I feel great regret I had to leave Helena behind, but I had no choice. It was a matter of protecting her without upsetting her life. It was also a matter of my survival. I would love to get a message to her because I do miss her, care for her, and feel bad about suddenly disappearing, but please understand, I had absolutely no choice. It was a split-second decision to leave Paris immediately or lose everything. The Flores family controlled me, and in some ways, they still do. If they ever find me here, they'll kill me. If they know you are in contact with me, they will torture you for information, and kill you, too, make no mistake. Do you understand?"

He paused and Summer could feel him trying to gauge her reaction. His tension was enveloping her, sending a chill up and down her spine despite the midday heat. "I understand," she croaked.

"I would like to get my sister out of Mexico. She's no longer safe there. I'm certain she and Helena are both being watched, you're right about that. You clearly have no idea how dangerous and risky this all is."

"I get the picture."

"Do you, though? How did you find me? Recognize me?"

"We came to your restaurant because my mom wanted to see where her pottery went. We had a Caribbean trip planned either way. My family comes to the Caribbean islands every few years, and we hadn't been to the Bahamas yet. We always pick a different island. I recognized you because of your eyes, your long lashes. I remembered them. I also remember the tone of your voice. Your disguise is pretty good otherwise. Had you worn sunglasses, I probably never would have figured it out. The rest of my family hasn't. I found Hermosa because Helena told me she worked for a large hotel in Mexico City. I called around. I would have contacted her eventually so, consider yourself lucky we just talked. Now, I won't risk it."

"I see. Here's what I suggest. You forget you ever saw me, and you lose Hermosa's information."

"Ok, no problem. I take it you don't want to contact Helena then?"

"I do. Here, use this email to contact me. The other email address will be yours. The password is here. Do not contact me from any other email address. I won't answer. Please wait until I contact you first. I'll give you further instructions how to get a message to Helena. Don't contact the restaurant as others read the emails here and please, do not call me on your phone. Ever. Also, don't talk to Helena about me, using your personal email or phone. She can't know where I am. If you do, I'll know. I know where to find you. You remember what happened to Adriano? You cross me, you and your family will pay. Do you understand?"

"Yes, got it. Secure sources only. What about Hermosa? Can I help there?"

"Let me think about it. Please, don't do anything until you hear from me. It's for your own safety, Summer, and for Hermosa's too. The Flores family is very influential and far reaching in Mexico and New York. If someone approaches Hermosa, they will know before you can get a sneeze out. Do you get the danger?"

"Yes, I do. I won't do or say anything until I hear from you."

"Good. I hope I can trust you. I'm taking a big leap of faith here. I don't think you really do understand the danger and I hope you never find out first-hand what happens if you mess up." Casi paused. "Tell your mother, we get a lot of compliments. If she sends us her business cards, we can pass them out whenever people ask about her work."

"Thanks. I'll tell her. Listen, don't worry. I won't do anything to harm you. I believe in second chances. You can trust me."

"So you said. You may not intend to slip, but one unchecked move can ruin all I have worked for and endanger you and your family. The Flores group is ruthless. You are clueless. Really, sooo clueless. I'm happy here. I'm making an honest living, and I will protect that with my life. I always wanted an opportunity like this. I don't expect you to understand. You never lived in fear, I suspect."

Summer shook her head, no.

"Bye and forget you saw me, until I contact you. Don't disclose my whereabouts to anyone, least of all your family. They won't understand."

Summer nodded, "Who would I hear from if Carlos isn't the right name?"

"Just C." Casi put his sunglasses on and walked past the bar to the office, leaving Summer to trail behind him. The meeting was adjourned. Summer shuffled through the sand, her legs leaden. She was shaking from the aftershock. Motioning to Jasper, she waved and pointed toward the parking lot. Her voice sounded hoarse.

"Let's go."

CHAPTER XLI

Never Lie to Those You Love

In the taxi, Summer sat back and took deep yoga breaths, thankful she was still alive. She opened the window to let the ocean breeze wash over her face. She had just experienced one of the most stressful lunches in her life. Still trying to digest what she had done, she replayed the scenes in her head, trying to remember all that had transpired. Details mattered. Something about Carlos's confession resonated with her. She could only imagine how difficult his life had been and still was. It now made sense to her why Helena liked him. Underneath his tough exterior, he had a sincere quality. There was definitely a likeable human being in that tough exterior shell. She imagined, he probably needed the armor to survive his former boss and life.

"I was worried you were ditching me for that guy. I was debating what I would tell mom. Summer decided to ditch Sundance for a job at the Sea Grape Garden."

"Hilarious, Jasper."

"Well, you have to admit, that was a really long talk about ceramics. Even mom wouldn't buy that one."

"We talked about the island. He moved here recently. I got some great pictures for mom."

"Not a bad life."

"So, what are we doing for the rest of the day?"

"Well, I don't know about you, but I plan to go for a swim, then hit the gym."

"I'll join you for the swim. Are you packed?"

"That will take me all of ten minutes with time to spare."

"Of course. Where did mom want to have dinner tonight?"

"In the hotel. Not sure which restaurant."

"Ok, then. Let's go for a swim. I need to get my beach bag in the room. Meet you in five."

"Right. That means twenty. If you aren't down in twenty minutes, look for me in the pool. And don't talk to any strange men along the way."

Summer smirked at him and walked hurriedly to the elevators.

On her way to the room, she stopped ever so often to look over her shoulder. The hotel had long hallways that weren't always active in midday. People were out. She was happy to discover the maid's cart across from her room. Entering carefully, she listened and looked before proceeding. In the bathroom, she splashed some cold water on her face before grabbing her packed beach bag. She rushed out of the room, lest the cart moved, and raced back to the elevator.

Spotting Jasper on the foot end of her mom's chaise, she waved from afar. As she approached, he took off his tee shirt and started moving toward the water.

"Hi, guys. Jasper, pool? Mom, you coming?"

"No, Francois and I just swam. He went to get us ice coffees. I'm staying right here. I've been dreaming about that coffee since breakfast. It's my afternoon treat. You two go ahead."

After swimming, Summer was cornered by her mom.

"Jasper said you went back to the Sea Grape Garden for lunch today. Any special reason?"

"No. I just really liked it there, the food is so good. I also wanted to surprise you with some great pictures of your pottery on location. I'll send them to you after I edit. Mr. Blabbermouth ruined my surprise."

"Thanks. How thoughtful. Jasper said you talked to someone at the restaurant. Who was that?"

"Yeah. One of the guys who works there. We talked about your pottery. He said they get a lot of compliments. You should send them business cards to give out. Why, what did Jasper say?"

"Nothing different."

Summer tensed up. Damn her brother. Her eyes were hidden behind a falling lock of hair and sunglasses. She hoped her mother wouldn't notice her nerves kicking in. Fooling Cara was an art no one in her family had perfected.

"What time do we leave for the airport tomorrow?"

"Around noon. Be packed and ready at the taxi line."

"Ok, what time is dinner?"

"We're meeting in the lobby at 7:45pm. Not sure which restaurant yet. Working on that."

CHAPTER XLII

Communication Is Key

The next morning, when Casi left his apartment, he bumped into Rose.

"Hi, Rose. How was your week end?"

"Hi, Casi. Good. Thanks for drinks the other night. My friend, Taryn, was really impressed with the place."

"Thanks. I hope that means you'll both be back."

"Taryn left last night, but I'm around for a few more days. I just may. Are you going to the pool now or are you off to work?"

"I'm going to work, but I hope to get a swim in this afternoon."

"Ok, maybe I'll see you then."

"What day are you going back to Miami?"

"Wednesday night."

"Any interest in dinner Tuesday night?" Rose's smile could melt glaciers.

"Yes, that would be nice, thank you."

"Great. See you later. We'll make plans."

When he got into his truck, he couldn't believe how bold he had become. In the past, he waited until girls solicited him; they always did. He had been too busy and too shy to ask anyone out. Helena was the sole exception and that took two tries before he dared.

When Casi arrived at the office, he had a spring in his step. He was looking forward to his date with Rose. He planted himself in front of the computer and knocked out his orders. Island living was splendid in so many ways, but getting orders filled in a timely fashion required aggressive organizational skills. He kept a running list and ordered things in bulk, but it still was challenging to anticipate proper amounts in advance. He kept his truck ready in case he needed to do a quick pick up at the airport. Many of their shipments came from the United States. Express overnight delivery was costly.

By the end of the week, a personal order Casi was waiting for arrived. He tackled that box first. It contained numerous pre-paid, non-contract cell phones. He put three back in the box after adding numbers and labeling them. Then, he redirected the shipment to Summer Crenston in New York City. No return address. He sat down to send her an email.

"Dear S,

I'm sending you a package today which should arrive in New York midweek. It has three secure cell phones. Open and activate the one with your initial on it. Please use it to call me at the number programmed in it. If at any time you change your mind about anything we discussed, just destroy the phones and forget you ever saw me. I will understand. Our communication is not without danger for both of us. Hope you and your family had a good time here. Don't share any information.
C

He reread it three times before pressing send. It was excruciatingly hard to trust, but he had a good feeling about Summer. He also suspected, he scared her sufficiently.

CHAPTER XLIII

Choking on Secrets

Summer checked her new email account daily for a note from C. When it finally came a week later, she smiled. She was in business. It was killing her not to share information with her family, but she knew what they would say. "Back off, Summer. You're playing with fire. A cartel is not to be messed with."

She could hear their warnings ringing in her ears, windchimes in gale force winds. She knew sharing anything at all would elicit an immediate family intervention.

Summer craved an inside story of the cartel's operations. She also truly cared about Helena and maybe C and his sister, too. His story had struck a chord with her. She felt a desperate sincerity beneath his veiled threats. Time would tell. She hoped she wasn't making a mistake in trusting him.

In the meantime, Summer activated the phone marked S. The other two phones were labeled H and He. Was she to forward them? Summer emailed C.

Hola C,

The package arrived. I will contact you in the morning around 9am your time, unless I hear otherwise. I'm still on board and awaiting your instructions.

Cheers, S

The next morning, at 9am on the dot, Summer called C. He picked up instantly.

"Hello, Summer, I see the phone is working. These are non-contract, pre-paid cell phones, secure and untraceable. When the balance is low, the funds need to be replaced immediately, or you'll lose the phone number, so let me know. I have you covered for a while."

"Ok, got it. Thank you."

"The other two phones are for Helena and Hermosa. I labeled them. 'He' is for Hermosa. You will give Helena her phone when she comes to the United States. Don't clue her in long distance. Give her the phone at the festival in Park City, not before. Definitely not in New York City. Understood?"

"Yes. What about Hermosa's phone?"

"We can't send it to her. Her mail is being checked and no doubt, she is being watched. The package needs to be hand-delivered to her at her place of business by a fellow Mexican. Someone who won't look suspicious. If you can find someone trustworthy, I will pay for the flight, hotel, and travel expenses. The person delivering cannot be clued in. They need to just physically hand her the box and tell her to open it privately. Don't even think about doing this yourself as you and your family are well documented in Flores' world."

"How will she know what to do?"

"The cell phone has two numbers programmed into it, yours and mine. The box also contains a clue that will alert her the phone is from me. Trust me, she'll know when she discovers it."

"Ok. Do you want to tell me what the clue is? The box is sealed."
"No."

Summer heard the conviction in his voice and knew not to push. "Alright. Off the top of my head, my mother's landscaper is

Mexican and he goes home every December. He stays there through the winter holidays. The timing could work. Maybe I can ask him?"

"Is he trustworthy? Will he tell your mother?"

"I really don't know."

"Well, you need to be sure or keep looking."

"Ok, I'll see what I can do. You don't think I should do it myself?"

"Absolutely not. Your blonde head would stick out like a white radish in a black bean dish. Besides, Fernando knows you and your entire family. He would know about your arrival before you checked into your room."

"Really?"

"Yes, really. Remember when your mother's tablet was stolen in Paris?"

"Yes."

"Your brother had no clue he was being shadowed. The delivery person has to be a random Mexican. Someone no one will notice, someone who blends."

"Ok, then. I'll see what I can do."

"When you find someone, send me their name and contact info. I'll arrange for a prepaid flight and hotel room in Hermosa's hotel."

"Sounds good. How much time do I have?" Summer looked at her desk calendar.

"No deadline, but the sooner we get to her, the better. She's in danger."

"Right. I'll be in touch."

"On these phones only."

"I'm aware. Bye."

"Summer?"

"Yes?" She whispered nervously.

"Thank you."

Before she could reply, he was gone.

CHAPTER XLIV

Heard it Through the Grapevine.....

Visiting Cara in her studio, Summer sat at the table with a view of the driveway.

"I like your new work, Mom. Have you decided on your Paris exhibition dates yet?"

"Thanks! Not yet. Since we're all going to Sundance in January, I decided to wait until spring. I wanted to discuss the dates with you because if we all go to Paris together, maybe we can rent the apartment on rue Malher again. What do you think?"

"I think that would be great. I could plan my Paris screening for that week. I'll email Madame de Fontenay and check if the apartment is available in April, around Easter. I know they usually like to come back from Southern France by May. Does that work for you?"

"That would be perfect, honey. It gives me time to save money and finish my work. It's also a great time to be in Paris. I'll run it past the boys. Francois is totally flexible."

"Sounds good, Mom. I'll also need to check with Mimi to see if the theater is available. I'll shoot her an email and let you know." Summer observed the landscaping truck pull into the driveway. "I'm going to the kitchen for a snack. Do you want anything?"

"No, thanks. I'll be busy in the studio for a while longer."

Summer watched the landscaper unload his gear. She planned to catch him by the sliding doors on the other side of the house. Hurrying to the kitchen, she slid the door open. Stepping outside, she waved at Miguel. He was blowing the fallen leaves into a neat pile, a total useless gesture in Summer's estimation. One good gust of wind and they would all be scattered again, before the town collected them at the curb. When she approached, he turned off his blower.

"Hi, Miguel. How are you?"

"Hi, Summer. Good. Are you visiting your mom?"

"Yes. What about you? Are you going home to Mexico, again?" Summer smiled sweetly.

"Yes. It'll be nice to see the family."

"Where's home? Are you near Mexico City?"

"Veracruz. It's on the coast, about five hours from Mexico City."

"When are you leaving? Do you have your ticket already?"

"Not yet. Couldn't decide on the date."

"Listen, Miguel. I have a proposal for you. If it doesn't work, no problem."

Summer carefully explained she had an important package that needed to be hand-delivered to a young lady in Mexico City because it was valuable.

"This isn't anything illegal, is it?"

"What? No! Of course not. I promise you. It is valuable, so I want it hand-delivered by someone I trust. If you can do it, your flight to Veracruz, through Mexico City will be paid for and your hotel for two nights as well. Are you interested? Can you do that?"

"I think so. When would you pay me?"

"The ticket and hotel will be prepaid before you leave. You'll get an email with a ticket and the hotel information attached. I'll give you travel money and the package when you leave. You'll deliver the package to a lady who works in the hotel where you'll be staying. What day do you think you want to leave?"

"I was hoping to go early, around December 15th."

"Perfect. Here, write down your information. I'll need your email, phone number, and address in Mexico. The package is small, so keep it with you in your hand luggage. It's electronics. Also, my mother doesn't need to know about this, ok?"

"Is the package for someone special?"

"Yes. Someone very special. My friend who can't go to Mexico himself, wants to send a holiday gift. He asked me if I could help. It's important to him."

"Ok, I can do it."

"Thank you, Miguel. It means a lot."

That night she emailed C.

Hi C,

I sure miss Bahama weather. We're having a cold spell, and it's threatening to snow soon.
I found someone to make the drop. Below is his information. He would like to fly to Mexico around Dec 15th. He'll be visiting family in Veracruz for the month. I'll give him detailed instructions about the drop the day of his departure before he leaves for the airport. I'm confident he'll manage to personally hand it to 'He.'
Regards,
S

The next morning, she had her reply.

Hola S,

I remember what NY winters are like. Really brutal.
Thanks for your quick work.
A prepaid ticket was emailed to Miguel from Delta. He is on their flight out of JFK Airport on Monday at noon. His hotel reservation at the Hotel Marquis Reforma is prepaid for two nights.
If he needs additional nights to find 'He,' just let me know. 'He' may be off or not working one day. We don't know her schedule.
When the drop is made and he wants to leave, I'll arrange his connecting flight to Veracruz. Just tell him to email you his planned itinerary. I want no direct contact. Keep me posted when the drop is made or if there are any complications.
Muchas Grazias,
C

The next morning, Summer had breakfast with Jasper and her mom.

"So how is job hunting going, Jasper?"

"Not so well. I had a few leads, but nothing materialized. I'm hoping after the holidays I'll have more luck. No one moves at bonus time in my world."

"Well the good news is, you'll be here and available when Helena arrives. In the meantime, I'm benefitting from your writing skills so I can't complain."

Jasper perked up. "When is she coming?"

"After Christmas, just in time for New Year's Eve. We have to think of something stellar to do. Any ideas?"

"I'll check into it. Is she staying here or with you in the city?"

"With me in the city, but we might be here a night as well. She's so excited to come. She'll be flying home after Sundance. You have your ticket, right? We'll need your help pitching."

"Yes. Mom bought me a ticket."

"Good. Samson is coming too. His boss said he could write about it and have a partially paid vacation."

"What's he doing for Christmas?"

"Not sure. The holidays will be hard for him without Natalie and us."

"Guys, the frittatas are ready. Come get your plates," Cara hollered from the kitchen area.

Summer walked to the granite counter and plopped herself onto one of the counter stools.

"Thanks, Mom. Looks awesome."

It felt good when things fell into place. Summer worked hard to make that happen. Now, she would be on pins and needles until Miguel delivered the goods. She hoped things would go as planned. She didn't want to think about the consequences if they didn't.

CHAPTER XLV

Don't Go Breaking My Heart…

Casi was getting ready for work when his secure cell phone rang. He looked at it in momentary shock. It was too far away to discern the calling number. When he recovered, he dove for it, lest it stopped ringing.

"*Hola*," he said in anticipation of hearing Summer's melodic voice.

"Carlos, is that you?"

"Hermosa! Thank God! I hope you're calling me from a private place." He heard a sob and a long pause.

"Yes. I'm on an outdoor terrace at the hotel. There's no one around. Where are you? I was so worried." She sniffled softly, regaining her composure.

"I'm safe. Not in Mexico. You can't talk to anyone about this call, you know that, right?"

"Of course! I'm not stupid. I was beginning to think I would never hear from you again. It's been really tense here."

"How are you? What's happening?"

"I'm ok, considering. I was being followed and harassed…..a lot. Fernando's people told me to contact them if I hear from you. At first he acted concerned, second time around, they were accusing me of hiding your location and after that, they were just plain nasty, threatening me, but I think they finally realized that you weren't contacting me."

"I'm so sorry. I purposely waited for the right moment --for things to die down. I knew they would be all over you. There's no way I would abandon you, you know that," Casi said adamantly.

"I know. I'm ok. I miss you. I dream about you all the time. Fernando's people haven't let up, they're just sneakier about it. I'm not being harassed anymore, but I'm sure I'm still being watched. They won't give up."

"No, they won't."

"Someone was in my apartment and went through my belongings, but nothing was missing. I feel like they're checking my mail too. Some envelopes are open when I get them. Who was the nice man who dropped your package at the hotel?"

"Nobody. Not important. Listen, Hermosa, I opened a restaurant. I have a legitimate business now. I want you to come here. I waited until it was set up and things cooled down to contact you. I can provide for us both."

"Good, because you can't ever come back here. They'll kill you. I think the only reason I'm still alive is they consider me bait. I feel like a bleeding fish with sharks circling."

"I know. Listen to me, you have to come here. You're the only family I have."

"They'll follow me, Carlos. We can't risk that. They'll kill us both."

"Are you happy where you are?"

"My job is fine. I can support myself, but I'm lonely in Mexico City. I miss you."

"Look, I'm going to hatch a plan for you to come, but you have to follow my instructions exactly. No arguments or questions asked. You have to fully trust me and listen to what I say, ok?"

"Ok."

"Pay attention, this is important. The phone you are using is secure, it can't be traced. Never call me on any other device. Keep this phone hidden on your body at all times, not your handbag, and don't use the phone indoors in case someone is listening. Definitely not in your home."

"I know, Carlos. My apartment has ears."

"Probably. It's so good to hear your voice. I miss you more than you know."

"I have to go back to work now."

"Call me whenever you can. I'll keep this phone with me. And Hermosa... I'll make a plan to get you here. I promise. Give me time to figure it out."

"Ok. I'm scared. Before Christmas, maybe?"

"I'll try my best. I love you, don't forget that."

"I love you, too." He could hear her sniffling again. It broke his heart.

When Casi hung up, his heart was beating so fast, he thought it would explode. Hearing his sister's voice tugged at his heart strings, but also made him fearful for her. His mind was racing. How could he get her out of Mexico unnoticed? It would take careful, methodical planning. He finished getting dressed, grabbed his wallet and left for the restaurant. He wondered if Hermosa would like the Sea Grape Garden and the Bahamas. In his heart, he knew she would be proud--he just hoped she would get to see it.

Two days later, Casi was on a flight to Florida. When he arrived, he called Rose.

"Hi, Rose. It's Casi. I'm in Miami."

"Casi! It's so nice to hear from you. What are you doing here? Why didn't you tell me you were coming?"

"It's an unplanned business trip. Are you free for dinner tonight?"

"Yes. Where are you staying?"

"I'm at the Loews Hotel in South Beach."

"Oh, nice. I can pick you up around seven thirty, and we can eat nearby on Ocean Avenue. That's a great restaurant area."

"Sounds good. Shall I make a reservation somewhere?"

"I'll handle it. This is my turf. I'm so glad you called me. See you later."

When Casi hung up, he went for a swim in the ocean. The weather was sunny and eighty-two degrees. He enjoyed a late lunch on the outdoor porch, overlooking the pool. Lingering over his coffee, he checked his emails. Nothing urgent. He went for a walk on the boardwalk and hit the hotel gym. Later, showered and dressed, he sat down to do a little research on small private security firms. He set up a few appointments for the following day.

At 6:45pm he went to the bar for a drink and to wait for Rose. The bar was mildly busy. A Latino security guard was standing at the end of it, chatting with one of the bartenders. Casi sat down next to him. When the bartender got busy with drink orders, Casi turned to the security guard.

"How do you like working here?"

"Not bad. It's easy, pleasant work most of the time, except for the occasional loud drunk, personal injury or petty theft."

"Do you work for an agency or for the hotel?"

"I work for the hotel, but I used to work for an agency before I came here. The jobs in the agency paid better, but they were unreliable. Sometimes, you're swimming in dough, and sometimes, you're counting pennies for groceries.

"Which are the better agencies to hire from, and are there any individuals who work freelance?"

"Yeah. A List Security is good. So is Star Security. They hire trained professionals. Are you looking for a job?"

"No, I'm doing research for someone who wants to hire. Are there any Spanish-speaking agencies?"

The man laughed. "This is Miami. Every agency has Spanish speaking guards."

"Thanks for the info. Do you have any favorite restaurants around here?"

"Yeah. Gloria Estefan's place, Larios. Good Cuban food. She also has a new restaurant called Estefan Kitchen in the Design District."

"Thanks. I'll be sure to try them."

Casi paid and walked to the lobby just as Rose walked in, looking fall color-coordinated and seasonally sexy in a fitted burgundy pencil skirt, cream silk shirt, and eggplant heels. She had a multi-colored, dark wrap slung over one shoulder, and her warm greeting heated Casi's insides. It was good to see her.

CHAPTER XLVI

The Great Escape with Some Distractions

The next morning Casi was up early. His nerves were wreaking havoc with his insides. Perhaps a morning run would ease his tension. At 7am he hit the boardwalk and to his surprise, it was bustling with activity. "Good morning, Miami," he muttered.

People were exercising everywhere. On his way back to the hotel, he picked up coffee and a sugar brioche. He showered, dressed, read the news on his laptop, and left early for his first appointment. He had three lined up for the morning and one for the afternoon.

Hours later, discouraged with the day's meetings, he lingered outside the building of his last appointment, wondering what to do next. He noticed a professional looking woman exiting the same office. She was standing alone outside the brick building, checking her phone messages. On a whim, he decided to approach and chat her up.

"Hi, do you work for IC security?"

"I do, whenever they have jobs."

"No luck today, then?"

"No. I was checking for next week."

"Any chance you would be interested in a free-lance job outside of the firm? It requires travel."

"Maybe. That depends what it is and where the travel takes me. What's it pay?"

"We can discuss it over dinner, tonight. This is strictly professional, I promise."

"Can you give me a clue?" She appeared interested.

"It's a very private matter, so I would prefer not to get into it here, near your office door. I'm not hiring your firm. The pay will please you, I promise."

"Ok. Here's my card. Text me with the dinner details, and I'll be there. It has to be a public place, though."

He looked at the card and replied with a winning smile, "Great, Maria. It will be."

Encouraged, Casi returned to the hotel for an afternoon swim and made a reservation at Lario's. Resting on a chaise by the pool, he sifted through emails on his smartphone. He texted Maria the time and place to meet him. She confirmed immediately.

Casi arrived at Lario's ten minutes early and ordered *sangria*. He eyed the door, his back against the wall. Maria arrived five minutes later, looking very professional in a black pants suit with a stiff-collared raspberry shirt. Her shoes were sensible, and her hair was in a tight bun.

"Hello, Maria. Thank you for coming. Can I order you a drink?"

"Thanks, I'll have what you're having."

Casi poured her a glass of *sangria* from his pitcher and asked Maria about her background. She slid a copy of her bio across the table with a referral attached. Maria explained why she started working in the security industry and what her experiences had been. As she talked, his eyes studied her face and hand gestures. Maria was from Cuba. Her parents came to Miami by boat when she was a young child. Her younger brother was born in the USA.

"Looks like I picked the right restaurant then. Have you ever eaten here?"

"Oh, I've been here many times. I like Gloria's places."

Upon further inquiry, Casi found out Maria's cousin got her started in the security business. She chose this line of work because she needed to make money and she hated the thought of being trapped in an office. Desk jobs bored her and she wasn't much of a homemaker. This line of work kept her out and around the city. She preferred being around people all day.

As Casi listened, he realized she was a good fit for his mission. Coming from Cuba, she understood the need to escape. When he had a good grasp of her qualifications, Casi explained his mission. He needed to get his sister out of Mexico unseen because she was in an abusive relationship. He painted a scary picture of a controlling boyfriend who kept her on a short leash. He laid out the difficulties, the terms, and his compensation for executing the plan. The final and largest payment would be made when his sister arrived in Miami safely.

"Does your sister agree with this plan? Does she want to leave Mexico?"

"Yes. She will cooperate."

"I can only make her disappear if she's on board completely."

"I promise you, she is. She's terrified."

He asked her what ideas she had to execute this Herculean task, and was surprised when she came up with a sound plan.

"Sounds like you've done this kind of work before, Maria. Can this transaction be done before Christmas? My sister would love to spend the holidays with me. We haven't seen each other in over three years."

"Yes. I can do it before Christmas."

"We need to get my sister a fake ID. That may be tricky on such short notice. Do you have any contacts or ideas?"

"I can possibly use one of my friend's IDs. I'll have to check. What does your sister look like?"

"She's five foot five, about one hundred and thirty pounds with black hair, brown eyes, and an infectious smile. I'll be happy to compensate your friend for the privilege of using her ID, if the description works."

"That surely will make things sweeter, Casi. Everyone needs extra cash before the holidays."

"Great. You'll do it then?"

"Yes, I'll do it." Maria nodded locking eyes with Casi.

"Can you meet me tomorrow to make final arrangements?"

"I'm working, but I could either meet you for lunch or after work."

"Lunch is good. Tell me where?"

"I'm working in downtown Miami tomorrow. There's an outdoor picnic area nearby."

"Text me in the morning and tell me where to meet you. I'll bring lunch."

They spent the rest of their dinner talking about Maria's growing family. Her brother was married and expecting his first child. She'd just separated from a boyfriend, but had close cousins and friends she hung out with in her free time. The Cuban community was tight. Casi was pleased with his selection. The advantages of going with an individual rather than an organized firm were tremendous. The less people privy to this operation, the better.

The next morning, Casi cancelled his remaining appointments and took a long walk on the boardwalk. For the afternoon, he scheduled a boat tour so he could see Fisher Island and experience the Miami waterways. Mission accomplished, he waited patiently for Maria's text. Once he received it, he picked up sandwiches and water bottles from the deli and hopped in a cab. He took a spare secure phone with him for Maria's use. She was delighted to receive it.

"Good thinking," she smiled, checking the contacts. "I assume these numbers are yours and your sister's?"

"Correct."

After lunch, Casi texted Hermosa to call him when she could. His meeting with Maria had ended well and he felt confident enough to give Hermosa hope. His phone rang in the late afternoon, as he was sitting on the hotel terrace, having an iced coffee.

"*Hola*, Carlos. I'm alone now. What's new?"

"How are you?"

"Nervous if you want to know the truth. I'm looking over my shoulder every minute." Casi could hear the tension in his sister's voice, and it tugged at him.

"As you should be until I get you out. I know that feeling all too well. Listen, I've been working on your escape plan. My friend Maria will contact you next week. Pack a small bag with your favorite things and have it ready. No big suitcases please, and none of your IDs will be needed. More importantly, don't make any large withdrawals at the bank. Leave the money. You hear me? Maria will give you instructions. Follow her lead, no questions. I told her you are running from an abusive boyfriend."

"Really? Ok. When is she coming? Do I need to do anything? Pay her?"

"No, Hermosa. Don't do anything out of the ordinary, just be ready starting Monday. I'm not sure what day Maria will contact you. Don't worry about anything. Leave everything in your apartment as if you were coming back after work. Leave a handbag with your ID in the apartment too. Only bring your absolute favorite things in a small gym bag or hand luggage. Maria will contact you at work. You'll leave from there. Do you have a locker in the hotel?"

"Yes, I can keep the bag in there, don't worry."

"Also, this is important, so listen closely. Do not refer to me as Carlos. My name is Casimir now. Skip last names entirely ok?"

"Yes."

"Again, this is important. Do not bring any IDs. We will provide all documents you may need, ok? And don't answer any unnecessary questions. Let Maria do the talking. You know what to do."

"Yes. I do. Years of practice. Oh, God. I can't believe it. I hope this works."

"It will if you follow directions. Maria knows what to do, trust her. Delete all messages after we speak and only answer the phone if you can speak in a secure place. If you don't answer, Maria or I will call you again. She has your number. Wait for her call and instructions. Do you understand everything I've told you?"

"Yes, I do. I really hope this works. I so want to see you, Carlos. I'm scared here."

"I know and you will. I have it covered. Don't worry. Trust me."

"I do. I'm wearing mama's cross you sent me with the phone. She'll bring us luck. See you soon.....hopefully. Bye."

"Smile. I'll see you soon, for sure."

When Casi hung up with Hermosa, he called Rose. He needed a diversion and she was the best distraction he knew in Miami.

"Hi, Rose. How's your day going?"

"Hey, Casi. Pretty well so far. Thanks for dinner last night. That was fun. Are you still here?"

"Yes. I'm done with business and I don't leave until tomorrow morning. Can I interest you in dinner at Cleo's?

"Sure. You're a fabulous date."

Casi smiled. "Thank you. So are you. Meet me there at eight?"

"Perfect. See you later."

Casi put on his sneakers, grabbed a water bottle, and walked to the hotel gym. Mission in motion, he was ready to focus on Rose. He wanted her company. His body responded to her, but he wasn't sure his head agreed. Getting entangled with a neighbor from down the hall wasn't the smartest move. He would have to exercise restraint. On top of everything, Rose asked a lot of questions. She rarely held back, and Casi had plenty to hide. Things could get complicated, but nonetheless, he couldn't resist the temptation.

CHAPTER XLVII

Pitching for Gold

Summer finished fine tuning her script and submitted it for copyright. She anticipated revising scenes with new information she hoped to get from C, but she figured she could always file another copyright for the final version. Together with Jasper, she reviewed her pitch over and over until they both were satisfied it was a strong package. She was happy Jasper agreed to help her. It felt good to have a partner. She suspected his help was forthcoming because he wanted to keep close tabs on her product. He didn't fully trust her to keep the Flores details skewed. What he didn't know of course, was C had scared her stiff. She no longer talked about going to Mexico or using anything but fictitious characters. She guessed Jasper thought Cara's stern warning scared her off, but Samson wouldn't have believed that for a second. Her older brother was infinitely more gullible than her twin.

Summer was anxiously waiting to hear from C. She knew her phone package had been successfully delivered to Hermosa. Miguel confirmed his drop by email. C's silence was killing her. A recent phone inquiry had gone unanswered. She had no choice but to be patient. Her next card would not be played until Helena arrived, not that she had a card worth playing, if she wanted C's cooperation. He was the dealer calling the shots. She hoped to strike a deal with him in Park City. Her gut told her he wouldn't be able to stay away. She would continue to be patient to score what she wanted—she was the woman with an ultimate goal.

The two weeks leading up to Helena's arrival in New York would be hard to endure, but Summer had enough to keep her busy. In the meantime, Helena's emails were ecstatic. Summer could tell she was beyond excited about her upcoming trip to the U.S..

Summer sent her film treatment package to a few industry insiders, confident her acceptance to Sundance would capture their attention. It was unlikely she would get funding quickly for her new proposal, but at least they would see she was working on her next project. Maybe she could arrange a few meetings at Sundance to pitch her next venture.

Jasper's input had been invaluable. Until now, she had no idea how intensely Samson and he had communicated throughout Jasper's ordeal. As they worked on the script together, she was amazed at the details that emerged. Samson and her mom also added a dimension she was unaware of. Had she really been that self-absorbed? Or just busy? The script was a well-rounded family effort and she realized she could not have written it alone. Now that she had talked to C, she understood Jasper's fear and knew how justified it was. Summer never guessed how dire Jasper's situation was until after Adriano was murdered.

"Was I really that clueless in Paris?"

"Yes," Jasper laughed. "Samson knew how swamped you were, so we decided to spare you the gory details. We also didn't want to worry mom too much. You know how she gets."

"Yeah, I do." Summer rolled her eyes.

"Adriano's murder really freaked me out. For a brief moment, I thought I was going to be next. I mean, Flores had no idea what Adriano did or didn't tell me. That's why his people stole the tablet.

As it turns out, Adriano told me nothing and they stole the wrong device anyway. Such a strange turn of events."

"Good thing. Did you notice anyone shadowing you before the tablet disappeared?"

"No. I was nervous, but I had no clue. Never saw anyone."

"This story could have had a very different ending."

"Thanks, Summer. Encouraging and endearing, as always."

Summer smirked. "I try."

Always quick to change the subject when things were heading south, Summer asked,

"So, what are we doing with Helena for New Years' Eve? It better be good. Topping last year's extravaganza will be nearly impossible."

"I'm working on a few party invitations. I thought we could take her to a Broadway musical. You're right you know, we'll never do better than the party in Paris, but we can do something different that's fun too."

"A musical would be perfect. I'll leave the entertainment up to you. My friends are all starving artists, so no parties in my circle. Is Francois coming back for the holidays?"

"Mom said he's coming after Christmas. He'll spend the Christmas holiday with his family and spend New Year's Eve with mom. Samson said Francois invited him over for Christmas, which I thought was really nice. They'll both be coming to Sundance with us."

"Oh, good." Summer smiled. "I'll have lots of support."

"Did Samson ever say what happened with Natalie?" Jasper inquired carefully.

"She cheated on him. He didn't want to talk about what really happened over Thanksgiving. He was totally crushed, but he sounds much better now. I spoke to him a few days ago."

"How did he find out?"

"He caught her. Went to her apartment unannounced one night."

"Oh, shit."

"Have you been in touch with Helena?"

"A little. We traded a few emails. Pretty benign, though."

"Well, she'll be here for a few weeks, so you'll have plenty of time to reconnect. If my movie gets funded, she'll be back for an extended period. I would definitely cast her."

"Agreed."

"So, are you going to help me pitch this script in Sundance?

"Me? Sure."

"Good. You wrote half of it, and I'm counting on your continued meddling. Your name will be all over the credits. You're more creative than you think."

"Thanks. Happy to meddle. Maybe I'm looking for jobs in all the wrong fields."

"Maybe."

CHAPTER XLVIII

The Devil Strikes Twice

Casi was sitting on the terrace of the Sea Grape Garden, enjoying the view, content to be back in his adopted home. Feeling the sun and salt spray on his skin was comforting. His restaurant gave him a sense of belonging he hadn't felt since childhood, when his family was still intact. That seemed ages ago, another lifetime entirely. Peter was his family now.

"*Hola*, Peter. Things were pretty busy while I was away, I see. Anything I should know about?"

"Welcome back, Casi. For starters, we need to order some supplies. I made you a list."

"Yes, I saw that. Thanks. Did everyone show up for their shifts?"

"Yes. We had a kick-ass birthday party here Saturday night, a table of twelve. They were pretty rowdy, so I put them outside. That table alone kept us mighty busy. We also had a few celebrities show up. They're staying at a private home on the island. Movie stars. No one I know. Ask Jenny if you're curious."

"Interesting. I'll check with her."

"How was your trip? Did you have a chance to relax?"

"I did. Got done what I needed to and had a little time to spare. I took a nice boat tour around the inlets of Miami, and I saw Rose for dinner."

"The blonde from your building?" Casi could see Peter's interest spike.

"Yes. She lives in Miami when she's not on the island."

"Oh, really? Did you plan to meet her?"

"No." Peter's curiosity amused him. "It just happened to work out she was available when I called."

"Well, look at that. I think she likes you, Casi." Peter's eyebrows danced.

Casi smiled, but he offered nothing more. He wasn't sure what to say. He couldn't tell Peter about Helena or that he still had hopes of sharing his life with her. He couldn't tell anyone. If Hermosa was here, she would understand. He would be on pins and needles all weekend, just thinking about her impending escape. Maria promised she would text him when they were *en route* to the airport. Until then, he would have to stay busy and not dwell on what could go wrong. If anything happened to his sister, he would never get over it or forgive himself.

As it turned out, the weekend was exceptionally busy. Peter was off, and he more than deserved it. He had been working almost every weekend since they opened. It was the last Saturday before Christmas, and Gracie wanted him around for a shopping tour. They also had a family holiday party.

"You should come, Casi. My daughter will be there."

"We can't both be out. It's too busy. I'd love to meet your daughter. How long will she be on the island?"

"Just a few days. Maybe you could slip away after the first seating? Jenny is pretty competent to cover."

"I'll see how things go. Thanks, Peter. You know I would love to. You guys are family."

"Thanks, man. You have an open invitation. I'll leave the address on your phone. It's at my cousin's this year. We switch off."

"Ok, I'll definitely try."

On Saturday, Casi assumed the manager's role with a frown. It really wasn't a position he relished, but Peter couldn't be expected to work 24/7 and they still hadn't hired an assistant manager. Peter was grooming Jenny for the spot, but right now she was still waitressing full time. Casi wasn't sure she was up to the managerial task.

The weather was picture perfect and tourists were flowing into the restaurant around the clock. Casi barely had time to breathe. He never left the restaurant from 10am to midnight. Sunday was no better. The flow of customers was constant. The vacation crowd was spending like crazy, and Casi was happy to collect their money.

Monday morning, Casi was still recovering from the weekend rush. He hadn't heard from Maria. He skipped his morning workout and arrived at the restaurant early to place orders and help restock the bar. The kitchen was too busy prepping to help with bar work, and they rarely went out of their lane anyway. Thank God, Peter was back. Together, with one of the bartenders, they carried case after case, restocking both bars. The other two bartenders weren't expected until noon. Everyone was working long hours through the holidays. Hopefully generous tips would keep them motivated.

"How was the party, Peter?"

"Crazy, man. We had live music, and everyone brought a dish. The food just kept coming. Gracie made jerk chicken and it flew off the table. We all chipped in for booze."

"Sorry, I missed it. I barely had time to go to the bathroom, it was so busy here. Tell me about the live music."

"I figured. My brother-in-law has a band. You know Jalen. He and some of the band helped out here when we were gutting the place. They play on week-ends at the hotels."

"I remember him. I didn't know he was your brother-in-law or that he was in a band. What does he play?"

"Guitar and his brother plays the drums. They have a guy on base, a keyboard player and a sax. Listen, enjoy the restaurant's success now, because after March, it slows down a lot. We'll have plenty of time to hear music then."

"Well, six months of steady business will get us through the first year. I'm hoping we can do events off-season too. Do you think Jalen might have time to play here one week-end?"

"Yeah. Over the holidays, he's pretty booked, but I'll ask him for the new year."

"What's the name of the band?"

"Jamaican Diamonds. They play mainly roots reggae, but some pop songs, too. Jalen is from Jamaica, you know. He came here for work, met my sister, Justine, and stayed. She sings in his band sometimes. She has a beautiful voice. Sang in the church choir growing up."

"How come you never told me this before?"

"You never asked. I could be telling you stories about my family every day. I have a huge family who gets into all kinds of mischief. You gotta come to my parties to find these things out. You're always invited, you know."

"Fair enough. I guess I've been so focused on getting the business up and running, I haven't had much time to socialize. Sorry."

"It's ok. There's time. You aren't going anywhere soon."

"Hopefully, not. This is home now. Let me know where the band is playing next. I'd love to hear them."

"Yeah."

Late Monday night, Casi finally heard from Maria. He was sitting on his terrace, relaxing when the secure phone rang. Her voice filled his insides with joy.

"Hi, Casi. I met Hermosa today."

"Thank God. Is she ok? How are you?" He held his breath as waves of relief circulated through his body.

"Yes, she's fine. A little nervous, maybe. She's packed and onboard with our plan. I haven't seen her boyfriend around. He must be working. Tomorrow is her day off, so we decided to have her come to the hotel midday. We'll work on changing her appearance, then skip out tomorrow night. There's a late flight we can catch to Miami. I booked it. I'll call or text when we're at the airport."

"Great. Thanks, Maria. Please be careful. Trust no one."

"Believe me, I don't."

"Safe travels. I look forward to hearing from you tomorrow."

"Thanks. I have this under control. Don't worry."

Casi let out a deep sigh. Exhausted from the week's tension, he fell into bed, but sleep eluded him for hours. Dark thoughts orbited his brain. He couldn't shake the feeling something was amiss. The next morning, he woke up tired. To ease his jitters, he went for an early swim. The breeze that blew in off the water was cool. He shivered, not knowing if it was the air or his bubbling fear.

Mid-morning at the restaurant, Casi sat at the bar when an alarming newsflash streamed across the TV screen. A seven-point five earthquake was rocking Mexico City and the infrastructure was crumbling like a crispy cookie. He let out a pained yell and stared at the digital glow in disbelief. The surrounding staff looked at him in alarm. Never had they heard or seen such a strong reaction from their hardened, silent boss. Eyes swiveled with concern.

Immediately, Casi retreated to his office to check his secure phone for messages, but there were none. For the next few hours, he stayed in the privacy of his enclosure and planted himself squarely in front of the laptop, absorbing every bit of news like darts to his chest. The terrifying images and witness accounts sent waves of nausea cresting through his insides. He could barely hold it together. The next forty-eight hours would be hell.

CHAPTER XLIX

Christmas Tinsel and Tangle

Summer was cleaning up her apartment in anticipation of Helena's arrival when she saw the earthquake news flash across her computer screen.

"Oh my God." She searched for updated incoming news and absorbed whatever she could find. The first images available were frightening-- crumbling buildings, cockeyed roadways with stranded cars, buried and injured people being excavated. Mother nature was fierce. Summer checked her secure phone and her 'special' email account to see if C had contacted her. Nothing. She wondered if he and Hermosa were reunited and safe. Why wasn't he contacting her? She looked at Hermosa's number on the phone and debated whether she should try calling her directly. She pressed autodial and waited. There was no answer. She left no message, lest she aggravate C. She tried his phone next, letting it ring over and over. Again, no answer and no message option.

Summer turned to wrap her Christmas gifts, the laptop beside her. For the holidays, she and Jasper bought theater tickets for Cara, Francois, Helena, and themselves. She was putting them in a holiday card, garnished with a decorative bow. For Jasper and Samson she got nice cashmere scarves, and for her mom, perfume. Her mother loved perfume and never left home without a spritz. Christmas would be spent with mom and Jasper. Ted, Summer's producer and Samantha, her mother's best friend, were invited too. Only Samson was missing.

The day before Christmas, Jasper picked Summer up from the train station. The snow was coming down in thick flakes, making it hard to see through the windshield.

"Hey. How's it going?" She greeted her brother, hugging him.

"Good. Looks like Ted isn't coming after all, but Sam will be here tomorrow. I'm glad you came early. We might be snowed in."

"Oh good. Sam is fun. Why did Ted cancel?" Summer pushed her sinking wool hat up over her eyebrows.

"He has relatives visiting from out of town. They popped up unexpectedly."

"Oh, he didn't tell me. Did you see the news from Mexico? The earthquake?"

"Yeah, I saw that. It was in Mexico City. Unfortunately nowhere near the Flores family."

"Ewww harsh, Jasper. That's not the Christmas spirit."

"Sorry. I heard from a friend in Barcelona that Jose isn't having much luck getting out of jail. His high-powered lawyer is a waste of funds. They will be trying him for drug trafficking and murder. He isn't talking, which is no surprise. The man rarely opened his mouth on a good day. He wouldn't get a deal, anyway, having committed murder. Might as well stay mum."

"Lovely. No news about Fernando? How is Jose paying for the lawyer?"

"I guess there's some money in an account somewhere or else it's being transferred from Mexico. I have no idea."

"Is that something you can find out, Jasper? It would be interesting to know."

"I can try, but my contacts in Barcelona are growing thin. I could ask Enrique if he heard anything or maybe email Maria at the bank. She loves to share."

As they drove up to their childhood home, Summer admired the sparkling lights and tinsel on the outdoor Christmas tree, front and center. Cara and the children had planted it years ago as a focal point on a grassy half-moon plot, encircled by a semi-circular driveway. The tree had been small and easy for short people to decorate back then. It had grown proportionately with hers and her brothers' reach and was now a huge, majestic pine. Beneath the thick layer of flakes and the colorful lights flashing, it looked Rockefeller Center regal, almost dwarfing their house.

"Did Mom make you help decorate the tree?"

"I did the lights and tinsel on the top half with a ladder. She did the bottom. Boy, do I need a day job."

"Looks nice. You're hired." Summer laughed. "Let the festivities begin."

CHAPTER L

Mother Nature's Sneeze

Casi's stomach was in knots as he waited for his phone to ring. Was his sister alive? Had he put Maria in danger? He couldn't unglue his eyes from the incoming news snippets. The earthquake and aftershocks had wreaked havoc in Mexico City. Not only were lives disrupted, but the infrastructure was destroyed, and communication and transportation systems were shut down. The airport was still closed. Try as he might, he couldn't reach Hermosa or Maria. Frustrated and ill at ease, he went about his work in a gloomy haze. When Peter popped his head in the office door to see if he wanted to have lunch, Casi could barely respond.

"You ok, man?"

"Yes." Casi croaked. Pausing, he looked up. "No, not really."

"I'm guessing you have family in Mexico City?"

"I know people there." He kept his misty eyes averted. Casi could feel Peter's thoughtful gaze on him as he looked down at his desk.

"Hope they're ok. Let me know if I can do anything for you." Peter shuffled from one foot to the other in the doorway, hand still on the handle.

"Me too. Thanks. What's for lunch today?"

"The specials are grouper with mango salsa and baked crab."

"I'll have the baked crab. I'll come join you in a minute. Thanks, Peter."

"Ok." Peter quietly shut the door.

When they were both working, they usually took their meals together. It was a good way to catch up on restaurant business. Casi enjoyed the social aspect, as well. If he didn't dine with Peter, he ate alone at the bar in front of the TV or in the office. He knew he was an enigma to his other employees, but that was fine with him. He tried Hermosa and Maria one more time to no avail. He slid the secure phone into his pants pocket and headed to the terrace. He needed a diversion, and Peter was it.

They usually ate early at the outside bar before the lunch rush started. When he exited the office, Casi saw Peter seated at the far end of the patio, away from all other employees. The man had the sensitivity of a hovering mom. Peter innately knew when he needed privacy, and his doting concern felt good, like a warm hug.

"The Jamaican Diamonds are playing at the Atlantis after Christmas. They're scheduled for a few nights. Want to go?"

"Yes. That would be great. I could use a night off."

"Good. Let me know when. If you want, I can have Gracie cover here for us. She's off from work over the whole Christmas week."

"No. Have her join us. Let Jenny be an assistant manager for a night. I think you're right. She can handle it. Chrissy can work the front that night."

"Great." Peter flashed him a bright smile. "You'll make the woman very happy."

"Which one?"

"All of them." Peter flashed him a smile.

Peter stuck to business over lunch, and Casi was thankful. After lunch, he took his coffee cup and returned to the safety of his office. He found it difficult to communicate when his soul was plagued and his emotions squeezed. He needed to be busy, alone. The updates on Mexico City were grim. The airport wasn't reopening, so there was no chance his sister could leave, even if she was ok. He guessed the airport would partially open so supplies could get flown in, but how long would it be before commercial flights could fly out? At this point, the best he could hope for was a phone call or a text message. He prayed Hermosa and Maria were alive.

Casi trolled the internet for any snippet on the Flores clan. He hadn't checked recently, in an effort to block them from his mind. Honestly, he preferred to never hear anything about his nemesis ever again, but he knew, at the very least, he should be keeping tabs. Luckily, no news surfaced. When he checked his email accounts, he saw that Summer had written.

Hi C,

I was horrified to witness the devastation in Mexico City. Did you hear from He or is she already safe with you?
H is scheduled to arrive in New York on December 30th. We plan to spend New Years' Eve at a Broadway show with my family. We'll do the usual touristy things. Mid-January, we leave for Park City, Utah. What are your plans for the Sundance film festival, if any? When should I clue H in and give her the phone? Please advise. Praying you and He are happily catching up right now.
Merry Christmas, S

Casi decided not to answer as he had no news on Hermosa. What could he say? He would wait a few days and hope for the best. As he was placing some orders for the restaurant, his phone pinged. An incoming message caught his attention. His heart lurched until he realized it was the wrong phone. He checked anyway. It was Rose.

Any other time he would have been excited to hear from her, but with the current pressures, he could barely muster a smile.

Merry Christmas, Casi,
Hope your holidays are wonderful. I miss the island.
See you in the New Year.
Warm Regards!

He sent back a smiley emoji followed by a thumbs up.

Same to you, Rose.

The restaurant was packed for dinner. Everyone seemed so happy and joyous, but then why shouldn't they be? They were on vacation, spending the holidays with their families and friends. Casi felt a tinge of jealousy. Despite his warmly decorated surroundings, he felt deeply conflicted and sad. A text from Hermosa could change his disposition in an instant. If only he would hear from her, but no message came.

That night, after closing, Casi patted Peter on the back.

"Good job today. Can you work half a day tomorrow? I'll handle Christmas Eve and day. I don't have any plans. Here, a little bonus for all your hard work. I would be working a lot harder without you." He handed Peter an envelope with cash.

"Yes, I can. Thanks, Casi. I hope your people in Mexico City are safe. Text me and let me know what night works for the Jamaican Diamonds. I'll reserve a table."

"Thanks. I'll do that. Merry Christmas, Peter."

"Merry Christmas, Casi. If you decide to close early, come to my house. You know you're always welcome. My family will keep you entertained and get your mind off things."

"I know, thanks. Hug Gracie for me."

That night, Casi went to bed early, but he couldn't sleep. He stared at the ceiling for what seemed like an eternity. When he got up hours later, he checked his phone. Still, no messages--not a good sign. He shuffled to the kitchen and made himself hot milk with honey. Hermosa had always made that for him when he was stressed and couldn't sleep. She was only two years older, but she had taken care of him when his parents were working and later, dead. The sweetened milk calmed him, and he finally fell asleep. His dreams centered around his sister.

CHAPTER LI

Missing the Mark

The next morning, Casi overslept. Skipping his morning workout, he showered and headed straight to the restaurant. It was December 24rth and he still had no message from his sister or Maria. The news from Mexico City deteriorated with each report. At least the day promised to be busy and keep his mind occupied. Many restaurants were either closed or had limited menu options. Casi decided to stay open for Christmas Eve and Christmas Day brunch. The restaurant's last seating was at 1pm.

Hidden in his office, Casi prepared bonus envelopes for his staff. Peter had hired a competent, wonderful group of people and so had Matias in the kitchen. Casi was thankful for his amazing crew. He had every intention of rewarding their dedication. The fact that they worked long holiday shifts was mitigated by financial rain. After the holiday rush, Casi resolved to throw his staff and their significant others a party. The restaurant's success called for it.

His messages to Hermosa and Maria continued to go unanswered. In his heart, Casi hoped it was just communication systems being sketchy and taxed. To make it through the holiday, he had to believe the women were ok. His sanity was at stake.

To keep busy, he helped set up for the day, stocking the two bars, checking flower arrangements, and moving tables around for larger reservations. It was another beautiful day in paradise. The sun shone, the ocean sparkled and the plants surrounding his restaurant emitted their irresistible fragrances. The island colors warmed his heart. Now, he just needed someone special to share all this beauty with. He prayed he would get some good news.

Around noon the restaurant started filling up. A group of 'beautiful people' wandered in for brunch. Jenny nudged Casi to let him know that these were the celebrities who were staying on the island. He found it hard to muster any interest. After they finished eating, Casi offered an exquisite papaya pudding and a glass of port wine on the house, sending Jenny to present it on Matias's behalf. They were thrilled. One of the guests cornered Jenny.

"Would it be possible to have a private party here one night?"

"You mean shut down the whole restaurant kind-of-party?" Jenny asked.

"Yes."

"After the holidays, I'm guessing. Do you have a date in mind?"

"Can I get back to you on that?"

"Sure. I'll give you my card. Call anytime. If I'm not here, ask for Peter."

"Great. I'll be in touch. You have a fantastic location." A megawatt smile attempted to bribe her, but Jenny kept her cool, like Peter taught her.

"We know. It's a pleasure to work here. Let us know when you have your date. We're getting booked up."

Christmas Eve was busy. Matias planned a special five-course meal with three entree choices. Casi had left the menu up to him. "Be creative. Surprise me," he said. Matias loved the autonomy and went to town with his appetizers. There were crispy lime chips with crab salad, *almond, bacon, gruyere crustini* on french bread, and mini puff pastries with the most delectable vegetable fillings. The entre' was a choice of fish, meat, or a vegan dish. Dessert was a choice of rum pudding or sorbet.

Interestingly, there were quite a few locals who came for the early seating. Casi was pleased. He credited Benny and Peter for that. Of course, they all asked for Peter and were disappointed he wasn't working. Jenny chatted amicably, filling the manager role. Casi was delighted to notice she had learned a few helpful social skills from her mentor. She handled herself like a pro.

Casi was happy Matias had excelled with his Christmas menu. The restaurant's reputation benefited from Matias's Herculean efforts. Casi was proud of his establishment and there were actually brief moments when he smiled that afternoon. When Benny and his family arrived, he felt particularly grateful. Benny's continued support had insured his old client base, while Peter and Tessa brought in a slew of new ones.

At closing time, Casi handed out the bonuses to those employees who weren't working the next half day. It felt exceptionally good to see their faces light up when they received their envelopes of cash. He was happy he could afford the gifts.

Casi was so busy Christmas Eve, he didn't hear or see the incoming text from Maria. When he discovered it, his heart skipped a few beats. Devouring it instantly, he reread it over and over.

Merry Christmas, Casi!
Airport is closed. Devastation here. I'm fine. Still trying to locate your sister. She didn't show yesterday. Went to her place today, but the building is damaged beyond repair. Nobody there. It was difficult to access. Roads closed etc. Will touch base tomorrow or when I have some news. For now, sitting tight. Wish I had better news. M

"Oh God," Casi moaned. "I need a Christmas miracle. *Please* protect my sister and get her here in one piece." He dropped his head into his hands and prayed like he hadn't done since he was a child and forced to go to church with his mother.

CHAPTER LII

Mistletoe and Snowflakes......or Just Flakes of the Human Variety?

Cara tiptoed out of her bedroom first on Christmas morning, happy to have the morning hours to herself. Armed with a peony mug of soothing rooibus tea, she planted herself in her favorite violet armchair in the niche off her country kitchen and checked emails. The compact space serving as her office had a cluttered desk facing a generous bay window, overlooking a miniscule backyard.

Once her Christmas greetings were answered, she turned to world news. The earthquake in Mexico City had taken a devastating toll. The pictures and death counts were heartbreaking. She thought of Miguel and his family and hoped they were fine. She wasn't sure where he lived. In England, a royal wedding was on the agenda, in Indonesia, Mount SInabung erupted spewing volcanic ash, disrupting flight paths, and in Iceland, a proposal to ban circumcisions was in contention. What really caught her ire was a blurb about Pakistan. Women were being attacked by a gang in Punjab. The women were being pricked with a needle and spinal fluid extracted to be sold on the black market to Islamic healers. In her wildest dreams, Cara could not have thought this one up. Unbelievable!

Done with her tea and thoroughly disgusted, she moved on to more cheerful thoughts, the continued planning of her Christmas menu. She had prepped everything the day before, except the puff pastries. Those needed to be made fresh. Cara shuffled to the kitchen and rolled out the phyllo dough, then washed and diced the vegetable ingredients, brewed a large pot of coffee, and went to shower. Later, she would roll out and fill the pockets and pop them in the oven.

Cara was thrilled to spend Christmas with her best friend, Samantha, and two of her three children. Francois would be coming the day before New Years' Eve and stay until the trip to Park City, so Cara felt somewhat appeased. She was happy Samson was spending Christmas with Francois and Luc. Sharing a meal with her boyfriend and his son was better than sulking at home, alone. There was something to be said for an intimate group during the holidays.

The day brought freezing temperatures and a blanket of snow, so Cara encouraged everyone to dress comfortably. The holiday meal would be a late lunch, stretching to finger foods through dinner. A choice of movies was lined up, and the fireplace was crackling, soft jazz playing in the background. Cara was not a fan of Christmas music. The stores had saturated her. Everyone was instructed to bring one gift for someone else. Names had been pulled out of a hat. Cara didn't want anyone to feel financial pressure.

Decorating the grand pine tree in the center of her semi-circular driveway had gotten her in the holiday mood. Every day at 4pm, the lights illuminated her small, two-story, home with its front and back porticos. She delighted in seeing the colorful lights reflected in the snow, from the comfort of her warm studio, kitchen, and dining room windows. The kitchen, with its own entrance on one end of the house, faced east, south, and west. The front entrance, opened to a foyer with the dining room and kitchen on the left and the living room straight ahead facing the back of the house. The den to the right had been restructured and combined with the laundry and mud rooms to make her studio space and faced north. The upstairs was comprised of three spacious bedrooms, each with their own bathroom. Summer had her own bedroom, but the boys shared the larger one. Cara had moved a stackable washer and dryer into the master bathroom for convenience. The configuration worked for her and provided open living and working spaces downstairs. The renovation had taken six weeks to complete, but it had been worth it. The house addressed her needs.

Cara hadn't decorated a tree after her children left for college as they often tried to take short holiday trips, but this year, she was inspired. She planned to leave the tree decorations up until Samson and Francois came. Decorating the tree with Jasper had been fun, despite his initial grumbling. Once the lights were up, he stood back and admired his handiwork with satisfaction. She knew he was secretly happy with the results. It made her laugh.

Indoors, her decorations were limited to white poinsettias, fairy lights around the fireplace, and colorful candles and holiday artifacts scattered throughout the living area. Her poinsettia ceramics brightened the sparkling white holiday table and a red rose centerpiece in a gleaming silver bowl echoed the holiday color. Cara's tables always looked festive and thoughtfully planned. She was the queen of details.

The holiday menu was comprised of apricot glazed duck, garlic mashed potatoes, maple syrup butternut squash with cranberries, green beans with almond slivers, and a rainbow garden salad. Sparkling pink wine and apple cider bubbled in the crystal glassware. The bourbon spiked eggnog and homemade Christmas cookies were ready to be distributed at movie time. The day promised to be a retreat for culinary satisfaction.

When Sam arrived around noon, Cara had just taken the first batch of phyllo dough appetizers out of the oven. Jasper was in the shower, and Summer was curled up with a fleece blanket by the fireplace.

"Welcome, Sam. Merry Christmas!"

"Merry Christmas, Cara. I brought some goodies from Nero's. Wait…is that mistletoe?"

"Yes, honey. Give me a hug and a kiss. Thank you. Nero's pastries are always welcome here, as are you. It's still snowing, I see. Did you bring your overnight bag?"

"Yes, it's in the car. Better get it now. Might slip later, when I'm too drunk on eggnog."

Cara laughed. "Better. Would you like a cup of coffee to start, or do you want to go straight to the good stuff?"

"I'll start with coffee and pretend to be civil. Be right back."

Cara left the door cracked for Sam and set out a fluffy pair of slippers. She poured her a cup of coffee, then checked on the second batch of puff pastries. Since lunch would be served late, she would titillate everyone's tongues with breakfast puff pastries filled with egg, gruyere cheese, spinach, tomato, and turkey sausage. Summer eagerly awaited the first batch, which was cooling on the granite counter separating the kitchen from the living space.

"My, that smells heavenly." Sam walked into the open kitchen area in her fuzzy slippers.

"Merry Christmas, Sam. Your timing is perfect. I've been waiting to devour a breakfast treat. Mom was holding out until you arrived."

"Merry Christmas, Summer. I can smell why. Where's Jasper?"

"He's primping for us ladies. He worked out this morning. I'm sure he'll be down pronto when he gets a whiff of these. Let's not wait for him."

"That's fine, girls. Eat while they're warm. Sam, here's your coffee. Come sit at the counter."

"Yum. Haven't eaten a thing yet."

"Smart woman. I did a lot of cooking. We're going to graze and lounge all day."

"How decadent. I love it. Your tree outside looks amazing."

"Thanks. I risked life and limb on that ladder. Merry Christmas, Sam," Jasper said as he made his entrance. He hugged Sam, then poured coffee into a mug.

"Just in time for breakfast I see." Cara winked at Summer.

The phone rang, and Cara picked it up.

Samson was calling from Francois's house. "Merry Christmas, Mom! What's for dinner?"

Cara laughed out loud and put Samson on speaker. She rattled off her menu.

"Merry Christmas! The critics present will weigh in on the first course. We wish you were here."

CHAPTER LIII

Santa's Helper Scores Big

Casi woke up early Christmas morning and immediately checked his phones. No news. He decided to skip the gym and go for a run instead. He needed to ease some tension. Despite the holiday, there were people out doing the same. Everyone within Casi's sight was with someone else. He wasn't a vindictive person by nature, but today he found it difficult to stomach everyone's joy. Why was his life so complicated? He knew he shouldn't feel sad, things could be worse. He could be in jail, like Jose'. Nonetheless, spending this particular holiday alone, depressed him.

Over the years, while working for the Flores family, Casi stopped caring about religion, was immune to it, but now, for some reason, he felt immeasurably sad because he knew how important Christmas was to Hermosa. She should have been here by now. Once again, the Flores family managed to place a hurdle in his lane. Having to sneak his sister out from under their noses had caused his delay in sending for her.

When Casi returned from his run, he went to his desk and pulled out a twelve-by-twelve- inch treasure box with various memorabilia. In it was the little *Santa Muerte* statue his mother had given him when he started working for Fernando Flores. He and Hermosa had always hated its obvious connotations, so he had buried it in the box with other keepsakes from home. Casi took the box with him, every time he moved. It was the first thing he placed in his suitcase. He lifted the exquisitely carved, four-inch bone statue out of the box and set it on his desk. Staring at it with disdain, his eyes traveled over the details—the little globe, the owl, the hourglass, the lamp, the scythe, and the flowing cloak, enveloping the skeletal woman's figure.

"I've never asked you for anything before. Please protect Hermosa and bring her home," he whispered. After a few moments of reflection, Casi crossed himself.

Dressing in black jeans, a black t-shirt, and black cowboy boots with red tips, he grabbed his phones, a red baseball cap, and headed to the Sea Grape Garden. At least he had that. At the restaurant, Casi was busy. The decorations and the mood were festive, so Casi lightened up, but deep down, it was hard to be truly joyful. Smiling took a Herculean effort. He longed for Hermosa and Helena more than ever. When he had a moment, he sent Peter and Gracie a warm Christmas message with a picture of the packed restaurant. It didn't look like he could leave any time soon, he wrote. He thanked them for their kind invitation. With his dark mood, he didn't want to go anywhere. Peter would read him like a book.

Around 2:45pm, Casi and his crew were cleaning up after the last lunch stragglers. He didn't usually help with clean-up, but he wanted to get his staff out early, so they could enjoy the holiday with their families. When the last employee finally left at 3:15pm, Casi retreated to his office with a bottle of premium tequila. He checked his phones, his email, and Cara's Instagram, followed by Summer's and Helena's. Pouring himself a double shot of tequila, he swung his cowboy boots on top of his desk. The golden liquid went down like silk, warming his frozen insides. After a while, he locked the office, checked the kitchen, which was left spotless, and walked to the terrace through the entrance door. The folding terrace doors were already locked for the night. He poured himself one final shot of tequila and sat morosely, peering at the moody ocean. He wondered what the two women he loved were doing right now.

Casi reached home, thankful no one stopped him in on the way. Generally, he never drank and drove, but the roads were empty, and he needed his jeep in the morning. Once there, he changed into shorts and a tee shirt and sat on his terrace, brooding. He watched groups of people wandering around the grounds, laughing, hugging, and enjoying the spectacular scenery—some were dressed for a holiday meal, and some were just hanging out, but nobody was alone. Again, he picked up the phones next to him and checked for messages. There was only one, from Peter who thanked him for his generous bonus and urged him to stop by. Casi looked out over the sparkling water and sighed, closing his eyes and listening to other people's happy chatter. Time passed lethargically. He was jolted back to reality when an incoming text chimed on his secure phone. It was Maria. His heart beat faster.

Good News--A Christmas miracle.
H and I are at the airport. We're on standby for the next flight out to Miami. Pray we make it out tonight. Trying to get home to salvage what is left of Christmas. Will text you when we are seated on the plane. Things got a little complicated.

Casi reread the text before the information fully sunk in.

"Thank you, God," he whispered. He glanced back at *Santa Muerte,* on his desk. "She's alive. Now, get her to Miami safely. Please!" he said out loud.

He wiped a falling tear with the back of his hand. Days of built up tension, released in a single tear. Stepping inside, he paused briefly before the *Santa Muerte* shrine. Had the saint listened to his needs for the first time ever? He checked for flights to Miami. There was no availability that evening, but he was able to secure a first-class seat, early in the morning. Coach was sold out. He hopped into the shower, letting the warm water run over his face, extended neck, and back. It felt so good and sobering. After drying off, he put on boxers and packed a bag. He placed both phones on his night table and set their alarms. Before turning off the light, he sent Maria a message.

Merry Christmas, M,

God Bless you! If you need to pay someone off to make the flight happen, know that I have you covered. In the event you make it to Miami tonight, check H into the Loews. I have a credit card on file for her. Give her five hundred in cash. I will make transfers to your acct. Tell her to not leave the hotel until I come in the morning, and PLEASE make sure you aren't followed. Booked an early morning flight. Glad you both are alive and well. Praying for your safe return.

Thank you, C

The reply was immediate.

Have it handled. Don't worry. M

He prayed they made it onto the plane and out of Mexico unscathed. The fact they were alive was a Christmas miracle in itself. Anything could still happen, though. He wouldn't fully relax until he saw them up close. The tequila and emotional exhaustion wiped him out, and he blissfully drifted off to sleep, dreaming of happy things--his long-awaited reunion with his beloved sister.

CHAPTER LIV

Any Day can be Christmas

The next morning Casi woke up to blaring alarms. He checked his secure phone. Had he dreamt that Maria texted him or was it real? The new messages from Maria assured him it was real.

Finally made it onto the plane. No easy feat. Sitting on the runway now. Waiting for takeoff. H is fine.

The next text said,

Taking off. Sat on the runway for 3 hours.

That text came in at 1am. The following text at 4:15am was the one Casi was waiting for.

Landed in Miami. Setting H up as discussed. Going home to sleep. Awaiting further instructions in the morning.

The final text was from Hermosa.

We made it. The hotel is beautiful, and I will sleep like a princess. Anxiously awaiting your arrival.

Casi jumped out of bed, showered and dressed in record time, then grabbed his IDs, credit cards, and some cash from his home safe. Minutes later, he was in a taxi to the airport. He could barely contain his excitement. After he checked in for his flight, he texted Peter.

Leaving for an unplanned trip to Miami. Can you cover for me for the next couple of days? So sorry for the late notice. Emergency. Will be in touch. Boarding now."

Within seconds he had a response.

No worries, man. Got you covered. Say Hi to Rose.

Casi laughed.

When he landed in Miami, he texted Maria.

Headed to Loews. Transferred money to you. Don't talk about this mission to anyone, family included. Thank you. I'm forever in your debt. Room number for H?

Her reply came quickly. He was surprised she was awake.

You are welcome. Good Luck with everything. Call if you need ANYTHING. Rm 413. Merry Christmas.

Thanks. Payment transferred.

Casi texted Hermosa, he was on his way. She responded by sending a smiley emoji with heart eyes. Half an hour later, Casi drove up to the Loews Hotel. He grabbed his bag and hurried up to Hermosa's room. When she opened the door, he dropped his bag, opened his arms, and welcomed her into his embrace. Hermosa wept with joy, clinging to him, and sobbing into his crisp, white linen shirt. He stroked her shiny black hair, to calm her down. When he held her at arms-length to get a good look, he saw multiple bruises on her face and exposed arms.

"How are you?"

"I'm a little banged up, but ok now. I'm so happy to be here. Come sit down. I ordered us breakfast from room service so we could talk in private. Are you hungry?"

"Starving. I haven't eaten yet. I was too nervous."

"You? Nervous? I don't believe it. I've always been the nervous one."

When they sat down with their coffees, Hermosa filled Casi in on the earthquake. She had been at the supermarket when it hit. Cans had flown off the shelf and pelted her. When the shelf tipped over, it knocked her out, burying her under its contents. A nearby ambulance was called, but she ended up coming to and decided she was ok. She would be bruised, but no stitches were needed. The paramedic who evaluated her decided she did not have a concussion. There were more dire cases to tend to, so they parted ways. Luckily, she had cash and her secure phone on her body because her handbag, along with her other phone, and IDs, disappeared in the rubble. Someone gave her a ride to the hotel and she hid in the laundry area. At night, she stayed in the employee lounge. Her travel bag was already stashed in her locker at work, the keycard in her pocket. The keys to her apartment were in the lost handbag, so she never ended up going back there after the earthquake. When phones started working again, she saw Maria had contacted her. Hermosa went to Maria's room for a make-over and together they departed for the airport when it reopened.

"Maria told me later that my building was uninhabitable. No one was allowed in, so I would have lost everything, anyway. I'm so thankful I wasn't home, and my bag, already in my locker at the hotel. It contained my favorite clothes, jewelry, travel cash, and our family pictures. I would have been very sad to lose those memories."

"The memories of our childhood and parents are here." Casi pointed to his head. "And in here." He tapped his heart. "Nobody can take those away. The fact your purse was found and never claimed may be a good thing for us. They might count you as missing, one of the dead."

"I know. Maria said the same."

"Tell me about what happened after Fernando came back. I know Jose is rotting in a Barcelona jail, forever."

"Yes, he is. And that is where that animal belongs. Fernando, at first, was happy you made it out and transferred the money out of Europe, but once he realized he wasn't hearing from you, things turned sour quickly. His guys visited and threatened me. They told me in explicit detail what would happen if I heard from you and didn't tell them. For a while, I noticed them hanging around. They were there when I left for work in the morning and when I came home at night. Not every day, but more often than I would have liked. I'm sure they bugged my apartment, and it wouldn't surprise me if someone at work was paid to spy on me. It felt horrible and made me very anxious."

"I'm sorry I didn't get to you earlier, but I knew they would have your every move shadowed. I waited for good reason. I also wanted to have a chance to set up a new home for us."

"I know. Honestly, I think the earthquake helped me leave unnoticed. That and Maria's red-haired wig and fake ID. She thought of everything. I looked completely different after her makeover. I looked like a bad version of Paulina Rubio. Remember when she had red hair?"

Casi laughed. "Yes. Tell me more about your life in Mexico City, your friends, your work."

Hermosa filled him in on everything--their mutual friends, cartel gossip, her work, and her life in general, which was pretty sedate.

"What about you? You look different. What did you do?"

Casi filled her in on his surgeries.

"I see you also got rid of that ugly skull tattoo. Was it painful to do that?"

"Yes. It was. That's why I left the roses."

"They look nice. The blue rose looks better than the skull."

"Yeah, sure does. There was an unsightly gap between the two magenta roses when I got rid of the skull, and my skin was damaged. The laser removal treatments were expensive and painful, so I switched gears. Adding another rose was the best solution."

"I like the way it looks now." She reached for his hand and turned his arm back and forth to examine the three roses.

"Listen, Hermosa, I'm going to stay in this room with you. I want to be close, just in case. I think the hotel is sold out anyway. I was lucky to get you this room. Someone cancelled or left early, I think."

"That's fine. Can we go for a walk? Or do I have to stay in the room? It's such a beautiful day, and I slept a few hours."

"No, we don't have to stay here. Let me show you the boardwalk. It's beautiful. I want to also make a hair appointment for you today. Maybe change your hair style a little. We'll get you cool sunglasses and a few new outfits. It can't hurt to change your appearance immediately."

"Sounds like Christmas to me."

"Having you here is Christmas, Hermosa. I love you. Life is good now. We're together." Casi leaned over and hugged her so tight, she gasped. He rarely showed emotion like that.

CHAPTER LV

Brother and Superhero

Casi enjoyed Hermosa's enthusiasm at discovering the beauty of Miami. Her excitement was infectious. After buying her a pair of Ray Ban sunglasses in the hotel and a stylish straw hat, he steered her to Lincoln Road and waited patiently as she chose a few sundresses and one formal dress for an occasion still unknown. She also picked six basic pants and a dozen tops. He bought her two bathing suits and cover ups, so they could enjoy the hotel pool and beach. Shopping on Lincoln Road was a pleasure as the stores were side by side and plentiful. They stopped for a late lunch, sitting amidst the palm trees in the center of the pedestrian walkway.

After lunch, they dropped their purchases in the room and spent the afternoon on Collins Avenue. One of their last stops was a shoe store where Camila picked out a beautiful two-tone leather handbag with matching pumps. She ended her shopping spree swooning over the sandal selections and picked out one dressy black number with a medium heel and criss-cross straps and one casual sandal, a soft camel leather with colored jewel studs and a low heel. It was a good starting wardrobe. On the way back, Casi insisted on adding a peach cashmere wrap and two cashmere sweaters, one black, one off-white.

"Those go with everything, and you'll need them at night when it gets breezy off the ocean. Let's stop and get you sneakers and exercise gear, too. I exercise almost every day. Maybe you'll join me? We could both use a new pair of sneakers. Yours look pretty dated."

"I've never owned such beautiful clothes. Are you sure you can afford all this? Thank you so much, Carlos."

"You're welcome and yes, I can afford it. It's my pleasure. Only one thing, don't call me Carlos anymore…ever. My name is Casi, now. You have to remember, ok? For now, I'll call you H."

"Yes. I will. Sorry. H is fine."

For dinner, Casi took his sister to Espanola Way, where they sat outdoors, sipping frozen margaritas. It was an easy walk from the hotel. They shared a Mexican meal and reminisced about the good times when they were younger, and their family was still happy and intact. They stopped in the little white church on Lincoln Road and lit candles and said a prayer.

Back at the hotel, Casi briefed Hermosa on what would happen next.

"Listen, H. We'll spend one more day in Miami and leave the following day."

"Why? I love it here. I thought you lived here now."

"No. I don't live here. I just came here to pick you up."

"Where are we going? You know I don't have an ID. Maria used one from a relative to get me out of Mexico, but she took it back."

"I know. I have a passport for you. I secured it back when I got my own, in Europe. Your name will be different and you'll have to get used to it rather quickly. Instead of Hermosa Ortiz, you are now Camila Santos. I'm Casimir Santos. You're still my sister."

"Camila. Camila and Casimir Santos, I like it. I hope I remember my name. Don't get me drunk or I may not," she giggled. "I'm glad you're still my brother. You haven't told me where we're going yet."

"It'll be a surprise. Let's just enjoy the day tomorrow and get used to our new names. Practice using them. One step at a time."

"Ok. I think I'll get ready for bed now, I'm really tired. It was a wonderful day, Casi. Thank you for everything. It couldn't have been a better Christmas, even if it was a day late. In fact, I can't think of the last good Christmas I had. Last year I spent it alone because I didn't want to go back to Tampico. We'll consider the 26th our personal Christmas."

"Yes, it was a nice day, Camila. And from now on we'll spend Christmas together no matter where we end up."

The next morning, Casi woke up before Camila. He tiptoed out and went for an early morning run on the boardwalk. On his way back, he picked up coffees. When he got to the room his sister was showered and wearing one of her new dresses.

"You look lovely."

"Thanks! I feel good. What are we doing today?"

"Well, we can start with breakfast in the hotel, then we'll do a little sightseeing. Would you like to go on a boat ride, to the beach, or see the art district, Wynwood?"

"Can we do all three?" Her face was lit.

"Yes. Let's start with the boat ride. We can go to Wynwood for lunch and spend the afternoon on the beach. I made a hair appointment for you at five. By then the sun is gone from the beach here. Sound ok?"

"Perfect."

"I'll be showered in a few minutes. Have your coffee, and get ready for a fun day." He turned the TV on and let her watch the highlights of Miami featured on the Loews channel. They spent the day as typical tourists would, enjoying each other, the sights, the atmosphere, and their freedom. It had been a very long time since they spent an unencumbered day with each other. When Casi dropped Camila at the salon at 5pm, he sat guard outside and checked his emails. He thought of calling Peter, but decided to email instead. He wasn't ready to talk about his sister yet. He wanted to introduce her when they were ready and finished with the judicious editing of their past lives.

That night they had Cuban food on Ocean Avenue and went to bed early. Camila's new hairstyle was a long layered look with magenta high lights that shone in the restaurant light. Casi was so happy spending leisure time with his sister, he couldn't stop grinning. They walked back to the hotel underneath the majestic palm trees, admiring the art deco architecture of South Beach. Stopping at the Versace mansion, they enjoyed the shadowed gardens and the sights and sounds of their surroundings—the beautiful buildings with their architectural details, the street musicians, and the soft sound of the ocean, visible through the line of lit palm trees, standing tall like regal sentries.

Camila looked at her reflection in a shop window. "I don't even recognize myself anymore. I look so glamorous."

"Good. That's the idea."

The next morning, Casi bought Camila a suitcase set for her new purchases. They shared a lovely, late brunch on the terrace and around four, they left for the airport.

"Now, will you tell me where we're going?"

"You'll see when we check in. No big public reactions, please."

"Right." Camila smiled knowingly.

An hour and a half later, they were happily settled in their seats on the plane.

"I've never been outside Mexico, and now, I'll have visited the US and the Caribbean within three days. Not bad for a new beginning," Camila whispered.

"No, not bad at all."

"I'm excited to see the Bahamas."

"You'll love it there. It's different from Tampico, in a good way."

"Everything is different from Tampico."

CHAPTER LVI

Precious Cargo Arrives Safely

Summer checked her email and was thrilled to finally see a response from Casi. She opened it immediately.

Hello S
Good News. My sister is safe and with me.
H should be arriving soon if I remember correctly.
Again, please don't give her the phone or tell her anything until you are in Park City. And definitely don't tell her where I am. I can't risk that, I have my sister to consider now.
H will most likely want to come see me, and I'm sure FF's people in New York will be watching her. (and you.) Be aware and careful. They may try to talk to H or worse, threaten her, so if she knows nothing, she'll be safer. So will you. Play dumb. I'll be in touch in January.
Hope you had a good Christmas.
Happy New Year,
C

Summer decided to respond immediately.

Dear C
I'm very happy to hear your sister is safe and with you. The earthquake looked crippling.
I was worried. You must be thrilled. H is arriving in two days. She'll stay with me, until we leave for Sundance. Maybe you'll meet us in Park City? LMK, S

The days following, Summer waited and checked for an answer, but by now, she knew Casi only responded when he was ready. He didn't answer texts, and he only emailed when he had an agenda. She secretly hoped that she would gain access to him through Helena. If it meant flying to the Bahamas, she would do it in a flash, but she also didn't want to anger Casi or endanger him. That would be counter-productive. She'd follow his instructions and move at his pace, annoying as it was. Hopefully, her patience would pay off, and he would come to the Sundance Film Festival. She'd hit him with her collaboration proposal in person. In a separate email, she sent him her and Helena's travel itinerary—dates and hotel. As usual, no reply was forthcoming.

When Helena arrived, Summer and Jasper took her out for a welcome dinner the first night.

"I'm so excited for the festival. I hope I brought the right clothes."

"Helena, you're a model in Paris. You always look incredible. You'll set the standard, trust me."

"Thanks, Jasper. I looked at red carpet pictures of previous years, so I'm somewhat educated. One of my clients let me borrow some beautiful dresses. I hope they'll be fine."

"I'm sure they are, Helena. Summer can take you shopping in New York if you forgot anything."

"Oh, yeah. I brought extra money for that. I dreamed of shopping in New York. I can't leave here without something new."

"Let's wait till after the new year if it's not urgent. Everything will be in clearance and much cheaper." Summer chimed in.

"Ok. What are we doing New Years' Eve?" Helena asked, looking back and forth between the siblings.

"We're going to a Broadway show and a party or two. Jasper lined up the parties so I can't vouch for Jasper's friends or tastes, but the show, *Tina,* will be good."

"Hey, at least my friends do parties! You'll have fun Helena, I promise you."

"I'm sure I will. Just being with you both is fun."

They spent the rest of the dinner chatting about mutual friends, the film's anticipated reception, Paris, the possibilities of making a new movie, Samson, and anything else that came to mind-- except Carlos. Summer didn't bring him up, and neither did Helena.

New Years' Eve was a blast, and Helena seemed to reconnect with Jasper. Secretly, Summer worried about that, but she didn't say anything. The following days, Jasper took Helena sightseeing around New York while Summer worked. Another afternoon, Summer took Helena shopping. The days flew by.

On their last night in the city, Summer took Helena to her favorite neighborhood, Mexican restaurant.

"You know, I never heard from Carlos again. It made me so sad for a long time." Helena confessed, sipping her margarita.

"I know." Summer smiled empathetically.

"I wonder if he's ok. I still worry about him."

Her concern made it hard for Summer to look at her. She sipped her drink and looked down. "I'm sure he is. He didn't end up in jail like Jose, right?"

"True. I also hope Hermosa is ok. I thought about her when the earthquake hit Mexico City. So scary. I know Carlos worried about her, alone in Mexico City."

"Yes, that was scary."

"Do you think he went back to Mexico?"

"I doubt it."

"I suppose not. The newspaper said he took money from the people he worked for. I wonder if it's true."

"For all we know, it was money he was owed. Who knows? I bet he's hiding somewhere safe."

"This Mexican food is delicious. Carlos would love it. He made Mexican food for me sometimes—guacamole, *tamales, tacos* and rice with beans. Margaritas made with premium tequila were his favorite."

When the bill came, Summer paid it. "Tonight is my treat."

"Again? Thank you! I'll take you all out in Park City one night."

"Deal."

Helena got up to go to the restroom while Summer waited for her credit card. When Helena didn't return for a while, she slid into her coat, grabbed Helena's faux fur jacket, and walked toward the restrooms. In the hallway, she spotted Helena up against the wall, cornered by a man who leaned into her in a threatening manner. As Summer walked up, scrutinizing the man, she noticed he was Mexican. He frowned when he saw Summer approach and abruptly stopped talking. He whispered a final threat, then brushed past Summer to the exit. She took a long hard look but decided she had never seen him before. Scurrying after him, she saw he left alone. When she turned back, Helena was on her heals, looking ashen. Helena grabbed her arm.

"Let's go. I'll tell you what happened outside."

"Are you ok? He didn't hurt you, did he?"

"No, he just scared me," Helena whispered.

Helena looked around the street as did Summer, but the man was gone. As they walked back to Summer's apartment, Helena shared what had transpired.

"He said he's friends with Carlos and asked if I knew how to get in touch with him. He wanted to know if I had seen him in New York. I said no, not since he left Paris. He told me if I hear from Carlos, I should contact him. He gave me his number." She held up a lined index card with a letter and a number on it. "He said if I didn't follow his instructions, bad things would happen to me."

"Did he say his name?"

"No." She handed Summer the card. The initial A and a number were scrawled on it.

Summer shuddered. There was no doubt in her mind, Casi had not been overly prudent. They were being watched, and Casi was truly in danger. In fact, he was fighting to stay anonymous. "What a life," thought Summer.

She surmised his love for Helena must be real if he was willing to risk another person knowing about his whereabouts. Summer knew how careful she would have to be, moving forward—his life depended on it. This was no joke. When she got home, she emailed him.

Hola C,

Having a wonderful time with H in New York. She looks great. Still talks about you with great sadness. Took her to a Mexican restaurant

in my neighborhood tonight, just the two of us, and she was cornered by a Mexican man when she exited the ladies' room. At least, I think he was Mexican. He threatened her and gave her a number to call if she has any contact with you. Attached is a copy of the card.
I've never seen him before, and I frequent this restaurant a lot. Of course, this being New York, a city of eight million people, that means nothing. We're leaving for Sundance tomorrow. I won't leave her alone anywhere from here on forward. Any thoughts?
S

Cara spent New Years' Eve with Francois. They enjoyed the Broadway play with Summer, Jasper, and Helena, then separated. Their night was spent in a restaurant nearby, until the ball dropped and the crowd around Times Square dispersed. Although they had a wonderful time, Cara could feel an undercurrent of uncertainty. Francois was warm but distant. Something was on his mind and he had yet to share it.

"Is everything ok, Francois? Did you enjoy the theater?"

"Yes. It was great. Everything is fine, *cherie*."

Cara couldn't shake the feeling that something unpleasant was bubbling under his composed exterior. Hopefully, he would tell her soon. The suspense was numbing.

Cara stayed the night in the city, in Francois's studio apartment. After New Year's Day brunch, she split none the wiser. He and Ted met at work. The following days, she barely heard from him. When she stopped by the gallery over the weekend, he didn't have much time, and he was unusually quiet when they went to dinner. His silence was hurtful and unsettling. She hoped their trip to Park City would shed some light.

CHAPTER LVII

Home is Where the Heart Is and Your Best Buds

When Casi and Camila arrived at his Baha Mar apartment, he was tickled by how impressed his sister was with his new home. Her eyes widened as she did a slow-motion, three-sixty sweep of the premises.

"You own this magnificent apartment? Wow. It's nicer than the hotel in Miami."

"Yes. I own it mortgage-free. I also own my restaurant, although I do have a silent partner. His name is Benny. I pay him a small percentage of the profits. He sold me the restaurant for a good price, so it's a fair deal. So far, I've done pretty well since we've opened." Casi glanced at his sister, thoroughly enjoying her reaction. "I think you should relax here tomorrow. Enjoy the hotel and the beach, and let me get caught up at work. I'll get you a pass, so you can use all the hotel's amenities. Go for a massage or a facial. Treat yourself. You deserve it. Until we open a bank account for you, I'll give you some cash. You can come see the restaurant another day."

"Tomorrow? I'm so excited to see it. And I have cash. I took small amounts out of my bank account in Mexico City on a daily basis. I couldn't leave with no cash at all."

"I knew you would do that, even though I told you not to. Well, you're lucky the earthquake took care of your disappearance. As far as the restaurant goes, I want to have a chance to brief you. Our stories have to match. I work with a very intuitive guy. He'll know immediately if something doesn't add up."

"Ok, Carlos. I understand."

"NO! That's exactly what I'm worried about. No more Carlos! Carlos died along with Hermosa in the earthquake. Don't even call me that when you think we're alone. It's Casi, always."

"Sorry, I forgot. I guess it'll take a little time to get used to."

"You cannot make those kinds of mistakes, Camila. We'll pay with our lives, if someone overhears, becomes suspicious, and digs. Another reason I want you to take a day or two to acclimate."

He looked at her, exasperation showing in his eyes.

"I promise to be more careful. I know the consequences if we're found out. I'll remember from now on."

"Ok, so here is your room. It has its own bathroom. I gave you the bigger of the two extra bedrooms."

"It's so pretty. I love it."

"We can go shopping and get whatever else you need in a few days. Everything is cheaper in town. The hotel shops are for emergencies only."

"Yes. Same as Mexico."

"Yes. In the meantime, you can make a list of things you need—toiletries, favorite snacks and whatever you may like for your room. I'll take you shopping as soon as I can. So, freshen up, unpack and relax. Can I get you a drink?"

"Yes. A glass of cold water, please."

"Come. Let me show you where everything is in the kitchen. Then I need to check my emails and do a little work. Tonight we'll have dinner here at the hotel. I'll show you around the grounds, so you know where to hang tomorrow."

"Good. It's really nice here. I like it."

"Great, because I love it here. It's my home, and I hope yours, too."

"Thanks, Casi. I'm grateful to be here. I'm sure I'll learn to love it too."

He noticed the hesitation In her voice.

He showed her the kitchen layout, handed her a glass of ice water, and let her get settled in her room. Crossing the living room, he picked up his travel bag and dropped it in his own bedroom suite. He unpacked and sat down at his desk to check emails. He gulped when he read the email from Summer. Not that there was ever any doubt, but now his fears were confirmed. Fernando Flores was still actively looking for him. He always knew that would be the case. That's why he chose his new residence with great care.

The Bahamas wouldn't be on Fernando's radar unless someone tipped him off. Fernando would be searching for him in South America. That's what they had talked about when they brainstormed about where they would retire. He hoped he could trust Summer. He also prayed Helena wouldn't slip, if he decided to contact her. He was putting his life and trust in others, and it scared him. Maybe he should skip Sundance?

The thought of not seeing Helena choked Casi, always torn between his head and his heart. His soul still ached tremendously for her. Looking at her pictures on Instagram was pure torture. He searched the internet for Airbnb listings in Park City near Summer's hotel and found a few simple cabins. He would have to decide quickly because they could be gone as the festival drew nearer. All the good cabins were long rented.

When Casi was done with work emails, he texted Peter that he was back. He also asked him if they could see the Jamaican Diamonds soon.

Sure, man. What about tomorrow night?

Tomorrow works, he texted back.

Will the restaurant be open late New Year's Eve, or are we still closing at ten? The phone is ringing off the hook.

Yes. We're closing at ten. Last seating will be at eight with a fixed dinner menu only. We'll reopen New Year's Day at noon with the fixed brunch menu Matias and I decided on. No changes. The staff has worked hard, and I want to give them a little personal time over the holidays. I can't afford to close entirely.

No worries. The staff will be thrilled. Thanks. We're booked solid. See you tomorrow.

Yeah, see you tomorrow.

Over dinner Casi and Camila spent a lot of time reminiscing about their childhood. When they took their coffee mugs to the beach after dessert, he caught her up on his hasty departure from Paris and his time abroad. The only thing he left out was his love for Helena. He would save that story for another night. Given his revolving door history with women, Camila didn't ask.

Casi was up early the next morning. When he returned from his run, Camila was waiting, coffee ready. He joined her on the porch with a cup of fresh brew.

"I'm going to be happy here, Casi. This is so, so beautiful."

"Yes, it is. And the people are incredibly nice. You'll see. I'm going to shower and go to work. I'll see you tonight for dinner. Don't answer your phone, unless I'm calling you. Enjoy your first day of exploration. Don't forget to hug a flamingo. All the tourists do that. After today, you're no longer a tourist. When the restaurant is less busy after New Year's, I'll take you around the island like a native." Casi smiled at his sister and gave her a wave as he headed to his suite's bathroom.

When he emerged, dressed for work, she was gone. He peeked into her room and saw that she was unpacked, all clothes neatly hung in the walk-in closet or folded in the drawers. Her few toiletries were organized on a shelf in the bathroom, and her dirty laundry was in a plastic bag on the floor of the closet. Her bed was made, but the curtains were left wide open, displaying the spectacular view. He made a mental note to show her how to work their appliances.

At the restaurant, Casi let Peter brief him on the days he missed and what needed to be ordered. Peter had Casi up to speed in minutes and he again felt fortunate to have such a competent wing man.

"Thanks, Peter. Did you and Gracie have a good Christmas holiday?"

"Yes. We missed you, though."

"Thanks."

"How was Miami?" He winked.

"Really good. I like it there."

"The concert starts at ten tonight. Are we still going?"

"Yes. Bring Gracie. I have someone I want to introduce to you both."

"Not Rose?"

"No."

"You are full of surprises, man."

Casi chuckled. In his mind, he was still trying to get Camila's story straight.

CHAPTER LVIII

Family History Deconstructed and Reconstructed

When Casi drove home around four, he was still working out the fine points of Camila's story in his head. He checked his messages and noticed one from her. She had sent him a picture of herself, hugging a flamingo. Casi laughed. It warmed his heart, knowing she would be there when he got home.

Peter was going to eat at the restaurant and oversee the dinner shift, then meet Gracie and Casi at the Atlantis later that night. Jenny would cover the restaurant after ten. She was still a little green, but Peter assured Casi she was doing a stellar job. Peter continued to groom her as his assistant manager and was confident she would get there.

The monkey wrench was Matias. When Casi and Peter weren't around, Matias felt he outranked Jenny and made sure to let her know in no uncertain terms. He had no patience for Jenny's mistakes and didn't mince words or spare feelings when he disagreed with her managerial decisions. More than once, he made her cry in frustration. Peter always managed to smooth things over, telling Jenny she needed to toughen up, not let Matias bully her. Casi witnessed these talks and worried about her skin not being thick enough for Matias or difficult guests. She was young and would gain confidence over time.

Once home, Casi texted Camila from the parking lot. She was still by the pool. He found her quickly, spotting the coral bathing suit and coverup he had bought her in Miami.

"*Hola,* Camila. Did you have a good day?"

"The best. I splashed in the water a few times, had a picnic lunch by the pool, and went for a facial. Can you tell?" She took off her sunglasses and lifted her face.

"You always look beautiful to me, but I can see your skin is glowing. So, are you ok with dinner at eight and a concert around ten?"

"Yes, I'm ready for anything."

"Good. I'm going upstairs to rest for a bit. See you inside."

At seven thirty, Camila emerged from her room in black cotton trousers and a muted turquoise silk shirt. She had a black cashmere sweater over her arm and a small black handbag with gold trim over her shoulder. Black dressy heels closed the deal.

"I'm ready. Where are we going?"

"I see you did a little added shopping for our date. Nice handbag. We're going to have dinner at the Atlantis Hotel. Before we go, let me add something to your stunning outfit."

Casi pulled out his single gold hoop earring, placing it in the center of his hand. He extended his open palm to Camila. "Remember this? Do you still have the other one?"

"Yes! Wait." Camila ran into her room and came back seconds later with the other half.

"This one is yours now. Mami would have wanted you to wear them both, along with the necklace I sent."

Camila's hand immediately went to her mother's small gold cross around her neck.

"When I saw this, I knew I could accept the phone you sent. Thank you, Casi. Let me put the earrings on." She was smiling ear to ear.

"Wait. There's one more thing." He handed her the little black silk box from the jeweler in Brazil. Camila opened it and gasped. She took out the diamond pendant necklace and held it up to the light.

"Oh my God. It's beautiful, Casi."

"Welcome home. It's the companion piece to the diamond in my ear. I wanted you to have the other one, to continue our tradition, so we are always connected like we were with mom's hoops. Ying and yang, infinitely interacting forces."

"We don't need jewelry to be connected, Casi, but I love it. Thank you so much." She smiled, tears swimming in her eyes.

"Go put it on. Don't ruin your make-up with tears now. You look so pretty in your sea colored shirt. I'm so proud of you."

Camila walked to the mirror and secured her jewelry. She admired the diamond necklace from all angles, beaming.

"I never owned anything so magnificent. It's shorter than mami's necklace, so I can wear them together." Camila hugged him and he kissed the top of her head.

"Well, get used to it. You'll have nice things now. We're not going to be poor anymore. Or dependent on others. We make our own money moving forward. Alright, let's go, princess."

Over dinner, Casi briefed Camila about his current life. He told her about Peter, Matias, the restaurant dynamics, and why he decided to buy Benny's restaurant and make the Bahamas his home. He also rehearsed their edited story. They grew up in Mexico City, not Tampico. Their father died in a car accident, and their mother was ill and died of medical complications. He tried to stay close to the truth, so they wouldn't get tangled in lies, but he omitted the pressures the cartel put them through. Over dessert, he showed her Helena's picture and told her how much she meant to him. He shared the dangers of seeing her again. Helena was being watched by the Flores clan. When he told her about his opportunity to see her again in Park City, Camila looked alarmed.

"She's beautiful, and I understand how much you must love her, but is she worth risking your life over? If Fernando is having her watched, he will surely find you, too. You know that. We just found each other again. Why risk everything?"

Casi nodded. "I know."

"If her movie is popular, she'll be recognized by everyone. One picture next to her, and you're exposed."

"Yes, I know that, too. I can't meet her in public, only in private. She isn't on anyone's radar yet. She's a budding actress. A nobody."

Camila nodded. Casi continued.

"I want to see her one more time, Camila. I need to tell her why I left. It's unfinished business that I can't let go. I need to settle this before I can move on emotionally. She meant so much to me."

"Trust me, she figured out why you left, Casi. I'm so scared for you to go to Sundance. There will be press everywhere. I'm frightened someone will recognize you, the people she worked with on the film or a trained journalist who knows about the drug bust. You look different, but I don't, so I can't go with you, right?

"Right."

"I'll be so, so nervous if you go."

"I know, but please understand, I have to do this. And by the way, at some point, we can discuss plastic surgery for you, if you want it."

"I don't want plastic surgery, but I would like to get my teeth fixed."

"That we can start right away, Camila. I did that here on the island. Let me know when you're ready, and I'll call the dentist and orthodontist for appointments."

"After the holidays, maybe."

"Ok, no problem. Listen, I've tried to forget Helena, because I know she's reaching for the stars and working hard to make it in the film business. I doubt she would be happy living a simple life here with me. She has her own dreams to follow, but I need to know for sure. I need to hear it from her. I can't move on until I know there's no future for us."

"When would you go? What are the dates of the Sundance film festival?"

"In a few weeks."

Casi watched his sister's shoulders sink, and a worried expression cross her face. He knew she didn't really understand because she'd never experienced that kind of love. Neither had he before Helena. His love was like an addiction.

"Let's not think about this now. Let's go have a fun night. I'm eager for you to meet Peter and Gracie. They're my best friends on the island. Peter has treated me like a brother."

"If they're your best friends, I'm sure I'll like them too. They must be good people. Do they know about Helena?"

"No. No one does, so don't mention her. The reggae band we're seeing includes some of Peter and Gracie's family members. I'm considering them for the restaurant, so let me know what you think. It occurred to me we could clear the outdoor tables after dinner on a Saturday night and have dancing. The bar generates a lot of money. Come on, we can walk to the club from here."

"Sounds good."

They walked in silence, each lost in their own thoughts. Casi knew he had loaded a lot on his sister in just two nights of information sharing, but he also knew she was smart and strong. She just needed time to process. A night of music would be a perfect diversion.

Casi looked around the club for Peter and Gracie, spotting them in a booth toward the front. He smiled. Leave it to Peter to get a prime spot on a busy night. He took Camila by the hand and threaded his way through the tables towards the booth.

"Hello, Gracie, Peter. This is Camila. My sister."

Casi could see surprise register on their faces.

"Welcome to the Bahamas, Camila," Gracie gushed, finding her composure quickly. "Casi told us absolutely nothing about you, so I apologize if we look shocked. Come sit down. So nice to meet you." She patted the seat next to her.

"Your sister? Now, why you keeping that pretty thing a secret? Are there any other surprise siblings I should know about? Step parents? Favorite aunties? Sticky cousins with nine fingers?"

"No, I just have one sister. Our parents are both deceased. I got Camila out of Mexico City because her home is in shambles, and her future was uncertain after the earthquake. She lost everything. I'm keeping her here with me now. She'll help us out at the restaurant. She's also a trained accountant, so she can help me with bookkeeping. I was thinking maybe she could be in charge of planning special events since we never seem to have the time to do that. She could work closely with Matias." Casi winked at Peter.

"Good decision to keep her with you, Casi. Keep your family close. Welcome to the island pretty Camila." Peter flashed his warm, beautiful smile. To Casi, he whispered, "You're going to let that poor girl walk into the fangs of Matias's kitchen? I thought you loved her?"

Casi laughed. "Don't underestimate her, Peter. Camila can fend for herself. She took care of me when I was younger."

Casi could see Camila relax. She was already chatting with Gracie and sipping a glass of fruity punch.

"Can I pour you some rum punch, man?" Peter pointed at the pitcher.

"Is it good?"

"Would I be drinking it if it wasn't?"

"Good point. I should know better than to ask, you being our star bartender and all. Nice table, by the way. I won't ask how you managed that." He grinned at Peter and winked. "Now, tell me about the band."

CHAPTER LIX

New Life, New Worries

The next morning, Camila and Casi arrived at the restaurant before anyone else. Camila had nagged him to take her, promising to be on her toes. The drive there was peaceful. Casi enjoyed watching his sister marvel at the spectacular water views along the way, photographing everything into her memory. When he pulled into the parking lot, Camila clapped her hands together.

"This is amazing, Casi. Mami and papi would love it. Your own restaurant on the beach! What could be better? All we need now is a boat. I saw a little harbor near your apartment." She jumped out of the car. "I can't wait to see everything. Wait! What is that incredible scent?"

"Ylang ylang. Intoxicating, right? I fell in love with the fragrance and the location. In the spring, we'll plant more. The building was pretty run down when I bought it, but Peter assembled a small crew, and we renovated-- we gutted, painted, expanded the decks, and added the hurricane proof roof. Remind me to show you the before pictures. Of course we hired the roofer, plumber, and electrician, but everything else we did ourselves. I kept the decor simple, but maybe you'll have some ideas." He unlocked the kitchen door.

"Nice kitchen. Spacious. Wow. Look at that fridge!"

"We have more than one, but don't get too excited. You won't be spending much time in here. The chef kicks everyone out, even me. He's from Chile and he came with his own people. He treats the kitchen like his fiefdom."

Camila laughed. "When does he come in?"

"He's probably at the fish market right now, driving everyone crazy." Casi laughed at the visualization. "He'll be here too soon. Let's enjoy the quiet while it lasts."

They entered the hallway and peered into Casi's office on the left. Moving on past the restrooms, they made a right into the main dining room.

"Oh my God. This is beautiful! I love the pastel pottery against the white brick walls. Where's it from?"

"That's made by an American artist I met in Paris. There's a story behind that, but I'll tell you another day. Check out the view! Let me open the sliding doors. We have more tables outside than inside now. I just added five more. We also have a great outside bar that people love. See all those benches? We installed them for people to sit on while they sip their cocktails and wait for a table. They're filled most nights."

"I love everything you did. There's nothing I would change. I love the whitewashed wood interior and the beautiful outdoor stone work with the bar. It's a perfect mix--the clean, simple interior, the beautiful stone exterior, all the big windows and sliding doors that let nature in, and the nicely organized patios. The only thing I might add is an outdoor fire pit or an outdoor oven. How much of the land do you own?"

"I own all the land past the last bench on either side, including the sea grape trees. Funny you should mention an outdoor kitchen. We wanted to build a pizza oven and grill opposite the bar over there on the employee parking side. I'll need special permits for that. We'll make that next year's project. In the spring, we also want to plant our own organic garden over there. We already laid the foundation. Customer parking is on the other side, and there is plenty of it for the size of the restaurant."

"That sounds wonderful. Tell me about the chef again."

"His name is Matias, and he's crazy. Be warned. He's a good chef and very serious about his craft. He wants to build a reputation. His girlfriend is the pastry chef."

"Can I see a menu?"

"Sure. We prepare seasonal local fare. Everything is served fresh. I wanted to do themed nights too, but we've been so busy, I haven't managed one yet. Perhaps in the new year."

"I can start planning a *Cinco de Mayo* celebration, maybe."

"Yeah. That would be awesome, Camila. I would love that. I thought you could handle all our special events. Peter and I never have time for those. We're barely keeping up with the day to day. I get requests for special events all the time. "

"I would love to help with that. I saw so many special events at the hotel in Mexico City. I did their book keeping so, I know what they entailed. I'm a quick study. I can help you with the accounting too, if you need to be freed up. Just tell me what you need."

"Ok, we'll figure it out. Let me show you the office. Matias and his sous chef will be here any minute. They'll make us coffee and breakfast."

As they walked back in, they heard activity in the kitchen.

"Morning Matias. Let me introduce you to my sister, Camila."

"Sister?" Matias cocked an eyebrow and ogled Camila.

"Yes. She barely escaped from the earthquake in Mexico City. She lost her home, so she'll be working here, starting tomorrow. Camila is an accountant. She can help me with the book keeping and ordering. I would also like to put her in charge of special events, so you two will work together on special menus."

Matias scrutinized Camila for another moment, then stepped forward, hand extended.

"Welcome aboard, Camila. We could use a little more help around here."

"*Hola,* Matias. I look forward to working with you. I already love your menu and how your kitchen looks. It's so well organized. You must have put a lot of thought into the layout."

Casi held his breath. Matias didn't like anyone but his staff in his kitchen, even when he wasn't there.

"Thank you, Camila. Let me show you around." Matias issued a rare smile. Casi took a step backward in disbelief.

"Thank you, Matias. I would love that." Camila gave Matias her brightest smile, turning her back to her brother. Casi watched in awe as Matias responded by explaining his kitchen's stations and who manned them. As his people arrived, he introduced them, one by one. Casi retreated to his office. When coffee was made, Camila brought him a cup.

"Matias liked the idea of a special themed night for *Cinco de Mayo.* I think he and I will work out just fine," she announced. Can you show me where the garden plot will be? I want to see how much space we have."

Casi took a sip of his coffee, eyes on his sister. He was having a hard time believing what he witnessed. He searched her face for a hint of sarcasm, but there was none.

"Sure. Let's go out through the kitchen while we still can."

"Matias, how was the fish market this morning?" Casi stood at the entrance of the kitchen.

"Good," Matias grunted. "I got everything I needed."

Camila moved closer to Matias, looking into his eyes, "Any ideas you have for a themed night, let me know. Hopefully, we can plan something together, way before May. Perhaps we can do a Chilean night?"

"Thank you, Camila. Right now we need to unload the truck. We have fresh fish that needs refrigeration. Have your coffee and let's talk later. A Chilean night would be awesome. I have ideas." He flashed her a smile.

"Of course. Can I help you?"

"No, we've got it. I'll find you when we're done prepping for lunch." Matias nodded.

"No worries. I'm going to go look at the garden space now. We can also discuss what you would like to see planted." She smiled back at Matias, as they passed through the kitchen to the patio.

"Peter is off this morning, so I'll need help restocking the bars." Casi added as they exited.

"Ok. The others should be here soon."

Outdoors, Casi showed her the perimeter of the intended garden.

"We also want to add lemon and fig trees."

"Will they grow here?"

"Yes."

They discussed planting and timing. Camila liked the space and was full of ideas. She made a list on her phone to discuss with Matias. Back inside, through the front door this time, Casi walked Camila to his office. He showed her the surveillance cameras, his vendor spreadsheets, and briefed her on the ordering schedule.

"Of course, the schedule changes all the time, but these are our main suppliers for liquor, specialty condiments, tools etc."

"Nice system."

Camila picked things up remarkably fast. She had the same training in accounting as Casi, so he wasn't surprised. Balance sheets and billing practices, were easy for her to decipher.

Some things were universal. Casi quickly realized his sister would be helpful in more ways than one. He hoped everyone would make her transition seamless. His biggest concern, Matias, appeared to accept Camila right from the start. Peter would be speechless. Isa too.

"Come, let's go back out and let me introduce you to the rest of the staff. Peter manages them. Jenny is his second in command. Chrissy is our main hostess." Tessa does PR on a part- time basis and occasionally subs as a hostess. You'll meet her eventually.

"Hi, Jenny. This is my sister, Camila. She'll be helping me in the office and take care of special events, moving forward. Her home in Mexico City was destroyed, so she's staying in the Bahamas now."

"Hi, Jenny. Nice to meet you."

"Hi. I never knew you had a sister, Casi. Welcome to the island, Camila. I'm sorry about your home. The past week must have been tough for you. What did you do for work there?"

"I was one of the accountants for a luxury hotel."

"Nice. Perfect background to help your brother." She turned to Casi. "When is Peter coming today? I need help setting up and the bars need restocking."

"I gave him the morning off. He'll come after the lunch shift. Matias will send someone to help me with the bar."

"I can help you set up, Jenny. Show me what to do."

"Thanks, Camila. First, we need to set the tables and make sure all the stations are stocked. Come, I'll show you."

Retreating to the office, Casi called the dentist and made a consultation appointment for his sister. Next, he opened Summer's email and drafted an answer.

Hello S,
Sorry to hear about A. bothering H. I know who he is. Not surprised. I'm only surprised it took him this long to get to you.
I'll let you know if/when I come to Utah. I'm still undecided. Enjoying my time with He.
Thank you again for your help and trust. Keep H safe, and yes, don't leave her alone in NY. There's a good chance A won't go to SFF, but others might.

Thanks, C

On impulse, he pulled up his Airbnb reservation and confirmed it. Next, he booked his flight via Atlanta. He needed to see the love of his life one more time. He wouldn't let her slip through his fingers without a fight. Summer didn't need to know he was coming, yet. The element of surprise always worked well for him.

CHAPTER LX

Sundance Fever.... When the Stars Realign

S alt Lake City International Airport was shining with stars, their handlers, producers, and the usual idle talkers. The elite of the film world was descending on Mormon country and being whisked eastward to a small enclave in the Wasatch Mountains, charming Park City. Summer and Helena were bubbling over with excitement. They had made the executive decision months ago to arrive in Park City a few days early. They wanted to get their bearings and perhaps ski for a day or two at the Canyons Resort. Jasper and Samson were particularly stoked to ski at Deer Valley. Cara and Francois were arriving two days later, as were Hope and Ted.

The first full day there, the four of them skied the canyons and had dinner on Main Street. A rented car allowed them to scoot around town. Helena loved quaint Park City, so Summer decided not to complicate matters by giving her C's phone before she heard from him. If he didn't show, Helena wouldn't be distracted and could concentrate on what they were there for-- to promote Summer's film.

Besides, Helena and Jasper were having a grand time together. Just in case, Summer activated Helena's secure phone and carried it with her. Carrying three phones was cumbersome, but under the circumstances, made perfect sense. If C came, it would interrupt their blissful, well-orchestrated schedule, but if he supplied the information Summer wanted, she could make it all work. Priorities!

The next morning, while the boys went skiing at Deer Valley, Helena and Summer decided to visit the local shops on Main Street and peruse all the festival locations. Over lunch, Summer sent C a text, asking his whereabouts. As usual, he didn't reply. She checked all the phones, but there were no messages. Before heading back to their hotel, they toured the other grand hotels, which were filled to capacity. In anticipation of pitching her new script, Summer was curious to see who had made the trip from L.A.. Helena wanted to see celebrities. Exiting the Deer Valley Ski Resort, Summer recognized a well-known producer and approached him for a possible meeting with Jasper. Having Helena there to dazzle him helped her case. To her surprise he promised a meeting.

That night, wiped from skiing, the boys suggested dinner in the hotel. Given the altitude and its effects, the girls agreed. They were definitely feeling it. Just as she and Helena headed to the dining room, Helena's secure phone buzzed with an incoming text from C. He was here and he wanted her to call. Since C hadn't replied to her earlier texts, Summer decided he could wait an hour or two until dinner was served.

After dinner, Jasper and Samson disappeared to their room. Skiing two days had left them with jelly legs and little energy to spare. Helena, aglow with excitement, insisted on dragging Summer to the hotel bar. So much for altitude fatigue. Summer acquiesced, but in her head, she was mapping out how to best break the news of Casi's arrival to her friend. They found a high bar table with a little privacy, and Summer went to order drinks. When she returned to the table, Helena was chatting with two men. Summer waited patiently, quietly sipping her cocktail.

"Cheers. Listen, Helena. I need to talk to you about something private. Can you give me your attention?"

"Sure, Summer. You look serious. Is something wrong?"

"No, not at all. I have some…news." Summer paused and whispered, "Carlos contacted me."

"Whaaat? When? Where is he?"

"Shhh, talk quietly. He contacted me in New York, but he gave me strict instructions not to tell you until we were in Park City. He suspected you would be watched in New York, and he was right, wasn't he?"

"Was he in New York?"

Summer shook her head. "No. He sent me a package prior to your arrival which included secure phones, one for you and one for me. He wants to talk to us on a secure line only. He doesn't want any calls to endanger you or be traced back to him. I think he might have arrived here today. I just saw his message. Do you want to see him? Or talk to him?"

"Yes! Of course. Where is he staying?" Helena's breaths came out in excited spurts.

"I don't know. He didn't tell me. You have to call him, but you need to be careful where you call from. We could be watched here too, like New York. I suggest we go back to the room."

"Ok, let's take our drinks with us."

Back in the room, Summer turned on the bathroom faucet, handed Helena the phone with C's number, and pointed to the toilet seat. She quietly closed the bathroom door, leaving Helena perched on the throne. She flicked the switch for the electric fireplace and laid down on the couch, enjoying the warmth. It was frigid outside.

She checked her messages. Hope had texted her arrival time for the next day. Ted, Francois, and her mom were also arriving in the late afternoon. Summer was thrilled her support team was confirmed.

When Helena emerged from the bathroom, with red-rimmed eyes and a flushed face and neck, Summer gave her a hug.

"He's here," Helena whispered. "He wants us to come see him, tonight. I have the address. He said it's very close. Ten minutes away."

"Maybe pack a little overnight bag, just in case? We can leave it in the car until you decide what to do. I have a feeling you two might have a lot to discuss."

"Good idea. What is our schedule tomorrow?"

"We have meetings and a couple of screenings. That will be our schedule most days. First meeting tomorrow is at 10am. Listen, Helena, I haven't told anyone about him contacting me. My family doesn't know, and I think it's best if we keep it that way. His life is in danger, and the fewer people who know, the better. He took a really huge risk coming here. Do you understand?"

"Of course," she whispered inaudibly, nodding. Her wide-eyed expression was telling.

Within half an hour, they pulled into a private, semi-hidden driveway of a mediocre canyon chalet. Summer sensed Helena's uncontained excitement erupting. She was ready to jump out of her seat when the car pulled up to the log cabin, stopping next to a parked jeep.

"Listen, Helena. He looks a little different. I just want to give you a heads up."

"Different? How? He's ok, though, right? How do you know?" Helena was breathless.

"Yes, he's ok. Different in a good way. I video chatted with him from New York," Summer lied. "One more thing and this is important. Don't mention the new script. He doesn't know about it, and it probably would be better if we don't spring it on him the first night. Just spend tonight catching up on personal things, ok?"

"Ok, I agree."

"Let's go. Leave your bag in the car. Let me know what you decide before I leave."

"Ok."

When C opened the door, Helena jumped into his arms, almost knocking him down. It was an emotional reunion as Helena couldn't keep her tears from flowing. C held her tight and comforted her as she cried, stroking her hair and back. Summer keenly observed his eyes moisten, but no tears came. He didn't move a facial muscle as he looked over her shoulder at Summer. When Helena calmed down, he offered them drinks. Helena's eyes didn't leave his face, and her mouth curved into a tantalizing smile.

Summer looked around the rustic cabin. It was a two-bedroom ranch with an open living space, a stone fireplace with iron scrolled hardware beside it, a comfortable, faux leather couch and an iron and wood coffee table, facing the fire. Two taupe velvet armchairs flanked the length of the coffee table. A large stone counter divided the kitchen from the living space and also served as a dining room table. The bedrooms were small, but had the essentials-- beds, dressers, and built in closets. The cabin had a cozy vibe with decorative metal sconces, fleece blankets, and patterned moose pillows.

"Thank you for bringing her, Summer."

"Sure, C."

"What? What did you call him?" Helena interjected.

"I'll let him explain." Summer smiled at him. "How's your sister?"

"She's good, thank you. She's home taking care of things while I'm gone. Girls, my name is Casi now. I had to take an alias to become invisible."

"Casi? Home where?" Helena asked. "Mexico City?"

"No. My sister's home in Mexico City was demolished in the earthquake. She lost everything. She's staying with me now. Outside of Mexico."

"How long are you staying in Park City?" Summer asked cautiously.

"Not sure. A few days, depending on how things go."

"Would you like to come to the festival? I can get you passes," Summer interjected.

"Thanks. Not tomorrow, but I'll let you know."

"I did as you asked. You'll have to fill Helena in on what you want her to know." Summer said to Casi. "I'll leave now and let you two catch up if that's ok? I'm really tired. Thanks for the drink."

"Thank you…for everything." His eyes met hers, and they studied each other for a long moment. Nobody smiled. Helena interrupted the silence.

"I want to know everything."

"Well, maybe you can stay here tonight?" He turned to Helena, his face expressionless.

"Yes. Summer, will you pick me up tomorrow morning, or should I take a taxi?"

"What do you want me to do, Casi?" Summer looked at him.

"It might be better if you pick her up." His tone was brisk. His eyes studied her face again. Summer knew he was wondering if he could trust her. It worked both ways, didn't it?

"Fine. I'll be here at 9:40am. We have a meeting at ten in another hotel. Helena, walk to the car with me. Good night, Casi." The two women walked out, and Summer handed Helena her little overnight bag. She leaned in to whisper, so Casi, who was standing in the doorway watching, wouldn't hear.

"Call or text me if you need me to bring anything in the morning. And…listen, if you feel unsafe at any time, just call me, and I'll come get you. Even if it's in the middle of the night, ok?"

"Thanks, Summer. I'll be fine. See you tomorrow." Her face was serene as she walked back to Casi. Helena rested her chin on Casi's shoulder as she threaded her arms around his waist from behind and locked them around his tight abs. Summer smiled and waved as they both bid her goodnight, before closing the door. Love like that sure must be nice, Summer thought as she backed out of the driveway in her tinny, rental car.

CHAPTER LXI

Love or Semantics?

When Summer left, Casi loosened Helena's grip around his waist and turned to gaze into her eyes. He kissed her passionately, blissful seconds skipping by. How he had longed for her all these months! He didn't want to rush her, despite having the intense urge to just rip her clothes off and have her on the kitchen counter. The hot need simmering in his lower parts was hard to restrain. Blood was pumping way too fast through his veins, and Helena, who was like putty in his hands, made it exceedingly difficult to pace himself. Her body arched toward him, responding to his every suggestion. He looked at her closed eyes, slightly parted lips, and let his lips travel down her neck line. Helena moaned and ran her fingers through his hair. With her other hand, she pulled his shirt out of his pants, running her fingernails gently across his chiseled back. Casi unbuttoned her shirt while continuing his kisses down her neckline to her cleavage. Lifting one breast out of the lacy bra, he let his tongue tease her nipple. Helena leaned back against the counter, letting her shirt slide off.

Having trouble with his shirt buttons in her excitement, she unzipped his pants instead and let her hands roam. Casi wrapped his muscular arms around her, and carried her to the bedroom, gently placing her on the bed. He continued undressing her and himself with slightly less restraint, letting his lips glide over various body parts while listening to her small intakes of air. An electric fireplace warmed the bedroom and offered romantic lighting for their highly anticipated reunion. Once horizontal, his restraint was abandoned for unbridled passion.

Helena and Casi spent most of the following hours talking and making love. He filled her in on his departure from Paris, his new life, and his travels. He told her about his sister's recent arrival in his new home after the earthquake, leaving out locations and all the carefully orchestrated details of her escape. He left out her name change and the names of all his new friends. He briefly sketched out the past few months, omitting names, places, and the type of business he had.

"Hermosa and I cannot go back to Mexico, ever."

"Or Paris," Helena added.

"No, I will not travel to Paris, Barcelona or New York either."

"How will I visit you if you don't tell me where you are?"

"You can't. We'll have to meet and make sure you aren't followed. If your movie career takes off, we'll not be able to see each other at all, I'm afraid. Look, it isn't that I don't want you to know where I live. I choose not to tell you for your own safety. And mine. Fernando's people will continue to shadow you and bother you for a while. Trust me on that. I worked for him long enough to know that for sure. He doesn't let go and if someone crosses him, they generally don't live to talk about it." He could see Helena process this silently.

"You mean to say, I need to give up my dream of becoming an actress if I want to be with you?"

"Yes. I have no choice, if I want to stay alive. If you decide that you want us to be together, you would have to choose to go under cover permanently, change your name and your appearance."

"There has to be another way. You do look different you know."

"But you don't. I might be able to fool strangers, but not the people who have known me since childhood. There is no digital or paper trail leading to Carlos Ortiz, I made sure of that, but I can't change all my physical attributes nor do I want to. You and now Summer, are the only possible links they can use to find me. If I didn't love you so much, I would never have taken this risk and come to Sundance. My sister thinks its suicide. She's worried every day I'm here."

"I do love you and I understand how risky this is. I realized that in New York when someone threatened me."

"Yes, Summer told me. No decisions need to be made now. Let's enjoy the few days we have together. Keep the secure phone, but be careful where you call me from. It's best used outside, alone, or in places with background noises. I'm going to give you a security briefing before you leave. If we want to stay in touch, you need to follow my instructions closely and whatever you do, try not to lose the phone. It'll be our only connection."

"That and Summer's phone, right?"

"Yes."

"Don't worry. I'll be super careful."

"I know this arrangement is far from ideal, but my life has always been complicated. I've had no choice in the matter. This is the most freedom I've had since childhood." His eyes hardened.

"I'm sorry. You know my heart belongs to you. Let me digest all of this. I feel overwhelmed and I can't make any decisions right now. You know, Summer is pitching another script here at the festival, and if she gets funding, I have a chance at being in another film. We've already had one successful meeting. I have a good feeling about this opportunity."

"I understand. How much money does she need to make the film, and what is it about?" Casi was curious.

"If she makes it independently, at least half a million, but we're trying to get it funded by a studio, obviously." Helena paused.

"What is it about?"

"I can't tell you. I signed a confidentiality agreement. You have to ask her."

"I see you have secrets too."

"Speak to Summer. It's standard industry procedure not to talk, especially if they are still pitching the idea and don't have funding yet."

He studied her face and detected uncertainty. He'd ask Summer in the morning.

Leaning over and straddling Helena on the bed, he used his fingertips to trace her profile, neck, and all her curves, ending his travels between her thighs. Helena closed her eyes. Just his touch made her body ache and arc. Teasing her with his erection, he entered her warmth.

Casi woke up first. He showered before Helena stirred.

"Good morning, Sunshine. You need to move it if you want to be ready for Summer."

"What time is it?"

"8:30am. Would you like some coffee?"

"Please. What are you doing today?"

Casi handed Helena a mug with coffee, just the way he knew she liked it. "I'll sightsee a little, work a little and catch a movie, maybe. Let me know what the good ones are."

"I'll ask Summer and text you. Will I see you later?"

"That depends on your schedule. Text me when you have a break. I won't be far. We can only meet here. Out and around is too risky."

Helena sighed and nodded. "Here is fine." She swung out of bed and stretched. Casi's eyes trailed her to the bathroom. He loved her curvy behind. She was the sexiest woman he had ever bedded. Few women equaled Helena, nor had anyone ever stolen his heart the way she had.

At 9:30am, Casi sat down on a barstool with a view to the driveway while Helena applied make up and primped in the bathroom. When Summer's car pulled up, Casi quietly scooted to the door and greeted her outside.

"Morning, Summer. Helena is almost ready. I need to talk to you alone for a moment."

"Sure."

"Helena and I shared a lot of information last night, but I don't want to tell her where my new home is or my new last name. Can you continue to keep this private?" Casi searched her face for a reaction. She showed little.

"I think so. I have so far. Not even sure I know your last name."

"Thanks for that. Just tell her I contacted you out of the blue and sent you the phones. I need your commitment, one-hundred percent. If you ever need to reveal my whereabouts under duress, send me a warning asap. Can you live with that?" His face and body were rigid, statue-like.

"You will continue to have my commitment. However, I would like to ask a favor in return."

"What is that?" Casi clipped, not moving. He had wondered when that was coming.

"I would like to meet with you later tonight to discuss something. I can't get into it right now. That discussion will take time. Helena and I need to be punctual this morning."

"Fine. Text me before you come. Can you give me a clue what it's about?

"No, not now. Helena is coming."

"There you are. Is it ok if I leave a few things here, Casi? I'll be back tonight."

"Yes. Good luck with everything today."

Summer noticed his voice softened substantially when he spoke to Helena.

"Thanks, *mon amour.*"

Casi kissed Helena as she passed by, then looked back at Summer. Their eyes met, but once again, nobody smiled. What did she have up her sleeve? He knew tonight would reveal the real reason for her exploratory visit to his restaurant. Summer was a woman with an agenda, but could she be trusted?

CHAPTER LXII

The Price of Anonymity

"So, how was your reunion?" Summer gave Helena a sideways glance while driving.

"It was wonderful. I'm so happy he's here. I still can't believe it," her friend gushed.

"Jasper and Samson asked about you at breakfast. I told them you slept in and ordered breakfast in the room. Jasper was disappointed. He wanted to practice his pitch on you. He'll meet us there. I told him we needed to run an errand on the way."

"I feel bad lying to Jasper."

"I don't. He's been through enough. He would freak if he knew Casi was here. It's for everyone's safety, my family doesn't know. We're ten minutes from the hotel. Let me quickly brief you on who we're seeing today. We can catch up on Casi later, ok?"

"Yes."

When Jasper, Helena, and Summer left the meeting, they were pumped.

"Jasper, I had no idea you're such a good story teller. They loved your pitch." Helena nudged Summer and winked.

"He's an even better business man," Summer chimed in.

"Well, since I helped Summer write the script, I feel very vested in the project."

"I really benefited from his input and lack of employment. I don't know if I would have gotten it done without him. In fact, I know I wouldn't have. I was so busy with the Paris film up through September. Jasper developed the rough draft from the outline I wrote, on his own." Summer looked at her phone. "Mom just texted me. She made a dinner reservation for all of us at 7:30pm, downtown. Hope and Ted will be there too."

"Ok, great. What about lunch? Are you all starving, or is it just me? All that talking made me hungry." Jasper patted his stomach.

"Me too," Helena agreed. Summer glanced at her and smiled. "Hmm."

"Back to the hotel, or should we stop along the way?" Jasper asked as he stopped for a red light.

"That cafe over there looks nice." Helena pointed to a place called Bridge Café and Grill.

"Done." Summer agreed. "We can go straight to the screening after. I have the tickets with me."

Dinner that night was a crowded event. The Crenston family, Helena, Francois, Hope and Ted all met in downtown Park City for a happy reunion. Hope and Summer discussed Hope's cinematography schedule and the logistics of her shooting the next film if funding came through. Helena and Jasper talked movies in general. Samson and his mother caught up on Samson's life in Paris without Natalie, and Ted and Francois discussed sales in the gallery. Everyone was engaged. The following night would be the premiere of Summer's film, so plans were hatched for an early supper in the hotel for those who wanted it so they could primp afterwards.

Following dinner, everyone scattered. Helena and Summer went back to their room so Helena could pack her overnight bag. Summer noticed her excitement. She exuded nervous energy as she screened clothes deciding to discard or pack. They ordered dessert in the hotel to bring to the cabin along with the sparkling wine Helena had picked up after lunch. Casi's fridge had looked pretty scant the night before.

When they arrived at Casi's around 10:30pm, he was waiting. He opened the door as soon as they pulled into the driveway and looked up and down the street. Summer realized that she and Helena hadn't talked about him all day. Every minute, she and Helena were surrounded by others which made it virtually impossible to chat privately. In the car ride over, they were both silent, each lost in their own thoughts. Or perhaps they were just tired, recharging their mental batteries after a long interactive day. Summer guessed it was stressful for him, waiting in the cabin all day. Helena hopped out of the car, bottle and desserts in hand and ran straight to Casi, kissing him on the lips.

The logs in the fireplace were aglow and the cabin had a warm, pleasant pine scent. Casi had tastefully arranged stemmed glasses and cocktail napkins on a tray in the center of the counter, a bottle of champagne next to it. Pillows and blankets were strewn in the seating area around the fireplace, and the lighting was dimmed to a romantic setting.

"Long day, and I thought about you every minute. We brought dessert." Helena smiled.

"And I bought champagne for us to toast your success with. How did the meeting go this morning?"

"Very good. Jasper made an amazing pitch," Helena shared happily.

"Jasper? The banker?"

"Yes. He and Summer wrote the script together so they pitched it together." Summer noticed Casi's face clouding. His mental cogwheels were in motion.

"I see. Good evening, Summer. So things went well?"

"Yes. They did. We generated some interest."

"That's good."

Casi's short answers and lack of follow-up questions unsettled Summer. Granted, he was a man of few words, but he was also intuitive and smart. She sensed he knew she was holding something important back. Perhaps he already suspected that her script had something to do with her request to talk. His silence made her breathe faster. When Summer was nervous, she generally overcompensated by talking too much. She would have to pace herself and choose her words carefully. She thought about how to start.

"Champagne, everyone?" Casi asked without looking at her.

"Yes, thanks." She hoped it would lighten his mood.

"Me, too." Helena chimed from the bedroom. "I'll be right there. I'm just going to hang my clothes for tomorrow."

"So what's on your mind, Summer. What can I do for you?"

Summer watched Casi pop the cork expertly and pour the champagne. His arms were so muscular, she couldn't help but wonder if he had ever hurt people with his strength.

"Did Helena mention what my script is about?"

"No."

"Ok. I'll be honest. That's what I wanted to talk to you about."

"Ok, I'm listening."

Summer took a deep breath.

"Just hear me out, please, before you comment." She paused and looked at Casi. He waited, eyes fixed on her.

"My script is loosely based on F&S Enterprises and how they stole ceramics from various art venues and copied the work. How they unloaded the originals on the black market in Europe and laundered money in newly purchased restaurants and real estate. I will touch upon the drug operation and how that enabled business expansion. I also want to include the brutal trail of dead drug users from a too potent mix. I've changed all names and places, adding a good deal of fiction to the story to make it more Hollywood. I was hoping you could help me fill in some of the blanks. I need background information. The story ends with the bust."

"I suspected you wanted this kind of information. Do you realize how dangerous this is? People have been killed for less. You know about Rosalis, right? He just joked about a drug lord and ended up shot eighteen times. Mexicans don't tell a cartel joke without looking over their shoulder to see who is listening, and you aren't even joking. This is a really bad idea."

"I'm presenting this as pure fiction, Casi. My team and I have done a good amount of research, but there is only so much we have access to, short of going to Mexico and snooping around. You know, this is information obtained from just reading newspaper articles. Virtually anybody could write about this and piece together the same story. I would love to get some authentic company and cartel background from you, a few unique inside stories. I would be happy to show you my script so far, and I'll change anything you think is too risqué. I want to protect you, not expose you."

"Summer, it is all too risky. All of it. The whole project. And you wouldn't be protecting me. You would be protecting yourself and your family by not doing this. Surely you realize, you would be inviting the media to dig and sink their teeth into the story all over again."

"But this is fiction, I can change anything," Summer protested. "I can incorporate stories from other cartels too, for shock value, so it looks like a cross section of cartel stories, not just about you or the Sinaloa cartel." Summer paused and looked at Casi. His eyes looked dark and his demeanor was unreadable. Gone was his welcoming smile.

"You're playing with fire, Summer. Why do you want to endanger your family? Honestly, if it weren't for me, Fernando might have harmed your brother in Barcelona. Let me sleep on this. I can't agree to anything tonight. I'm not sure I want to be involved, but I feel like I might have to be, just to save you from yourself. You are quite a stubborn woman."

"Please, get involved. I want your input. And yes, I am stubborn. My family tells me all the time."

"If I advise you to change certain things, will you listen? Just so you understand, I still live looking over my shoulder, every second of the day. I sleep with weapons within reach, and if it weren't for Helena, I would have never, ever risked coming here or talking to you. It's a calculated risk that could possibly backfire terribly, for all of us. Besides my sister, Helena is the only person I cared for in my former life, and I always had to hide those feelings publicly. I never introduced Helena to Flores or anyone affiliated with him and I sent my only sibling away to Mexico City to keep her safe. That wasn't an oversight. It was a calculated decision."

"I realize that."

"Do you? I wouldn't want that fact known, though. I came here to redeem myself and to ensure Helena's heart didn't stay broken, which I know it was. Mine was too. I didn't want her to think I ditched her because I truly care for her. I never wanted to hurt her. Having said that, your project scares me. There will be repercussions."

"If we change the story enough, why would Fernando care?"

"He may not. Or he may lash out full force. It depends on how you deliver it and if he feels threatened. I can see you're intent on telling the story. A word of advice. The more you disguise it, the better. Is Jasper's name going to be on the script?"

"Yes, he's the co-author. I understand your concern. My family agrees with you. My brother insisted I make the story fictional and change all names, characters and places. I think he agreed to co-write, so he could keep an eye on what I was doing. My mother wouldn't let me travel to Mexico to do research. The man who confronted Helena in New York scared us sufficiently for me to make a few more changes to the script. Look, Casi, I generally write comedy, not documentaries, so I assure you, this will be advertised as complete fiction. I promise you."

"You don't understand. It doesn't matter if you call it fiction. You're missing the point. It will still be recognizable by virtue of who is making the movie. Your promise to me, means nothing. If Fernando perceives it's about him, and he chooses not to like it, there is no telling what he'll do. He is unpredictable. I've known him all my life and I never knew what he would do from one minute to the next when he was angry. He's a loose cannon. You're lucky Jose is in jail. If he wasn't, you wouldn't make it to the first day of filming."

"Why don't you look at what I wrote? I'd like to share the script with you. Change whatever you like, then let's talk again."

"Bring it tomorrow morning. Let me read it before you shop it around the festival and attract the wrong people. I'm in no way agreeing to anything until I see it. On the contrary, I'll probably try to convince you to drop the project. There is no doubt you'll find my arguments compelling, if I really let loose."

"Ok. Understood. I'll bring you a copy. It's by no means final, and like I said, I'll be happy to edit scenes. I want your input. I'm prepared to listen."

"I also want to hear your pitch."

"Ok. Now?"

"No. After I read the script."

"Thanks for the drink, and thanks for listening. Helena, I'll see you at 9am sharp. I'm leaving. I'm beat."

"See you in the morning." Helena replied solemnly. Casi walked Summer to the door and lingered, filling the doorframe as she stepped outside.

"Summer, does anyone in your family know I'm here?"

"Hell, no."

"Make sure it stays that way," he clipped as he hovered over her with a menacing stance. Summer felt a chill run up and down her spine as she nodded. Was he threatening her?

CHAPTER LXIII

Cartel Business, Sour Grapes

The next morning Summer printed out a copy of her script in the hotel's business office and met Jasper and Samson for breakfast at 8am. She wanted to tell them about her interaction with Casi, to let them know where Helena was and where she was going, but she couldn't decide if she was more scared of him or her brothers' reactions to her meeting. She decided to keep quiet. She desperately wanted Casi's story and so she needed to play by his rules. If Helena weren't lodging at his cabin, she might have shared the information with someone in her family, but she realized it would just complicate matters. Casi's parting reaction the night before had scared her profoundly. Nonetheless, she was not backing down.

When she arrived at the cabin, she honked, not wanting to go inside. Casi and Helena came out to greet her. Summer rolled down the window and handed Casi her script.

"Here, you can mark it up as you see fit. I'm open to all of your suggestions. I also have an extra ticket to the screening of my movie tonight. Do you want to come?"

"I would love to, but no, thank you. I can't. I'll look this over and let you know what I think tomorrow. Last night made me realize that you have no sense of the danger you're stepping into. If you pitch to the wrong people or disclose the wrong details and word gets out, you're putting yourself and those you love at risk. I don't think you fully understand, Summer. You never had to live in fear. Did you give this script to anyone else?"

"No, only the synopsis. You have that too. It's attached. That's what we've been pitching and we purposely kept it vague."

"Don't give anyone else a copy until we go over it together. Got it?"

Casi's dark eyes stared at her. The corners of his lips were turned down, and there was a crease between his heavy brows. She could feel the strength of his conviction. Summer nodded, tongue-tied. She just wanted to get out of there. She was still feeling spooked from the night before, and Casi's threatening demeanor was making her knees turn to blubber.

"Did you hear me, Summer?" He leaned down to the car window and scowled.

"Yes, Casi. I heard you. I'll wait for your feedback," she stammered, looking at her hands. As she pulled out of the driveway, she kept Casi in her sight. She wondered if he was really in Park City alone, or if he had some people stashed away, listening and watching in a neighboring cabin. What was Helena thinking about all of this?

"How was your evening, Helena?" She looked at Helena from the corner of her eye, keeping her eyes on the road.

"Fine. We had dessert, a little champagne, talked a lot, and went to sleep."

Summer waited for more, but Helena looked out of the window, silent and preoccupied.

"Did Casi say anything else about the script after I left? What was your impression?"

"Not much. We talked about other things. He asked me if I was definitely committed to the movie if it gets funded."

"What did you answer?"

"Yes."

Helena's unusual silence was making Summer thoughtful. Did Casi get to her? Was she scared too? Have second thoughts?

"Is everything ok, Helena?"

"I don't know. I'm confused. I love Casi, but his situation scares me. I want to be with him, but I also want to continue my career. I loved acting in your movie, and if this film gets made, I would like to be a part of it, but Casi feels I can't do both. He hasn't said he wants me to quit, but I feel that he might if we get funded. He's scaring me. Also, if I want to be with him, I basically have to go under cover and give up my dreams, my life, my friends. I don't know if I'm ready to do that. His whole life frightens me, and what happens if he's exposed? My life could be ruined too."

"No doubt, his life so far was scary, but in his defense, he's trying to change that. Do you have to make a decision right now? Can't you continue life as is and see if your feelings crystalize later? It might hit you one day that you can't live without him or that you can't give up your career. You'll know what you need to do when the time is right. Surely, he'll grant you some space to think about it. You only had two nights together after being apart for eight months. A lot has happened in those eight months."

"Yes. That's true. He says I should take whatever time I need to decide, but then he tells me how much he wants me with him. I do love him, and I want to be with him. I don't know what to do."

"Enjoy the time you have now. Let's see where the festival takes us. Possibly nowhere. If he truly loves you, he'll be patient and let you decide."

"I think you're right. It's difficult to make a life decision when I don't even know where he lives and what his new life is like. What if I don't like his new life?"

"Well, there is always that. It's a leap of faith. It sounds like he lives a more subdued life in a smaller place than Paris or New York. Would you miss city life?"

"Yes, very much."

"Hmmm, well, maybe you should ask him what his day to day looks like and what you would be doing if you were to go. Get a mental picture of his life without necessarily knowing the location and see if it appeals to you. You don't have to know the exact town or city to get an idea, right?"

"I suppose. And another problem is, I don't speak Spanish. I imagine he settled in a Spanish speaking country."

"I don't know. You'll have to ask him. Maybe not. And even if he has, you can learn Spanish. You might want to either way."

"I guess. I can't decide this today or tomorrow. I need time. Which meeting are we going to this morning?"

"No meeting. We have a screening, lunch with a few industry people, and a 'talk' this afternoon. Hope set the lunch up with some of her L.A. contacts. Ted and Jasper will join us for lunch and the talk. Then we go to the hotel to get ready for our screening. Get excited."

"I am. I wish Casi could come."

Summer watched Helena strike a pose on the red carpet as she, Hope, Ted and Jasper waited in the shadows. Cara and Francois went into the theater to secure their seats. Helena dazzled in a form-fitting, midnight-blue cocktail dress and giant fake ruby earrings. She was an absolute natural on the red carpet. In that instant, Summer couldn't picture Helena being happy in Casi's sea side restaurant for the rest of her life, but she knew that Helena would have to arrive at that decision herself. Destiny was a matter of choice.

CHAPTER LXIV

Prison Without Walls

Casi poured himself another cup of coffee and sat down at the counter with Summer's script. He was still feeling the warm afterglow of a passionate night. He wondered how he had survived without Helena for eight long months. The last two nights had been magical and he sincerely hoped, she felt the same. He wondered if she would give up her stardom track, but he had serious doubts. He noticed how she lit up when she talked about the possibility of starring in another film directed by Summer. She had a successful modeling career too, but it appeared she was a lot less passionate about that. It paid the bills. He suspected he would have to be very patient and wait for her to think this through. All he needed was a sliver of hope to hang on, but how long should he wait? Put his life on hold? Maybe until she finished her second movie, if it got funded. He guessed less than a quarter of what was pitched had a shot, and even fewer films got funded by big studios. He wasn't thrilled with his prognosis, but he would do what he needed to. He would wait. Helena was worth it. She completed his life, but only if she remained committed to him. They needed to be on the same page, or resentment would percolate.

He turned his attention to the script. As he read the first few scenes, his skin crawled. It became immediately apparent that he would be forced to work with Summer if only to protect everyone from cartel payback. The American girl was fearless, but clearly, she didn't know better. In this case, ignorance was bliss. One good scare from Fernando's friends and she would change her tune, but Casi wanted to prevent that at all costs. A confrontation could have serious backlash for him as well. He decided to give Summer the background she wanted. A few good stories about Jose's killing methods, like the one of poor Diego, should set her straight. He wrote a few reminders in the margins.

When Casi looked up from the script it was lunchtime and his stomach was growling. He had made numerous suggestions and notes in the margins and he was satisfied with his first review. Since there was little but the breakfast basics in the refrigerator, he bundled up to go out. He needed to take a break and digest the darker side of his life on paper. It sure didn't help him forget his past to regurgitate the life he had shelved with good reason. He put on his black- knit slouchy hat and dark-lensed sunglasses. On impulse, he turned back and grabbed the script from the counter. It wouldn't be smart to leave it lying around. As he walked towards the door, he heard a car pull into his driveway. He froze. Looking out the window from a safe angle, he observed a black Mercedes SUV next to his rental jeep. Two men with dark sunglasses sat inside, talking. His heart was pounding. He noted the license plate and waited silently, not moving a muscle.

Moments later, the SUV pulled out, turning in the opposite direction and left. Casi breathed out. He waited a few more minutes, checked all the windows, set the alarm, and exited with his passport, plane ticket, and wallet, in case a quick departure was needed. He hopped into the black jeep and drove into town, looking out for a black SUV in the rearview mirror. He didn't see it.

He stopped at a diner for a hearty lunch, keeping his eye on all restaurant activity, especially near the door. He kept his hat and sunglasses on but shed his black sheepskin jacket and magenta scarf. Sitting in the back, near the kitchen, he was assured a quick exit in a pinch. His jeep was strategically parked by the kitchen door. After lunch, trying to kill time, he drove to a shopping center and picked up a few items in the drugstore and supermarket. Stopping in a clothing boutique, he bought his sister a violet fleece jacket with elaborate detailing and a long, lavender cashmere wrap with a ruffled border. He had the saleslady gift wrap it as he searched the store for Helena's gift. In the end, he decided on the same cashmere wrap in a sky-blue to match her incredible eyes. He added one more in winter white for Summer.

For himself, he picked up a thin, lined, quilted rain jacket in an emerald green, which would be perfect for a boat on a cool day. He also selected sunglasses with a mirrored reflection. Snow and water both required UV eye protection. The sales girl approached him from behind.

"Those look great. Did you see this green cashmere sweater? It matches the jacket you chose. I also have a beautiful light green and blue muddled scarf that works beautifully with the two. You could wear it all with blue jeans, and it would look awesome." Casi examined her lay out on the counter and agreed.

"Ok. I'll take it all. Do you have the cashmere sweater in a different color? I could use one more."

"Yes. It comes in royal blue, lilac, raspberry, and cinnamon. I think I have your size in all of them."

"I'll take both the royal blue and raspberry. Thanks."

"You're lucky. We have a cashmere sale, thirty percent off. Can I ring you up, or do you want to shop some more?"

"I'm good."

Casi left the store feeling great about his purchases. He had left most of his old winter clothes in Paris when he fled. The only coat he had was the black sheepskin he wore when he ran to the airport. The rain jacket would come in handy during the rainy season in the Bahamas. After his shopping spree, he drove through town but didn't stop. He called Peter to check on the restaurant.

"All's good here, Casi. Your sister has been great, managing orders. She catches on quick."

"Good, I knew she would."

"What has me captivated, is how she has Matias eating out of the palm of her hand. You have to see it to believe it, man."

"She has her charms, my Camila." Casi laughed. "Thanks, Peter. I'll be back in a few days. Tell Camila I'll call her tomorrow."

When he hung up, he sent Camila a text. He texted her daily on the secure phone, knowing how worried she was. Heading back to the cabin, he checked the rearview mirror. Near his cabin, he circled the neighborhood a few times to make sure he wasn't being followed.

When he arrived, he studied the tracks in the driveway. They looked the same as when he left. He backed the jeep into the driveway in case a quick departure was necessary. Carrying his purchases into the cabin, he noticed everything looked the same as he left it. It appeared no one had entered. Relieved, he put the wrapped gifts on the counter and went into the bedroom to organize his clothes. Whatever he didn't need or was dirty, he put into his suitcase. Casi liked to keep his belongings together for a quick exit. Once organized, he made himself coffee and continued to peruse the script. A few more things came to mind and he jotted them down. When he was satisfied with his additions, he showered, but first, he placed a chair in front of the main door and set the alarm.

Changing into black wool trousers and a pale pink cotton shirt, he pulled on his new royal blue cashmere sweater. He threw on his shearling, new blue/green muddled scarf, black slouchy hat, and mirrored sunglasses. He had a ticket for Helena's premiere, and he intended to use it. He bought it weeks ago, long before he booked the cabin. It was an aisle seat in the rear of the theater.

Casi got there early and sat in the jeep until it was close to starting time. Walking in with a crowd of people, he entered the theater and found his seat. Announcements and introductions were made on stage. There would be a Q&A following the screening. Thankfully, the lights dimmed quickly and the movie started on schedule.

When the credits had run and the applause subsided, Summer, Hope, Ted, and Helena were introduced on stage. An industry professional fired off questions and Casi noticed how skillfully Summer responded. On occasion, she deferred to Hope, the cinematographer, for technical answers or to Ted when it was a producing insight. He had to admit, he had enjoyed the film and appreciated its comedic voice. Summer had done a masterful job directing Helena and her co-stars. Before the last question was asked, Casi slipped out and hurried to the jeep. Once in the cabin, he turned on the TV to see if there was any local coverage. While he waited for word from Helena, he continued looking over the script. It would be a late night. As he sipped a mimosa in Helena's honor, his phone alerted him of an incoming text. Helena wasn't coming.

CHAPTER LXV

A Mother's Pride

Cara was excited to be at Sundance with Francois and her children. How life had changed since her first Paris trip, a little over a year ago. Her only regret was that Samantha couldn't join them. Sam was in the throes of a plum interior design assignment, which couldn't be delayed. Business was always a priority, especially when you worked for yourself. Similarly, Cara had labored around the clock to get her own orders out before traveling to Park City.

She enjoyed the action at Sundance--the movie star sightings, the screenings, the talks and most of all, dinner with her family on a nightly basis. Even if everyone was doing their own thing during the day, they convened over dinner and swapped stories, sightings, and general information, all of which was deliciously entertaining. The atmosphere in the hotel and at the festival was electric and Cara thrived on the sensory overload. She knew for most of the film industry, this was business as usual, but for her sedate life, this vacation was intoxicating. Many industry insiders only came to network. They barely went to screenings as most had seen the strongest contenders at private screenings months earlier, but for Cara, it was all a gigantic thrill. She enjoyed the films, the electric atmosphere and loved seeing the film elite hang out in their hotel.

Being able to share this experience with Francois was particularly rewarding. His artistic background and interests made him the perfect companion and fellow critic. They discussed and dissected everything as if a paycheck depended on it. Francois's insights and artistic eye amused Cara and broadened her viewpoints. Summer, Hope and Ted added the icing to the cake with their unique comments and inside information.

When the night of Summer's movie premiere arrived, Cara was just as excited as her daughter. She had seen the rough edits in various stages, but seeing the final cut on a big screen with a live audience was over the top. She hoped that Summer would get good reviews. Of course you couldn't please every critic, but if the comments were mostly good, Summer could possibly score another funded proposal. That was the ultimate goal--more work. When you worked on one project for well over a year, it became a big chunk of your life. Validation made it all worthwhile.

Cara and Francois got to the theater early to witness the red carpet fanfare. After Summer and Helena had their moment, she and Francois went inside to secure seats. Cara was so proud of how well Summer handled everything and Helena, well, she just looked like a mega movie star. Cara settled into her seat and glanced around the theater. All of Summer's anticipated guests were present, waiting. She knew Summer appreciated the support. When the lights dimmed, Cara sunk into her seat and reached for Francois's hand.

The Q&A started immediately after the movie ended, but a bulging bladder made it difficult for Cara to concentrate. After the introductions, before the first questions were launched, she sprinted up the aisle to the bathrooms, in the hopes of avoiding a line. As she passed the seated audience, she searched their faces for their post-screening reactions. She was delighted to witness a sea of smiles.

Approaching the rear of the theater, Cara spotted a familiar face. Her stomach lurched. Was that the man from the Sea Grape Garden Restaurant in the Bahamas? She was almost certain it was him. What was he doing at Summer's premiere? Somewhere in the deep recesses of her brain, she was making connections. He was here for Helena's movie debut. Carlos Ortiz came to see Helena! Cara wondered if Helena knew he was here. A chill crept over her, and it definitely wasn't caused by her exploding bladder. What should she do with this explosive information?

CHAPTER LXVI

Evil Knows No Borders

After tingling, pre-premiere stress, the industry after-party was the place to celebrate. Summer's film was well received and she had every intention of making the most of marketing her next proposal to anyone willing to listen. At midnight, after an awesome time, her mom and Francois left the party. Samson, Ted and Hope followed a half hour later. Summer, Jasper and Helena stayed until well after one, networking like their next meal depended on it.

When they entered the hotel lobby, Jasper bid the girls good night, barely stifling a yawn. Summer and Helena stopped to get water bottles from the bar area. While waiting, Helena texted Casi, promising to stop by in the morning. She felt bad she missed an evening with him but business was business. She knew he would understand. Sending a second text, she confirmed dinner for the following night as well. Waiting for his reply, she was approached by a man who appeared out of nowhere. Helena instinctively slid the secure phone into her beaded handbag.

"You better be careful with that script you're pitching. I hear it's about F&S enterprises." Helena said nothing, but Summer was quick to reply.

"My script is fictional and not about anyone or any organization in particular. How do you even know what my script is about?"

"I hear things and I try to protect our common interests."

"Whose common interests?"

"Let's just say, I represent Mexican business interests. We don't want our privacy invaded by someone who doesn't have a clue about anything. You know what I mean?"

"No, I don't. My script is pure fiction with some inspiration from current news articles."

"We may have suffered a small setback in Europe, but that doesn't mean we aren't working to regroup," he continued. "Think long and hard before you make a mistake that could jeopardize your family or ours. We're a strong group, and we don't want to be in the spotlight."

"Are you threatening me? I told you, my film is pure story-telling, not a documentary. All names, characters and actions are fictitious, I assure you. Take that back to your business interests."

"I hope so, for your sake, *chica*." He turned to Helena. "Any word from Carlos?"

"No." Helena whispered, emphatically shaking her head.

"Be warned," he glared at Summer.

Summer hoped the butterflies going berserk in her stomach didn't give her away. Her adrenaline was pumping, and her face twitched uncontrollably. Before she could respond again, the man turned and exited the hotel. Fear took over and the girls hurried to the elevator. Summer texted Helena on the secure phone.

Don't talk about anything in the room. He could have planted a listening device while we were out.

Next, she texted Casi.

Helena and I were just approached by a man who asked about you. He threatened us. FF's people are here. We're fine for now. Safe in our room. Talk tomorrow.

The next morning, Helena and Summer slept in. Helena texted Casi their change of plan. Between the party and the late-night scare, the girls didn't fall asleep until the early morning hours despite bolting the door and pushing a weighted chair in front of it. They showered and slinked downstairs for a very late breakfast, still jumpy. Hope, Ted, and Jasper were lingering over coffee. Samson, Cara, and Francois were already out.

"Morning guys. Where is everyone?"

"They left early for screenings. Dinner tonight is at eight. We have a reservation at the hotel." Jasper smiled. "Good night, wasn't it?"

"Yes. Good all around." Summer smiled as she surveyed the room.

"I heard from one of the studios this morning. They're interested in seeing your script. They want to meet back in New York. I set up a tentative date for Ted, you and I. I'm also waiting to hear from the L.A. group we met with the other day."

"Oh, good. Let's talk about this later. I'm still fuzzy." Summer scanned the restaurant again. "There's a screening at 1:30pm I want to see. After that, Helena and I are going to do some errands. How about you?"

"Sounds good. Hope, Ted and I are going to screenings at one and three thirty. This is what we're seeing." He pointed to a highlighted film schedule.

"Have fun. We're seeing a comedy." Summer pointed to their chosen film on his schedule.

"Of course you are."

Late afternoon, Helena and Summer pulled into Casi's driveway after circling the block several times to make sure no one was following them. She parked her car on the street in front of the neighboring cabin. Through the window, Summer observed Casi sitting at the counter with his laptop, waiting for them. When he spotted them, he moved to open the door.

"Hello. Congratulations on the good reviews." Casi smiled curtly.

"Hi, Casi. Thanks."

He closed the door behind them. "Tell me what happened last night? What did the guy look like?"

"We had a successful night and attended a party after the screening. When Helena and I got back to the hotel we were stopped by a Latin man. He approached us from behind as we were getting water bottles. He asked Helena if you had contacted her. She said no. He also asked me about my script. He wanted to know if it was about F&S Enterprises. It wasn't the same guy from New York. That I know for sure."

"Buckle up. This is only the beginning. If you move forward with this project of yours, this won't be the only time you'll encounter backlash. I warned you."

"Yes, you did. I assured him my story was pure fiction. I refuse to be intimidated. Did you look over the script?" Summer appeared to look tough, but in truth, her legs were liquid Jell-O.

"Yes. We have a lot of work to do if you're still serious about moving forward. How much time do you have?" Casi studied her, probingly.

Summer ignored his penetrating expression. He unsettled her. "We're free for the rest of the evening, and yes, I'm moving forward."

"Helena, can you get us something to drink? Summer and I need to have a long talk."

"Sure, Casi."

Two hours later, Casi leaned back in his chair and placed the script pages on the table. "I think we covered the important things. Once you revise the script, send it to me again. Trust me, it is controversial enough, so making these changes will only buy you a little peace of mind, if anything. You don't want someone to sabotage your set while you're filming, or threaten you and your crew with bodily harm. People will be dropping your project like dead flies if they feel threatened, contract or no contract."

Summer felt whiplashed. "No. I don't want anyone to get hurt or drop out. I can live with these changes."

She suspected Casi knew what he was doing. She would rather accept his rewrites than give up.

"Do you want a margarita? You look like you could use one." Casi inquired in a dry tone.

"No, thanks. I think I want to get back to the hotel and take a breather before dinner."

"Summer, I'm going to skip dinner tonight and stay here. Pick me up in the morning?"

"Yes, I figured that."

"Check your texts before you come tomorrow," Casi added.

"Ok?" Summer prompted, not wanting to ask. She pulled on her navy down jacket and hot pink fleece hat and headed to the door.

It was dark out and she was spooked leaving the cabin alone. Once in the car, she locked the doors and left quickly, merging onto the main street in a rush. She checked the rear-view mirror, but noticed nothing in particular.

At the hotel, she decided to valet the car instead of parking and walking from the dark, lot. In the lobby, she looked at her cellphone. There was enough time to run to her room and review the script one more time. Grateful for the people in the elevator and hallways, she bolted her door and turned on the electric fireplace, throwing herself on the sofa. She could only imagine Casi's former life. This was more stress than she cared to handle, but she was determined not to back down. She felt confident about her script and could envision the scenes.

Summer arrived at dinner a few minutes late. Jasper had ordered her favored cocktail, which she gratefully accepted. She was thrilled to see everyone chatting excitedly. They were half way through the festival, and so far, everything had gone according to plan--well, almost everything.

Her mind wandered back to the script changes Casi insisted on. His hair-raising accounts about cartel retribution had shocked her to the core. As a result, she let him change the locations, characters and some genders. The art forgeries were no longer ceramics, they included small bronze sculptures. The cities of interest were no longer Barcelona, Paris and Monaco, but Rome, Naples and Sicily. Instead of working with the Moroccans and Russians, they were in business with the Sicilian mafia. Summer didn't like some of the changes per se, but she didn't want to cross or question Casi. He clearly had a grasp on the cartel's pulse. His stories about Jose's violent warnings and retribution murders made her blood curl. She replayed her earlier dialogue in her head as she sipped her strawberry daiquiri and shuddered. Was Casi right? Had she bitten off more than she could chew?

"Why am I changing the city names and the product when you're giving me graphic details of Jose's executions? Isn't that even riskier?" She'd asked him.

His reply was instantly forthcoming.

"No. You don't understand how the cartel mind works. The places and product are a dead giveaway, especially coming from you. Flores knows your family. That in itself is dangerous and shouldn't be in the forefront at any cost. Neither should the business he still runs legitimately. The detailed brutality and enforcer stories, he will be proud of. They show how tough and thorough he is with people who cross him. Those accounts will only get him added respect in his world. People already fear him. This confirms they have every reason to."

"Good God. Ok, I'll trust you on that." Summer recoiled at the memory. Her mind wandered as she shivered in her seat.

"Summer, are you listening?" Jasper nudged her back to reality.

"What? No, sorry. What did you ask me?"

"Where is Helena tonight?"

"She's really tired from last night. She decided to have supper in the room and relax in a scented bubble bath."

CHAPTER LXVII

The Best Confessions are Made Under Water

Helena was indeed relaxing, in a heavenly hot tub…with Casi. They were chatting, sipping champagne, kissing and looking at the stars. It was a clear, crisp night and she was wearing nothing but the Brazilian tourmaline earrings Casi had given her. Her hair was piled haphazardly in a loose knot on top of her head. The earrings shimmered around her face as they caught the light. Casi thought she looked stunning. It touched him his celebration gifts had moved her to tears. Since he had forgotten to give Summer her gift after the script review, he let Helena choose which cashmere wrap she wanted, and to his surprise she chose the winter white.

"These earrings are from Brazil? They're beautiful! Is that where you live?"

"No, I traveled there when I left Paris. I'm happy you like them."

"I more than like them. I love them! They're pink! I'll think of you whenever I wear them and I plan to wear them all the time. Tell me about Brazil." She sparkled inside and out. Casi gathered her in his arms and painted a romantic picture of the sights and sounds of Rio as the amniotic water bubbled around them and his hands encircled her breasts.

Earlier, after Summer left the cabin with script changes in hand, Casi turned to Helena.

"We're moving to a nicer cabin. I switched my Airbnb today. For security reasons. Same owner, so it was easy. Don't unpack your bag. I want to leave immediately. Let's pack the rest of our belongings and get out of here. We'll have cocktails in the other cabin."

Circling the neighborhood a few times, he pulled into another driveway not too far away. The cabin interior was not unlike the first one, but it had the added perk of an outdoor hot tub in the deck. Casi turned it on before they unloaded the jeep.

"I didn't bring a bathing suit."

"You won't need one. The deck is private. Would you like a glass of champagne?"

"That would be lovely."

"Considering your encounter last night, it doesn't hurt to move around. You were shadowed. I think whoever confronted you was at the party. Maybe he overheard Summer pitching the script to someone. Or maybe he was looking for me by following you."

"Do you think he was following us all week?"

"Hard to say. Probably not. I would have noticed something. I think he tailed you at the party."

"Summer and Jasper were talking about the script with a few people. Do you think the guy will keep watching us?"

"Who knows? He might have been on a fishing expedition for the big event. Just be careful. Don't go to unsecured, dark areas. Try to be aware if anyone is tailing you and don't call me from questionable places. I think he was trying to scare you and he managed to do that, didn't he?"

"That he did. I'm scared. Summer isn't backing down though."

Helena leaned her head against the edge of the hot tub. "Mmm… this feels so good. This was so worth the switch!"

"Agreed. Are you hungry yet? I have dinner in the cooler we brought from the other cabin. We can eat whenever you want. It only takes a few minutes to heat."

"I'll take another glass of bubbly first, please."

Casi refilled her glass and smiled as he looked into her glistening face. Time spent with Helena was always wonderful.

Toweling off after the bath, Helena slipped into a silky violet lingerie slip and struck a sexy pose.

"I'm ready for dinner."

Casi threw her a white, terry-cloth spa robe.

"Here, wear this, or you'll be dinner."

"If you insist," she whispered in his ear.

Touching his semi erection, she teased his ear and lips with her tongue and planted little kisses along his neck, letting her hands wander across his back. Casi let out a low growl and tied her robe in the front.

"Hold that thought until after dinner."

He turned on the oven and slid their food onto a baking sheet while Helena searched the kitchen for plates, silverware, and water glasses to set the table. The electric fireplace warmed the room, adding a diffused, warm light. Helena lit a candle and placed it table center. It started snowing outside and the wind whistled softly through the window cracks. The robe felt good on her moist, heated skin. She refilled their champagne flutes and added a carafe of water to the table.

"Are we staying with champagne or switching to wine?"

"Champagne is good. I have a second bottle in the fridge. Dinner will be ready in a few minutes."

"Casi, how do you really feel about the script? Do you think it'll cause trouble for us, or are we fine with your changes?"

"I think if anyone else made the movie, it would probably be fine, but since it's Summer and her family who wrote the script, Fernando will be watching. If he decides he doesn't like what he sees, you will undoubtedly find out. You're on his radar because of me. Sorry about that, but it is what it is. Sometimes, he makes decisions based on his mood, and with me and a large chunk of money gone, I'm sure his mood is as foul as a pig trapped in a pond. He has a volatile personality as it is." He opened the oven and checked on dinner, then continued.

"Then there is Jose, his enforcer. We're all fortunate he's in jail. He was the one I feared most. He loved to bait Fernando, get him riled up, just to be dispatched to bully and hurt people. They were a dangerously impulsive and combustible combination. I was so happy to be in Paris while they stayed in Barcelona. It gave me room to breathe." He sliced some bread and put it on the table.

"Jose has so much blood on his hands, I don't know how he sleeps at night. He's a dangerous psychopath, with a seriously sadistic streak. He's also a frustrated gay man who refused to come out of the closet. Somehow he couldn't reconcile his sexual urges with what was expected of him by his family. He never killed a man, without stripping him down first and touching him. What scares me is, he was training Fernando's two nephews, Julio and Luis, to be enforcers too. I was happy when they stayed in Mexico."

"How did you manage them?"

"I barely did. I had no choice. I kept the lowest profile possible and only talked when needed. I managed the company books meticulously and stayed out of everyone's way whenever there was trouble. I rarely made mistakes. Didn't dare. Fernando trusted me for that reason. I was the quiet guy who handled the investments." He slid their dinner onto waiting plates, arranging the food artfully. "Sit. Dinner is served."

"Why did you never tell me any of this?"

"To keep you safe, Helena. The less you knew, the better off you were. I didn't want to scare you and possibly lose you. I couldn't bear that thought. You were my bright spot. I made it my priority to keep you happy and far away from Fernando and Jose. I never wanted them to know we were close. I never talked about you, so they wouldn't realize I cared. If they knew how much I loved you, they would have exploited my weakness for sure." Carlos stopped to choose his words carefully. "For Fernando, women were disposable. I moved my sister to Mexico City for good reason. Hard as it was to be separated, sending her away was the only way I could protect her. I wanted her to have a chance at a better life, away from the Flores family and the Sinaloa cartel, but honestly, once you grow up in a cartel environment, you never fully get away. They always find you, if they want to."

"I'm so sorry, Casi. I hope they never find you or your sister."

"I will always be looking over my shoulder, but at least now, I have money. I can run. I hope I don't have to. My business is doing well, and I like where I settled."

"You do look different, hard to recognize. That helps, I'm sure. I love your new look."

"Thanks. Face to face, Fernando would recognize me, though. We spent too many years together. If he looked into my eyes, he would know."

"If I were to go under cover with you, what would I do?"

"Work with me? Raise a family? You would need to stay close. Being in the public eye would be impossible. You would have to give that up. I know it's a lot to ask. That's why I want you to take time to really think about it. I would love to have you in my life, but you have to be aware of the risks and want to be there. Know what you'd be giving up. Basically, your freedom and your identity. I love you, but I won't trap you against your will. Neither of us would be happy."

"I need time, Casi. I love you too, with all my heart, but I worked so hard for this opportunity. I don't know if I can walk away right now. This is an impossible choice."

"I understand. I'll wait… for now. We can stay in touch and try to figure out ways to meet in random places. Time will tell you what you need to know. I'm sure of that."

"Ok, I don't want to lose you again." She reached across the table and closed her hand over his. Casi circled her wrists with his warm hands and gently guided her around the café table to straddle his lap. Sliding his fingers into her robe, he explored her warmth.

"Right now, I'm more interested in checking out your new lingerie, *mamacita rica*."

The next morning, Casi texted Summer the new address on the secure phone. He turned to Helena, who was still lounging in bed with her coffee mug.

"Now that we know Fernando's people are here, take all your things with you in case I have to leave."

"You aren't planning on leaving unless something is wrong, right?"

"Right."

"I plan on seeing you tonight, you know."

"And I, you."

She finished her coffee and walked to the shower.

"You coming?" Helena smiled over her shoulder.

Casi followed her, dropping his pants along the way.

A short while later, Casi was dressed and standing by the window, holding his coffee mug. There were no suspicious cars lingering or passing by as far as he could see. He watched Summer pull up to the street curb.

"Summer is here."

He walked to the door and waved Summer into the cabin.

"Hi, guys. I like your new digs." Summer did a three-sixty sweep. "A little less cabin and a lot more luxury hotel room."

"Thanks. Same owner. Small upgrade. We moved last night. Please delete both addresses from your phone right now."

"Right. Will do. Your landlord needs to plow the driveway. Good thing you rented a jeep." She pulled out her phone and under Casi's watchful eye, deleted his messages.

"Would you like some coffee?" Casi held up the freshly brewed pot.

"Half a cup with lots of milk, please."

"We have a little gift for you, Summer, to congratulate you on your film's success." Casi handed her the beautifully wrapped gift bag.

"Oh my, thank you! May I open it?"

"Yes."

Casi watched Summer pull at the rose silk ribbon and tear the wrapping. When she pulled out the sky-blue cashmere scarf, her face lit up.

"This is beautiful! My favorite color. How did you guess? Thank you both so much."

"Your welcome. Enjoy it. What are your plans today?"

"We have more meetings, screenings, the usual. I'll bring her back tonight."

"Fine. Just text me before you come. I'm checking passing cars a little more closely, now that I know Flores' people are here."

"Got it. Listen, Casi, I probably won't be able to rewrite the script until I get home, but I promise you, no one will see it until all the new changes are done and you approved them."

"Glad to hear it. Maybe you can come for breakfast tomorrow morning? I thought of a few more changes I'd like you to make,"

"I can do that. Thanks for the coffee. Helena, I'll be waiting in the car."

"See you both, later." Casi clipped.

"Coming," Helena chimed, kissing Casi passionately on the way out.

Summer knew she had a hard time tearing herself away from his embrace. Again, she wondered what passion like that felt like.

CHAPTER LXVIII

Ignorance is Bliss Compounded

The last twenty-four hours were pure hell for Cara. She wrestled with whether she should tell Summer and Helena who she had discovered at the premiere. She wanted to give Helena some much needed closure, but a larger part of her wanted to keep them both safe. She decided Helena was better off not knowing about Carlos. She was a beautiful girl, inside and out, who deserved better. She had the opportunity to go places, be successful. She didn't need a ball and chain. No, she would spare Helena renewed heartache and not tell the girls she saw Carlos lurking in the theater.

Cara was also plagued by the possible consequences of Summer trying to converse with a hunted drug felon. She could just imagine Summer naively asking him to fill in the blanks in her script. Good Lord! Countless people had died at his posse's hands, many from forced drug overdoses, some from merely breathing in their vicinity. The articles she had read about the Flores posse painted them as ruthless killers when it came to protecting their investments.

Now, a good portion of their ill-gained assets was in the hands of the French and Spanish authorities. Served them right. And to think that Jasper had unknowingly handled their investments at the bank. Cara shuddered when she thought about that.

Summer's and Jasper's safety was her first concern. Frankly, she didn't care if Helena loved the guy, the girl needed protecting. She would stay silent for now, but keep her eyes open to make sure he didn't approach her family. If he did, she wouldn't hesitate to alert the police. Or should she do that regardless? She needed to think about this. She couldn't discuss her discovery with any of the men in her group. They would only complicate things. It would have to be her decision.

The next morning, while Francois was still sleeping, Cara searched the internet for news on the Flores family and Carlos Ortiz. Jose Flores was still charged with murder and rotting in jail, as he should. Fernando Flores appeared to be back in Mexico, handling business as usual, and Carlos Ortiz's whereabouts were unknown. Cara studied the picture of him. The man she saw here and in the Bahamas looked so different, but he reminded her of Carlos Ortiz. There were striking similarities. Those eyes! She had to admit, she had doubts. What if she was mistaken, and the man just looked similar? She couldn't be one-hundred percent sure, but why was he popping up everywhere?

Before Cara and Francois left their room for breakfast, she sent a group text to her children to see if anyone was up and wanted to join them. While seated in the main dining room, sipping coffee, Summer appeared.

"Hi, Mom, hi, Francois. What are you up to today?"

"Morning, Summer. We're going to do a little shopping, have lunch in town, then, go to a one thirty screening. What about you and Helena?"

"Our meeting this morning was cancelled, so maybe we'll see you in town."

"Where is Helena now?"

"Resting. What are you having?"

"She missed dinner too. Is she feeling ok?"

"Yes. It's just been a lot these last few days and she's not a morning person. She likes her down time, and she doesn't eat breakfast anyway."

"I guess she doesn't look like that without concessions. We slept later than usual this morning. Oh, look, our omelets are here."

"Looks yummy. Can I get a coffee to go, please?" Summer smiled at the waiter.

"Samson and Jasper are on their way down for breakfast. Sure you don't want to stay?"

"No. I'm going to grab a muffin from your basket and go. I have some emails to send, and then we're off to town. I'll see you later." Summer took her goodies and scampered off in a hurry.

When Francois and Cara left the hotel in their rental car, they spotted Summer at the traffic light, leaving the hotel grounds. Cara pulled up behind her, one car separating them.

"Oh, look. The girls are in front of us. We should follow them into town." Cara squinted when the car in front of her turned left and she ended up behind Summer. "Wait, do you see Helena? I only see one head."

"Me, too," Francois agreed.

"That's odd."

Cara followed Summer in the direction of town, but then Summer made an abrupt right turn into a residential area.

"Where is she going? Is this a short cut?" Cara followed.

After a few more turns, Summer pulled into a driveway. Cara drove past her, turned around, and looped back, slowing down at the house Summer parked at. Cara observed her daughter entering the cabin, chatting with Helena and a man. She grinded to a halt a few doors down. It was the man from the Bahamas! She was certain. Rolling forward, she swerved nearly crashing into a parked car.

"It looks like the girls have a meeting after all," Francois remarked.

"Yes, it does and I'm not sure I like this meeting. I'll have to talk to Summer." Cara frowned.

"Why? Who is that?"

"Let's just say, if it is who I think it is, he's a really shady guy."

CHAPTER LXIX

Can't Fool Mother... Forever

Summer pulled into the cabin's cleared driveway and turned off the engine. She was preoccupied, wondering what script changes Casi wanted her to make so, she didn't notice the car slowing behind her. He had completely altered her script already; her story was barely recognizable. Secretly, she was worried he would try to kill the project and talk Helena out of participating. She soon realized, Casi was a man of his word.

Over coffee and eggs, he shared some memories of growing up in a cartel environment. His first-hand experiences were mind-bending as far as Summer was concerned. She had never heard of such brutality and she cringed as she listened, yet she wanted to hear it all, every last gory detail of knee caps broken and men thrown to the sharks or skewered by fire pokers. If Casi was willing to share, she was a captive audience. Could everything be used, or reenacted, if the script got funded? Questionable, but Summer didn't want to miss a single, jarring event. Some of this information could be used in a background narrative.

Casi's former life was heartbreaking. His father was forced into the cartel as a runner. According to Casi, he was a gentle man who had worked in the ceramics factory before it went south. Dealing with drugs displaced him, and he never quite found his footing afterwards. He was killed by a rival gang while trying to make a delivery, gunned down in his car, which then skidded off the road. It was he who urged Casi to learn accounting, so he would be spared from the brute life. His father recognized his son was also not cut out for cartel dealings.

"If you have a specific skillset, you have a chance at a different life," he had reiterated to his son, but Casi wouldn't leave his sister behind to get a job in Mexico City. Instead, he taught Camila, who was two years older, how to balance a budget. He wanted her to have the same marketable skills, so he paid for her education with his hard-earned money, selling off family assets to complete the task after his father passed. His plan paid off. She had been able to find a good job in Mexico City, before he was forced to leave for Barcelona with Flores. They both cried when she left, but he knew it had been the right choice. He was consoled by the fact she had a brighter future ahead. She escaped the bowels of their world. Since she was a woman, no one objected to her leaving. He wasn't afforded the same freedom.

It shocked Summer that Casi had turned into a seemingly well-balanced, sane person, despite his checkered past. She recognized why Helena found him appealing, although she still felt Helena could do better, but who was she to judge? Love falls in the most unlikely places.

When she and Helena left the cabin they were both shell-shocked from Casi's stories. A little shopping therapy would serve them well to get their minds off the terrible things they'd heard. It would take time to digest those unthinkable atrocities.

"Had you ever heard any of this before, Helena?"

"No, never. I didn't know anything about his life in Mexico. He never talked about it."

"And you never asked?"

"No. I sensed he had an unhappy childhood, and didn't want to upset him."

"No wonder he wanted to run away at the first opportunity. I would choose to go undercover, too, if I were in that situation. He had nothing to lose and everything to gain."

"I can't imagine living in such an oppressive environment. It makes me so sad to hear it. He's such a good man, not deserving of such a rotten past," Helena replied.

After wandering through a few stores in an attempt to clear their heads from lingering dark thoughts, the women went to the planned screening. It was a dark drama, more than they could handle given their morning, so they walked out. Casi's stories had gotten to them. Summer checked her phone for messages. There was one from Samson and three from her mother.

"Helena, I'll meet you back at the room. Can you take my bag up? I want to call my mom and see what's so urgent."

"Sure." Helena scooted off to the elevator and Summer called her mother from the lobby.

"Hi, Mom. Helena and I just got back. What's up?"

"Can you come up to my room? Francois is in the gym."

"Ok."

Five minutes later, she was facing her frowning mother.

"I'm not going to beat around the bush. I was driving behind you this morning, thinking you were heading into town. I was shocked to find out where you stopped. I saw Helena and the man from the *Sea Grape Garden Restaurant* in the Bahamas, standing by a residential cabin. Don't deny it. The guy looks like Carlos Ortiz. Is it him?"

"You followed me? What the hell?" Summer sat silently for a minute, trying to reign in her racing thoughts and gauge her mother's anger.

"Not purposely. I thought you were taking a shortcut to town. I want the truth, Summer. He's a dangerous criminal. The police are looking for him on three continents. My guess is that the Flores goons are looking for him as well. I read somewhere that he disappeared from their radar… or maybe not? However, if they are looking for him and find him while you're with him, you'll be collateral damage. What are you thinking?"

"It isn't quite as it appears, Mom."

"Really? Well, set me straight, then, or I'll call the police right now. I was contemplating doing that when I saw him at your premiere. Now, I know where he's staying."

"No, Mom! Please don't. Carlos was at the premiere? Are you sure?"

"Yes. I saw him there. He sat in the back. When I went to the bathroom during your Q&A, I saw him. He was wearing mirrored sunglasses indoors. Now, get to the point. What's going on here? Did he contact you or Helena?"

"He contacted me because he wanted me to arrange a meeting with Helena. They still love each other. When he fled Paris, he never had a chance to say good-bye, as you know, so this was his chance to see her again. She doesn't know we saw him in the Bahamas and that he lives there now. He doesn't want her to know, in case the cartel contacts her, so please don't tell her. He wants to protect her."

"And who is protecting you? Why are you putting yourself in a dangerous situation like this? Are you out of your mind? If Flores's people come to murder him for leaving their organization and you're with him, what do you think will happen to you? Do you have a death wish I don't know about?"

"Mom, look, I know you're right. We're leaving in a few days. I won't go there anymore, ok? Please don't rat him out. He's not a bad man. He's had a terrible childhood and life so far because of the

Flores group. He fled Paris and is trying to make an honest living in the Bahamas."

"With whose money? Give me one reason why I shouldn't turn him in. Why I should believe what he's telling you? And don't say Helena. She's better off without him. That relationship will never work out."

"She knows that but she loves him, and as far as I can tell, he deserves a second chance at life. He got sucked into the cartel against his will when he was young and poor. Sit down, let me tell you his story, but this has to stay between us. You can't tell Francois, Jasper, or Samson, ok? Promise, please."

"I'll decide after I hear the story. Talk."

An hour later, completely spent from information gathering in the morning and dispersing said information to a most challenging audience in the afternoon, Summer hit the hotel bar. She texted Samson and Jasper to join her for a drink.

"So, how was your day?" She asked Jasper wearily.

"Pretty good. I heard back from another studio. They want to hear our pitch tomorrow over breakfast." He looked pleased with himself. "Let me fill you in."

"Oh, good. Which one and where are we meeting?" Summer tried to look excited.

"Well, that's the bad news, they want to meet us at 7am. It's Violet Sky Studios."

"Oh, God. Here in the hotel, I hope?"

"Yes. That's the good news. How did you guess?" He laughed. "They're leaving the festival early, so that's the only time they had."

"Ok, then." She turned to her twin.

"What's going on with you? How's the skiing been?"

"I'm done for this vacation. It was fantastic. I have some news too. I heard from Natalie. She wants to meet when I get back."

"You're kidding! Watch out. Once a cheater, always a cheater. I wouldn't trust her. What did she say?" Summer frowned at her brother.

"She apologized and wants to talk. That's all." Samson looked happy.

"Don't get too excited, Bro." Jasper shook his head. "In my experience, Summer is right. Cheaters are cheaters."

"I would like to hear what she has to say, nonetheless."

"I don't know. Keep us posted. What are we doing for dinner tonight?" Summer changed the subject. She knew her twin wasn't going to budge.

"Nobody made a reservation, so I guess we'll eat here." Jasper shrugged his shoulders.

"Can you make one for 8pm and text everyone? I need a little down time in the room. Long day."

"Sure."

"Listen Jasper, I may be adding to our script, so don't be surprised when I change our pitch a bit tomorrow. In fact, let me do the talking this time."

"Changes? Like what?"

"Well, I was talking to someone in the industry and they had some good suggestions. I was thinking of adding some childhood flashbacks for some of the cartel members and throwing in a few grisly stories about how the cartel settles scores. It will add needed background and dimension to the characters and maybe camouflage who we're talking about. Also, I might change the product from ceramics to sculptures."

"Really? Will that work? Give me some examples."

"Ok, fasten your seat belt. It gets ugly. I'll give you the abbreviated version. But first, let me say thanks for arranging the meeting. Good work. If I weren't so spent today, I would show a lot more enthusiasm. It's been really great having you here."

"You're welcome. I'm actually enjoying myself. So let me hear what you got. Did any movies at the festival influence this change?"

"Yes, that too," Summer lied. She hoped Samson wouldn't notice. He generally knew when she was full of it.

After Summer left her brothers, she pulled out her secure phone and texted Casi.

Hi C

I can't bring Helena tonight. We have an important meeting at 7am and need to prepare for it. FYI, my mother recognized you at the premiere and asked a lot of questions. I think she's cool. Don't worry. Helena doesn't know anything. I didn't tell her. Will touch base tomorrow morning after our meeting. S

At eight the Crenstons, Francois, Ted, Hope and Helena assembled for their last night together in Park City. Hope, Ted, and Samson were leaving the next day. After dinner, Summer, Jasper and Helena met in the bar to discuss the script changes and write a new pitch. Their last opportunity to pitch their proposal was key. The festival was coming to a close, and it had been a good run. Before the industry insiders scattered, Summer wanted to cast her last line. She only needed one good sponsor for her next project. Either way, Summer's success at the festival was everyone's success, so it stood to reason that the final days would end on a high note…except maybe for Helena.

CHAPTER LXX

Houdini Couldn't Do It Better

When Casi reread Summer's text, his skin crawled. Cara Crenston should have been a bloody detective! Her power of observation was uncanny. He supposed artists were wired that way. Damn! How did she recognize him in the dark theater? He was wearing sunglasses and a slouchy hat down to his eyebrows. He had absolutely no sense of whether Cara could be trusted or not. What if she called the cops? Casi shoved his dinner into the oven and poured himself a stiff drink to relax and think. After dinner, he called his sister.

The next morning, after an encouraging breakfast meeting, Summer and Helena drove to Casi's place. Summer intended to drop Helena and go to the film festival hub for a director's talk. Afterwards, she planned to have lunch with her mom and do some damage control. Francois and Jasper were skiing one last time before their imminent departure. Summer needed to be sure that her mother not do wrong by Casi. She was scared of the consequences. If Casi thought she was crossing him, now that she had the information she wanted, he might turn on her. What if he stopped trusting her? Her project would die.

It was apparent that Helena was excited to spend a full day with Casi, the only one they would have before leaving. She chatted happily as Summer's thoughts wandered to her midday speech.

When she and Helena arrived at the cabin, they noticed the jeep wasn't there.

"Did you text him, Helena? Does he know we're coming?"

"I texted him and told him we would be here around ten. We're a little early. Maybe he went to get groceries?"

"Did he respond to your text?"

"No, he didn't."

"Let's wait a few minutes. I don't want to leave you."

"Why don't I go check. Maybe he returned the jeep early?"

Helena got out of the car and knocked on the front door. When there was no reply, Summer watched her hesitantly peer through the picture window. She came back to the car, frowning.

"Summer, I think he's gone. I don't see any of his belongings, and there's a note with a key on the counter." Her face clouded and she looked like she was going to cry. "He left without saying good bye, again! I hope he's ok. Do you think that guy from the party found him?"

"No. I think he left early. You might have to get used to that, Helena. He's a hunted man. When he senses danger, he bolts. No time for goodbyes. You can't fault him for that."

"I guess. I wish I knew where he lived. Do you know? I can't go another eight months without seeing him." Panic showed in her face.

"No, I don't," Summer lied. She was becoming quite proficient. "Listen, it's better you don't know. You can always contact him on your secure phone. I'm sure he'll answer as soon as he can. He genuinely cares about you. That's obvious. He put himself at great risk to see you."

"I know. It still makes me sad. I would like to have a normal life with him. I missed him tremendously when he left Paris. I felt a sense of loss… like someone died."

"I know that, and no, I don't think he was discovered," Summer lied again. "Do you want me to drop you at the hotel? Or do you want to come to lunch with me and mom?"

"I think I'll go back to the hotel and get a massage. I've wanted to treat myself all week. Now seems like a good time. I won't be good company anyway."

"That sounds like an excellent plan. Maybe Jasper will join you at the pool later. The boys will be back from the mountain around three, they said. Text him."

"I'll do that. Thanks. Jasper always manages to cheer me up, and I haven't had any alone time with him."

"Yeah, I'm sure he's been wondering why. He probably blames me."

The previous evening, after dinner, Casi spent a good portion of the night on the phone with Camila.

"Listen, Casi, you had a pretty good run. Don't be stupid and mess up now. Come home while you still can."

"I hate leaving without saying good-bye…again."

"She'll understand. Please, come home. Get out of there before Summer's mother does something crazy or forces Summer to turn you in. I'm begging you."

"Summer wouldn't do that. Her mother, I'm not so sure about. I'll change my flight." When he hung up, he called the airline and packed his few belongings. He was bummed Helena didn't come one last time. She was the highlight of his days and nights in Park

City. He had little interest in the movie screenings and the industry talks. It was a different world, one he didn't particularly care about. He slept poorly that night, tossing, turning, and waking at the slightest sound. In the pre-dawn hours, he showered, cleaned up, and left, returning the jeep at the airport.

He checked in and completed the security screening. Once at the gate, he emailed the cabin owner about his early departure. A business emergency required his immediate attention, he wrote. Next, he texted Camila and let her know he was boarding his flight shortly. She would be relieved. His message to Peter was brief too. He thought about what he would tell Helena, but the right words didn't come to mind. What could he possibly say? He felt like he was letting her down again. He decided to wait until he landed. Maybe he could speak to her. Hearing her voice, he would be able to gauge how upset she was.

Leaving Helena felt equally bad this time around. Casi had no idea when he would see her again, although now, they could communicate on the safe phone. Either way, his heart stung. He wasn't hopeful that she would be happy living under cover. No, the best he could hope for was an occasional secret *rendezvous* at a remote destination. The thought depressed him, but also gave him a glimmer of hope. At least she would be in his life. He would take whatever he could get.

Right now, he couldn't see her giving up any film possibilities, but maybe time would change that. He would try to be patient. The flight attendant interrupted his thoughts as she announced boarding for first class passengers. Casi was happy to leave the cold behind. The winter climate was not for him.

When he landed in Atlanta around lunch time, he texted Helena.

Can you talk?

The reply came quickly.

Yes.

He called her from his connecting gate.

"Hi. Are you ok?"

"Yes and no. Where are you?"

"At an airport, far away."

"I miss you already. I was going to spend the whole day with you today. Why did you leave? Did anything happen?"

"Yes. I couldn't risk staying. I'm sorry."

"What happened? When will I see you again? I need something to look forward to."

"I don't know at this moment, but I promise you, we'll make a plan soon, ok?"

"Ok. For Easter, maybe? I can't wait eight months again. Please. That was just too long."

"I know. I want to see you too. I really enjoyed the few nights we had, but it wasn't nearly enough. I promise we'll make arrangements soon. I have to board. I have a connecting flight. Enjoy the rest of your vacation, and good luck with everything. Keep me posted on what you're doing. You're surrounded by good people. Be thankful for that. Call me whenever you can, but please, please make sure no one is around to listen when you do. My sister knows all about you so you can call any time, ok?"

"Good. Thanks again for the beautiful gifts. Safe flight. I love you, Casi."

"I love you too, *mi tesoro*. See you soon. I promise." He heard a soft cry as the phone disconnected.

CHAPTER LXXI

Home Sweet Home

When the plane touched down in the Bahamas, Casi felt like kissing the ground. He exited the baggage claim area and spotted Camila's megawatt smile. She was waving frantically and blowing kisses, which made him laugh. When they exited the airport together, the warm Caribbean breeze caressed his face and calmed him instantly. He opened the window and closed his eyes as Camila drove and chatted away, clearly ecstatic he had returned safely.

Casi was thrilled to have left the icebox weather behind and the unrelenting stress in the Wasatch mountains. He didn't feel that pressure here and he sure didn't need a reminder of how it felt. He couldn't wait to see Peter and his restaurant family.

"Can we stop by the Sea Grape Garden on the way home?"

"Sure. Peter is itching to see you. He kept fishing for information about your trip, but I didn't share anything, just mentioned you were meeting an old friend. That's it."

"Thanks. Let's keep it that way. I'll tell you all about the trip over dinner, when we're alone."

"You better!"

When Casi pulled into The Sea Grape Garden parking lot, he was at peace. He had developed a special love for his beach hideout and its colorful cast of characters. He couldn't imagine life without them anymore. It was a world he embraced.

"Welcome back, Casi. We had a busy week. Did Camila tell you?"

"No. Can you fill me in, Peter?"

"Yeah! Have a seat. Want a drink?" Casi basked in the warmth of Peter's care. It was good to be home. He felt safe here. But in the dark recesses of his brain, he wondered if Summer could contain Cara Crenston.

CHAPTER LXXII

Sunny Skies Ahead

By the time Summer, Helena, Jasper, Francois, and Cara touched down in New York, she had a movie deal. Violet Sky Film Studios had made an offer.

"We should wait till we hear from the others," Jasper suggested.

"I don't know, Jasper. This isn't like banking. You usually jump on opportunities in my world. Movie financing is really, really hard to come by. Maybe we can stall a little by reviewing the terms?"

"Whatever you think, Summer. I can impede the process with a list of questions. That should buy us some time, so I can fish for a counteroffer."

"Ok. Listen, let's keep this offer between the two of us until the deal is signed. Things can still go south, and I don't want to get anyone too excited. Especially Helena."

"Yeah, ok."

"Did you tell mom and Francois?"

"No. I thought you should do that."

"Let's not tell them either. Mom is a little unnerved about the cartel aspect. I think she's secretly hoping we won't get funded. She's had a change of heart."

Jasper laughed and nodded. "I get how she feels. I've had my doubts, too."

Summer grimaced but said nothing. She was dying to fill Jasper in but knew she couldn't. He would back off immediately. Helena approached them with her suitcase, so they stopped discussing the proposal. Once all the bags at the carousel were collected, Jasper hugged the girls good-bye. He was going home to Cara's house, while the girls were headed into the city.

"I'll come into the city for dinner before you leave for Paris," he promised Helena.

"Good. I would like that. See you soon, Jasper." She hugged him and blew him a kiss as they got into a taxi.

"I feel bad I didn't get to spend more time with Jasper in Park City, but between Casi and you, I was busy every minute."

"I think he was a little disappointed, but he'll get over it. He doesn't know about Casi. He still thinks I hogged all your time."

"Well, we'll make the last three days count before I have to leave. And I do plan on coming back. Are you coming to Paris at all?"

"Not for the moment. Right now I'm so busy here. We're thinking of springtime perhaps, for my mom's opening at Francois's gallery. I might also do a screening with Mimi if it works out."

"Oh, good!" Helena perked up. "I can help with that."

That night, Helena was lying on Summer's bed as Summer unpacked her clothes.

"I really love that blue cashmere scarf Casi gave me. I'm so wearing that tomorrow. You know, I'm really sad you're going back to Paris. It was fun having you around."

"So am I. I would love to stay."

"I see no reason why you can't do modeling jobs here in New York. Why don't we contact a few agencies? We'll email some tonight, what do you think? Maybe we can get you an appointment before you leave."

"Really? Let's try. Life in Paris was boring and lonely after you and Casi left. I'm tired of the agency and the work I do there. I always get the same type of jobs. It pays well, but I'm so bored."

"Fashion week is coming up in February. Let's see if we can get you into a show or two. That would be the best way for you to break in here. I'm the research expert in this family, so let me see what I can find out. Can we work on your computer? I'll need to access your pictures."

"Yes. Here's my portfolio."

"Let's see. Wow, Helena, these pictures are amazing. I'll make a few calls tomorrow morning. You never know."

Two days later, Helena had an appointment with Wilhelmina Models.

"I'm so nervous, Summer. What should I wear?"

"Wear something casual that shows off your fabulous figure. Your skinny black jeans and that cream silk shirt maybe? Oh and wear your over the knee boots and Casi's cashmere wrap for good luck."

"Ok. That sounds comfortable and classy. I'll wear his earrings too. They add a touch of color."

"Perfect."

"Can you come with me?"

"Yes, but I'll wait outside."

"No, come in with me. We could say you're my agent."

"Hmmm, let me think about that one."

When Helena left her job interview, Summer was waiting outside.

"How did it go?"

"Good, I think. They want me to come back tomorrow for a 'go see'. I'll have to hurry to the airport. It'll be rush hour traffic at four. Will I make it?"

"It's doable. I'll bring your suitcases to the last stop. Text me. I think it'll be worth the effort. New York Fashion week is a big deal. It could launch you here."

"Ok. Thanks, Summer. It would be amazing if this works."

"Don't thank me yet. Trust me, the fashion world is fickle. They can change their tune twenty times until tomorrow."

"In Paris, too. It's the nature of the business."

"Jasper said he would meet us for dinner later. Let's go have a drink first and put a hex on the agency."

"A hex?"

Summer laughed. "I'll explain over drinks."

CHAPTER LXXIII

Changing Worlds Bring New Opportunities

After Helena returned to Paris, and Casi reviewed the rewritten script giving his stamp of approval, Summer and Jasper concentrated on fine-tuning their newest proposal and film synopsis. Negotiations with Violet Sky Film Studios were long-winded, but eventually, successful. The content was never the issue. The hold-up was a question of budget. Jasper's background in finance proved to be extremely helpful in hashing out several costly details. None of the other film studios had come through. They all dragged their feet as expected. Summer's instincts had been right to grab the first opportunity and run with it. Before the ink on the contract was dry, Summer was scouting for cast and crew. Jasper, Ted, Hope, and Helena were on board, so she knew her dependable core group was back. However, this film needed so much more participation than the last. The cast and crew would be substantially larger.

Pre-production would take more than a couple months, but they were well on their way. Every day was filled with meetings, scheduling, interviewing, and auditions. The days were long, and Summer was perpetually tired, just like in Paris. Jasper now fully grasped the unglamorous side of movie making as he worked alongside his sister, but he rarely complained. He seemed to embrace the experience. He also temporarily stopped interviewing for banking jobs. He didn't have time, and besides, he was getting a paycheck now. In early February, Summer sent Helena an email sharing the good news.

Dear Helena,

Good News! We have a movie deal. Jasper, Ted, and I started working on pre-production. Hope is confirmed as our cinematographer. Other than that, nothing is set. C sent me his final blessing, so the script is locked (although I always make adjustments before and during shooting). Will keep you posted as things develop. Are you still confirmed?

Love, Summer

When Summer received Helena's enthusiastic reply, she smiled.

Yes, yes, yes! I would be thrilled to work with you again. Any part in the movie is fine. When do we start filming?

Helena's interview regarding fashion week had gone well, but there were no firm offers on the table. Fashion week was around the corner and the chances of Helena participating were slim. Most models were booked far in advance, but Helena didn't give up hope. There were always last-minute changes, and maybe she could be that desperately needed backup. She cc'd Summer in an email she wrote to the agency, letting them know her schedule was flexible, a gentle reminder she was still available and interested.

Helena's emails made Summer realize life in Paris was uneventful-- her friend was busy, but not particularly happy. Work wasn't fulfilling. Coming home to a nice but very empty apartment, the one she had once shared with Casi, depressed her. While she was thrilled she had her own place, Helena missed his love and support. When a few of the other models asked about sharing the place with her, she turned them down, she confided to Summer. While the company would have been nice, she craved privacy. Uninhibited long talks with Casi, kept her sane.

"Occasionally, the agency pays me to put someone up from out of town, and I'm happy to oblige, but I don't want a steady roommate anymore."

Summer understood. She liked her own space too.

She replied to Helena,

Don't have a set starting date yet as we are still at the beginning of pre-production. We're hoping to shoot in late Spring, early Summer if all goes as planned, but it never does, does it? This project is more involved than the one I directed in Paris. The more moving wheels there are, the longer pre-production takes. Yes, I've been in contact with C. He doesn't know we have funding from a studio. I'm not ready to tell him yet. Please don't share this news with anyone either. You know the drill. Privacy, safety and all……

Summer and Helena communicated about their interactions with Casi, but Summer continued to be very careful in regard to his whereabouts. From what she gathered, he was very much entrenched in his new restaurant. Having his sister there had enriched his life and softened his demeanor. She noticed it in his more frequent communications. He was indebted to her for keeping her mom at bay and it showed in subtle ways.

Luckily, Cara had agreed to stay silent and not contact the police, but it had been a hard sell. It went against her mom's righteous grain. Summer strongly appealed to her mom's empathy, detailing Casi's miserable childhood in Tampico. Arguing until she turned blue, she finally secured Cara's promise that she would abstain from notifying the authorities in Park City and New York because Casi had nothing to do with the art thefts. He merely did the bookkeeping. This was a bit of a stretch since he was fully aware of the drug distribution aspect, but Cara miraculously acquiesced in exchange for Summer's promise not to travel to the Bahamas or Mexico. Jasper was still in the dark about everything. So were Samson and Francois. The Crenston girls knew how to keep a secret under duress.

Three days before fashion week was set to begin, Summer heard from Helena.

Bonjour Summer,
I'm coming to New York! One of the models working for two design houses broke her leg in a skiing accident over the weekend. I'll be taking her place. I can stay an extra week if you need me. Let me know asap before I book my flight. I'm so excited to come back!
Bises, Helena

Summer was thrilled.

Yes, book an extra week or two! We'll need you to read during auditions. Perfect timing. Send me your travel itinerary when it's final.
Love, Summer

Summer searched for her secure phone and called Casi. As expected, he didn't answer.

CHAPTER LXXIV

A Rose has Thorns and the Peony, a Short Bloom

asi's life in the Bahamas was hectic, yet peaceful. He and Camila were extremely busy in the restaurant however, not having the constant cartel pressure, afforded them inner peace, and the opportunity to enjoy each other and their beautiful surroundings. He was also spending quality time with Rose. She had come down for a vacation week and made it a point to visit the restaurant several nights. Casi welcomed the distraction. Rose was fun to banter with.

However, unlike Helena, Rose asked a lot of intrusive questions. Casi enjoyed her company, but kept her at arm's length, often excusing himself when he was short on answers. He knew she was ripe for seduction, and the temptation was hard to resist, but her close proximity and insatiable curiosity posed problems for him. He didn't want ripples in his smooth existence to turn into seismic waves. Rose could easily cause a tsunami—such was her nature. Tourists looking for an island adventure were more his speed. No muss, no fuss. Camila agreed and overlooked the occasional visitor emerging from his bedroom in the morning. Despite knowing the odds, he still had his hopes pinned on Helena.

Camila watched the cat and mouse play with Rose from afar. One morning, when she and Casi left their apartment together to go to work, Rose was lurking in her slightly open apartment doorway. The opportunity to be introduced had not yet presented itself, so Rose didn't know Casi's sister was living and working with him. That night, Rose appeared at happy hour in a low-cut, barely there, nude, lace dress. Camila observed Rose positioning herself at the outside bar, facing the camera, ensuring herself maximum exposure on all fronts. Rose irritated Camila. She rolled her eyes at Peter as she dropped off a container of limes at the bar.

"That woman is trying harder than Giovanni Dos Santos at practice."

"He's a Mexican soccer star?"

"The best."

"I thought so." Peter laughed. "She's been after Casi's ass since we opened."

"She lives in our building. That's way too close for comfort. I pray he doesn't think with the wrong body parts."

"I doubt it. He could have had her months ago," Peter assured her as he mixed drinks.

"She keeps showing up like a bad penny."

"Don't worry, Camila. She'll go back to Miami soon. She's never here for that long."

"Personally, I hope she leaves tomorrow." Camilla raised her water glass with a cheers.

Peter laughed and winked.

In his office, Casi watched Rose on camera and felt a stir. He knew she was on a fishing expedition, and his resolve was weakening. He also knew Camila had no use for Rose and her antics. As he got up to walk outside and say hello, his secure phone rang from inside his desk drawer. He dove for it.

"Hi, Casi, It's Summer. I called you yesterday."

"Hello. Been busy. How are you? Everything ok?"

"Great. Listen, I wanted to run something by you. Helena is coming back to New York to work at New York Fashion week. She also has to read for me in auditions, so she'll be here for at least two or three weeks. My script got funded."

"Congratulations. That was quick. What's next? When is she coming?"

"Thanks. I was thinking… I would love to sit with you one more time and go over some areas of the script that could use a little tightening. Maybe the three of us can meet somewhere?"

"That would be possible. Not here, of course. She doesn't know where I am, right?"

"No, only my mom does, and she's agreed to forget she knows as long as I don't travel to the island or Mexico. Perhaps we could meet in Miami? Or anywhere else of your choosing?"

"Miami would be perfect. When?"

"End of February. I don't have her flight information yet. As soon as I get her schedule, I'll let you know."

"Fine. I hope you haven't changed the script too much after my last viewing."

"No, I haven't. You'll see."

"Ok, let me know when you want to meet and………Summer?" Casi took a deep breath.

"Yes?"

"Thanks. I'll be happy to see you both."

"Thank you. I won't fill Helena in until she's here." Summer smiled. She still had his trust.

"Good. Who funded your script?"

"Violet Sky Film Studios."

"In full?"

"Yes."

"Congratulations, again."

"Thanks. See you soon, ok? Be well."

Casi disconnected the phone and stared into space. Just what he needed to resist Rose--the promise of seeing Helena. He opened his laptop and googled Violet Sky Film Studios. They had an office in New York at the Kaufman Sound Stage complex. That meant Helena would be in the U.S. for a while. Of course, he wasn't sure where they would be shooting. He definitely wasn't going to New York again, ever. He didn't like the city. There were so many nice places halfway between. The options were plenty. The thought of seeing Helena in a few weeks aroused him.

When Peter came to tell him Rose was asking for him, he told Peter to lie and say he left to do an errand.

"You sure, man? She looks ready to pounce."

"Yes, I'm dead sure. She lives down the hall from me. Not a good set up on any level. I like clean breaks. Are you trying to stir the pot and get me in trouble?"

"Clean breaks are tough on an island this small, but ok, you got it." Peter laughed. "Maybe your pot needs a little stirring, but Camila sure will be glad you're hanging tough."

"I can imagine." Casi laughed, rolling his eyes. "We need to get my sister a date, Peter. I'm her only focus right now. That's painful at times."

"You know Matias has a thing for her, right?"

"He has a girlfriend. I don't need a war on my turf. You are a troublemaker, today. Keep looking."

Peter winked, laughing. "I'll keep my eyes open for the right guy."

CHAPTER LXXV

Traveling Incognito

Rose left the island without incident. So did most of February. Casi's trip to Miami was fast approaching and he could think of little else. Helena still had that power over him. When Camila asked to join him in Miami, he gave her a hard no.

"You can come next time. Summer and I'll be working and I need time alone with Helena. We only have a long weekend. Please understand. I need you to stay here, and mind the restaurant anyway. We're so busy this season."

"Peter and Jenny can handle things, but ok, I'll stay. Next time, I want to come."

"Fine. If there is a next time."

"There will be. You're completely obsessed with her."

"I am. She may change her mind though."

"Well.....that's what I want to evaluate. I'll know when I meet her."

"Ok, Camila. Next time, I promise." Women, he thought. He knew enough not to argue. The key to good relationships with the opposite sex was to find a compromise before the arguing got heated. That tested strategy saved time, and money on apology gifts.

To feel protected, Casi contacted Maria Alfaro for his Miami sojourn. She was delighted to hear from him. Not telling her what she didn't need to know, he made clear what he required for his stay.

He wanted to know if anyone was tailing the girls from the airport and he wanted his back covered while in Miami. Maria was a skilled professional, and he trusted her. She was on board.

"I'm available," she replied immediately. "How is your sister?"

"She's great. She sends her regards. Unfortunately, she won't be coming. I need her to stay and cover for me. I'll be in touch with my itinerary, and I'll text you when I arrive."

"Fantastic."

He would have to explain to Maria the name Hermosa stayed in Mexico with his sister's old life and her alleged abusive boyfriend. For enough money, she could forget a name and keep her lips sealed. A soft sell approach, letting her know these decisions were made for everyone's safety, including hers, should seal the pact.

When Camila drove Casi to the airport, she was uncharacteristically silent. He knew she was nervous to see him go.

"Camila, I know you had your first dentist consultation a while back. I made you an appointment to move forward with your teeth. I want to see your improved smile when I get back, not that your smile isn't pretty now. It should help keep your mind off me. Don't worry." Casi looked over at her from the corner of his eye. Seeing her face light up, encouraged him. He continued, "We had a good holiday season, so I have the money to pay for everything. I fluffed up your account yesterday."

"Thank you."

Camila still had no idea how much money Casi really had. He felt she was better off, not knowing. It would just make her nervous. It was easier to give her a weekly paycheck and feed her account for the occasional extras, as needed. Earning her own money empowered her and made her feel productive. In an emergency, she knew where to look for most of his financial records. She would faint if she knew how wealthy they really were.

"I'll still worry about you, nothing can change that. Don't think the dentist's pain killers will mask my concerns. Having said that, I'm excited to finally get my teeth fixed. They always bothered me. I wouldn't mind getting eyelash extensions too. I saw a lady in the restaurant with them, and they looked so good."

"Do it. The money in your account will cover both." Camila cracked a smile. "God really smiled on me when he made you my sibling. I couldn't have bargained for a better brother."

"I know," he teased.

"Ok, we're here. Please take care of yourself, and don't be stupid. I can't lose you again. Bring back pictures this time."

"Thanks, will do. I'll see you in a few days. Be ready to answer your special phone. Keep it on your body."

"It's here." She pointed to the pocket in her dress. "Safe trip. *Adios. Hasta pronto.*"

CHAPTER LXXVI

Sun, Surf and Glorious Sex

When Casi landed in Miami, he gathered his luggage and hailed a taxi. The ride from the airport warmed his heart. He enjoyed the breathtaking water views, approaching the bridge to South Beach. Paying the driver in cash, he checked into the hotel, while sweeping the busy lobby. Summer had left her credit card on file for both rooms. He replaced his reservation with his own card, making sure Summer's room was on a different floor. After unpacking, he put on swim shorts and sprinted to the boardwalk for a run and ocean swim. It was almost dinner time when he returned, and his thoughts drifted to Rose and their last dinners in Miami. He obviously wouldn't be calling her this trip, but she crossed his mind. After cleaning up, he had dinner at the hotel bar, alone. He sent Maria the girls' flight information and a few close-up pictures.

The next morning, he went for a jog on the beach. Dipping into the waves after running, he relished the salt on his skin. He rinsed off at the outdoor showers and walked to the spa for a massage and haircut. Back in the room, he called Maria with more instructions.

"If they're being tailed, let me know before you get to the hotel."

"I'm on it. Don't worry."

Satisfied, he went for a late lunch by the pool, bringing his laptop. Lingering over coffee, he checked his emails and studied the current cast of characters. Hotel life in Miami was never dull. When the sun disappeared behind the high-rise buildings, he went back to his room to primp for the girls' arrival. He tried to relax, lying on the bed, but his stomach was doing summersaults in anticipation of seeing Helena.

At 6:30pm Maria texted; she had found the girls. She was driving a few cars behind them, but didn't notice any tails. Casi paced his room. The knots in his stomach were tightening. Soon after, there was a knock on his door. Helena entered with her rolling suitcase and a giant shoulder bag, sporting a huge grin. He grabbed her bags, not taking his eyes off her, and plopped them inside. Taking her into his arms, he kicked the door shut with his foot. They held onto each other for what seemed like an eternity.

"Oh my God, Casi. I missed you so much," Helena whispered. "I was nervous the whole plane ride that you wouldn't be here." He reversed her baseball cap, flipping the bill backward and kissed her, taking in her scent and the softness of her hair and skin.

"Summer made me wear the hat with big dark sunglasses the whole flight. She wore them too," Helena shared nervously.

"Why would you think I wouldn't be here? I want to see you! Summer's idea is good. I appreciate the effort. Where is she?"

"She's unpacking in her room. She said to text her if we want to have dinner together, but she's fine with meeting us in the morning, too. She's tired. She's been working so hard. What do you want to do?"

"I would love to have dinner alone with you."

Helena slid her arms around Casi's waist and teased his lips. "Me too. In or out?"

"You decide."

"Can we have it downstairs in the hotel? I've been cooped up in that airplane."

"Yes. Why don't you get settled and text, Summer. I have a quick call to make before we go."

"Ok."

Helena unpacked a few clothes, then disappeared into the bathroom with her toiletries and phone. Casi called Maria and spoke to her softly in Spanish.

"Two of us are going to have dinner in the hotel restaurant. Are you still here?"

"Yes. I'm in the lobby."

"Please feel free to order yourself anything you want on my tab. Room 424. After we finish dinner, you can go. I'll text you later about tomorrow. It won't be early."

"Thanks. No problem."

"For the next few days, text me if anything looks amiss. Anytime. Day or night."

"Got it. Enjoy your dinner. So far, I see nothing concerning."

When Helena exited the bathroom, she was dressed in a form fitting off-white linen dress. Her hair was up in a knot, and a dark pink lipstick turned her full lips into a deliciously ripe raspberry. When she bent over to slip on her gold sandals, Casi saw her neckline shift to reveal a silky pink bra. He inhaled through his teeth. To him, she was still the most beautiful woman in the world. He couldn't wait to peel back the petals enveloping her luscious curves.

Two hours and two glasses of wine later, he had his chance. He could feel his heart pounding as his mouth closed over her puckered lips inside their hotel room door. Hands fumbling, bodies gyrating, heat rising they wrestled with cumbersome clothes. Urgent needs fueled a record removal of her dress and his shirt. She slid her fingers down his back to his buttocks as he unzipped his linen pants and let them drop to the floor in a puddle. Pushing her against the wall, he stepped out of his pants and loafers, letting his fingers slide over her body and into the hot area between her legs. Helena groaned.

"Don't stop." She arched her back, pressing against him and tilted her head back. He let his tongue travel down her extended throat to her cleavage as he unhooked her silky bra and removed her panties. Helena slid her fingers through his thick, black hair with the newly bleached tips.

"More."

She drove him wild. He thrust into her, burying himself deeper and deeper in her warmth. Her body quivered from the rush of his need. When her limbs turned to jelly, he lifted her by the hips and lost himself in her steam and throaty cries. Her arms around his neck, legs wrapped tightly around his hips, he carried her to the turned down bed. Lying on top of her and pushing deeper, he felt her peak as she let out a cry. Then he let go. Two months of longing, built up inside him, exploded in one glorious, climatic moment. He buried his face in her hair and collapsed on top of her as her body went limp.

"Oh, God, Casi. I need you. I want you… forever."

CHAPTER LXXVII

Bad Memories Don't Die, but a Good Future can Override Them

The next morning, Casi ordered breakfast to the room. A night of passionate sex left them both fatigued and ravenous.

"Do you think Summer will mind?"

"No, she's easy. I bet she slept in too. We can invite her to lunch instead.

"Sounds like a plan."

Helena's phone chimed.

Casi reached for it on the night table and looked at the screen. A text from Summer.

Went for an early run this morning and just had a light breakfast. Meet you in the lobby at 10am? Maybe we can find a quiet corner on the outdoor side terrace?

He handed the phone to Helena after reading it.

"Good. This gives us an hour to get ready and for me to make a few phone calls. Tell her, yes."

When Helena hopped in the shower, Casi texted Maria and called Camila and Peter.

By 10:15am, he and Summer were seated in a secluded corner, shuffling papers. Maria was having a cup of coffee and reading the newspaper three tables away. Helena left for a beach walk, sporting her baseball cap and sunglasses.

"Take a moment to look over the last revised script. I made very few changes."

Casi nodded.

Summer sat back, sipping her coffee. She noticed the same woman from last night, sitting a few tables away reading the newspaper.

"What do you think?" She asked, turning her attention back to Casi.

"It's still hard for me to swallow, but it looks fine."

"Right. Any other thoughts?"

"There are a lot of truths Fernando may recognize, but I think some of those facts may hold true for drug cartels in general. The only thing I absolutely object to is any mention of my sister or Helena as possible characters. Any reference to them needs to go."

"I understand. I've tried to focus on the rise and fall of the business with flashbacks of the early years. However, people have families and relationships. I'm interweaving unlikely relationships in Europe without pointing fingers at my family. The thing is, Casi, there have to be women and family members somewhere in the story. Girlfriends, wives, eye candy, contacts.......sex sells in the cinematic world. Any ideas?"

"I don't know, Summer. You're the writer here. Maybe make the bank contact female, or Fernando could be married and cheating. He would be if he was married, I assure you."

"Ok. Now we're going into a good direction. Tell me about Fernando's and Jose's relationships."

"Whew…let's get refills. This may take a while." He motioned to the waiter and pointed to their cups. "Fernando tends to abuse women, then sprinkles them with lavish gifts, so they stay quiet, and Jose is a macho gay man in denial. He's also a sadist who thrives on seeing people suffer, as you already know. He's not a well-balanced individual or a happy, openly gay man like your friend, Ted. He's deeply conflicted and filled with self-loathing. Of course you're never privy to what goes on behind closed doors, but I have heard a few things over the years that ring true, crazy as they sounded." Casi paused as the waiter approached with a coffee thermos.

"Wow, ok. It sounds like we have something good to chew on. Let's start with Fernando."

"Did you know that Fernando has two children in Mexico with two different women?"

"No. Tell me more. This is exactly what I need."

A couple hours later, Helena returned to check in.

"Hi, are you two interested in lunch by the pool or are you going to have a working lunch?"

"I think we'll join you. Summer, we can continue later."

"Sure. I need to process some of this anyway. I wouldn't mind some sunshine. I'm chilled to the bone. Can we sit somewhere with a beach view?"

"Yeah, for sure. Let's go next door to the Ritz. Lunch is my treat."

Letting the girls walk before him, he eyed Maria and texted her.

After eating, Helena and Casi went for a walk along the surf. Summer went swimming in the ocean, then back to her room to shower and change. She planted herself in the shade with her laptop and worked until she and Casi regrouped in the late afternoon, around four thirty. Casi met her in the lobby for an abbreviated work session before dinner. An hour and a half later, he leaned back in his chair.

"Let's call it a day. My brain is fried from rehashing bad memories. We can continue in the morning if you have more questions. Do you want to join Helena and me for dinner tonight?"

"I think I'll pass. I wanted to look at the stores on Lincoln Avenue and maybe grab a salad there. I'm still full from lunch. I plan to go over this material tonight, so we can fill in the blanks in the morning."

"Ok. See you on the side patio around ten again?"

"Yes, sounds good. Have fun tonight."

When Casi got back to the room, Helena was stretched out on their bed in a raspberry silk slip, listening to the radio. When she heard him enter, she propped herself up on one elbow and waited with an inviting smile. He stopped dead, feasting his eyes on her alluring presence.

"I was going to discuss dinner plans with you, but I think that may have to wait."

"Good, because I had other ideas." She pointed her fuchsia-lacquered toes and stretched her lithe body, reaching her arms over her head, then towards him. Casi flicked the light switch off and shed his clothes, not taking his eyes off her.

Desire flooded through every pore and lust raged through every muscled ripple as he slid on top of her, letting his hands travel upward inside her slip. Her skin felt like liquid satin. Her arms and legs welcomed him, enveloping his heat. She never failed to stimulate his body and soul, every nerve ending climaxing him to a colorful explosion.

CHAPTER LXXVIII

Miami Heat...Cold as Ice

Casi woke up early for his daily meditative run on the beach. Helena was still fast asleep when he quietly shut the door behind him. The sun was lazily scaling the sky, but not yet scorching its diminutive subjects. Miami's infinity beach was empty except for a handful of early risers and the trusty hotel staff, setting up neatly rowed beach chairs in preparation of the daily onslaught. Most of the early morning activity took place on the city's four-mile boardwalk, simulating an anthill during peak production. Running on the hard-packed sand with a faint ocean breeze pleasuring his hot face helped Casi clear his mind for the next marathon meeting with Summer. Reaching back into the darkness of his past was mentally draining, more than he would have liked to admit. He thought he had buried those sinister memories forever.

Over dinner, he and Helena had broached the serious subject of their future.

"Where are we headed as a couple?" he asked her after sex. He hadn't really wanted to go there because he knew it was too soon, but he couldn't help himself. The two months after Sundance had been difficult, especially with Rose circling like a vulture. He hoped Helena felt as frustrated as he did. It was way too soon to propose, but he was ready to commit.

Their talk, late into the night, settled nothing, their future still unresolved. Helena wanted to be in Summer's second movie. Casi assured her he would wait the duration of the production, but he wasn't sure after that. He wanted her to understand he couldn't hang on forever. She needed to cut him loose, if she had no intention of ever settling down with him. The suspense was torture.

"I love you, heart and soul, but eventually, I want a woman in my life who will actually be there in the morning. Someone I can see and hold every day. Someone who will care for our children and be happy doing so. Those are my needs. They're simple, but they're important to me."

Helena told him she was on the same page in principle, but she wasn't quite ready to settle down yet. She needed to follow her dreams and see where they would take her. She felt cheated since some women could have it all, but she understood Casi's checkered past didn't allow for normal freedoms. It was a hard choice for her to make at this time. She was at a crossroad in her life and she resented not having the liberty to follow her dreams and still have the man she loved in her life. It was a steep price to pay.

"Let me work with Summer on this project and see where it leads. Maybe I'll get it out of my system. If I don't do it, I'll always have regrets."

Casi knew all about regrets. He also understood wanting to follow dreams. Owning his own business, far away from the shackles of his childhood was his utopia. He resolved to be patient with Helena and hope for the best because he wasn't ready to let her go. In fact, he couldn't fathom a life without her. She was his drug, his addiction, his one love. The thought of not having her in his life physically hurt his insides. His future was complicated, but he was tenacious, a survivor. No matter what happened, he would fashion a life he loved for himself and his sister and hopefully, Helena, too.

He called Camila after his run, to vent. She was the only person Casi talked to regarding personal matters. He spent years keeping things bottled inside. Camila listened, often offering little advice. There was a time to share frustrations and a time to listen or advise. His sister recognized what he needed when. She was a smart, intuitive woman, and she felt her brother's pain. Besides, what could she say? She didn't even know the woman in question.

On his way back to the room, Casi picked up two *café au lait* and sugar *brioche* from the French bakery on Ocean Avenue. He texted Maria to arrive at ten. He also stopped by the concierge's desk and asked him to make a boat reservation for the afternoon. When he got to the room, Helena was awake and showered.

"Good Morning. Hmmm, that coffee smells so good."

"It is good. Let's have it on the terrace. I brought some *brioche* too."

As he sipped his coffee, he turned to Helena, studying her profile in the striped sunlight. "Listen, I know the life I'm offering you is filled with uncertainty and secrecy, so I want you to have time to think about our discussion last night. It would tear us apart if one of us wasn't happy. I'm here now, and it's fun, but there is something missing in my day-to-day life. It has been for the last ten months. Your love on a daily basis. Don't wait too long to decide. I think that strain in itself will change things for us. Nothing ever stays the same. Relationships evolve, and need to move forward and grow. If they don't have the chance to do that, they become stale and die a slow, painful death. For now, let's drop the subject and have a good day, but try to understand what I'm trying to say."

"I do understand what you're saying. But I can't pretend to be ready if I'm not. You'll give me at least until the film is done, right? Please, Casi. You promised."

"Yes, I'll try."

He got up and threw his empty coffee cup into the garbage. Heading into the bathroom, he turned on the shower to get ready for his meeting with Summer. When he reappeared, he dressed in shorts and a tee shirt.

"Come pick us up for lunch around noon. We'll do something fun for the rest of the day. Something vacation-like."

"Ok, good. I think I'll hang out by the pool this morning. I have a good book to read. See you later." She pulled on her bathing suit as he watched, feeling an arousal coming. He cupped his hands under her chin, looked into her precious sapphire eyes, and kissed her softly on the lips. Then he turned and left without another word. When he closed the door behind him, he thought he heard her sigh.

Around noon, Helena was back, circling around their table. Casi waved her over.

"We're done. How would you girls like to look at Miami homes from the water? I reserved a boat for the afternoon."

"That sounds awesome. I'm in. Helena?"

"Yes. I'd like that."

Casi thought he detected a trace of disappointment.

"I'll get some sandwiches to go and we can have a picnic on the boat. I'm going to change into a bathing suit and grab a few things in the room. We can meet in the lobby in a half hour. Sound doable, ladies?"

"Totally," Summer replied, packing up.

Casi followed Helena up to the room. He closed the door and stared at her moping face.

"What's wrong?"

"I thought you and I would spend the afternoon together… alone."

"I wouldn't have felt right, ditching Summer."

"I know you're right. I just feel like we don't ever have enough time alone. You're spending more time with Summer than with me this weekend."

As he packed a small backpack, he replied carefully, not wanting to hurt her or lose his patience.

"Helena, I agreed to collaborate on this film for your sake. I have zero interest in going over Summer's script for hours. I agreed to do it for everyone's safety and because I wanted to see you this weekend. Trust me, I'm putting myself at risk every time we meet."

"I thought you were just going to do damage control on the script, not rewrite the whole damn thing for days."

"Yes and no. I'm giving her what I think is safe to tell, but I'm also helping restructure certain scenes to make sure they aren't offensive to the Flores family. There are no guarantees Summer will listen to me and do as I suggest, but I have to try. She can still change things at any time and sell me out. I have no recourse, and she knows it. It would have been so much smarter if I had left Paris and never contacted anyone. I got myself into a mess here, but I'm making the best of it…for you."

"I would have never given up looking for you. It was my idea to look for Hermosa in Mexico, you know."

"And I appreciate the thought, but what good would it have done? Hermosa didn't know where I was, and you would have only endangered her and yourself. The damage control I'm doing now is necessary for all of us. You both are clueless when it comes to the danger involved. Enough said. Meet you downstairs. I'm going to get some drinks and sandwiches. Let's have fun and enjoy the afternoon." He slammed the door behind him, leaving her speechless.

Casi was in heaven. They were cruising the waterways of Miami in a 30-foot motorboat. The captain was a young man who knew all the juicy gossip about who lived where and what scandals happened in the fabulous homes and waterways. He was pleased to see that the girls were lapping it up. Helena's mood visibly lightened, and by the time they were back at the dock, she was laughing and tipsy from the *Sancerre* Casi brought.

Seated around the dock, were sketch artists offering caricatures and portraits, with a choice of Miami backgrounds. Casi encouraged the girls to pick a style and paid. Helena chose a portrait style with a Versace mansion background while Summer opted for a caricature with a waterway background. Casi perused the various Miami scapes and picked a beach view with the iconic illuminated Art Deco architecture of South Beach and an aerial shot of the Miami skyline surrounded by its waterways. Pleased with their purchases, they headed back to the hotel, agreeing on a late dinner. It was their last night together and Casi wanted to end the weekend on a good note. He consulted with the concierge for an unforgettable reservation.

He chose the Gotham Steakhouse in the sprawling Fontainebleau Hotel. Casi liked the lay-out of the restaurant. He studied the extensive wine list and took a picture of it for Matias and Peter. At the bar, Maria enjoyed an appetizer with a direct view of their table. He noticed she was drinking water. Seated, facing her, he had a full view of the entrance. Dinner conversation was light and jovial. They talked about Helena's experience at New York fashion week and about their impressions of Miami. After a delicious dinner, the girls went to the ladies' room, and Casi paid the bill, carefully counting out his cash. When his cell phone alerted him of an incoming message, he looked at the screen.

Blonde approaching your table. Been checking you out.

Casi looked up from the text to see Rose. He studied her as she walked toward him. She looked exceptionally fine in a form-fitting violet cocktail dress, and amethyst, swing earrings. Her hair was up in a messy bun and showed off her long neckline and striking jewelry. He jumped up to greet her, and pocketed his phone.

"Casi? What an unexpected surprise! How are you? Did you just get to Miami?" She smiled and flung her arms around his neck just as Helena and Summer turned the corner.

"Rose! So nice to see you. You look rather beautiful tonight." Casi smiled graciously.

"Thank you. You look nice yourself. What are you doing here? Business or pleasure this time?" Obviously flattered, Rose shifted closer to him. Eyeing Helena, he took a step back.

"Business. These are my associates." He gestured to Helena and Summer nearing the table. Rose turned and surprise registered on her dainty features as she faced two equally beautiful women.

"Hello, I'm Rose, a good friend of Casi's."

"Hello, Rose. I'm Jasmin, and this is my associate, Sarafina. Nice to meet you." Casi was thankful for Summer's quick reaction. Helena looked stupefied, or was that annoyed? Rose smiled and turned back to Casi. "Are you here for a few days? Do you have time for dinner?"

"Not this time. I'm leaving tomorrow morning. This was a quick weekend trip." Summer motioned to Casi. "Sarafina and I will wait for you in the lobby." She grabbed Helena by the arm and gently pushed her toward the exit.

"You sure do surround yourself with nice-looking business associates. When are you coming back to Miami?"

"No plans right now. Business is concluded, but I'll let you know if I do return."

"Let me introduce you to my friends. We're having birthday drinks at the bar. Can you join us?"

"Thanks, Rose, but I don't want to be rude. The ladies are waiting. We're staying in the same hotel, and sharing a ride. I'll see you next trip or on the island. Have a wonderful evening. This is a nice place for a birthday celebration. Is it yours?"

"No. Too bad you can't stay. See you soon, ok?" Rose leaned in to give him a telling hug. She lingered a second or two longer letting her signature scent waft up Casi's nose. He found it intoxicating. Over Rose's shoulder, he saw Helena watching them from the exit. He gave Rose a warm smile and threaded his way through the tables with Maria in tow. She was watching every move in the room from a respectable distance.

"Sorry, ladies. We can leave now." Casi put a hand on each girl's back and guided them toward the taxi line. Summer thanked him for the lavish dinner and marveled over the wonderful food. Helena said nothing, until they were in the taxi.

"Who is Rose?" Her face puckered like sour lemons.

"She's a friend who lives in Miami."

"So this is not your first trip to Miami?"

"No. I've been here a few times for business."

"What kind of business?"

"Let's talk at the hotel. Jasmin, thanks for your quick thinking, tonight. I really appreciated that."

"No worries. All is well. Will I see you before you leave, Casi?"

"Sure, but it will have to be early. I'm leaving the hotel at 9:30am."

"Right. When I'm up, I'll text you guys."

When Casi and Helena got to the room, Helena turned to face him.

"When did you have dinner with Rose? How do you even know her?"

"I met her in a restaurant one night."

"Did you sleep with her?"

"No, I didn't. We're friends."

"Will you when I'm gone?" Her arms were crossed over her chest, and she was staring at him with a combative expression.

He approached her, placed his hands on her upper arms and gazed into her stormy face. Helena had never exhibited jealousy before. Casi had to admit, he was flattered.

"Look, Helena. We had a beautiful day and a wonderful dinner together. Don't ruin our last night arguing about intangibles. For your information, if I wanted to sleep with Rose, I could have done so months ago. I chose not to. Haven't I shown you how much I love you and want you?"

"I'm sorry. I don't want to be jealous. I never worried in Paris because I knew I would see you every night. I always trusted you. These long lapses between short visits are so difficult."

"Not just for you. And that was the point I was making last night. Long distance romance will only work for so long, then something or someone has to give. It's only a short-term solution."

"Casi. There's no one in the world I would rather be with than you, but the idea of giving up my identity and a career I may love is an impossible decision to make right now. It's a lot to ask of anyone."

"I know that, and I'm trying to be patient and give you space. I wish we could live together risk-free, but that's a luxury I may never have. Loving me comes with a price. It's up to you if you want to pay that price. I hope you will. I promise I'll do my best to give you a good life, but there are never any guarantees, are there?" He pulled her into his arms, rocking her back and forth. "Happiness comes from within. Only you know if you are truly happy. I know that I finally am in my life. Your love would complete it, but only if you feel that way too."

"I don't know what I feel. I do know that being with you makes me happy, but working with Summer on set makes me happy too. It's challenging and exciting."

Not wanting to rehash last nights' conversation, he changed the subject. They weren't getting anywhere and he needed to lighten the mood.

"I like the name Summer gave you. Sarafina Santos has a nice ring to it, don't you think?"

Helena couldn't help but laugh. "Yes, it does. How in the world did she come up with that so fast?"

"Summer is a creative thinker and quick on her feet. She never ceases to surprise me."

"Me either. She was quick with her answers in Park City, too, when that man threatened us. She's the reason I got my first film role and my first modeling job in New York fashion week. Summer makes things happen." Helena lifted her head off his shoulder. "Wait. Did you just propose to me?"

"Not yet. When I do, there will be a lot more to it." His lips closed over hers, and he felt her melt into his arms. He tried to savor the sensation, imprint it on his brain because it would have to sustain him for the next few months.

CHAPTER LXXIX

Reunited Love Scatters Like Dust......Until Further Notice

The next morning Casi was up and packed by eight. While Helena was showering, he went down to the lobby for coffee. Waiting in line, he bumped into Summer, who was just returning from a morning run on the boardwalk. She was wearing black biker's shorts and a tank top. Casi had never noticed Summer's muscular arms and shoulders before. They were always covered in an effort to avoid sun exposure. She had a lighter skin tone than Helena and burned easily. She also looked very fit. He wondered if she lifted weights.

"Hey, good morning. How was your run?"

"Good. It's crowded out there, today." She mopped her face with the bandanna around her neck.

"Every morning. That's why I run on the beach. Can I get you a coffee? Or a water bottle?"

"Yes, thanks. Water, please. There's something I wanted to ask you or at least mention." Summer shifted her weight and leaned in closer.

"What's that?" Casi lowered his head toward her.

Summer whispered. "A Latino woman has been watching us all weekend. Did you notice her?"

Casi smiled and lowered his voice too. "Yes. She's with me. I wanted to make sure we weren't being followed. You're pretty observant."

Summer pushed her sunglasses up into her wavy blond hair and looked at him, silently evaluating. She was inches from his face, and he seized the moment to admire her mesmerizing, ocean-colored eyes. They were different than Helena's, lighter and almond- shaped.

"Really? Well, thanks to you, I've become more aware of my surroundings. So, were we?"

"No. We weren't." Casi's lips turned up at the corner in amusement. "Listen, Summer. I wanted to thank you for having Helena's and my back. You've been a really kind friend." He was standing so close, he could smell her shampoo mixed with sweat. Summer didn't back away.

"Your welcome. It works both ways. Thanks for having my back with the script. I believe in second chances, Casi. I want you to have yours. I think you deserve it." A spark passed between them, like the almost touching of fingers and souls in Michelangelo's mural gracing the Sistine Chapel's vaulted ceiling. Close connections didn't happen often in Casi's world but when they did, it was life-affirming. He felt a warm rush through his body, not necessarily the sexual kind. Before he could reply, Summer turned to walk away.

"Thanks for the water," she said waving the bottle over her shoulder. He studied her muscular physique as she sprinted away. She was a remarkable woman, he thought. So different from Helena, who tended to be an open book and a touch needy. Different from Rose too. Rose was sexually confident and a fun-loving busybody. Summer was driven, fearless, self-sufficient, stubborn and very smart—she was a complex woman. Casi wondered about the men in her life.

Back in the room, he sipped his coffee while Helena listlessly pulled on black leggings and a long, sky blue and white, pin-striped shirt in anticipation of her flight back to New York. The baseball cap was resting on top of her hand luggage, sunglasses perched on her head.

"I feel like we never have enough time together. Can we make the next vacation longer, just the two of us?"

"We both have such busy schedules, but yes, we can try." He could see that his answer frustrated her.

"When am I going to see you again?"

"I don't know. Once you start working on Summer's film, you'll have no time. Maybe we can meet before the filming starts?"

"That's at least three months from now."

"Yes, it is. My business doesn't slow down until May. It would be difficult for me to leave for more than a weekend. Do you have a different suggestion?"

"Yes. Why can't I come visit you where you live?"

"Helena, that's out of the question. I'm never going to share where I live, unless you come to stay. Let's not argue about this. We'll stay in touch and make a plan soon. Right now, May looks like the best time for both of us unless you can come back for another long week- end in Miami?"

"No. I'm going back to Paris next weekend and won't be back until we start filming. I can't take more time off work. I'm not even sure if we're filming in Europe or New York first. Summer hasn't confirmed a schedule yet."

"We'll figure it out. It doesn't have to be today. Come on, let's go have breakfast. I have to leave soon." He gently nudged her toward the door.

Helena made a face and hugged him, clinging for an extra beat. He felt a tug at his heart strings. Nothing would be decided at this moment; their schedules were too up in the air. As he hugged her, he sensed her vulnerability.

At the airport, Casi's flight was delayed, so he called Camila. She picked up on the first ring.

"Where are you? How was your trip?"

"At the airport. The trip was good, but leaving this morning was difficult. This long distance stuff stinks."

"Yes, I imagine it would. Do you have a next meeting planned?" Casi could hear a touch of fear in her voice.

"No. Maybe May."

"That's only three months away. Not terrible."

"True, but not ideal either. Listen, my flight was delayed. I'm at the gate. We're leaving forty- five minutes late. If anything changes, I'll text you. How's everything at the restaurant?"

"Well, there's been tension in the kitchen. I think Matias and Isa are waging a silent war. I've been having lunch with Peter."

"Hmm. I vote to keep Matias. How are your teeth?"

"Good. My new smile will dazzle you sooner than you think. I visited the dentist."

"Great. Can't wait to see you. You're picking me up, right?"

"Yes, I'll be the woman with the longest spider lashes on the tarmac. By the way, I gave Peter the day off since you'll be back. He needed it. I have to go. Jenny needs me. See you later."

When Casi arrived at the restaurant, Matias came out of the kitchen to greet him, a highly unusual gesture. The man rarely left the kitchen except to go out the kitchen door or to the bathroom.

"Welcome back, Boss. Can I talk to you when you have a chance?"

"Sure. Now?" Casi wondered about the warm welcome. This must be urgent.

"Yes. Can we go outside?"

"Let's take a walk by the ocean. I missed our beach."

As they walked down to the sand, Matias looked anxious.

"I have some bad news. Isa and I are splitting up. We've been having problems for a while, but this past week was hell. I think she'll give notice later today. I wanted to talk to you first."

"I'm sorry to hear that, Matias. Can I help in some way?" Casi listened patiently as Matias gathered his thoughts.

"Yes, let her go." His eyes met Casi's.

"Ok. Do you mind me asking what happened?" Casi held his breath.

"She wants to get married, and I don't. We've been fighting like feral cats. She isn't the right woman for me. I know that now."

Casi exhaled. "I understand. Relationships are hard, but they are even harder with the wrong person."

"So true. I'd like to continue working here. I like the creative freedom you give me, and I enjoy island life. I was wondering, do you want me to look for a new pastry chef, or do you want to handle it yourself?"

"Do you have someone in mind?" Casi was immensely relieved Matias was staying.

"There's a girl who works at the Atlantis who may be suitable."

"Ok, when Isa gives notice, let's get her over here and have her prepare a few signature dishes for us. If she passes the test, I want to check out her references and work history. In the meantime, I would also like to advertise the spot, just in case. You and I will decide together who we hire. I want you to work with someone you like. Tight kitchen quarters require that." Matias nodded, relieved. "Thank you, Casi."

"Also, I know you may want to go home for a visit at some point. I'm thinking of closing the restaurant for a month in the summer. I'm not sure when exactly, but I'll let everyone know as soon as I decide. Maybe we'll keep that announcement quiet until Isa leaves."

"Of course. Thanks."

"One more thing, I wanted to start renovations soon, give the outside of the building a facelift, and build the outdoor oven. I'll want your input for the outdoor kitchen. I have to discuss the timing with Peter. Keep that under your hat for now, too, ok?"

"Of course. An outdoor kitchen, that would be fabulous." Matias's face lit up. "I have all kinds of ideas for that."

"Good. Hold on to them. You, Peter, Camila and I will discuss this together."

"Ok, thanks. I have to get back to work, prepare for lunch." A grin lit up his usually dark features.

"Don't worry, Matias. Breakups are hard, but they pass. Consider this a new beginning. The next chapter in your life."

"I'm ready."

When Matias left, Casi sat down on a bench by the water and called Peter.

"Hi, got a minute?"

"Yes. What's up?"

"Matias just told me that Isa will be giving notice. They split up, and she wants to return to Chile, I hear. She hasn't told me herself yet. Did you notice any problems?"

"Yes, I noticed some sour faces for a while now. They always speak in Spanish when I'm around, so I don't know what they're saying, but body language speaks volumes, you know?"

"I do."

"While you were away and Camila was at the dentist, I heard some angry clanging of pots and pans. I was scared someone would end up with stitches, it got so heated, but it was handled in the kitchen. I stayed out of it."

"The minute she gives notice, I want to advertise the position. Do you know anyone who may be interested?"

"Not off the top of my head. I can have Tessa put the word out when you tell me to."

"Yes. I was thinking Matias should sit in on the interviews since he has to be happy working with the person."

"Of course. Not everyone will put up with him. Isa was exceptionally quiet."

"Do you see any other surprises coming?"

"No."

"When you come in tomorrow, let's talk about the next few months. I'm thinking ahead to the outdoor renovations. Getting estimates and a schedule in place, you know? I also want to close the restaurant for a month sometime between May and October. Let me know what your thoughts are about the best month to close."

"Ok. Did you have a good time in Miami?"

"Yes, very good. See you tomorrow."

The next day he and Peter mapped out their schedule for the spring and summer months. Camila and Gracie agreed to work on the fruit and vegetable garden in the coming weeks, finalizing its contents with Matias. A fence would be embedded on the short retaining wall they had already set as a boundary. Fresh, nourishing soil would be added to the five- hundred by eight-hundred square foot plot. Casi wanted the outdoor oven built by April in time for Easter festivities and the Bahamas Family Regatta, the third week of April. The outside of the building would be worked on simultaneously. All work would hopefully be completed by mid-May, before the Long Island Regatta.

"The best months to close up are August, September, or October. Tourism is at an all-time low then. People generally don't like to come to the island during hurricane season," Peter added.

"Let's close in August. If we have any storm damage, we'll need time to take care of it through October. Also, schools start in early September so staff with children can't travel then. Will you tell everyone so they can make their plans?"

"Sure. When?"

"After Isa leaves. Let me run all this past Camila too. You can tell them the month off will be everyone's paid vacation. I just gave everyone an extra week, but we had a good winter and they worked so hard. This would be in lieu of a raise this year."

"Thanks, Casi. We got holiday bonuses, so that's more than generous."

That night, Casi went over the schedule with Camila, who was fine with everything.

"Can we afford it all? The summer months will be slow."

"Yes, I think so. I'd like to develop and expand our special events for the slow months. We have a good local following. Maybe Tessa can advertise the restaurant for weddings and private parties. Be creative, Camila. Look at the official Bahamas calendar of events with Peter and come up with themes for the slow tourism months. Also, maybe we can do a different international night every week and advertise it. Drop flyers each week at the hotels."

"Sounds good. *Cinqo de Mayo* is in the making and Easter will be the first special event. Matias and I are talking about it. Between private parties and you being gone, I haven't had a lot of extra time. I'll research and plan international themes starting in April. The first international night will be Chilean. I promised Matias.

"That's fine. We've done well this winter. Next year, we can throw in some more special events."

Before bed, Casi texted Helena.

Just worked on my business schedule. I will be free to meet you from mid-May on. The month of August is also good. Keep me up to date on your film dates, so I can book us a special trip. Hopefully, your starting date is late in June. Call me when you can talk. I love you, and miss you.
C

CHAPTER LXXX

Lust in the Kitchen…. And Blooming Romance at the Bar

The following weeks brought a lot of change at the Sea Grape Garden. Isa gave notice and left the island in a huff. A new pastry chef was hired, another woman. The girl who Matias had suggested did not pan out, and even Matias had to agree, after tasting some of her concoctions, she lacked innovation and skill. Some additional interviewing proved to be successful. They collectively settled on a woman from France who had interned at one of the large hotels and wanted to stay in the Bahamas. Matias was thrilled.

Amelie was young, pretty, and extremely competent. The kitchen dynamic was restored, the *brigade de cuisine* back in its rightful place. Now, there were three horny, Spanish men, salivating over a pretty French girl, who had no trouble handling them with grace and humor. Luckily the cooks and dish washers were all locals, either married or spoken for.

The border fence around the raised vegetable garden was erected with sturdy chicken wire, and topsoil was trucked in. Additional fruit trees were planted around the perimeter of the employee parking lot, and edged with mulch, but the dirt lot parking was kept as is. Casi wanted to maintain that rustic feel. Benny heartily agreed. He came around to help with the placement of the trees so they would thrive. Camila and Gracie planted the new garden with unbridled enthusiasm. Gardening tools purchased, the two ladies rolled up their sleeves and got to work. It was a pleasure watching them dig in the dirt, while loudly discussing placement of said vegetables. When Matias added his opinion to the mix, things got heated. Peter and Tessa took pictures of the progress, which were posted on the restaurant's Instagram. The candid shots were endearing and humorous but always tasteful. No faces were revealed, only slanted straw hats at a working angle.

"We gotta document this. They look like they're five years old making mud pies," Peter noted.

"And they act it, too. I saw Camila swing a worm under Gracie's nose. She was wearing gardening gloves, of course." Matias laughed. His mood had lightened substantially with Isa gone.

"Oh, that must have gone over well. I'm surprised I didn't hear her scream in the restaurant."

"I heard it in the office. I ran out through the kitchen to make sure they didn't find a dead body," Casi added as he listened in.

"Good Lord, you have some dark thoughts, man." Peter laughed.

If only he knew, Casi thought.

When Casi wasn't working, he was thinking about Helena. They managed to talk every week-end, but during the work week, they only managed to text. The time difference made communications difficult. She sounded increasingly sad when he spoke to her, and it worried him. He missed her like crazy, but he was too busy to dwell on what couldn't be changed. Rose hadn't come down since he saw her in Miami, and he was secretly glad. The occasional tourist fling worked for relieving his sexual tension.

On a slow night, Camila and Casi were introduced to an American businessman who had recently arrived from Panama. Peter, who still worked the outside bar in a pinch, recognized him as a repeat customer and started chatting him up. The man's date had cancelled last minute, and he decided to stay and dine at the bar.

"Let me introduce you to the owners of the Sea Grape Garden, Casi and Camila. I'm Peter, the restaurant manager. What was your name again?"

"Nice to meet you all. I'm Stefano Salas. I work for the Hilton organization here on the island. I was in Panama until a few months ago. I really enjoy coming to your restaurant. The ambiance is special, and the food is spectacular. You have a good chef."

"Thank you, Stefano. Our chef is from Chile. We like him, too." Camila smiled warmly. "What do you do for the Hilton?"

"I work in management. In Panama, I managed the onsite retail stores and here I'm more of a general business manager. Are you planting a garden on the premises? I noticed some changes."

"Yes. That's my pet project. Thank you for noticing. We planted some fruit trees, and now, we're adding an organic vegetable garden for the chef."

"What a great idea! You certainly have the space."

Peter winked at Casi. "Can you get me some lime twists?"

"Sure." Casi turned to Stefano. "Excuse me. Duty calls. You're in good hands with my sister." When he returned with the lime twists, other people were seated at the bar, but Camila and Stefano were oblivious, deep in conversation. Casi noticed Stefano's appetizer had arrived and he was eating while chatting animatedly with his sister. Peter was busy filling drink orders but managed to look up and smile. He raised his eyebrows and nodded his head toward Camila. Eyebrows dancing, he indicated a love connection.

By the end of the evening, Camila had a date, her first since her arrival in the Bahamas. Peter proudly took full credit.

"I waited and searched for the right match. I think this guy might be it," he joked. "Just give me the green light; I can be on the look-out for you too."

"No thanks. I'm good," Casi clipped holding up his hand in a stop signal.

CHAPTER LXXXI

Let the Junkanoo Planning Begin

The month of April flew by for the Sea Grape Garden collective. They had obtained the permit for the outdoor oven, and it was in the final stages. Peter's demolition crew was back and doing a marvelous job coordinating with a very decisive Matias, who wanted his outdoor kitchen just right. The plumber who ran the gas line was impressed with the result.

"I'll be back with my family for a pizza dinner," he promised.

"Good. I'll make sure you get treated right when you come. Anyone who works on my restaurant becomes part of the extended family," Casi promised. The grill and oven looked great, and he couldn't wait to fire it up.

The outside of the building was power washed, and stone repairs were made. Peter wanted to be done in time for the Junkanoo Carnival and Music Festival, which started the first week of May, so he kept his work crew on schedule, despite a fussy Matias.

Camila had her own goals. She wanted the garden planted and growing before her *Cinqo de Mayo* celebration, so she could gloat over her bunches of cilantro. Once the garden was planted, she and Gracie moved on to discussing flowerbeds on either side of the restaurant's front door. They couldn't agree on what to plant. Casi settled the discussion after talking to Benny. He vetoed flower beds entirely and opted for a series of huge, hip-high, round, textured terra cotta planters with ylang ylang and hibiscus. Around the planters, he opted for pampas grass placed in a mixture of sand and pebbles within a stone border to keep the mix from washing away or growing between the stones in the walkway. The employee patio was adorned with equally large, simple terra cotta planters, jam-packed with various herbs. The patio's planters matched the more elaborate front door ones. They stood tall, near the columns and overflowed with bougainvillea, the plant that had captured Casi's love when he first saw the property. Benny was thrilled, clapping his hands enthusiastically when he came to collect his quarterly check.

Peter's ulterior motive for wanting the restaurant completed by carnival time was his family's musical investment in the Junkanoo celebration. The Jamaican Diamonds were scheduled to play everywhere, including at the Sea Grape Garden for two nights. Gracie and her sister were singing with the band and various cousins were marching in the parade. Casi hoped to increase his local business with all the festivities. Peter's family and friends alone could fill the restaurant for a number of nights.

Casi was pleased the outdoor work was completed for his own reasons. His trip with Helena was tentatively planned for late May. He wanted to kill two birds with one stone and island-hop in the Caribbean for two weeks. He figured it would give him an opportunity to gauge how Helena reacted to island life, without disclosing where his new home was and he could scout possible new restaurant locations at the same time. Sitting in front of his laptop in the office, he startled when Camila walked in.

"So, where are you planning to take your girlfriend this time?" Camila asked as she peeked over his shoulder.

"I want to stay in the Caribbean. Perhaps, do a little island hopping. If you need me, I can be here in a flash. I was thinking Aruba, Barbados, Saint Martin or Saint Thomas, maybe. I would like to check them out for business reasons, too, if we ever decide to expand."

"If you're thinking expansion, Miami would be nice. I really liked it there."

"Really? I like Miami too, but the US is too difficult to get into if you don't have citizenship. Lots of immigration issues and regulations for new businesses."

"I suppose. Well, for now, I'm very happy here."

"Me too. I'm so glad we're done with renovations. The rest is just maintenance. Now we can concentrate on profit."

Camila's eyebrows shot upward. "Then why are you looking for another project already?"

"Just thinking ahead."

"So tell me the truth…are you taking Helena around the islands to see if she'll like island life?"

"It's scary how well you know me." Casi smiled.

"I know how you think. Don't get your hopes up too much. Everyone likes to visit an island, but living here would give many island fever, especially if they're used to big city life."

"Are you experiencing island fever?"

"No, not yet. Right now, I'm too busy to even think about it. Ask me again in the slow months."

"Ok. How is the *Cinqo de Mayo* planning going?"

"So far, so good. Matias is easy to work with. We think alike. The menu is set. I'm just working on decoration details and promotion with Tessa."

"You're the first person to say Matias is easy to work with. Did you drug him?" Camila laughed and shrugged her shoulders. "I think Isa leaving and Amelie arriving has calmed him. She keeps all the men in the kitchen in a good mood with her chatty, cheerful disposition."

Casi turned back to his computer. "I was thinking…maybe Helena and I could meet in Aruba and just relax for the first week. From there we could fly to Saint Martin or Saint Thomas and charter a sail boat to take us around all the little islands nearby. What do you think?"

"I don't know. Am I invited? Three on a boat might be tight." She placed a hand on her hip and tapped her foot.

"No, sorry. Next time for sure, Camila."

"In that case, it sounds good."

Camila's *Cinqo de Mayo* celebration, around the corner, had Casi excited. He hadn't had authentic Mexican food in a while. Camila didn't cook much anymore, since they worked through dinner most days. The few nights they didn't, they took dinner home. The reservations for the event were trickling in and it looked like they would have another full house.

Their first international night, a Chilean fest, a few weeks earlier had been rather spirited. Little did Casi know the *Cinqo de Mayo* celebration and the International nights would be tame compared to the junkanoo events. The junkanoo festivities left Casi gasping for air and in need of a royal rest. Even his abundant energy level was taxed after Bahamian partying.

CHAPTER LXXXII

A New York Minute turns Deadly

March pre-production dragged into April for Summer, Jasper and Ted. Summer was still far from ready to start filming, despite working around the clock. The anticipated start date was pushed from early May to early June until further notice. While most of the crew was in place, courtesy of Ted, her ever-efficient producer, the cast was proving to be a problem. Summer's main characters were cast, but she was still missing a few important supporting roles. Ironically, Helena was cast as Fernando's mistress, Casi's nemesis. Summer also wanted to play up Jose's repressed sexuality by adding a hidden boyfriend, but she hadn't yet found the right man for the part. She wondered if Casi could guess his type. She texted him asking his thoughts. Jasper's character was cast as a woman.

To add to Summer's frustration, one of Hope's previous projects was running later than planned, and she wasn't able to come to New York for casting calls. The cinematographer wasn't crucial for casting, but Summer wanted Hope's opinion. so the audition tapes were discussed over video chat and Zoom. Hope finally arrived in late April, just before their trip to Europe. They held one more week of intensive auditions, settling nothing. The rest of the time, they prepared for Italy. Casting calls would have to be resumed in May after their location- scouting trip.

Summer hoped they could start filming in New York in June and make Italy the second leg, in August. Filing the necessary paperwork in Italy would take time as Italian bureaucracy was notoriously slow. She wanted to get the ball rolling in early May when they visited to finalize location decisions. Even that was tight, she thought.

Francois's gallery in New York was gaining momentum, but unfortunately, Ted's time was divided between working for Summer and training his replacement. He would be needed on set from June to September and in pre-production prior to June. That was not without its complications because Francois couldn't return to New York until after Cara's show, in April. He was busy in Europe until May and totally relying on Ted to keep the gallery afloat. It frustrated him that Ted wasn't fully committed to sales in the gallery, thus adding more pressure. Summer knew her mom missed Francois and felt bad she couldn't help out in the gallery, but she was swamped with her own ceramics business. Everyone was juggling it seemed and hanging on by a mere thread.

Summer was sad she didn't have time to attend any of her film's screenings after Sundance, but pre-production was all-consuming. In general, that wasn't a terrible problem to have as she was thrilled to be working, however, she would have liked to bask in the sun of success occasionally. "When it rains, it pours," she thought morosely. Unlike her last film, she had studio backing this time, which was extremely comforting. The person assigned to them helped Ted handle the budget, paperwork and press.

With Helena's help, Summer orchestrated a special showing of her film in Paris, the Saturday and Sunday night after Cara's Friday night gallery opening. Helena and Summer arranged the showing with Mimi in the little Montmartre theater they had used as home base the previous year. Claude and Pierre, Ted's reliable gay friends, were in charge of notifying everyone who worked on the film. They also helped with publicity. It was heartwarming how everyone pitched in to make things happen.

Cara's art opening in Paris was scheduled for a Friday night, the week-end after Easter. Everyone arrived the Wednesday before. She was planning to stay until the following Wednesday, while Summer, Jasper, Ted, and Hope would stay through the weekend, then depart for Italy on Monday morning. They rented the de Fontenays' apartment for one week, which was substantially cheaper than a hotel. Madame Balon, the trusted housekeeper, was happy to welcome everyone back. To show her joy, she cooked her famous *poulet a la moutarde* with potatoes *au gratin* for her American charges and left it in the refrigerator with a welcome note. The *coup de gras* was her surprise dessert, her world class *clafoutis*. If only she could have heard the orgasmic sounds surrounding her meal that night. Arriving in Paris and finding this extraordinary feast waiting was the pinnacle of Madame Balon's love.

"Oh my God! I cannot believe Madame Balon cooked for us. We need to get some wine for this extraordinary meal," Cara exclaimed as they discovered the bounty. "This meal alone is worth renting here."

"She didn't leave any recipes, did she?" Ted joked.

"No, those will be buried with her," Cara replied, laughing.

"I brought you guys some wine," Samson volunteered as he helped carry their bags inside. "I figured you would need some basics, so I got a few groceries for the morning as well."

"Bless your heart. What a considerate son you are."

"Gee, thanks, Bro. Is it enough for five people?"

"Yes. You are covered for tomorrow morning. After that, you're on your own. I only promise to make reservations moving forward." His eyes twinkled.

"Fair enough. Thanks, Samson. That was really thoughtful. We're toast today." Hope smiled warmly.

"You're welcome, Hope. So glad you all are back. Missed you guys."

CHAPTER LXXXIII

Paris Reunion ……Short and Sweet…..but Sour for One

Arriving in Paris on Wednesday gave Summer and her group a few days to check on the screening plans and notify additional friends. She called Pascal, her Paris fling from last year and he appeared happy to hear from her.

"Of course, I'll come to the screening Saturday night."

"Bring any friends you would like," Summer offered.

"*Merci,* will you have time after the screening?"

"Yes. We'll have a little party afterwards at the theater--some wine and finger foods, so plan on staying. We can chat then."

"Are you free for dinner one night? So we can catch up… alone?"

"Only tomorrow night. My mom's gallery opening is Friday night, the screenings are Saturday and Sunday, and Monday I'm leaving for Italy to scout locations for my next film. This is a very abbreviated trip. I wish I could stay longer."

"Tomorrow will work. I'll text you where to meet me. Is 8pm good?"

"Yes. Fine. You're invited to the gallery Friday night, too. My mom's *vernissage.*"

"*Merci*, I'll come. I can't wait to see you, Summer. *Salut. A' demain.*"

The night of Cara's *vernissage* was fun, but not terribly lucrative. The gallery was crowded, but only one piece sold. Francois didn't seem terribly concerned.

"We're just getting the word out. Collectors will come back, and look at their leisure. Don't worry, Cara."

"I want to be successful for you, Francois." She leaned in to kiss him tenderly on the lips. "I'm having a fabulous time, though, so thank you for that."

Summer watched the interaction and smiled. Her nerves were temporarily lulled by the sparkling wine and love vibes, but she was starting to feel jitters about her upcoming screenings. Would the audience like her film?

"Francois is sweet to her," she remarked to Samson. "Hey, do you think my screenings will be as well attended?"

"Don't worry. Your crew and friends alone will fill half the theater both nights."

"I never checked with Mimi how ticket sales were going. I didn't have time with the auditions and all."

"Listen, if Helena comes through, half the modeling agency will be there. Plus, I have a friend covering press for you, so I can be your proud brother and not work the event. I think we're good. Stop stressing."

"I hope you're right. By the way, what's going on with Natalie?"

"Nothing much. I saw her a couple times, but things have changed."

"Sorry."

"It is what it is. At least we're talking. Does Mimi have a boyfriend?"

"Not that I know of." Summer grinned. "Why? You interested?"

Samson smiled and shrugged his shoulders.

The next day, Summer and Ted assembled the press kits on the kitchen table and bagged them for the evening.

"Mimi wants us at the theater an hour and a half before opening. She said the theater is almost sold out. She invited the press beforehand for wine and cheese and a private showing. The crew have vouchers, but all the other seats generated tickets, both nights."

"Great," Summer muttered, distracted.

"Mimi will introduce you, Hope, and me before the screening. Afterwards, she'll ask a few questions in a Q&A format. She said if there are any questions you want her to add, you should let her know."

"That's so nice of her. Do you have any in mind?"

"What do you think? Here, I wrote them down. Take a look and see if you want to add anything."

Summer looked at the questions Ted had written.

"This looks good. I can't think of anything for the moment other than I'd like to plug my next film, so maybe we can give her some material on that? Keep it vague though. Maybe we can attach a synopsis to the press kit?"

"Ok. Let's think about the wording."

"Maybe give her the synopsis of our most recent pitch? Actually, I need to look it over first. Jasper and I made a ton of changes to the script after Sundance. I'm not sure it's still accurate."

"Ok. Can I see the new script?"

"Yes. I think you'll be surprised when you see what I did."

"Summer, nothing you do surprises me. I am in a constant state of shock around you and your projects."

Summer burst out laughing. "Thank you, I think."

Summer and Ted arrived at the theater two hours early, greeting Mimi warmly.

"Mimi, it's so good to see you. Thank you so much for all your help and hard work. I'm so thrilled to be here again." She turned to look around, pleased at what she saw.

"Nice to have you back, Summer. This brings back good memories. I had fun preparing for tonight. It's nice to see you too, Ted. You look '*super*'."

"You too, Mimi. Snazzy dress."

"*Merci*." Mimi smiled warmly and squeezed Ted's arm.

"We brought you a few additional questions to ask, our press kits, and a brief synopsis of Summer's next project. Maybe we can talk about that with the press before they leave and at the end of the Q&A?"

"Oh, yes! I want to hear all about it. Come, lets lock your things in the office and get to work. Would you like coffee or water?"

"Water, thanks."

"Hope, my brothers, and my mom will be here later. They'll be happy to help. Let me know what you need done now, Mimi."

"Natalie too?"

"No. She and Samson broke up. He's still recovering."

"Oh, sorry. I'll make sure to keep him entertained."

Summer noted a devious twinkle.

"That would be nice." Summer smiled. "I know he likes you!"

"Really? Take a look around the theater and reception room. Do you want to make any changes?"

"No. Everything looks fabulous, Mimi. Thanks so much. We'll just put some promotional materials out. Is this spot, ok?"

"Yes. The caterers will bring more food while we watch the film. The bar is already set. I hired a friend to take care of that. I think we're ready."

Summer looked around. The stark white walls were decorated with stills from the film, and a beautiful spring flower arrangement graced the media table.

"Everything looks great, Mimi."

By the time the press left and the theater reopened for entry, Summer was ready and excited to see everyone. The press party had gone well. One by one she greeted former crew members and their families and friends. When Helena made her grand entry, Summer had chatted with almost everyone.

"Summer!" Helena squealed with delight. "I'm so happy to see you." She embraced her friend.

"Helena, you look spectacular. Where do you find these outfits?"

Summer admired Helena's long, multi-layered, black lace top and crimson silk crepe, cropped pants. Right down to her black lace pumps, she looked fabulous. Helena's crimson lips broke into a smile, lighting up the room. In seconds she was surrounded by admirers, Jasper included.

"*Bonsoir*, Jasper. Don't you look handsome." She leaned in and kissed him on both cheeks.

Jasper looked flustered to Summer's amusement.

"And you are quite the shining star. Nice to see you, Helena."

"Ok, everyone. Find your seats. We'll have time after the screening to talk. I would like to introduce our VIPs," Mimi announced at the door of the party room.

When the Q&A after the screening wrapped, everyone migrated back to the adjoining conference room. The bar was set up on one side and the buffet with colorful finger foods on the opposite side. The space was filled to capacity, standing room only. Many of the guests spilled over into the theater to sit and talk. Summer sat in the back of the theater, chatting with Helena.

"We plan to have all our locations set by the time we leave Italy. We'll have to make quick decisions and hope the authorities are receptive to our permit requests. So far, we're still on schedule to start shooting in New York in mid-June. Worst case scenario, we'll start after the July 4rth week-end."

"Good. Casi and I will be vacationing in late May, I think."

"Where are you going?"

"He hasn't told me yet. It's a surprise."

"It will always be a surprise with him. Wish someone would whisk me away," she sighed. "Just make sure I can reach you by email and the secure phone, ok?"

"Of course. Don't worry. I'll be there. I was thinking of coming to New York in May before I meet him. Do you need me for anything?"

"I might. I'll let you know."

"I'm booked through April and the beginning of May. I told the agency not to book me after May 10th. I could be in New York the second week of May."

"Book it. On second thought, wait. Let me talk to Ted and Hope first, and I'll confirm the dates with you in a few days. Hope will be staying with me, so you might have to stay at my Mom's place with Jasper. We'll work it out somehow."

"As long as I don't have to stay with Ted. He still doesn't like me, I think."

"Not true. That's just his style. He's very professional."

"If you say so."

"I cast most of the big parts. I think it would be nice for you to meet the other actors. I could have you read with them prior to shooting."

"Ok. Just let me know as soon as you can, so I can plan ahead."

"I will."

Summer got up to mingle. Refilling her glass with sparkling wine, she looked around for Pascal. The wine relaxed her, or maybe it was the hum of a successful night? One more evening to go, but the important reunion and fete had been a success, and it felt great to be celebrated for all the hard work her core group had organized. The cast and crew had accomplished so much in a remarkably short time with her Paris film. Summer felt a little sad about leaving old friends so soon, not knowing when she would see them next. She felt especially sad, leaving Pascal, who had faithfully shadowed her every night. They had reconnected so seamlessly.

"You have to plan a trip to New York," she urged him before she left.

Cara was miffed. Francois had come to the screening Saturday night but was on the phone outside through half the party. His behavior was annoying her. What could be so important on a Saturday night that couldn't wait? When he returned, the news got worse.

"I have to work tomorrow, Cara. I need to be in the gallery early to prepare some paperwork for a shipment that needs to go out first thing Monday morning. I can't come to the second screening. I have an important business dinner tomorrow night."

"Ok. Do you want to meet up after the dinner for a drink or on Monday then?"

"I don't know yet. I'll call you."

Cara was perplexed. What was going on?

When she called Francois Sunday night after the screening a woman answered his phone. Cara swallowed hard. She thought she had the wrong number. She paused and asked for Francois."

"*Ne quitte pas*," the woman clipped with annoyance.

"Are you still at your business dinner? Who just answered your phone?" Cara quizzed him.

"No. I'm at home. This is still business. I couldn't get to the phone quick enough. Esme picked up for me."

"That's bold. I won't bother you then. Do we have plans tomorrow?"

"Let me call you tomorrow morning. I can't talk now."

"Can't you call me later? I would like to plan my day."

"I may be tired. Let's talk tomorrow."

Cara disconnected the phone, feeling gravely disappointed. Was he putting her off? This just felt wrong. He had sounded so distant on the phone, not like his usual warm self. Who was this Esme?

The next morning she made breakfast for everyone as they packed and got ready to go to the airport. Around noon, Francois finally called her. He sounded tired. Her flight wasn't until Wednesday, and she had hoped to have a few days alone with him. It appeared it wasn't meant to be.

"Cara, would you like to have dinner on Tuesday night?"

"Well, that would be the last possible chance, Francois. I'm leaving Wednesday if you remember."

"Yes, I know. Sorry. I've been really busy. Shall we meet at Les Petites Bouchees at eight?"

"Ok. Should I stop by the gallery later this afternoon?"

"No. I will be swamped all day."

"Is Esme an artist you're working with?"

"No. She represents a few good artists, and she's looking for gallery space to show their work. We may work out a deal."

"What kind of a deal?" Cara's stomach felt queasy.

"She is considering subleasing part of my gallery space for a brief period."

"Really? Where will you show your artists' work then?" This deal sounded odd to Cara.

"We're still working that out. I want to keep one wall for my artists. I have the New York Gallery too."

"What about Annabel?" Cara visualized his colorful gallery assistant.

"We would share Annabel for that time period. Cara, Let's talk over dinner. I have to meet Esme."

"Are you meeting her for dinner again?"

"Yes. She prefers to meet at the end of the business day. I cannot say no."

"Does she now? Is she aware that your girlfriend is here for only two more nights?"

"I don't discuss my personal life with her, Cara. If I don't work by her schedule, I might lose the deal to another gallery. Surely, you understand that this is a time sensitive matter. I'll see you tomorrow night, ok?"

"Ok." Cara heard someone calling Francois as he hung up the phone. She was only here for a week. Couldn't he clear his calendar for this brief period? She didn't like the sound of Esme. Was he trying to keep her away from the gallery, so she and Esme wouldn't meet? It sure felt that way. She was so disappointed.

Cara spent Tuesday morning at Galerie Lafayette, appeasing herself with shopping therapy. She couldn't figure out the change in Francois's demeanor. Was he dating someone else in her absence? Esme? After lunch at the corner café, she cleaned up the apartment and packed. It was time to go home. That evening, she walked to the restaurant. Getting there early, she waited at the bar. Francois arrived twenty minutes late and looked tired. He had come straight from work, and he appeared regrettably short tempered, something

Cara had never seen before. They ordered *kirs.* She hoped it would relax him a little.

"So how did things go with Esme today?"

"Why are you so interested in Esme? If I make a deal with her, I'll tell you, but for now I'd rather not talk about it. I'd rather talk about other things besides business."

"You always share gallery business with me. Why is Esme such a big secret?"

"She isn't. I just don't feel like rehashing business with you after a long, tiresome day. I want to relax," Francois snapped.

"Fine. What would you like to talk about?"

"How was your day?"

CHAPTER LXXXIV

Sailing the Caribbean…..Pirate or Refugee?

Casi and Helena were meeting at the Ritz-Carlton Hotel in Aruba. The destination had remained a surprise until two days before Helena's departure. She cheered when the ticket arrived in her email. Having never traveled to the Caribbean Islands before, she was tingling with excitement and anticipation. The thought of seeing Casi and feeling his hands on her body made her insides quiver. She quickly repacked her suitcase, throwing in extra bikinis and sun dresses.

The morning of her departure from Charles de Gaulle International Airport, Casi received a confirmation text. She was checking in for her flight to Oranjestad, which was scheduled to leave on time. Her trip was a night flight with one stopover, so he knew she wouldn't arrive until the next morning. Casi arrived a few hours before Helena. His flight from the Bahamas was less than an hour. Shortly after touching down, he checked into the hotel and dropped his suitcase in the suite. He stopped to marvel at the ocean view from his small terrace, taking in the expansive scenery. It reminded him of his arrival in the Bahamas after fleeing Paris. What a difference a year made. Once again, the sun's inviting rays warmed his heart as he gazed into the sparkling turquoise horizon. Helena would love it here.

Casi used the time before her arrival to get settled. He slid open the sliding doors, letting in the breeze and leisurely unpacked a few cottons and linens, hanging them in the closet. He placed his toiletries over one of the two sinks in the bathroom and unpacked his shoes, placing them on the closet floor. Flinging the clothes he had worn on the plane over a chair, he changed into colorful board shorts, a white t-shirt and rainbow flip flops. The rest of his clothes would stay folded in his suitcase until he needed them. Old habits die hard-- he was always ready to flee at a moment's notice should a situation call for it.

Secretly, Casi was pleased Summer had summoned Helena to New York first, before Italy. He would make sure Helena arrived rested and ready to tackle the long hours a film set required. The work was grueling—twelve-hour days, short tempers, and endless stretches of waiting and wilting on set, if he remembered correctly from Paris.

For their three weeks together, prior to shooting Summer's film, Casi had mapped out special plans—sightseeing on the islands, coveted restaurant reservations and a sailing jaunt. He was intent on making this a sweet birthday trip. Spoiling Helena was not without merit; he intended to do a soft sell on island living and convince her to stay in paradise with him...forever.

While exploring the hotel grounds and adjoining footpath connecting Aruba's neat line of luxury hotels, his phone sent him an alert that Helena's plane had landed. Instinctively, he turned and walked back to their hotel to wait in the lobby and consult with the concierge regarding dinner reservations for the next few nights. He also secured a rental car. It would be fun to give Helena a private island tour and at the same time, satisfy his own curiosity. So far, the island looked very commercial to him, but he had only seen the hotel strip coming from the airport. He ordered a cup of black coffee and plopped himself into a comfortable armchair with a view of the main entrance.

Helena arrived, appearing tired, but looking beautiful nonetheless. She mimicked a teenager in her strategically ripped jeans and casual, white-lace crop top, exposing a strip of tight abs. A strawberry and gold braided rope accentuated her small waist. Her smoldering lips were lined in ripe cherry, and her eyes were accentuated by a musty brown shadow, a few shades lighter than her hair. She carried a small strawberry colored handbag trimmed in camel leather, matching her ballet flats. Over her shoulder, she slung an oversized, two- handled straw bag with colorful beach appliques. The porter behind her, rolled in a set of emerald luggage, one large and one smaller hand luggage. She looked like she belonged on the front cover of the Vogue vacation issue. Observing her from his corner perch, Casi noticed all eyes shifting toward her in quiet admiration. He felt a burst of pride this gorgeous creature was here to see him.

Not spotting him, Helena approached the check-in desk. Finished with his moment of quiet enjoyment, Casi rose and sauntered toward her. When she turned and saw him, her face lit up. She dropped her straw bag on the suitcase and sprinted into his arms.

"Casi. Oh my God, it's so good to see you."

"And you, my love. Did you have a good flight?"

"It was long, but I was so excited about the destination, it was hard to stay put in my seat. Thanks for sending the car service to the airport. I was worried I would get here and not know Where to go."

Casi chuckled. "Of course you would. You're a big city girl. Did the destination surprise you?"

"Yes. I was thinking of South America."

"Anywhere in particular, there?"

"Argentina, Brazil, Chile….I really didn't know."

"Good guesses. Come on. Let me show you our room. I got here early and checked us in. We have a beautiful ocean view. Are you hungry?"

"Famished."

"Good. Me too. We'll drop everything off and have lunch by the pool."

"This place is incredible. I love all the palm trees and cool vegetation. When I left Paris it was grey and wet. The view from the plane before landing here was magical. I can't wait to explore."

"No rain here. That season hasn't started yet."

Casi's first few days with Helena passed in a passionate, blur. One night they celebrated her thirty-second birthday with a candle light dinner on the beach and another night they dined at an Argentinean steak house, listening to tangos and boleros while sipping spicy red wine. The ensuing night was hotter than chili peppers. In their travels around the island, Casi soon realized that one side of the island was lined with mega hotels and nicer residential homes, while the other was peppered with local housing and wild terrain, but little else. He enjoyed vacationing on Aruba but he definitely didn't see it as a place he wanted to open a business at. The successful restaurants were all located in hotels, for protection he imagined. Nonetheless, he and Helena had fun exploring the island, the downtown shops and each other.

His dose of reality came when he checked in with Camila a few days later.

"Camila, it's as if we never parted. Our daily life in Paris was equally harmonious. Helena isn't a party girl, despite what she does professionally so we were happy with a sedate life. We get along so effortlessly and just enjoy being together. The last few days have been wonderful, good for my soul."

"So happy to hear that, Casi. But remember, you're on a luxury vacation. Real life can be slightly more challenging, especially if someone feels trapped on an island."

"Don't push clouds over my head, Camila."

"I don't mean to, but I need you to have your eyes open. Island life is not for everyone, and don't forget, you're a hunted man. One wrong decision can cost us everything. I'm concerned about someone recognizing her, which could lead back to you. How would she handle that?"

"How can I forget? I'm careful. We're keeping a low profile here. Don't worry so much. Everything alright at the restaurant?"

"Yes and no. Stefano says hello. He came here Saturday night to flirt and ask me out for Sunday. I really like him."

"Glad to hear that. He appears to be a decent guy. The same goes for you, by the way, in regard to being vigilant. Don't slip up and tell him something you shouldn't. What was the no?"

"Peter went home early yesterday. He hasn't been feeling well. Been tired a lot, not his usual energetic self."

"I'll call him later. Hopefully, it was just too much partying at the Junkanoo. Are you managing alright?"

"Yes, everything is under control. The big festivities have passed. We just have the regular dinner crowds, and they are thinning. Lots of locals lately, which is nice for a change. Hurricane season is around the corner, and that makes me nervous. Peter and I were talking about it the other day, and he got me thinking. We should prepare."

"Ok. When I get back, we'll work on getting storm shutters and setting up preventative measures. I'll talk to Benny. He's survived a number of hurricanes on the island."

"Yes, that would make me feel better. I have another call coming in. A supplier. Talk later?"

"Yes. Take care and call me if you need anything."

When Casi hung up, he immediately called Peter. His call went to voicemail, so he left a brief message.

Having spent a honeymoon-quality week in Aruba, Casi and Helena flew to their next destination. His research had convinced Casi to skip sailing around the ABC islands, Aruba, Bonaire, and Curacao, in favor of the Leeward Islands. They would spend the next seven days on a sail boat, powered by a professional staff, touring Saint Martin, St Barths and Anguilla.

Helena appeared slightly uneasy about this venture, having never been on a sailboat before. The first two nights in Saint Martin were spent in a luxurious hotel while the boat was prepped for departure. Casi enjoyed the natural beauty of the gated La Samanna property. He and Helena shared long beach walks, swam in the infinity pool, and chatted over exquisitely prepared meals on an elevated outdoor terrace, overlooking the cove.

The hotel's private beach and beautifully manicured grounds were magical. Luscious green vegetation and colorful tropical plants lined hidden pathways leading to the main building from various bungalows hugging the coast.

The hotel's Alice in Wonderland appearance inspired Casi and helped him form a vision of what his new restaurant should look like. One of the highlights of their stay was a private tour of the hotel's wine cellar, a maze of cool stone walls built into the rocky cliff beneath the hotel's main building. It harbored an impressive wine collection and the *sommelier* who lectured them impressed

Casi with his knowledge and forthcoming collector's advice. The morning after their wine tasting tour, they left for town to buy snorkeling gear before boarding the sailboat.

There's something unpredictable about being encapsulated in close quarters on a sailing vessel that can either bring out the best or worst in people. While most of mankind enjoys an afternoon of smooth sailing on a comfortable deck, not everyone is meant to be a sailor when the water gets choppy. The down side of living on a boat is that your immediate well-being is tied to the weather. Helena proved not to be sea-worthy and by the third day, tempers flared.

The first couple days on the boat had been idyllic as they hugged the land and docked frequently. Saint Martin and St Barth were in close proximity to each other, so they spent part of their days and evenings ashore, exploring the islands and dining locally. The shopping area of St Barths was quaint and lined with beautiful little shops, so Casi encouraged Helena to pick her own birthday present. She picked a gold ring with a cushion shaped, pink tourmaline to compliment the earrings from Brazil. The beaches in Saint Barths were a short ride from town. One popular lunch spot and beach was near the tiny airport's landing strip so they marveled at the low flying planes overhead as they ate. They rented a mini car and drove to all the famous beaches—Gouveneur, Nikki, Saline and Shell Beach. The next day they moored at Colombier and snorkeled.

Night three on the boat, the weather changed. So did Helena's disposition. She turned green and unbearably cranky. The choppy sea was a reflection of changing air and water currents. Helena retreated to the cabin to lay down, placing a bucket beside her bunk. That night they anchored close to shore, just in case.

"How are you feeling?" Casi asked that evening.

"Like a spoiled milkshake. When will this end?"

"The captain says it should blow over by the morning, maybe earlier. Do you want to have some dinner?"

"No. I can't keep any food down. I don't know if I can do three more nights of this."

"We can stay close to land and leave the boat during the day."

"Good, because this is torture."

"It will pass, I promise."

Out of the blue, Helena asked, "What do you do at home for entertainment? Have you seen Rose?"

"Rose? Maybe once or twice, since Miami."

"Do you see her socially?"

"Not much. She's a client, you know."

"She likes you, Casi. I could tell."

"We're just friends."

"Does Camila like her?"

"I don't know." In an effort to kill the inquisition, he made a split-second decision to not offer Camila's sentiments.

"Why can't I visit you in your new home and meet Camila?" Helena continued to whine.

"You know why. What you don't know can't hurt you. Whether you notice it or not, you're being randomly watched. You most certainly will be followed on set in New York, so be careful where you talk to Summer. Fernando's people will try to scare you again. Trust me, you are better off not knowing anything about my whereabouts."

Casi looked at her defiantly. "I don't want to endanger Camila, either. What for? To satisfy your curiosity? You're not making a commitment to me. We enjoy each other's company, which is fine for now, but we don't have a lasting commitment, de we?"

"How can we? There are too many secrets. We don't have a normal relationship. You can't visit me and I can't visit you. I never meet your family or friends. I know nothing about your current or past life. I feel like we lived in a bubble in Paris. This relationship feels isolating and wrong on so many levels. It's not healthy or normal. I hate this." Helena stomped her foot in frustration.

"I'm sorry, Helena. Life isn't perfect or smooth sailing all the time. There are always concessions to be made and bumps in the road. Unfortunately, we have a few more than most couples."

"I know that, but I still think you could sneak me in and out of where you are."

"I choose not to. It's risky. If we get spotted on vacation, we can leave. I have worked too hard to rebuild my life. You just don't understand how easily things could go downhill for me. One mistake and I have to run and start over. I can't keep doing that. It's tiring and hard to build something from scratch over and over. I don't expect you to get it, but I do expect you to trust me and respect my judgment."

"It's hard to trust someone who never shares." Her voice pitch rose.

"I've already shared more with you and Summer than I have with anyone. Where I come from, if you share too much, you end up in a box looking skyward. Camila and I made it out of Mexico because we kept our mouths shut and waited patiently for the right opportunity. We were diligent and covered all bases before making a move."

"You never told me about that either. You tell me nothing." Her hands are thrown up into the air for emphasis.

"That's the way it has to be, Helena. I 'm already taking a big risk seeing you and traveling with you. That is all I can offer."

"If I'm such a big liability, maybe we should rethink our relationship." A deep frown contorted her even features.

Casi sighed, exasperated by her cantankerous mood and pouting face. Turning to the cabin door, he placed his hand on the hardware. "I don't want to fight with you. I worked hard to plan a nice trip for your birthday, for us, to show you how much I care. Appreciate it. Enjoy it. Keep it in your heart. If you can't make a commitment to live undercover with me, and you no longer want to meet on vacation because the arrangements don't suit you, I can put you on the next plane to New York. Just say the word," he said firmly.

Before Helena could answer, he slammed the door behind himself, leaving her stunned. He never spoke to her so harshly, but he was tired of her whining. There was no regret in his actions or stern words. She was being unreasonable, and for the first time, he had run out of patience.

Helena was acting like a spoiled child. It was a side Casi had never seen and he was bothered by her lack of empathy for his personal safety and precarious situation. Maybe Camila was right. This union would never work long term. Helena was incapable of escaping her past and present for a foray into the unknown. Maybe she was star struck, or maybe she lacked maturity and was too scared. What Casi knew for sure was that she wasn't ready to join him and he was seriously beginning to wonder if she ever would be. Timing was everything in life.

CHAPTER LXXXV

Land Lubber Trumps Sea Blubber

The next morning, the sea had quieted down, and the sun smiled invitingly on the sailboat and its inhabitants. Helena woke up in a better mood. She'd slept with the bucket next to her, while Casi opted to stay on deck, sleeping under the stars. When she emerged, he had already gone for a cleansing morning swim and rinsed off on deck. They were anchored near a different beach in St Barths. They were staying for another day before departing for Anguilla, the last island in their floating travels.

"Good Morning. Would you like some coffee?"

"Yes, please." Her eyes traveled over his tan, muscular body.

"How are you feeling today?" His concern was genuine.

"Better, but my legs still feel wobbly."

"So what are your thoughts? Do you want to leave? There are flights out of St. Barths. I checked." He swiveled around to make sure no one was in listening distance.

"No. I'm sorry, Casi. I was frustrated and nauseous yesterday. I didn't mean to act ungrateful. I love being here with you. It's just … when I think of our future or lack of it, I feel anxious and upset." She reached for his hand.

"Why don't you just enjoy life now, live in the moment. Tomorrow brings no guarantees. We can figure things out later or maybe they'll just evolve naturally over time."

"It's hard for me to imagine a future without you. I've missed you tremendously since you left Paris. It saddens me that we can't have a normal relationship, that we have to live secret lives in hiding all the time." She wanted him to bridge the distance she felt in her heart.

"It wouldn't be a normal life either way if you become a film star. They don't have normal lives." Casi frowned.

"But our situation makes it even worse."

"It makes it impossible. So enjoy the time we have and accept it for what it is…temporary pleasure. I'm thankful for each day away from Fernando and for each day I can spend with you. Try to see things through different lenses. Our future will crystalize one way or another."

"I'll try." They were getting nowhere.

When one of the crew members approached, they fell silent. Casi was happy for the interruption.

The fourth day on the boat, in Gustavia, was idyllic. Helena calmed down and reverted back to her pleasant self. They toured a few of the island's residential areas and had an early dinner at Le Tamarin. Casi took in the restaurant's incredible location. He shot pictures of the gardens from various angles to share with Camila and Peter. That night the sea gave them a much needed break. They slept peacefully. The following morning, they woke up half way to Anguilla. The calm waters had allowed for a more romantic night.

Over breakfast, the captain approached them to confirm the travel itinerary.

"We're off to Road Bay for lunch and some afternoon snorkeling off Sandy Island. I thought we could check out Prickly Pear Cays Park to see some marine life. We'll circle the entire island. Tomorrow, we'll head back to San Maarten and stop at the Dutch port for a late lunch. You can do some shopping in Philipsburg."

"Thanks, Captain." Casi smiled. "That sounds wonderful."

When the sailboat docked in San Maarten the next day, Casi knew Helena was happy to disembark. They spent the day walking around the port area. In the late afternoon, they checked into La Samanna, retrieving their luggage from storage. One last night at this wonderful place would realign their stars. They could have their laundry washed and repack for their last destination, St.Thomas, in the British Virgin Islands.

They arrived at the St Thomas Great Bay Resort in the late afternoon by private plane. Casi felt right at home. The resort reminded him of the Bahamas. Sitting on the terrace of the Coconut Cove Restaurant, Casi felt at peace. He reached across the table for Helena's hand. "So what do you think of island life?"

"I love it. I prefer living and sleeping on land, though. The sailboat was great on the calm days, but I like a stationary bed at night-- a fluffy, soft, padded bed with silky sheets and quilted covers."

Casi laughed. "Fair enough. I might even agree with that. Could you see yourself living on an island? Or is it too boring?"

"I don't know. I love it now, but perhaps all year, every year may be too much of a good thing. It would have to be a bigger island than St Barth. I still like the excitement of big city life. And hurricane season would scare me. What about you?"

"Yes, that could definitely be scary. I think I'd like it as long as I could leave whenever I wanted. I would have to try it for a while." He changed gears. " So...I thought we could explore St Thomas tomorrow. Walk around town and have lunch or dinner down there. What do you think?"

"Let's hang here in the morning and go after lunch. It's so pretty here."

"Ok. Would you like to go snorkeling to the Baths of Virgin Gorda tomorrow? It's a short boat ride."

"No! No more boats this vacation. Can we go snorkeling here?"

"Yes. I'll check where is best. I hear Sapphire Bay is nice. We can rent a jet ski there."

"Good. That sounds like fun."

Two days before leaving, Casi called Camila. He still hadn't heard back from Peter.

"How is everything?"

"Everything in the restaurant is under control. We were very busy over the weekend, but now things have slowed. Happy hour still gets a crowd."

"How is Peter?" Casi heard Camila take in air.

"Peter is out right now. He has to go for some medical tests, so I told him to take care of it before he comes back. Gracie filled in for him over the weekend."

"What? Really? He never called me back. What did the doctor say?"

"I'm waiting to hear from Gracie. We don't know yet."

"What are his symptoms?"

"He just said he wasn't feeling right and he's very tired. His body must be fighting something. Hopefully a virus and nothing more."

"I'll be home in a couple of days. Call me if you hear anything."

"Of course."

Casi hung up, feeling uneasy. He could tell his sister was being evasive, and he didn't like it. Peter would have returned his call if it was something minor. A pit was forming in his stomach. He tried calling Peter again, but the call went to voicemail. It wasn't like Peter not to call him back. Was Camila holding something back?

CHAPTER LXXXVI

Life and Death …A Thin Line Sometimes

The last couple days in St Thomas were emotional and testy. While Helena and Casi tried to enjoy their time, the romantic spell from Aruba was broken. When Helena became melancholy about her looming departure, Casi couldn't muster enough patience to deal with her complaints. His thoughts were with Peter now. He needed to get home.

"Helena, why ruin our last few days? We'll see each other when you're done filming in August. Stop complaining and enjoy the here and now."

"I know but it's more than three months away!"

"We just had three beautiful weeks together! Think about that when you're sad or struggling, but honestly, you won't have time to be sad. Don't you remember how busy you were when you were filming in Paris? You were up at 4:30am and exhausted every night."

"Yes and you were there to pick me up, encourage me, and care for me. I needed that. I wish you could at least visit me on set."

"That's impossible. Please, you're making this difficult. We'll stay in touch and make plans once your schedule with Summer is set. Now, let's focus on having a nice day. We're still here, together." When had she become so needy? It was starting to bother Casi.

When Helena finally left for the airport, she clung to Casi. He stroked her hair and back gently, holding her close. Kissing her good bye, he reminded her they'd see each other in three months. His heart would have stung more had he not been so worried about Peter. His head was already in the Bahamas, wondering what was wrong. A few hours alone on the terrace of the Coconut Cove Restaurant helped him gather his thoughts and leave for the airport with a plan. He checked his work emails and called Camila from the taxi.

"Hi, my flight leaves at four. I'll be home for dinner. Are you coming to pick me up, or should I take a taxi?"

"I'll be there."

"How is Peter?"

"Let's talk when you get here. I'm kind of busy right now." She sounded tired.

"Fine. Can you text me Gracie's work number?" He wasn't going to let it go.

"Casi, let's talk first before you call her. Gracie and Peter need a little time alone right now. They're dealing with doctors."

"What's going on? Tell me."

"Peter isn't well. I'll give you the details when I see you. Safe flight. Love you."

Before he could protest, she hung up. He felt sick with worry.

When he landed a few hours later, Camila was waiting.

"How was your trip? You look good, rested."

"Thanks. Tell me about Peter."

"Peter has stage two prostate cancer. He started radiation therapy. We're hoping it works. He's been really depressed Gracie said. And… he's not a good patient because he's never really been seriously ill."

Casi gasped. "Oh my God. I had a feeling it was bad, but that's treatable, no? Where is he going for therapy?"

"Doctor Hospital. Gracie says they're hopeful."

"Why didn't you tell me?"

"Peter asked me not to. He made me promise."

"Why? Can you drop me at his place?"

"He wanted you to enjoy your trip. He said there was nothing you could do for him right now, and Gracie filled in for him, so we managed at the restaurant. He's expecting you. I warned him you would come immediately. Just know, he gets tired easily and has to run to the bathroom a lot. Go easy on him. Don't scare him more than he already is. He's had a lot of tests these past few weeks. It's taken an emotional toll." Casi listened in silence, processing.

When they arrived at Peter's house, Gracie opened the door and hugged Casi.

"How is he, Gracie?"

"It's been a rough couple of weeks, but hopefully, the radiation therapy will eradicate the tumor they found. Say a prayer. The worst part is his mood. He's been beyond crabby."

"I've been praying since I heard. What can I do for him?"

"Take his mind off things for a bit. He's out back. He had a treatment this morning. They told him to rest because he's been dragging, but that's partly emotional. He's a terrible patient."

"How long will he do radiation therapy?"

"Five days a week for three or four weeks. He knew he had a small tumor and we were watching it, but the doctor said it grew in size, and IMRT radiation was necessary. The treatment only takes fifteen minutes every day. No surgery is needed at this time. We hope this will do it."

"Me, too."

"Here, I made a pot of green tea. Can you take it out to him?"

Casi took the tray from her and walked out to the backyard. Peter was slumped in a wicker armchair, pretending to read the newspaper, his eyes half closed.

"Green tea delivery. How are you?"

"Casi. Hey. I'm alive, man."

"Glad to hear it. I need you, you know."

"Yeah, I know. I plan to be back. Just needed a minute to get through the damn tests."

"No worries. Take all the time you need. Camila said Gracie is better than you anyway." Peter grinned and perked up in his chair.

"Not even dead yet, and the woman is already 'snakin' my job?"

"Don't worry. I'm back. Your job is secure. I only let the women rule when we take a much needed break."

Peter chuckled, sitting up. "Good move. Only let them think they're in control. I've been doing that for years. The secret to surviving marriage."

"Right. I hear good things about the radiation treatment you're doing. It makes you bounce back like Superman."

Peter laughed and stood. "Yeah, man. I'll be ripping up tree roots and swinging rum cases with my pinkie when I'm done."

"That's right, but for now, take it easy. Sit down. Can I pour you some tea? Gracie wants you to drink this green stuff."

Peter stretched and sat back down.

"Yeah, but put a teaspoon of honey in it. It needs help. Tell me about your trip, Casi."

"It was wonderful. Have you ever sailed around the Leeward islands?"

"No, tell me about it."

An hour later, Camila and Casi said their good-byes to Gracie at the front door.

"That is the perkiest I've seen him since you left, Casi. I'm glad you're back. You lift his spirits."

"So am I. We'll get through this together, Gracie. I promise." He leaned in and gave her a long hug.

"See you tomorrow. If you need me to take him to the hospital or do anything at all, let me know. I'm glad to help."

"Thanks, Casi. We're good. He'll be back at the restaurant shortly. I think he needs to go back to regular life. This has been mentally draining on him more than anything else."

"Of course!"

Back in the jeep, Camila and Casi chatted about Peter's downward spiral.

"I knew something was up when Peter was uncharacteristically quiet. He didn't smile or joke, just did his work quietly as if he was in pain or dragging. At first, I thought it was because you weren't here. Then Gracie called me."

"Listen, Camila. We need to get supplemental health insurance for ourselves and our permanent employees who aren't covered by NHI Bahamas. This is a reminder and a warning. We have the most basic plan right now."

"Ok."

"In the interim, can you check into getting us an international group health plan first thing tomorrow?

"Yes."

"Good. The sooner, the better. I want Peter to have the best care. I can't even think about losing him."

CHAPTER LXXXVII

From the Idyllic Italian Seaside into the New York Fire Pit

Summer fell in love with Naples, Italy's southern, third-largest city. A day trip and forty minute ferry ride to the island of Procida sealed the deal. She wanted to film at these colorful locations. Southern Italy spoke to her-- the narrow, winding streets of Santa Lucia, the Castel dell'Ovo in the sea and the incredible harbor, Naples biggest economic boom. The area was alive and vibrant like its people. Procida had its own charms. The island's landscape of pastel, staggered houses hugging the hills was a filmmaker's dream. The colorful boats neatly docked along the cobblestones, and the clothing hung out to dry along the buildings' sunny side, added to the eclectic beauty of the landscape and lent the island an exotic bazaar quality. Eateries scattered along the water's edge provided atmosphere and good food.

"Filming here will be so much fun. This is so quaint and lively. I love the architecture, the majestic buildings and the cobblestone streets. The harbor and all those winding alleys create a mysterious atmosphere. What do you think, Hope?"

"I agree. I think you should write a spooky church with skulls into the script. Old black-clad women carrying crosses and winding around the San Gennaro Catacombs. Do drug trade deliveries on flaming red Vespas with Mount Vesuvius in the background.

"Creepy. Yeah, we'll definitely adapt the script to the location. Keep those ideas coming."

Ted stretched and looked at the girls. "This has been an eye-popping few days. Really inspiring. I think I got most of the paperwork we'll be needing. I only have a few more stops before we leave. I'd like to get some company names that might be of service to us when we film. I can email them from New York if I establish a contact. What are we doing tomorrow, for our last night in Naples?"

"I don't know. Any thoughts, Jasper? You're the foodie here." Summer looked from one man to the other.

"I think we should go for Neopolitan pizza again. We haven't been to Brandi yet. That's where pizza was invented."

"I don't know. It couldn't be better than La Notizia. That was pure pizza heaven." Summer smiled at the memory.

"Let's find out by comparing."

When Summer and her posse returned to New York, auditions resumed. Spending valuable time carefully scouting possible locations in Italy had helped Summer visualize and finalize her mental picture of the film. She could easily imagine her actors on location. Within a few weeks, they finalized the cast and had the studio lock in signed contracts. Pre-production was almost done.

Equipment was organized, and all New York permits secured. The one thing that still needed filling in was crew. Hiring the right people was crucial. Given their timing, they decided to postpone shooting until after July 4rth. Summer notified Helena, who decided to go back to Paris until filming was set to begin.

"It will give me time to possibly work a little, check on things at home, pay my bills and repack before I take off again."

"Are you having a good time with Casi?"

"Yes. I'll tell you about that when I see you. I'm finding it hard to separate, though."

"I would imagine so. How is he?" She was picturing Casi's strong, silent, soft-spoken presence. The man had left an impression on her in Miami.

"He's handling our impending separation better than me."

"I bet he's just not showing it as much. Listen, Helena, Jasper, or I will email you with the exact dates of when you need to be here. Rest up, and I'll see you soon, ok? Oh, and pack lots of sexy clothes for your character. It will save us time looking here."

"Ok, I'll see what I can find. Send me an email with some suggestions."

"Will do."

Helena was on set, looking sexier than ever as Fernando's girlfriend. The shooting schedule had been delayed and revised three times, but finally, they managed to begin in July. Jasper was in charge of keeping everyone on schedule, while Ted took care of all other logistics like adjusting the Italy travel dates from early August to September. They left themselves a two week break between the New York and Italy shoots to ship and regroup. Summer was thankful Jasper was helping Ted as co-producer. Jasper catered to the cast and crew's whims, which freed up Ted's time for the important stuff. This time they would be taking a basic crew with them to Italy, so travel plans were slightly more complicated. Summer was thankful the studio assisted with travel accommodations.

The long, hot hours on set were exhausting, and things moved slowly at first, but each day yielded results. Summer soon realized they would need extra time in New York. She was glad Ted had postponed Italy to the second week in September. The cast and crew appreciated having Labor Day week end off.

The first days in August were steaming. Tempers flared when some of the crew started to overheat and feel overworked. By the second week, Ted got the studio's approval to hire extra people to move things along more efficiently on set. Everyone was wilting, especially those not used to New York City humidity in August, like Helena. She was staying with Jasper just north of the city and each morning they drove in. Traffic at that early morning hour was light. Summer noticed a change in their interactions. They appeared comfortable, and somewhat smitten with each other.

"So, how are things working out with Jasper?" she asked Helena one day.

"Great. He keeps me on schedule, and he's fun to work with and hang out with after work. We've been too tired to go out, so we stay home and gossip."

"Have you heard from Casi?"

"Yes, but I've missed a lot of his calls. I'm usually on set or in transit with Jasper, so I can't talk."

Summer nodded. "You can always text."

"Not the same. Anyway, I feel more removed when I can't see him or hear his voice. Our relationship is complicated and the distance doesn't help."

"Yeah….long-distance relationships are challenging, but the strong ones usually survive if you stay committed. Alright, let's get you into make-up. You need a refresh."

Summer looked around for Jasper. He was talking to Hope. She caught his eye and waved him over.

"Just wanted to check how things are going with Helena? She seems to be wilting a little more than usual."

"Fine, I think. She's having trouble with the heat, so we need to make sure she hydrates."

"Ok. How are things at home?"

"What do you mean?"

"Is she ok staying with you and Mom?"

"Yeah. Mom isn't around that much when we get home. She's always in the studio. Helena and I usually have dinner alone. Why? Has she said something?"

"No. Just checking…"

"Don't worry. I'm taking good care of her."

"I'm sure. You aren't getting involved, are you?"

"What? No. Where is this coming from?"

"Please don't. I need her to focus. Hope also noticed she's a little off on camera. Hopefully, it's just the heat. Keep an eye on her, ok?"

"Sure thing."

One morning, toward the end of shooting in New York, a new crew member cornered Helena.

"How's it going? Can I get you some water?" He reached for the cooler.

"Hot. Yes, thanks."

"Have you heard from your boyfriend recently?"

"What? Who? You mean Jasper?"

"No, the other one. Carlos."

"No. He's not my boyfriend anymore. How do you know him?"

"Family friend."

"I see. He disappeared off the face of the earth. I've moved on as you can see. Excuse me."

The man grabbed Helena by her wrist and leaned into her, the rim of his baseball cap banging into her forehead.

"Listen. If I find out you're lying, you'll be sorry…you read me?."

"Let me go. You're crazy. Stay away from me."

Helena walked over to the make-up chair for her refresher. Her knees were shaking, sweat dripping down her back and she was beginning to feel faint, in desperate need to sit and get misted with revitalizing rosewater. How did these people pop out of the woodwork with no warning?

Anxious about a reprisal , she looked around for Summer, but her friend was busy directing. There was never a moment Summer wasn't surrounded by people. She would have to wait until the end of the day. Touch-up completed, she walked around the set, looking for Fernando's snitch. She spotted him, working as a grip and snapped several pictures on her phone. He must have just been hired, because she hadn't noticed him the first week. From a distance, she observed who he interacted with. Was he the only mole? Jasper walked up behind her.

"How are you holding up in the heat? Can I get you a water bottle?"

"I'm fine. I just had one. Who hired the new grips? You or Ted?"

"Ted hires and fires. Why? Is something wrong?"

"I'm not sure. I'll let you know. I'm still on break. Want to get some iced coffee?"

"Sounds good. I could use a caffeine lift."

At the end of the day, Helena sent Casi and Summer the pictures she had taken using her secure phone. Casi texted back within minutes.

That man is Fernando's nephew, Angel. Fire him as soon as possible. He's shadowing you and wants to get an insider's view of the film content. Who hired him?"

Ted, but I'm sure he was unaware. She added a frowning emoji.

Tell Summer to get rid of him and watch your back. I bet he isn't working alone. Can you talk? Call me in fifteen minutes.

Yes.

When Helena called, Casi picked up on the first ring.
"*Hola, mi amor*. I miss you." His voice was soothing.
"Miss you more."
"How long has Angel been there? Has he bothered you before?"
"I think he's new on set. I've never noticed him. He threatened me today, asked if I heard from you. Of course, I said no. I think he was the guy who scared me in the restaurant in Summer's neighborhood. I'm not sure, though. He wears hats and sunglasses. Hard to tell."
"Make sure he doesn't go to Italy with you. Shall I contact Summer, or do you want to handle it?"
"Can you, please? I'm at the Crenston's home and can't talk that long."
"Ok."
"When am I going to see you and where? I really need to see you," Helena whispered.

"You're shooting in Italy through September, right?"

"Yes, last I heard. We're down to the last few days in New York. Then we have a two-week break, but I need to go home to Paris and take care of things before Italy. I'm not free until after the movie is done. October is the earliest I can meet."

"Ok. Keep me posted, and I'll book something. I won't be able to get away after October, so hopefully, there won't be any more delays. My busiest season is from November to March."

"Where shall we meet?"

"How does South America sound?"

"Good!"

"Ok, done. Let me try reaching Summer. Night, my love."

Sprawled on her bed in her underwear, Summer enjoyed a moment of pure bliss. Her air conditioner was cranked to high and she was wiggling her bare, sweaty toes in time to soft tunes on her ipad, drowning out the hum of New York city traffic. Her eyes fluttered between open and half shut. These hot days on location were draining her. Luckily, Hope was out getting food, giving her some much-needed time alone. Tonight she would eat, shower, and go to bed early in anticipation of another 4:30am wake-up call.

From the locked drawer in her desk, she heard her secure phone chime. Could she lift her tired bones off the bed? She leaned over to grab her cotton robe off the chair and felt around for the key in the pocket. Swinging her tired legs off the bed, she unlocked the drawer. The phone stopped ringing just as she got the drawer open. She looked at the screen and perused messages.

"Holy cow."

She quickly called Casi back. He picked up immediately. She said hello and let his comforting voice glide over her. "Hello, Summer, how've you been?"

"Good. I just saw your and Helena's messages. This is alarming news."

"It is. How is the filming going?" His voice soothed her.

"Good, I guess. We're all moving slower than molasses in this heat, but miraculously, we're almost done in New York. Hopefully, Italy will be less problematic. Who is Angel?"

"I hope so, for you. He's Fernando's nephew. Listen, you need to get rid of him and anyone hired with him. He's not only harassing Helena, he's watching your every move, checking out every scene you shoot, and undoubtedly trying to get his hands on a script for Fernando."

"Geez. There are only two full scripts on set, and one is always in my possession. Jasper has the other and he has strict instructions to never put it down. Standard procedure. The actors only get the scenes for the day in advance. Even so, this is scary. I'll make sure Angel doesn't go to Italy with us. We only have a few more days left in New York, so I don't know if we can make crew changes now. I'll talk to Ted, my producer."

"I remember Ted from Paris. What are your Italy dates?"

"We have a short break to pack and prepare, then we fly out after Labor Day, on September 5th. We'll be there for most of the month."

"Be very careful who you hire. I assume you're only taking a few people from New York?"

"All the important crew, who I know well, and the actors, of course. We already hired additional help in Italy. They're all union people."

"Still, everyone has a price. Be aware."

"Yeah, thanks, I'll try. I'll have to talk to Ted about screening people better. He hires and fires. I'm really oblivious to everyone who isn't an actor. It's hard to be on top of every detail. Impossible, really."

"I can imagine. How are you feeling?"

"Exhausted, but happy to be working. How about you, Casi? Are you well? Your sister?"

"All good here. Thanks."

Summer heard him pause as if he wanted to add something, but there was just lingering static.

"Goodnight, Summer. Get some rest. Good luck moving forward and call me if you have any other concerns."

"Thanks, Casi. I will." She hung up and tried to picture him at his beautiful restaurant. She wondered if he was happy there. He sounded content. Living on an island was like being in left field. Summer shifted her attention to the picture Helena sent of Angel. She barely remembered seeing the guy. Debating whether she should call Ted or speak to him in the morning, she decided she was too busy on set. Everyone wanted a piece of her there. She picked up the phone and called Ted.

"Ted, we need to talk. Are you alone?"

"Yes, thankfully. I'm in an air-conditioned room sipping a big glass of chilled rose. It's heavenly. What's up?"

"Don't ask me how I know, but we have a mole for Fernando Flores on set."

"Noooo. Are you kidding me? Who?"

CHAPTER LXXXVIII

Summer Trade Winds Shift at the Sea Grape Garden...but not the Arancini

Casi looked up at Camila over the rim of his wine glass. They were enjoying a peaceful dinner on the patio of their restaurant. A gentle trade wind brought welcome relief from the days' heat. The sun was setting, in a fiery blaze of spectacular colors and he was listening to the water gently lapping onto the shore. They both were lost in their own thoughts. The restaurant's happy hour crowd was slowly clearing out, and the more sedate dinner circle was arriving, but Camila and Casi paid little attention from their remote spot at the outer edge of the terrace. They were concentrating on sampling a new dish Matias had concocted, shredded lobster and mango *arancini* with a summer salad. After a busy day, it felt good to sit and enjoy a delicious meal, watching the silent fireworks on the horizon line, chatter and soft music relegated to the background.

Camila broke the silence. "Casi, there's something I've been meaning to ask you." She hesitated for a moment.

"What?"

"I'm not sure how to say this."

"Spit it out, Camila."

"I was thinking it may be time for me to give you some privacy and get my own apartment. Don't take this the wrong way. I'm really grateful for the roof over my head, and I do love living and working with you, but I think we both could benefit from privacy and our own space. What do you think?"

"Really? I haven't noticed. I like having you around. I don't have to worry about you when you're close."

"I wouldn't move far."

Casi sighed. "I knew I would have to loosen the reins a little at some point, but I didn't think it would be so soon. Can we check into an apartment in my building? Would that be acceptable?"

"I don't think I can afford that. I have money saved, but..."

"Don't be silly, Camila. We can afford it. I would feel so much better if I knew you were within reach."

"Are you sure? That would be nice."

"Yes, I'm sure. I'll check into it tomorrow. Let's see what's available. Does this have something to do with Stefano?"

"Maybe."

"I thought so. Just don't rush into anything, please?"

"I won't."

"So, I have something to discuss with you, too. I've been talking to Helena, and I would like to plan another trip with her. I was thinking of Brazil. Do you want to come for part of it? I would like you to meet her."

"Yes. When?" A smile spread over her lips.

"Sometime in early October. I also thought, if you want to do any plastic surgery, the doctor I used there is very good."

"I don't think so. Do you think I need it?"

"No. I'm just offering."

"What I would really like is a trainer who can teach me how to swim and help me be fitter like you."

"That's easy enough to do at the hotel. Do you want me to ask the lifeguards at the pool?"

"Yes. I'm too embarrassed to ask."

"No worries. I'll find the right person. I'll ask tomorrow morning when I go to the gym. Any other pending business?"

"How do you like the *arancini*?

"Not bad."

"Should we add it to the summer menu?"

"Not sure. Ask me tomorrow. Too many changes for one night."

"I think we should use it for a special themed night, but not on the regular menu."

"Agree. You tell Matias." Casi laughed deviously.

Camila smirked. "You stinker. We'll make it a special so Matias can try it out this weekend. He was so enthusiastic, I can't kill his spirit. Do you think Peter will be well enough to cover for us in October?"

"I certainly hope so. Maybe if Gracie helps? Let's see how he feels, but I think Jenny is capable enough."

"If Peter isn't well, I'll stay here, and you meet Helena alone."

"No, I really want you to come this time. I have to make a decision about Helena, and I want your input."

Camila eyed her brother. He sounded serious. "Sounds like a do or die decision."

"Maybe."

CHAPTER LXXXIX

Life Changes but only at a Snail's Pace, Please

"Morning Cyril. What are we starting with today?" Casi greeted the hotel's trainer, his regular work- out partner in the gym.

"Hey, Casi. Cardio?"

Casi looked around the gym. At 7am the place was still empty.

"How about we start with some yoga stretches, then cardio."

"Sounds good. I'll get the mats."

"Thanks."

"Before I forget, do you know a good swim teacher?"

"For children?"

"No, for an adult woman."

"Yeah, me. Who's the brave lady?"

"My sister. She never learned how to swim properly, and she's pretty embarrassed about it."

"No worries, man. You'd be surprised how many island people can't swim. I'll have her swimming in no time. I can work with her on my day off. This way she won't pay the hotel rate. Where does she live?"

"Here, with me."

"Oh, that makes it really easy. Give her my cell. We can figure out a good time."

"Perfect."

Casi stepped out of the shower. Wrapped in a towel, he trudged to the kitchen and grabbed a cup of Camila's freshly brewed coffee, adding a splash of milk. Granola and berries were his current morning favorite. He called the management office.

"Hi. Casimir Santos here. I was wondering if there are any condos for sale in my building?"

"Yes. Let me transfer you to Tiffany." Casi introduced himself again and briefed Tiffany on his apartment needs. When he hung up, he knocked on Camila's door. She opened it in her robe, coffee in hand.

"Morning. Good work out?"

"Yes. Cyril wants to teach you how to swim. Here's his cell. Call him to set up your first lesson. I fully trust him to be discreet. I also have Tiffany from the office coming in a few minutes. We're going to look at two apartments in the building. Hurry up and get dressed."

"Good God, you move fast. I'm showered. Be dressed in a few minutes."

"You didn't mention what size apartment you wanted. Is a one bedroom, ok?"

"Yes, more than ok."

Casi and Camila walked up a flight of stairs to 6D and waited for Tiffany. When she stepped off the elevator, they chatted briefly, then entered an empty apartment. Camila liked it instantly. The water view was spectacular and the apartment was freshly painted.

"What do you think?" Casi asked.

"It's great." Camila smiled. "How much is it?"

"The owner is asking 1,350,000."

"Oh my God! That's too much."

"The one downstairs is less," Tiffany suggested. "Let's take a look, shall we?" As they walked to the elevator, Casi whispered to Camila.

"Don't worry about the price yet. Let's find something you like first. Prices are always negotiable."

"Ok."

When they entered the apartment on the third floor, Camila circled attentively.

"This one might need a little work. What are they asking?"

"Nine hundred thousand. It's a little smaller than the one upstairs. The owner is very motivated to sell. He doesn't come to the island much anymore because his company transferred him to California. He used to live in Atlanta."

"Are there any offers on it?" Casi searched Camila's face as he asked Tiffany. Camila didn't look convinced.

"No, but it's generating interest with this recent price reduction, so don't wait too long if you like it."

"Thanks. We'll be in touch, Tiffany. Let me know if you get an offer or if anything else comes on the market under one million."

On the way to the restaurant, Camila called Cyril from the jeep. As the phone rang she turned to Casi.

"Stefano likes boats. He wants to take me out on the water. It's time for me to become a stronger swimmer."

"I could never get you into deep water growing up. You must really like this guy."

CHAPTER XC

Under the Campanian Sun...

The final days in New York were hectic. Ted fired Angel and two other men deemed questionable, the morning after Casi warned Summer. Despite being slightly short on manpower, they managed to muddle through and wrap as planned, which ensured that everyone had two weeks off to prepare for Italy. Ted wasted no time working his organizational magic. Summer realized she couldn't have gotten though the film prep without him. He, with Jasper's help, managed to organize and ship everything they needed to Italy, leaving early and arriving in time to receive all shipments.

In Italy, Jasper and Ted took care of the preliminary set up, shopping for staples, basic foods, and setting up drink deliveries. They confirmed hotel reservations, additional crew, rented a van and a truck with secure locks. Ted also made a point of introducing himself to all the immediate neighbors in Procida, the first place they were shooting. They, in turn, supplied the charming Americans with local resource tips. The friendly exchange resulted in a promise of being used as extras in the film. Ted left it up to Jasper to share this bribe with Summer.

He hoped if any concerns or problems arose, the neighbors would come to him first to troubleshoot. To his surprise, a group of women knocked on their door the next day with a proposal. For a modest fee, they offered to provide prepared foods daily for cast and crew. Why pay for expensive catering when they could do it better, they argued. Ted's instincts sent out distress signals, but he graciously agreed to try the arrangement. If the majority of his people were happy, it could work out just fine. He gave them a head count for the first three days and mentioned some diet restrictions.

Summer and her crew settled into their colorful rental house in Procida. Filming began the day after her arrival. While permits for outdoor locations were still being secured, the scenes in the Procida house could be shot without delay using the core crew from New York. Living and filming in the same location had its drawbacks, but luckily, all the shooting would center around the common areas and the outdoor terrace. The bedrooms were private and would thankfully remain so.

The group that arrived in Italy with Summer and Hope were the gaffers and sound technicians, hair and make-up and wardrobe. A handful of actors needed for the first scenes were also present and settled in a nearby hotel. The third and last group to arrive were the remaining actors who had been scheduled for the second week. Summer, Ted, Hope, and Hope's crew were staying at the house with the truck and equipment. Quarters were tight, but they made it work. Summer and Hope shared a bedroom, and Hope's crew shared another two bedrooms. Ted, in the double role of producer and production manager had his own bedroom since he needed a quiet place to organize and work.

The first day on set proved to be a challenge, but by the second day, a rhythm was in place. The food the neighbors delivered proved to be delightful, home-made Italian cooking. Everything was prepared with fresh ingredients, using local vegetables and fruits. The women set it up on outdoor picnic tables Ted had wisely set up along the garden fence, close to the gate. This kept outsiders away from the sets. The crew was thrilled. After the first food delivery,

Ted made a few minor adjustments for vegan and gluten-free diets, but the fare was so tasty and wholesome, everyone voted to keep the ladies in business for the duration of their stay. Ted paid the women each night in cash for their deliveries. To his surprise, different women showed up every day adding to the variety of dishes. One day, Summer staged the women chatting animatedly by the gate and filmed them. She promised to include the clip in her final version. Everyone was happy, and the ensuing smiles reached from Procida to Rome.

Make-up was done at the inn prior to arriving on set. A section of the house's living room served as a dressing and changing room behind make shift sheet dividers. A generator made sure the lights on set never failed. The only issue was bathrooms. There was only one guest bathroom. In an emergency, Ted offered up his bathroom to the core group. As a result, the occasional garden bush got watered, when the Italian ladies weren't looking. Summer knew this wasn't ideal, but she hoped the neighbors would turn a blind eye, since Ted also hired local gardeners to get the place back in order after they left.

Jasper, acting as co-producer and assistant director, stayed at the hotel in the mornings. He helped Ted manage actors' schedules, sending them to the set at Ted's prompt. Once the actors knew their schedules for the day, Jasper worked on set with Summer. All actors' concerns were directed to him, so Ted could focus on equipment, location permits, general paperwork and whatever else came up. Ted was accountable to the executive producer from the sponsoring studio. In New York, said producer had been on set, but not in Italy. They were flying solo here.

Dinner was provided in the hotel most nights, but people had the option of going out on their own dime. Few did. Since Jasper was located at the hotel he was also in charge of the pass van. He drove the actors back and forth when they were too tired to walk and ran the occasional errand for miscellaneous items. Everyone was deathly busy. While Summer, Ted and Jasper were in charge of the important aspects, they had hired enough crew to make life easier.

One night, over dinner at the Inn, Summer's eye traveled to Helena and Jasper, who were engrossed in what looked like an intimate conversation. Their eyes were locked, ignoring everyone around them. Summer was too far away to hear what they were saying, but she could detect a certain intimacy that made her nervous. Had this started in New York when Helena was staying at her family home with him? They were only at the beginning of their Italy adventure; there was no space for romance now. Jasper didn't know about Casi and Summer knew she couldn't tell him. She would have to talk to Helena. She didn't want her brother's heart to be broken. Damn, what was Helena thinking? Where did Helena stand with Casi? Did she still see their situation as insurmountable?

Summer's attention was diverted.

"Earth to Summer. Do you want some homemade strawberry *gelato* or *panna cotta* with plums for dessert?" Hope smiled and pointed at the waiter's tray laden with colorful ceramic bowls.

"Sorry. Strawberry *gelato* sounds like ecstasy right now."

"Jasper will drive us back to the house after dessert. I need to get to bed early tonight. I'm so fried. Good day of shooting, though."

"Yeah. I'm with you, Hope. Let me know when you want to go."

When Ted, Hope, and the lighting crew exited the van a short while later, Summer lingered to talk to Jasper. Opportunities to talk alone virtually never came up. People were everywhere.

"Hey, haven't had a chance to talk to you. How are things going over at the hotel?"

"Fine, so far. Nothing I can't handle. The biggest complaint is the Wi-Fi"

"Ted told everyone to get their own Wi-Fi. Did someone not listen?"

"Yeah. There are always those who don't, but we're working on changing that."

"How is Helena? Does she like her room?"

"I think so. She's on another floor, so I haven't seen it."

Summer was relieved to hear that.

"Listen, Jasper. I' m not sure where things are going between you two, but I wanted to give you a heads up. I know for a fact, Helena is still hoping to hear from Carlos, and when she does, she'll run to him. She told me as much. I'm just alerting you because I don't want you to be disappointed or get hurt when it happens."

"If it happens."

"I would wager a bet it will happen. They were very much in love, and I know she is still completely heartbroken over his disappearance. I think he's waiting until the dust settles to contact her. It would totally shock me if he didn't. Besides, I don't want any drama on my set." Summer peered at him over her shoulder.

"Ok. Noted." Jasper looked straight ahead at the steering wheel. "Summer, do you know something I don't?"

"Just be careful. I don't want you to be disappointed. Night, Jasper. Love you. You're doing an awesome job."

"Thanks. See you tomorrow."

CHAPTER XCI

Privacy for Camila Leads to Temptation for Casi

Casi was sitting in the office when his phone rang.

"Hi, Casi. It's Tiffany. A fabulous one-bedroom apartment on the 4rth floor is opening up and I would like to show it to you before it goes public. I think Camila will be pleased. Can you come today?"

"Sure. Let me check with her and I'll get back to you."

A short while later, Casi and Camila were standing in apartment 4F.

"The owner wants to sell quickly. He needs cash for a different investment. The apartment is move-in-ready. What do you think?"

"This is the same view as your apartment, Casi, only further down the beach. I love it." Camila gushed.

"Is the size good for you, Camila?

"Yes, it's bigger than my apartment in Mexico City. Is he selling it with the furniture? I kind of like it. Everything looks clean and new."

"I can ask. He didn't say. It isn't even officially on the market yet. We're still working out the details. If you're interested, leave an offer. Maybe we can do a quick turn around."

"I'll put in a cash offer for 755,000, furniture included. Let's see where that goes." Casi glanced at Camila and nodded. She was smiling from ear to ear.

"Ok, then. I'll let you know."

Two and a half weeks later, Camila was packing to move. Casi helped her carry her few belongings into the new apartment, early in the morning. The seller had come the day before to close and ship his personal items, his artwork and select costly electronics. He left all his cleaning products, so Camila rolled up her sleeves and got to work. The furniture and kitchen appliances had stayed, so she scrubbed them until they shone, lining all cabinets and drawers with wax paper. By lunchtime she was done. It took her one day to clean and unpack. Casi surprised her with a late lunch consisting of sandwiches and a celebratory bottle of champagne.

Camila was thrilled with her new home. The following night she invited Stefano over for dinner, her first official guest. Casi pretended to be hurt.

"Really, Camila? Shouldn't I get that honor?"

"You had the first lunch here, remember?"

"Yeah, and I brought it. Your generosity overwhelms me." They both broke into laughter.

Casi was sitting in his office, feeling blue. He hated coming home to an empty apartment, but of course he kept this sentiment to himself. Camila's excitement over having her own place was heartwarming to watch. She jabbered incessantly about all the things she was going to do to spruce it up. She and Stefano moved furniture around and set up a new flat screen TV. Oddly, Casi felt left out, like his opinion didn't matter. His thoughts were jolted back to reality when his phone rang.

"Hey, Casi. I have some bad news. You're not going to get rid of me yet. My doctor cleared me to come back to work. My treatment was successful and I got a good report."

"Wow, Peter, that's fabulous! I hate to admit it, but I've missed you around here. Camila just moved out, to another apartment in my building. I was starting to feel seriously abandoned."

"Really? Well, pretty boy, my ugly mug is coming back. I'll see you tomorrow, so stop moping."

"Great. I needed to hear that." Casi felt a shift in his mood. His spirits lifted, even more, that evening. It was Friday night and the restaurant was busy. Weekenders were arriving for happy hour and early dinner, many coming directly from the airport- one of them was Rose.

"Hey, Casi, I'm here for a few days. What's cooking?" She hugged him and he felt a warm rush. Damn, she looked good in fitted jeans.

"Welcome back, Rose. Great to see you. Can I get you a drink? We made a batch of fresh peach sangria tonight."

"Ooh, sounds delicious. I'm in."

"How long are you here for?"

"I'm staying through Tuesday. The past few weeks have been exceptionally hectic in the office. I worked through a couple of weekends, so my boss gave me a few extra days. I'm so happy to be back."

"I have to work tonight and tomorrow, but maybe we can have dinner Sunday night?"

"Sure, that would be nice. Any time for the beach?"

"No, not this weekend. My manager was out sick, and my sister just moved, so I have to cover all shifts, but now things will ease up. Did you come alone?"

"Yes. I just want to relax, lie by the pool, and swim in the ocean. I need some R&R."

"Cheers to that." He clinked glasses with her and chatted for a few more minutes. "Hey, I'll check back with you in a bit. I have some things to take care of. Don't distract my patrons too much with that irresistible smile of yours." Was he flirting with her? He must be seriously lonely.

Rose laughed. "You're the only one I want to distract, Casi."

Ok, now she was flirting with him. His thoughts wandered into dangerous territory.

Sunday night, Casi and Rose enjoyed an intimate, candle-lit dinner in a new restaurant, catching up on their respective lives.

"I'm still getting used to Camila moving out. What really hurts is she's so openly happy about it. I thought she would miss me."

Rose laughed. "We all love you, Casi, but girls like to have their own space. It's where we primp, sulk and do whatever we need to do alone. Don't hold it against her."

"She hasn't even come back to visit." Casi feigned a mournful expression.

"Oh, grow up. She has a boyfriend, doesn't she? She needs a little space from her overprotective brother."

"Right." Casi smiled and changed the subject. "A little more wine?"

After dinner, they strolled around the lit gardens and boardwalk of the Atlantis resort. Rose took Casi's hand, and for the first time, he let it be. The contact felt good and somehow, he couldn't bring himself to withdraw. Back at the Baha Mar, he invited her in for a nightcap, knowing full well he was getting himself into trouble, but for once, Helena was not on his mind. She hadn't answered his calls in over a week. What exactly was she doing in Italy?

Early the next morning, Casi opened the blinds and turned on the shower, leaving Rose to languish in his comfy sleigh bed with the spectacular ocean view. When one of his phones rang from inside his nightstand, Rose hesitated briefly, then opened the drawer. She reached over and picked it up.

"Hello? Long distance static attacked her ear.

"Hello?" After a long, silent pause, the person hung up.

CHAPTER XCII

Italian 'Bella Figura' Mesmerizes the Cast

Following two blissful, well-organized weeks in Procida, Summer was ready to film in Naples. They decided to keep the house in Procida as their home base. It was easier and safer to have their expensive equipment all in one place, in their driveway. Besides, given their established neighborly relationships, they now enjoyed a protected status on the island. However, the actors were relocated to the hotel in Naples, Ted had booked. Hair and make-up, wardrobe and all gaffers also relocated to Naples. All continued to work from a hotel room, while Jasper's suite was used for prop storage. The hotel provided breakfast, lunch, and finger food daily, but the food was a far cry from the neighbors' meals in Procida. Everyone had been royally spoilt. At night, the group was on their own in the narrow, cobble stone streets of Naples.

The difference between shooting at the house in Procida and in Naples was substantial. Naples was stressful and by the third day, they realized numerous things were inexplicably missing. Extra people had to be hired to protect the equipment and props and the truck had to be locked when no one was standing guard. There were always unknown shadows lurking where they shouldn't be, and Jasper and Ted couldn't cover all territories with the few men they had available. Security was increased, and even more difficult, had to be trusted. In Naples, everything needed to be nailed down. There were pickpockets everywhere, and minor thefts happened daily. Crowd control situations also arose, but Summer was oblivious to it all. Her focus was laser sharp, on the job at hand. She plowed through her agenda and scenes with complete precision, surrounded by a protective group who had her back. She couldn't be bothered with petty theft problems. She had men to handle that.

Once the additional, local security was put in place, miraculously, stuff stopped disappearing. What still made things challenging though was the oppressive mid-day heat. The actors' make-up had to be refreshed several times a day and all organic props were bought in triples, but everyone adjusted without complaining too much. Jasper and Ted worked around the clock to make this happen. Summer and Hope were thankful for the ability to concentrate on the important things without disproportionate distraction.

One night, after an especially long day, cast and crew had dinner together in Naples while security guarded the truck and van. The restaurant owner, Luciano, who personally took their orders, chatted boastfully about his recent truffle purchase.

"They come from Alba. It's the real thing, I assure you. Today we made a fresh *tagliolini* with butter, parmesan and white truffles. You will think you died and went to heaven, I promise you." He gestured by gathering his fingers together at the tips and kissing them loudly with his pursed lips. "I also made a fresh burrata with tomatoes and basil."

"That sounds delicious," Jasper replied. "What do you think, guys?"

"Yeah, let's get a few different pastas and share. We could use comfort food for energy; fuel for tomorrow. It will be another marathon day," Summer concurred. She looked around the table and saw nods of approval. When Luciano came back with their wine order, she invited him to sit at the table.

"Luciano, tell us about the truffles. How did you get them?"

"Ahhh, it's not easy to get truffles, especially the white variety. My brother lives up north and hunts for them, but it's become a difficult business. Last year, his best truffle-sniffing dog was poisoned. He cried like a baby when he told me. He didn't know if it was something the dog ate or drank, so now he carries water for himself and the dog when they hunt. He also puts a muzzle on the dog, so he can't eat anything unchecked. The competition to find the best and largest truffles is intense, but my brother is one of the best. He's a chef, too. Has his own restaurant, like me. Once in a while, he sends me some truffles in an air-tight overnight container. You're lucky you picked tonight to come here."

"Truffle hunting sounds like a difficult trade. I can't wait to try them. Thanks for sharing your story."

After the food arrived and Luciano was up to date on the movie being shot in his hood, he left the table and disappeared through swinging doors. The oohs and ahhs were probably heard in the far corners of the kitchen, where Luciano was scheming over his next dish. The truffle pasta was amazing. When Luciano reappeared, he brought a plate of *cannoli.*

"This is a Sicilian recipe from my grandmother. It's made with pistachios. Try them. It's better than sex," he laughed deviously.

"They look amazing. Dinner was delicious, Luciano. Thank you for both the meal and the truffle education. We'll definitely be back." Summer smiled. She was so tired, even smiling took an extraordinary effort. Now all she wanted was a soft bed, but she still had to commute to Procida.

The next morning, everyone slept in. They regrouped at nine to shoot until dusk. Summer noticed a mood change in Helena. Most days, Helena tried to stay close to Summer, but yesterday at dinner she sat at the other end of the table from Jasper and her. Today she was particularly withdrawn. Helena's moods were generally transparent, easy to decipher. She was literally the dead opposite of Casi's poker face. Perhaps that was what the man loved about her - she was endearingly genuine. When Summer got home that night, she checked her safe phone to see if Casi had called, but there was no message.

"Did something happen with Casi or Jasper," she thought out loud?

Too tired to give it further thought, she fell into bed. Before dropping into a long, exhausted slumber, Summer resolved to keep an eye on Helena.

CHAPTER XCIII

Goodbye to Naples and Helena's Confusion

By week three in Italy, everyone was feeling the strain of long hours on set. Summer and Hope were tireless, attacking every new day with close to the same enthusiasm, but everyone else was showing serious wear. Helena, usually perky, was wilting, her head drooping like a peony after a rain storm. Summer was worried about her. Jasper and Ted worked without pause, organizing daily schedules, and confirming and clearing locations as required, but they were fatigued too. There was one more week to get through before wrapping and Summer hoped they would conquer it without incident.

Over an intimate dinner, with Helena, Hope, Jasper and Ted, Summer noticed Helena flirting with Jasper. Her brother was clearly flattered, finding it hard to resist Helena's charms, which alarmed Summer. When Helena got up to go to the ladies' room, she followed, trying to casually chit-chat. After hand washing, she pulled Helena aside outside the loo.

"Listen, Helena, I'm not sure where this is going with Jasper, and normally, it wouldn't be my business, but in a director's capacity, I want to make two things crystal clear. One, no drama or involvements on my set until we are completely done shooting, and two, don't hurt my brother. He doesn't know and shouldn't know, about Casi. He genuinely cares for you and thinks you're unattached. If you're still pining for Casi, don't break my brother's heart."

"Casi cheated on me," Helena blurted out. "I don't know where we stand anymore. I'm confused. I truly like Jasper."

"Are you sure about that? I know Casi loves you."

"A woman answered his phone the other morning. I called his house early, knowing he wouldn't be at work yet."

"I believe you, and I'm truly sorry to hear that, but maybe you should consider resolving this first before you hurt someone else. A one-night stand is fine if you want revenge sex, but not with my brother, who truly cares for you. He deserves better. Did you even speak to Casi after that phone call?" Summer watched Helena squirm for words.

"No…not yet. I am still in shock, trying to decide what to do."

"Talk to him, Helena."

"Fine, Summer. I hear you." Summer let Helena stalk off in a huff. She didn't regret her warning. In fact, she felt good about it. Jasper was vulnerable and she wasn't going to let anyone mess with her brothers, especially not on her set, when she was their paycheck. Blood was thicker than water, no matter how sweet the water. Sometimes being the bitch suited her just fine. A whole movie studio depended on and trusted her. She was determined to deliver a better than excellent product. She expected the same professionalism from her cast and crew.

The next morning Helena came to the set with a new attitude. Now, Jasper seemed confused. For Summer, it was business as usual.

CHAPTER XCIV

The Morning After Pill is Hard to Swallow

The minute Casi woke up, he regretted his night with Rose. While it was a fun, satisfying experience, he didn't feel more than lust and warm friendship for her. His heart belonged to Helena, until she kicked him to the curb. As long as there was hope, he wouldn't give up on a future that included her. He seriously regretted his actions. How could he have been so stupid?

While in the shower, he wondered how he could disengage himself from Rose without hurting her feelings. He needed to undo his 'mistake', pronto. Rose lived too close for him to just walk away. This needed to be handled with care. Man, did he dread doing that. He wanted to bolt. He cursed himself for messing things up. In the past, he always left women before things got too heavy. Helena was the exception in his life. He didn't want to lose Rose as a friend and amicable neighbor, now that he was sprouting roots. He genuinely liked her. This definitely needed to be fixed before it went any further. Letting the warm water stream down his chiseled, tension-filled back, he contemplated his next move. He was in unchartered territory and felt lost at sea.

Behind his desk, at the restaurant, he had difficulty concentrating.

"What's wrong with you today? You look like you have trapped gas." Camila studied him critically.

"Nothing." He kept his eyes averted.

"I know that face. That is not nothing. What's wrong?" she persisted.

"I made a mistake last night. Rose stayed over." This was not a secret he could contain for long. His sister knew him too well.

"You did what? Now, what are you going to do? She's not going to let go easily, and we both live there. How awkward! Clearly, you weren't thinking with the right body part," Camila spouted, emphasizing every word with her racing hand gestures. "I move out and look what happens. *Oh, Dios mio.*" Her hands circled in the air and paused briefly on her hips.

"I know, I know. I was lonely and she was doing her best to seduce me."

"Alright, alright. Enough information. I'm staying out of this. This is your mess, so deal with it. Serves you right for cheating. When is she leaving?" Camila was back to waving her hands around.

"In two days."

"Good. You better talk to her before she leaves. Hopefully, time apart will help. I sure hope I don't run into her in the elevator. Does she know about your upcoming trip with Helena?"

"Stop. I'll deal with it."

"You better," she warned. "The last thing we need is a vindictive woman in our building. Really, what were you thinking? Wait. Let me answer that. You weren't." Camila shook her head in disgust, her hands back on her hips. "So, let's talk shop now. Can you look over my supply order and see if there's anything I'm missing, or is your brain complete mush?"

"It's working fine today, thank you. Let's see your order." No one dared talk to him like that, except his sister and right now she was on fire.

Thankfully, the rest of the day, Camila was busy. Casi noticed she chose to have lunch with Matias and the kitchen crew out back, instead of him. He overheard her, discussing kitchen orders with Matias. After lunch, she wordlessly handed him another list.

Casi waited to eat lunch with Peter who was arriving for the afternoon and evening shift.

"Hey, how are you feeling? Come sit down." Casi stood and gave him a hug.

"Hi, man. I missed being here. Place looks good."

"No big changes. Only little ones and I kept you up to date on those. Lunch?"

"I already ate with Gracie, thank you. She insisted. The last time she fussed this much over me, we were on our honeymoon. It feels good to be out of the house."

Casi laughed. "Be thankful. You have a good woman."

"I know, and I am. So what's new with you?"

"Funny, you should ask. I could use some advice."

Peter's eyebrows shot up. This was a first.

CHAPTER XCV

Don't Go Breaking My Heart.....

Casi left work before the dinner shift and invited Rose over for a drink. Sipping strawberry margaritas on his terrace, he broached the subject, thinking honesty would be the best policy. Without mincing words, he told her he wanted to backtrack and go back to being friends.

"Really, Casi? I thought we were friends first and took our friendship to the next level? Did I miss something here? Do something wrong? I thought the sex was incredible."

"We did take our friendship a step further, but we shouldn't have. I haven't been entirely honest with you. I'm still emotionally involved with someone long distance and I'm not ready to give up on that relationship, even though it's on shaky ground. She has to live elsewhere for work and it's been really hard on us. We only see each other every few months. Honestly, the relationship may not survive. It appears to be dying a slow and painful death, but I realized this morning, I'm not ready to let go yet. Forgive me, Rose."

"Well... I have to say, you came to that conclusion conveniently late. It doesn't make me feel particularly good. Why didn't you share that pearl earlier?"

"I'm sorry, Rose. Really! I value your friendship and had no intention of hurting you."

Rose sprung up angrily. "Right now, I'm very disappointed with you. We'll see where things go from here. See you around, Casi." She bolted for the door. Casi got up to follow, but she moved so fast, the door slammed shut in his face. He knew she was upset, but he sighed with relief that it was over and done. He could only hope that Rose would be mature enough to let it go.

Smoothing things over with Helena was a lot more complicated. He saw she called earlier and left no message. When he called her back, he received a punishing earful, which he humbly accepted. It surprised him that Rose had picked up his phone, thus causing irreparable damage. Over several lengthy late-night phone calls in which he prostrated himself, he managed to calm Helena down. The final conciliatory call was from his office, one morning. He checked into traveling to Brazil for their fall trip and wanted her to know he was moving forward with booking their next vacation.

"Please come to Brazil. I think what we need is time together to set things right again."

"I don't know if that's even possible. I feel like we're drifting apart. You have a whole life I know nothing about, and the distance is killing us. So is my imagination. Clearly, it's justified."

"Helena, I know our situation isn't normal or easy, but I do love you, and I want to make this right. I need you to come and spend time with me. It isn't easy for me to get away because I'm working hard, putting in long days, trying to build something good. I'm creating an honest future, I'll be proud of, and hopefully, you will too."

"Don't change the subject, Casi. You may be working hard, but your nights are free enough, or a woman wouldn't have answered your phone early in the morning. Was it Rose, Casi?"

"Helena, I already explained what happened. I'm sorry. It was a one-time mistake, and I regret it. The woman means nothing to me. If you were here, it would never have happened. You know that. I never cheated on you in Paris. I was horny and lonely one night and she was there."

"So what you're saying is, you can't be true to me when I'm not with you. How is that a functioning long-distance relationship? You're telling me with your actions, that long-distance love doesn't work for you. Ever heard of massage oil? Why should I still trust you?"

"Please, let's talk in person. I want to send you a plane ticket. Give me another chance. We're good together, and that is a rare thing to find. If you decide differently after this trip, I'll respect that, but give me another chance. It is my only infraction."

"I don't know, Carlos... I mean Casi. I don't even know who you are anymore. Or maybe I never knew to begin with. This might just be too complicated for me. Too many lies. Too much deception. Too many secrets. I need more clarity and honesty. You lost my trust."

"Do you still love me?"

"Yes, I will always love you, but that doesn't mean I can make this long-distance thing work. I want more, and I need transparency. You keep breaking my heart. You cheat, you disappear, and you don't share. Pretty soon, there will be no heart left to break. You are chipping away at the foundation of our love. For me, love and trust go hand-in-hand. There is no true love, without complete trust. You destroyed that."

"You know the reasons for my silence. It's always been for your safety. Let's talk in Brazil. Don't give up on us yet. I haven't. I refuse to. I know I made a mistake and I'm sorry."

"How many mistakes?" Helena sighed and waited. He didn't reply. "Ok... I'll come. I've always wanted to see Brazil. If nothing else, we'll have a nice vacation, but I'm making no promises. You hurt me, Casi."

"Thank you. I'll send you a ticket." Casi was exasperated and tired. He'd never dealt with relationship fiascos like this before. It was exhausting. He also never had to beg. He was always the one to call the shots, the one who broke hearts. However, Helena had the power to break his heart. They were hurting each other. He cursed at himself for compromising his relationship with her. He knew he would never find another Helena. Maybe there would be other women he could love, but not like Helena. She was his soul mate. He disconnected the phone and hung his head between his hands. He was in the same position minutes later, when Camila walked in.

"So, is your love life back in order?" she asked harshly.

"Who knows? Helena agreed to meet me in Brazil, but she's angry and hurt. I'm an idiot for screwing this up. I can't lose her, Camila. I want you to meet her this time. You're still coming for a week, right?"

"Yes, but no fighting in front of me. I want to enjoy Rio, not be a mediator. You have to promise me that."

"I promise. There'll be no fighting. I plan to fix this."

CHAPTER XCVI

Sounds of Brazil....Including the Dark, Unpredictable Side

Casi and Camila touched down in Brazil's Galeao-Antonio Carlos Jobim International Airport in the last week of September.

"I can't believe I'm really here," Camila gushed happily.

"Welcome to Rio de Janeiro." Casi hugged his sister and smiled. "What do you want to see first?" They were waiting for their luggage at the carousel.

"The Christ statue on Corcovado Mountain."

"That should be easy. What else?"

"The famous Ipanema Beach."

"That'll be even easier. Our hotel is on the beach."

"I'll be completely happy then. Look, our bags are here."

The next morning after breakfast, Casi rented a driver for the day and took his sister on a private city tour. They visited Sugar Loaf Mountain, a few museums, and consumed a late lunch by the beach. Completely exhausted, they had dinner in the hotel and went to sleep early. The next day they took a wildlife tour, returning to the hotel in the late afternoon. The third and last day alone, they hit the beach. They left before it got dark around 4pm. It was the start of winter in Rio de Janeiro and it got dark early. The temperatures dipped at night.

On day four, Helena was due to arrive. By that time, Casi had his sister up to speed on everything Helena. He was wondering how their first meeting would transpire. Over breakfast, Camila offered a solution that gave him the space he needed.

"I think I'll rest by the hotel pool this afternoon and give you some time alone. Today appears to be the warmest day yet, close to 80 F. I plan to enjoy it. You need to smooth things over before I meet her. If you want, I'll meet you both for dinner later. Just give me an hour's notice to clean up. If not, breakfast tomorrow is fine. Take the night to get your relationship back on track."

"Ok, thanks. That might be a better idea. I have some fences to mend, and it may take twenty-four hours."

"Good, I want no part of that."

"Understood. I'll text you in the morning."

Casi was waiting in his room when Helena arrived. She looked tired but happy to see him. However, there was a measure of restraint in her greeting. He was relieved she walked into his open hug, because the last thing he wanted was friction from the start. He knew they needed to talk, but he was hoping they could ease into it. Closing the door, he pulled her into his arms, holding her tight. He stroked her hair and whispered in her ear. "I'm so happy you're here. Thanks for agreeing to come. I think we need this time together."

Helena sighed. "*Bonjour,* Casi. That was most definitely the longest flight I have ever taken. Twelve hours! I was so happy to get off the plane this morning." Helena wiggled out of his embrace and looked into his eyes. "I guess I'm happy to see you, too." She touched his face with the palm of her hand, making his body react.

"Did you manage to sleep at all?" He looked at her with empathy, feeling warmth spreading through his lower regions.

"A little. Let me freshen up, unpack a few things, and then maybe we can walk around and have lunch?"

"Sure, no rush." He watched her open her suitcase. "I have a surprise. You always wanted to know more about my past, so I brought my sister. She'll be here for the first few days. You can ask her whatever you want."

"Really?" Helena stopped what she was doing and smiled. "You brought Hermosa? I can't wait to meet her."

"One more thing. We had to change her identity too. Her name is Camila now."

"Casi and Camila. Ok. Where is she?"

"She has some things to do today. We'll meet her for breakfast tomorrow."

"Oh, good. That will give us some time to catch up… and talk."

Casi nodded. He was so glad to see her, but he sensed a shift in their relationship. In the past their reunions started passionately. Today there was a careful distance. He began to worry if he could swing things back to where they once were. His feelings hadn't changed. The long gaps and the incident with Rose had damaged their bond and he was perceptive enough to realize that. She was hurt, insecure and he wasn't sure how to fix it or how to earn her trust again. He planned to fight for another chance. His one night of pleasure with Rose had life- changing consequences. Once again, he understood how one poor choice could change your destiny forever.

CHAPTER XCVII

Vacation Pleasure Takes a Wicked Turn

Casi and Helena spent the first night talking and making love. Their emotions ran the gamut from intense anger to conciliatory cries, but not one of these moments could have been skipped. It was a process. By the time Helena fell asleep in his arms, they were both emotionally spent.

When they arrived in the hotel's breakfast room, Camila was seated in a secluded corner, by the window, not far from the kitchen doors, ensuring a degree of privacy. Her handbag was on the chair next to her, facing the entrance. When she saw Casi, she motioned him to take that seat. Casi smiled. His sister, forever thoughtful, understood his needs.

Preceding Helena's arrival, Casi had briefed his sister on what Helena knew about her. She knew Hermosa had fled Mexico City after the earthquake and become Camila, but she didn't know under what circumstances. Casi opted to keep those operations vague. Camila and he had agreed on what Helena could know. He hoped his sister wouldn't perjure herself.

"Hello, Helena. How lovely to finally meet you!" Camila rose from her seat and warmly embraced Helena. "I have a little welcome gift for you. My brother is so happy you came, and so am I." She handed Helena a small, colorful gift bag, overflowing with colorful tissue paper.

"Hi, Camila. I've heard so much about you. It's nice to meet you, too. Thank you for the welcome gift. That's so thoughtful. I have something for you, too, from Paris. I'm happy to be able to give it to you in person." Helena handed Camila a small box with a card attached. She had brought both Camila and Casi a new scent. "Shall I open my gift now?"

"Yes, please do."

Helena peeked in her bag and pulled out a beautiful ocean blue, sheer beach cover up.

"Oh, this is beautiful, Camila! Thank you so much!"

"Casi showed me pictures of you. I thought it would look nice with your blue eyes."

"I love it." Helena got up and hugged Camila.

Casi sat back and watched the love fest. He could see that both women were making a concerted effort. He couldn't yet gauge how they really felt and he was nervous. He wanted the two most important women in his life to like each other, but some things were out of his control. It had to happen organically. The only thing he could control was the setting. Conversation flowed easily through breakfast, and when they were almost done, he interjected, "Before they kick us out, what would you ladies like to do today?"

"A city tour maybe?" Helena looked back and forth between the two of them.

"Let's do it. Casi, maybe we can ask for the same driver? He could mix it up for us, so we don't take the exact same routes, but still cover the main attractions for Helena."

"Smart thinking, Camila. I have his card. How about a boat tour of Guanabara Bay tomorrow? I need to book it in advance if you like the idea. I spoke to the concierge and he also recommends the day trip to Buzios, a former fishing village. I have the brochure, so you can decide. It's a two plus hour bus ride, though."

"The boat ride sounds wonderful. Sitting through a two-hour bus ride isn't so appealing at this moment. I'm still getting over the plane ride. Camila?"

"I agree. No long bus rides. There's enough to do here in Rio."

"Ok, then. I'll meet you girls in the lobby in a half hour? Get what you need from the room, and we're off."

The next few days were spent harmoniously on a boat tour, a hike to Vista Chinese in the Tijuca Forest National Park, and a tour of the beaches in the ecological reserve of Juatinga. At night, they took in a Samba performance and a few pubs in Ipanema. On Camila's last day, the girls went shopping while Casi caught up on emails. Her last night, they did a pub crawl in Lapa with Casi not drinking much and the girls getting tipsy. When Camila left for the airport the next morning, he was happy about how their time together had been spent. He escorted Camila to the taxi, hoping for some feedback, but she shook her head.

"Let's talk when you get home. I'm still processing my impressions. Please be aware of your security for the rest of the trip."

"I will. Text me when you land. Peter is picking you up. If there are any delays, he'll know. He has your flight information."

"Thanks. I had a wonderful vacation. Come home safely." She hugged him and got into the waiting taxi. Casi was frustrated she hadn't shared her thoughts, but he knew she couldn't be swayed.

A couple days later, Casi took Helena back to Leblon for some final souvenir shopping in the late afternoon. She wanted to get a gift for Summer and one or two others. While she browsed in and out of stores, Casi checked his messages and looked around at the crowds. It was close to dinner time and they had no reservation, so they chose a lively restaurant in the nearby *Ipanema* area on Rua

Visconde. The meal was served on beautiful colorful plates that reminded Casi of Fernando's factory. Lingering over coffee, Casi noticed a group of men enter. One of them looked uncomfortably familiar. His heart froze. He leaned over to Helena.

"Listen carefully, and don't argue or ask questions," he whispered. "Please walk to the door, keeping your head down, and go straight back to the hotel. Text me when you get there and don't leave the room. Lock the door and don't open it for anyone, regardless of what they may say. Do you understand me?"

She stared at him, searching, then nodded. He was sweating.

"Are you coming too?"

"I will pay and come, but I want you gone before I move. I see someone I know from Mexico. Please, go. Pack your suitcase and get ready to leave. Now!"

Clearly frightened by his serious demeanor, Helena put on sunglasses, scooped up her shopping bags and left unnoticed. Casi sat silently for a few minutes debating what to do. First, he needed to give her a head start. Perhaps he could slip out unnoticed too. He looked at the other men, but only recognized the one. Since the waiter was a no show, he put on his fedora and walked to the bar to pay, pulling out a wad of cash. As he waited for the bill, a hand forcefully slammed down on the bar beside him. Casi kept his head down. He noticed a prominent gold lion's head ring with ruby eyes on pudgy, squat fingers. He recognized Fernando's ring. It dawned on him why the restaurant's ceramics had looked so familiar. It was *Corazon de Leon* pottery!

"One beer over here," the voice next to him bellowed.

Casi recognized Felipe's voice. His mind raced. Did Felipe recognize him? Why was he here and why was he wearing Fernando's favorite ring? Where was Fernando? Good Lord, how he had dreaded this day. The waiter finally came and he paid without talking or lifting his head, leaving a generous tip. He walked to the door. A text came confirming Helena was safely in the room. He hoped he would get there without incident. When he exited the restaurant, the streets were crowded. He stopped to look around for a moment. Not seeing any familiar faces anywhere, he started walking past the side alley of the restaurant, where Felipe, who had exited through the kitchen, was waiting.

"*Hola,* Carlos. I thought that was you."

Casi didn't reply.

"I mean you no harm, I swear." He placed his hand on his heart. "I just want to talk. No one else recognized you, but I would know that walk anywhere. We spent too many years in close quarters."

"What do you want, Felipe? Is Fernando here, too?" Casi's face stiffened, poker muscle memory kicking in.

"Fernando is dead. His nephews are home, running for the cartel. I'm here on *Corazon de Leon* business. I swear. I'm staying at the Sheraton Grand Rio Hotel. Meet me there tomorrow morning at five. Room 313. We can talk privately before the others wake up. There's so much I want to tell you. Trust me, this is information you'll want. Please, Carlos."

"I won't meet you at your hotel, but I'll meet you at six in the Fairmont lobby."

"See you then. You know, you can trust me, Carlos. I have always had your back. Nothing has changed."

Casi nodded and turned to walk in the opposite direction of his hotel. When he was certain no one was following him, he turned back toward his room at the Miramar. Helena pounced on him as soon as he opened the door, clinging to him like a barnacle on a fishing boat until he pried her loose. He could feel her heart racing.

"What happened? I was so scared." Round wavering pools searched his face.

"I can't get into it right now. Please just do what I say. We're going to pack and leave early in the morning. Let me work on getting us flights out of here. Give me your ticket."

"Here, my ticket and passport. I already packed all my things. Shall I pack yours?"

"Yes." Casi sat down with his laptop and checked flight schedules out of Galeao. After a concentrated search, he booked two seats on a flight to Trinidad/Tobago, leaving at 11:30am. He wanted to leave earlier, but there was nothing that made sense. It was frustrating how few flights there were. Even fewer flew non-stop. Most direct flights went to major cities in South America and Europe.

"We are flying to Trinidad tomorrow. I would like you to leave here with our suitcases at 8am. I'll meet you at the airport. I'll take my own hand luggage. If anything goes wrong and I don't come, get on the flight, anyway. I want you safely out of here. I'll be in touch with further instructions. Now, let's get some rest. I have an early morning meeting."

"Meeting? With whom? I don't want to leave without you!"

"You won't have to. However, in the unlikely event that you do, either I or Camila will be in touch. Don't worry. I booked us a nice hotel in Tobago. It's right on the beach. I'll email you the details.

"Do you have to go to this meeting? Can't we just leave now?"

"No. I need to do this. I'm hoping it will give me some much-needed closure. Please, let's not talk about this right now. I need a clear head. Relax. Trust me. Go get ready for bed. We have a long travel day ahead, but at least you'll be closer to Paris. Your flight home will be substantially shorter."

"Casi, I'm scared. Is this what life with you will always be like?"

"I hope not. That's why I'm going to this meeting. I want to strike a deal."

CHAPTER XCVIII

Fernando's Legacy is Casi's Salvation

At 5:45am, Casi was seated in a remote corner of the Fairmont hotel lobby with two takeout coffees. Ten minutes later, Felipe appeared, alone. His face lit up when he spotted his former friend. Casi handed him his brew.

"Thanks." He took a sip. "Just the way I like it. I'm happy you came. I've thought about you a lot in recent months. So much has happened. I think I'll be able to give you some peace."

"How is that, Felipe? What happened to Fernando?" Casi clipped, poker face in place.

"Well... first things first. Let me start with Fernando's return to Tampico. He left Barcelona on a private plane as you may know, but he was completely shaken when he realized Jose didn't make it out. He blamed himself for telling Jose to get the extra stuff in the safe, including the antique ceramics. In fact, he never got over it. The guilt was killing him. He came up with all kinds of hairbrained schemes to break Jose out of jail, but we talked him out of all of them. Can't dig a tunnel in Barcelona without someone noticing." He laughed. "Can't say I miss Jose, that twisted piece of shit."

Casi nodded but said nothing.

"When Fernando realized that you weren't coming back, things went downhill fast. At first, he concentrated on the ceramics business, but he was so rattled about Jose rotting in jail and you betraying him, he started drinking a lot. He always liked to party, but this was really excessive. He was chasing every pretty skirt around town and got himself into trouble a few times when he hit on girls already taken. At first, I said nothing, hoping it would pass, but then he started making bad business decisions, so he and I had it out one night." Fernando paused.

"Another night, after we fought, he calmed down long enough to tell me what things were really like in Europe. He was so impressed with how you handled the financials. He trusted you, and he couldn't believe or understand why you didn't come back. It hurt him to his core. That I know for sure."

Casi remained silent and nodded again. When he said nothing, Felipe continued.

"About a year after he got back, he started to get tired of running around. It was taking its toll. One night at a birthday party, he met Ariela and they hit it off. She got pregnant pretty quickly and he decided to marry her. He really was crazy about her in the beginning. I was surprised he chose to settle down. I thought he had finally turned the corner, you know, matured. However, I was wrong." Felipe paused and sipped his coffee. "Soon Fernando was back to partying on his boat with his posse. They partied with other women and drank too much. He should have been home with his pregnant wife, but he didn't care. One night, they hit another boat full force and he catapulted overboard. No one was wearing life vests, of course. The others were too busy saving their sorry asses. They managed to hold onto the capsized boat until help came, but Fernando drowned. He was knocked unconscious on impact, and they couldn't find him in the dark, or so they said. They were all drunk and injured with broken bones. His child was born after the accident. Ariela had a girl, Arianna. They live with her parents now, but I help her financially. She works for me in the factory."

"That's decent of you. You were always the kind-hearted brother. I'm sorry about Fernando. When did he die?" Casi briefly locked eyes with Felipe before sweeping the lobby again.

"Thank you. He was doomed to self-destruct. He died recently, about a month ago." Felipe paused and shook his head. "You know, Carlos, I appreciated you putting the apartment in Monaco in a corporate account linked to me. I was able to sell it and get the money out. It helped make up for our other losses. I don't have to tell you that moving drugs is a capital- intensive business. Bribes are the biggest expense on the books, but they're necessary and keep us alive day to day."

"Good. The money from the apartment was meant for you. I'm glad you got it. Who is doing your books now?"

"Me, for the ceramics business. I learned from the best." He stopped to wink at Casi. "Julio and Lois for the other business. I'm not so sure they were paying the same attention to your work. They fight a lot. I stay out of it, though. I am strictly ceramics only. That business is still flourishing, Thank God. That's all I care about."

"Good for you, Felipe."

"You were also smart to pay off the cartel on that last shipment the day you left. I convinced Fernando not to tell them you took a large chunk of money with you. At first, Fernando was relieved you transferred the money, but once he realized you weren't coming back with it, and it wasn't traceable, he was angry and hurt. He talked about revenge, however, he soon realized if he told the cartel about the money, they would know how much you guys were making on the side in Europe. It could have hurt us in Mexico. They would have wanted a larger cut from us, so in the end, Fernando kept his mouth shut. All things considered, you were brilliant, paying everyone just the right amount to keep them quiet. I have no ill will toward you, Carlos. I understand why you wanted out, and that you needed money to get out. This was never your world anyway. You got trapped in it. And unlike Fernando, I recognize how dearly your family paid for that."

"Thanks, Felipe. For a short time, I was happy in Paris, but then Fernando and Jose resorted to their old tricks and things went south. I needed to seize the opportunity to get out for my own safety and sanity."

"What are you doing in Brazil?"

"I have my own company now, a legitimate one. I'm here on business."

"I'm really sorry about Hermosa. I heard she died in the earthquake."

"Thank you. I hope you didn't lose anyone from your family."

"No. I feel terrible you've lost your entire family. I hope you have someone special in your life. Everyone needs someone. Are you married?"

"No. Still single." He held out his ring finger, thankful he didn't bring his new watch to Brazil.

"Girlfriend?"

"No."

"Shame. I understand if you don't want to share more about your life. You're still a hunted man. At least you're off our radar, now that Fernando is dead. I'm not sure Julio and Luis know enough to care why you disappeared. Fernando only clued me in about the missing money. He'd never admit to anyone else funds went missing on his watch. They would have thought he turned soft. I wouldn't trust the nephews, though."

"I don't, and they won't see me because I'm never coming back to Mexico."

"You should be good then because they can't afford to leave. They're always in hiding these days. You look good, Carlos. I hope you're well."

"Thanks. What happened to Angel in New York?"

"He's still there. He got fired from his job at the Metropolitan Museum. Now he's working on distribution for Julio and Luis. What a waste. For a while Fernando had him keeping an eye out for you in New York but then they gave up. I keep trying to tell Angel to look for an honest job. He used to be a good kid until Fernando corrupted him."

"Sorry to hear that. I won't ever go back there either. I hated that city, especially in the winter."

"Never been. I wish we could stay in touch. Sometimes, I think about leaving too, but I'm trapped with the business. Things are so different now. Without Fernando, I have to deal with Julio and Luis and I can't stand them. They're too much like Jose, but not quite as bad. No one could ever be that bad."

"It's wise not to trust them. Watch your back, Felipe. How is your family?"

"The family is good. Business is good. We sell more ceramics in South America now, but we still have some loyal European clients. I travel down here once in a while, just to get away. I miss having you around, Carlos. You were always the one sane person I could lean on."

"Thanks. Are you traveling anywhere besides Brazil this trip?"

"Yes. Argentina. I might end up retiring down there. Or maybe I'll open a business, who knows?"

"Not a bad idea. You should give that some thought. I'm glad we talked. Do you need money to do that or to retire, Felipe?"

Felipe smiled. "No, my friend. Fernando left me in very good shape. Thanks."

"Listen, I have to go. Thanks for your update. It eases my mind a little. Be well and take care of yourself." He got up and grabbed his backpack. The lobby was starting to show morning activity and he wanted to leave before someone came looking for Felipe.

"You be well too, Carlos. You know how to contact me should you feel like it. Good luck with everything. Maybe we'll meet in Rio again?" Casi could see moisture creep into Felipe's eyes.

"Maybe." He hugged Fernando's brother and turned to leave before Felipe could see his face. He felt sorry for his only Flores friend, still trapped in Fernando's world. Had Carlos gone back to Tampico, his life would have been hell, with or without Fernando. Those punks, Julio and Luis, would have made him miserable. Felipe carved out his niche with the factory, just like he had done in Paris, with creative accounting. There is only so much freedom you have within the confines of cartel territory. Casi felt somewhat liberated as he sat in the taxi, *en route* to the airport. Meeting with Felipe had been well worth the risk. He cracked the window and let the cool morning air hit his face. He would not be coming back to Brazil either. It felt too good to be free.

CHAPTER XCIX

Cara's Changing World

Cara was sad Jasper had accepted the job in L.A. Just when she thought her children would all be back in New York, one of them left again. She was still hoping Samson might come back. He hadn't yet regained his footing after the break-up with Natalie, but he did enjoy his work in Paris. Nonetheless, she was hopeful.

The job opportunity in L.A. was too good for Jasper to turn down. The entertainment world was growing on her oldest son. He had enjoyed working with Ted and Summer and had demonstrated great people skills managing the various personalities on set. He was also a competent problem solver. His new job entailed more than those accomplishments. He was part of a team who selected worthwhile projects, evaluated the budget, then saw them through in a producing capacity. Ted had written him a convincing recommendation, sharing how impressed he was with Jasper's prowess. Jasper was definitely a people pleaser, a competent negotiator, could give a compelling pitch, and he was tight-lipped about new projects under consideration, a trait highly valued in the movie industry.

Summer, back from Italy, was working around the clock, editing her newest film. Since it was a complicated story, and she had seven weeks of filming to sift through, she would be buried for a while. Cara was happy she was nearby, even if she barely left the lab.

Occasionally, she traveled to Summer's vicinity for dinner and to offer a valued opinion on the latest edited scene.

Francois was still shuttling back and forth between Paris and New York, but as of late, he was spending more time in Paris. Ted was back at work and doing his best to drum up new business. The New York gallery hadn't taken off the way Francois had hoped. Cara felt like they were drifting apart. Lately, he appeared distant and stressed. Time would tell if their relationship would survive.

CHAPTER C

Nothing Ever Stays the Same....Not Even Home

Casi spotted Helena standing in line at the check-in counter. He walked up behind her and wrapped an arm around her shoulders. She jumped, startled, then melted into him.

"Thank God! I'm glad you're here. I was so worried." She leaned her head against his shoulder, nuzzling into his neck and wrapped one arm tightly around his waist. His muscles were tense.

"Everything is fine, Helena. We'll talk later, in private. It's good we're leaving early, though. We'll have a nice time in the Caribbean, I promise you."

"That's fine. I like it there." Helena stroked her hand up and down his back. She was comforted by his presence, and he felt touched by her concern.

"I'm just so relieved you're here." She breathed into his armpit.

Casi smiled. "Me too."

Lifting the suitcases onto the conveyer belt, he let Helena handle the tickets. Pulling his fedora low, he leaned back against the counter, and swept the airport with watchful eyes, No unusual sightings caught his attention. By now, he was pretty adept at spotting the suspicious. He could relax and enjoy the rest of his trip with Helena. Once the suitcases were checked, they hurried through security, picking the shortest line. On the other side, they located their gate. They had two-and-a-half hours to kill before departure.

"Let's go have breakfast. I'm starving," Casi suggested as he tapped his abs.

"Me, too. I was so nervous, I couldn't eat at the hotel. I didn't even have coffee."

"Nervous energy. Maybe stick with decaf? I'm having tea."

It was surprising how hungry they were. They both devoured omelets loaded with cheese and vegetables, buttered toast, and fruit cups. After breakfast, Casi waited outside the ladies' room. He quickly called his sister and shared their new destination, without telling her why they were leaving Rio early. He could tell Camila was suspicious, but he hung up before she could interrogate him.

"Helena says hello. I'll talk to you later," he cut her short. Helena had yet to exit the restroom. When she did, Casi went to the men's room. In one of the stalls, he took apart his backpack to make sure nothing unusual had been slipped inside, like a tracking device, one of Fernando's favorite tools. He found nothing.

Tobago was a welcome change from the bustle of Rio de Janeiro. It had a laid-back vibe and allowed Casi and Helena to relax at the beautiful Coco Reef Resort & Spa. The beach was spectacular, and the ocean view from their room, soothing for their frazzled nerves. Casi was happy to discover the fully equipped gym while Helena swam in the pool. Together, they enjoyed spa treatments and long walks on the beach. It was a true honeymoon experience and just what they needed to get their tortured souls back on track after the last twenty-four hours. The Wi-Fi worked, so Casi checked in with Camila and Peter. He was relieved to hear that all was well at the restaurant.

Casi thought about filling Camila in on Felipe, but decided to wait until he saw her. He knew she would be worried he was being set up. He was certain Felipe had been genuine and that he hadn't been tracked, but it would be difficult to convince Camila.

Helena enjoyed the first few days in Tobago. Casi was back to his usual, calm self. The cutting tension that had surrounded him, dissipated into the fragrant Caribbean air. His story about seeing someone from Fernando's circle in Rio was suspicious and she wasn't sure whether to believe him or not, but the fact he had switched their schedule so drastically at an added expense surely meant something. Seeing him relax again, eased her fears. Living with such uncertainty was not ideal and it left her mindful. Would life with Casi always be like that?

While he was in the shower one morning, one of his phones rang in his backpack. Helena hesitated briefly, then sprinted over to see who was calling. When she pulled the phone out of a side pocket, she only caught the area code before the screen went dark. She quickly looked up 242 online and discovered that it was the area code for the Bahamas. She sat down on the edge of the bed, her mind racing. Up until now, she had suspected he was based somewhere in South America. Was that where Casi lived now? It would explain his fascination with the Caribbean for sure. She resolved to do research in the hotel's business center when he went to the gym later that afternoon. His refusal to explain what had transpired in Brazil had her curiosity on high alert.

Helena waited patiently all day. Once seated in the business center, she checked her email. Summer had sent her an update. She was surprised to read that Jasper had accepted a job in the entertainment world in Los Angeles. She pictured him as an executive in training and laughed. Was this a permanent departure from the banking world? She would have to congratulate him.

Summer was busy editing the new film, spending ten-hour days in the lab. The film would take much longer to edit than the last since it had many more moving parts. At least a year, Summer confided. Hope was back in Los Angeles and working on another project, and Ted continued to work in Francois's gallery.

Cara was busy with new projects. She and Sam were working together for a new private client. Samson was fine in Paris, but contemplating a transfer. Helena appreciated the update. She had grown to love Summer's whole family and was invested in their well-being.

She turned her attention to the Bahamas. When she googled Casi's name, nothing came up.

She checked restaurants and their owners, but again, nothing. She could try checking for new businesses, too, since she didn't really know if he was in the restaurant business. He could have started any business. Tomorrow, she would continue her research. She wanted to be back in the room before Casi returned from the gym. She pressed reply to Summer's email and quickly tapped out,

Hi Summer,
So surprised to hear about Jasper's career change. Congrats to him. I know how Samson feels. I'm not looking forward to going back to Paris. I feel lonely there without the people I care for. Hopefully I can come back for fashion week in January.
We're having a wonderful trip together. Rio de Janeiro was fun and I really liked C's sister. Now we're in Tobago. I'll be back in Paris

next week. I think I know where C may be living. Let's talk when I get back.
Love, H

The reply was immediate.

I hope you're using the secure phone and Wi-Fi. Don't endanger him!

Rattled, Helena signed out of the hotel's Wi-Fi.

CHAPTER CI

Helena's Choices ....the Joys of Travel

When Helena arrived back in Paris, after eight days in Tobago and Trinidad, she felt rested, but deflated. She and Casi were back on track, but now they were facing an extended separation again. She couldn't shake the feeling that home was where your heart was, not necessarily where you hung your hat. Energized, she emailed her contacts in New York to let them know she was available for fashion week in January or February. She had missed September, but maybe she could work in the spring/summer show. Perhaps she could meet Casi in Miami for an extended weekend again? She also emailed Jasper to congratulate him.

Hi Jasper,
Congratulations on your new job! I'm thrilled for you. It must feel great to discover something you enjoy doing, although I would have never guessed your choice would fall in Summer's world. I hope you'll be happy in L.A.
I'm trying to come back to New York in January to work at fashion week. I'll keep you and Summer posted. Miss you all,
Love, Helena

A few days later, a reply came.

Hello Helena,
Thanks for the good wishes. I actually arrived in L.A. last week and just started work. So far, so good. We're casting for a new movie, and I suggested you to the director. You need to get a reel together as soon as possible. Talk to Summer. Maybe she can give you a clip from the current movie so you have more than one film on your reel. Normally, that's not an option, but she might relent and give you a snippet that has been edited. Keep me posted on the dates you come to New York. We may be holding auditions there, too.
Love, Jasper

Wow! Thanks, Jasper. I'll keep you posted, for sure!
I would love another movie part. Who is directing? What's the movie? I'll check with Summer about my reel. Where are you living in L.A.?
Love, Helena

A week later, Jasper answered.

Hey,
I live in Westwood. I found a temporary apartment not too far from the studio. Summer put a reel together for you and sent me a copy. She must really like you a lot to do that on such short notice. Did you get your copy, too? Will keep you in the loop re auditions. See attachment for movie details.
Love, Jasper.

Back at work, Helena was modeling for online fashion catalogues. After working on set for so many weeks and enjoying her leisure time with Casi, she couldn't get her head back into the agency's mundane assignments. They had her wearing scratchy winter fashions in the late summer heat. She was bored, and she missed Casi's warm embrace. Each time they spoke, her heart ached. His voice soothed her like a fleece blanket on a frigid night. She decided not to tell him about Jasper's possible acting offer in case it didn't materialize. Why upset him when there was no firm offer on the table? She knew he was hoping she would scrap her acting career for a less public life with him. As tempting as it was, she still wasn't ready to make that commitment. The quick exit from Rio had given her pause for thought. Now that she had a role opportunity, she would see how it played out.

A couple weeks later, she heard back from the agency in New York. They had booked her for fashion week, end of January. She let out a scream of joy. She immediately emailed Summer and copied Jasper. Should she come earlier for auditions, or was January fine? She also texted Casi. Would he be free to meet her somewhere? She checked her email hourly for their replies. Casi answered first.

Coming home to her empty apartment after long, tedious work days only made things worse. She floundered around like a fish out of water, walking from one room to the next in her confined space. Helena didn't care for the catty people she worked with and had maintained few friends. She desperately wanted to be in New York near the Crenstons or with Casi, wherever he was. She hadn't been successful locating him in the Bahamas when she did a new business search. Maybe he had a partner? Or maybe Summer was right, he just did business there and lived elsewhere. To make matters worse, she contracted a stomach virus and felt completely limp and nauseous. The approaching winter holidays also depressed her. What would she do for Christmas all alone? When Jasper answered, her spirits lifted.

Hi Helena,
Hope your summer ended well. We're holding open auditions the
first two weeks of November. Can you come to L.A.? You can stay
with me.
Let me know.
Love, Jasper

Her answer was swift.

"Yes! Confirm the dates and I'll book my flight.
Looking forward to seeing you, Helena

A few weeks later, she was on a flight to Los Angeles for a ten-day stay. Her stomach was still unsettled. Nerves probably, she thought. When she saw Jasper standing in the LAX airport terminal, Helena felt like crying. She gave him a heartfelt hug and bombarded him with questions about his family and job. They drove to his apartment, deep in conversation. Jasper pointed out various landmarks along the way.

"Los Angeles is so overwhelming and spread out. I had no idea! Is there a downtown area?"

"Yes, but it's not like Paris or New York. Los Angeles is more of a cluster of neighborhoods, set side by side, like a honeycomb effect. It has eighty-one cities and roughly ten million people. I live in Westwood, which is halfway between the beach and where I work, two places that are essential to me. I would have liked to live in Santa Monica, but it's too expensive, and the commute to work longer. The thing is, in L.A. you're always in your car. Traffic is horrendous, so if you can live somewhat close to work or drive during off hours, you're ahead of the game."

"Everything is so far apart. How long does it take you to get to work?"

"It varies. Usually, I give myself a half hour. Luckily, I have parking there. I've visited L.A. with my family a few times, so I already knew what I was getting myself into when I moved here. Hope says hello, by the way. We'll see her over the week end. She's working over in the valley right now."

"Oh, good. I'd love to see her. I saw Samson once or twice this past October. He's still sad about Natalie."

"Yeah, I know. I think she was his first serious love. Before her, he was the heartbreaker."

Hollywood wasn't half as glamorous as Helena imagined. In fact, it was tacky and had seedy characters hanging out of every crevice. The Chinese Theater was overrun with tourists, like the Eiffel Tower area in Paris, and the locals looked anything but spectacular. Over the week end, Jasper took her to Beverly Hills, Venice Beach, and Malibu, which she liked much better. They had brunch with Hope in Santa Monica at Back on the Beach and walked along the winding boardwalk, dodging bikes and skateboards. Los Angeles was nothing like Helena had imagined, although the beach area came closer to her expectations. It had its own culture, especially in Venice. The long boulevards in Los Angeles, with their endless traffic jams, left her feeling overwhelmed. It took ages to get from one destination to the next. What irked her was that there was no real city center she could walk through. There was something to be said for Southern California weather, but the sheer size of Los Angeles was paralyzing. Paris and New York were large cities, too, but with the *metro* or subway, they were totally manageable. On a positive note, the sun shone every day she was there.

Her first audition on Monday morning was an eye opener. The sheer amount of actors present was intimidating. Jasper had prepared her, telling her what to expect, but she was nauseous and nervous anyway. Summer's training came into play, and Helena tackled three different tryouts with confidence. She felt she delivered what was asked of her. Jasper agreed.

"You did well today, but just know if it doesn't work out, it's not a reflection on you. Auditions are random to some degree. So many factors are considered before a final choice is made. Some things are just out of your control. If the director had a different character look in mind, it doesn't matter how well you read."

"I'm beginning to get that message. So far, I haven't had much experience with rejection." Helena had sensed the desperation in some of the other people waiting to audition and could only imagine how many rejections they had endured. It hit her how lucky she had been when Summer picked her in Paris. It was her first and only audition. Hope and Summer taught her how to present on camera. She had learned so much from them and it was now coming full circle. Two good film opportunities right from the start had spoiled her. She was beginning to realize how much others vied for these chances and how competitive things truly were. One stint at Los Angeles auditions said it all. The conversations all around her were eye-opening. Was she cut out for this? What if there were big gaps between films? How would she survive? Casi had her back in Paris and she also had her agency jobs to fall back on. Would Jasper have her back in Los Angeles?

The second weekend Helena was in Los Angeles, she and Jasper visited the Getty Museum, the Grove and drove around to look at real estate. The homes were all so different. She liked the Spanish style homes best, but she choked when he told her the prices they fetched. The styles reminded her a little of Southern Europe. She was slowly warming up to Los Angeles, but she couldn't see herself surviving here. She felt lost.

Her last night, Jasper took her out for drinks and dinner. They flirted, laughed and felt completely comfortable together. One thing led to another, and Jasper kissed her on the way home. In another world, Helena would have welcomed the opportunity. However, remembering the hurt and rift Casi's affair had caused, she stopped herself from giving in to the impulse.

"I'm sorry, Jasper. I can't. I'm not over Carlos yet. It just doesn't feel right, especially if we end up working together. I hope you understand."

"I do. Sorry. I feel comfortable with you."

"And I with you. I feel like you and Summer are family. That doesn't mean I'm not attracted to you. You know I love you. I'm just not ready."

"I understand. Summer mentioned you might still be sad about Carlos. Let's get some sleep. It's been a fun week. I hope you get one of the parts. It would be great to work together again."

"Yes, it would. You've been a wonderful host. Thanks for everything."

When she took an Uber to the airport the next day, Casi was lingering on her mind. As nice as Los Angeles weather was, she was happy to go back to New York. She also wanted to call Casi. They hadn't spoken in ten days. Thinking things over on the plane, she decided she liked New York and Miami better than Los Angeles. Mid-flight, Helena felt nauseous again. Had she relapsed on the plane? She felt like she had an ongoing malaise. Germs circulated like fake currency in a game of monopoly through those confined airplane vents.

Back in Paris, she had work the next day. She did her best to hide her exhaustion and queasiness from the styling crew, not wanting to suffer the consequences of wagging tongues. They were already jealous of her travels. Every client was important and they expected her best. Things were so hectic, and everyone was so self-absorbed, they didn't notice her discomfort. She was wearing so much make-up, she could have died and still looked ravishing.

Helena started making ginger tea in the morning, to settle her roiling stomach. At lunch, she ordered warm, soothing soup instead of salad or protein shakes like the other girls. She was doing runway work that required concentration and stamina. She found it difficult to concentrate and came home dead tired at night. The jet lag was killing her, more than usual.

In the meantime, she and Casi talked regularly. They were planning their next trip for February, after fashion week. It was such a long way off, she wasn't sure if she would make it. She tried to focus on the positive in their conversations, but in reality, she longed to spend the holidays with him.

"Where shall we go in February?"

"I can only get away for one week this time. What do you think of New Orleans as a destination? We can go back to Miami another time."

"Oh, yes! I would love that."

"Good. I'll do some research."

"February is so far away. Can't we meet somewhere sooner?"

"This is my busy season, Helena. I really can't get away now."

"I suppose I can't either. I need the money. I've been gone so much, I hope I still have a job when I get back to Paris in February. My boss complained last time."

"But you were working in New York. He knows that."

"Yes, but I'm not making him any money. I have a non-exclusive contract in New York. I took a leave of absence to work at fashion week. Summer got me the job, remember?"

"Yes, I do. How is she?"

"Very busy editing. It will take a year to complete the film."

She thought of telling him about her time in Los Angeles, but again, she refrained. She would tell him in person. Besides, he was the king of secrets. She could keep a few of her own. Part of her felt guilty. Few people cared about Helena's well-being and success like Casi did. Her mother might have, but she was dead and her father had been absent from her life. The Crenstons had become her chosen replacement family.

Helena finished her runway job with her usual professionalism. She somehow managed to muddle through the week, hiding her upset stomach and frazzled nerves. She was starting to feel a tad better. It appeared the ginger tea was helping.

Over the weekend, Summer called for a video chat, the first since Italy. Although they had stayed in touch by email, it was nice to catch up in person. Summer was up to speed with her life. She filled Helena in on the film's progress, then shifted her attention to her friend.

"Hey. How was your runway job?"

"It went well, considering I had an upset stomach all week. The client was pleased." Helena smiled and filled Summer in on some of the details.

"Great! Tell me about Los Angeles. I spoke to Jasper briefly, and he said they liked you."

"Yes, the audition felt good, but then you never know in that world, do you?" Helena's eyebrows shot up.

"No, you don't. It really all depends on what the director is looking for. If you fit their vision, you're in luck. Did you like L.A.?"

"Yes and no. I liked the weather, the palm trees, the museums, and some of the neighborhoods. Jasper's apartment is great. So were the areas by the ocean; I loved Santa Monica, but I was surprised at how large and spread out L.A. is. It wasn't at all what I expected. I think I like New York and Miami better."

"Me, too. Jasper seems to love it, though. He likes the weather, his job, and he doesn't mind the driving. He always preferred warm climates. I wouldn't mind working there on a project, but I don't want to live there long term. So, what are your plans now?"

"Casi and I are planning a vacation to New Orleans after fashion week, in February."

"Nice. You'll like it there. The French Quarter is really fun. That might be Mardi Gras time. Check the calendar."

"Oh, fun. I'll do that. I can't wait to see him again. February seems so far away." She hesitated. "Summer, I think he might be living in the Bahamas."

Summer visibly stiffened and took a sip of her water, avoiding Helena's direct gaze on the screen.

"What makes you think that?"

"He received calls from that area code when we were in Tobago. I saw the prefix number and checked it."

"He may just be doing business there. It would make more sense for him to live in South America, don't you think?"

"That would be the obvious choice and I thought that was where he ended up, but now I'm wondering."

"Be careful, Helena. Don't discuss this with anyone but me."

"Do you know where he lives?"

"No. I don't. Honestly, I prefer not to know." Summer switched the subject with a cutting voice. "Listen, I have to go. I have an appointment. Talk soon?"

"Sure." It surprised her Summer didn't want to explore her findings. Why wasn't she more curious? Had Casi scared her?

CHAPTER CII

Helena's Surprise

Late November dragged into early December, and Helena still had no plans for the holidays.

She was completely cheerless. Yes, there would be parties at the agency and all over town, but her heart wasn't in it. She had done that for the past decade, and it had lost its allure. Now that she knew what it was like to have special people in her life, the parties where everyone drank too much and drugged their senses were as exciting as tooth extraction. She was so over that scene. She had lost her old party friends when she moved in with Casi. Her travels and New York jaunts further isolated her from the other girls at the agency. She wondered if she should call Samson and invite him to a few events, or suggest hanging out over the holidays. Summer mentioned that he was in touch with Mimi, but she didn't think they were dating.

Most mornings, when Helena left for work, it was still dark. Many nights, she came home in the dark as well. Winter gloom was getting to her. Once home, she had nothing to do, but eat and sleep. One morning, she realized, she no longer fit into her favorite jeans. They were snug, and she couldn't zip them up without inhaling and gasping for air. This was not a problem she was familiar with. How did this happen? Her tummy felt bloated and sore. She was beginning to think she had an ulcer. It was time to see a doctor.

She called and made an appointment for Saturday morning, so it wouldn't interfere with work. Later that day, she got a call from Jasper. Hearing his voice cheered her up immediately.

"Hi, Helena. I have great news."

"What is it?" He sounded so warm and cheerful.

"You got the supporting role. Congrats!"

"No! I did? Are you sure?" She waited for his affirmation. "Thank you, Jasper. What happens now?"

"First, you need to decide if you want the part. If yes, we need to get you an L.A. agent. We probably should get you an agent either way. I know this role wasn't your first choice, but I think it's still worth taking. It gets you working here."

"I'll have to think about all of this. I may have to rent out my apartment and take a temporary leave of absence from the agency again. They're going to be so mad. They're already annoyed with me."

"Sounds like you have some serious decisions to make. This is a good opportunity to break into Hollywood, Helena. Many would kill for this chance, but you have to want it."

"I always wanted it. Let me work out the logistics. Can you email me all the details?"

"Sure!"

"Who got the lead?"

"That hasn't been decided yet. I'll email you who got which part when I send you all the other information. Some things I can't disclose until contracts are signed. You know the drill."

"I understand. Thanks for thinking of me, Jasper. I know it's a good opportunity and that I wouldn't have gotten it without you."

"You bet. I have to run. Keep checking your emails."

Helena hung up and stopped in her tracks. Why wasn't she more excited? She should have been jumping up and down. After all, this is what she worked so hard for, wished for. She felt bad she hadn't displayed more enthusiasm. She knew Jasper had bent over backwards to help her and she loved him for it. If she decided to follow her Hollywood dream and give up on Casi, she could easily see herself with someone like Jasper. He was a good person, like Summer. But would she love him like she did Casi? Would there be the same kind of passion? Either way, her decision shouldn't be based on people, should it? Wasn't she supposed to follow her own dreams and hard-earned opportunities?

She tried to reconcile her emotions with the impressions of her changing world. Strangely, she didn't feel overly excited about going back to Hollywood. A year ago, she would have been ecstatic. Was she fearing failure or was it something deeper than that? She realized she had some soul-searching to do. Helena needed to talk to someone. She couldn't discuss this dilemma with Casi until her choice was made or Jasper either. She needed to talk to her best friend, Summer.

CHAPTER CIII

Lady Sings the Blues

Helena's long exploratory conversation with Summer helped, but she still couldn't make up her mind definitively. The conclusion they arrived at was since Helena was no longer happy in her current job in Paris, maybe it was time for a change--whether Los Angeles or New York remained to be seen. Summer gently pointed out that Helena was no longer in her twenties. At thirty-two, how long did she anticipate being a sought-after print or runway model? Or an actress if she didn't make it soon? Shouldn't she shoot for the stars now if she was going to try? Did she have a plan B? The clock was ticking.

"You can work as a print model when you're older. You just work for more mature brands," Helena explained.

"Do they pay well?" Summer wondered?

"Not as much as runway, of course, but there is work. It's an average salary."

"If you work as an actress, you'll also need a day job between films."

"I would continue to do print work in between films. I've done well with that for the last eight years."

The girls weren't getting anywhere quick. It would require reflection on Helena's part. What would make her happy? If she did the film in L.A. would she search for print work there? Or would she come back to New York and work with the agency that had already placed her at fashion week a few times.

Surprisingly, Casi never pointed out that she might age out of her career choices in any of their arguments. He was forever encouraging when it came to her work. He never sought to squash her dreams and she loved him for that. Other men would have rubbed her face in the reality of age-related careers. The one thing that would surely end both career dreams was an uncontrolled weight gain. If she couldn't fit into the clothes she modeled, her regular clients would disappear like lint on passing Velcro. She needed to put a lid on her eating. The funny thing was, she couldn't even remember eating more than usual. Was her metabolism changing now that she was over thirty? Or was it her appetite?

After a few sleepless nights, Helena decided to give Hollywood a chance. What did she have to lose? It was either now or never. She could rent out her apartment to someone at the agency and make the transition. If things didn't work out, she would figure out where to go from there. What was life without taking chances? Besides, having Jasper in her corner would be a plus. She could manage Los Angeles with Jasper's and Hope's friendship and support. That night she called Casi and told him about the movie offer in Los Angeles.

CHAPTER CIV

Peter.... a Bright Light Extinguished?

Casi was sitting in his home office, contemplating a trip to Miami. He felt like seeing Rose.

She always made him feel good, and he guessed, by now, she would have gotten over her anger at him. Deep down, there was a connection between them he couldn't quite explain. They had become friends and they each enjoyed the other's company. It wasn't the same kind of passion he had with Helena, but he was definitely fond of her and found her sexually attractive. Love was a different story.

Since Helena told him she had successfully auditioned for a movie part in Hollywood, he was fairly certain she would never join him in the Bahamas. Her phone call had pierced his heart, and the pain of their four-month separation was magnified to epic proportions. What budding actress would leave Hollywood once she was there and working? Until now, he dealt with their separation by keeping busy and seeking out temporary diversions. At least, he still had harbored hope. However, in light of these new developments, Rose was foremost on his mind and the best distraction he could think of.

When he shared his thoughts with Camila by phone one morning, she wasn't very sympathetic.

"Look, I understand you're discouraged, but give it some time. Helena may still come around. Now that I've met her, I know how much she loves you. That kind of love is hard to find in life. Trust me."

"I don't know. My head is spinning and I'm not feeling hopeful anymore. I was thinking of flying to Miami for a night or two. Rose could easily get my mind off Helena."

"What! Are you crazy? You had a wonderful vacation with the love of your life not so long ago, won her trust back with great difficulty, and now you want to see Rose? What's wrong with you? Stop thinking with your lower parts. It only gets you in trouble. What do you think Rose will expect after you sleep with her a second time? Are you ready for that? And…if Helena comes around, do you honestly think she'll forgive you twice?"

"Helena is not coming to the Bahamas, Camila. I know it."

"You don't know women, Casi. They can change their minds. Stop being a fool and get your stupid ass off the self-pity chair. Get back to work and wait patiently. If nothing happens in the next six to twelve months, you can visit Rose or hopefully, someone else by then. Give Helena a chance, for God's sake. She's conflicted, and I don't blame her. Living with a wanted man isn't exactly a future one dreams about."

"Oh, alright."

"There's stuff happening here you need to know about and be involved with. Peter needs your support. I spoke to Gracie this morning, and the news isn't good."

"Why? What's happening?"

"I'll fill you in at work. Vacation time is over. We need you here, body and spirit. Now get in your damn truck and drive to your restaurant." She disconnected the call before he could breathe. His sister sure knew how to get his attention.

When Casi arrived, Camila was waiting in the office.

"Hallelujah! You made it. Sit down and pay attention because I'm only going to say this once.

I had a wonderful time in Rio and truly enjoyed meeting Helena. Now I understand why you keep holding on to her. I can only encourage you to keep believing. She's worth it."

"Thanks. I know you're right, but I'm not feeling it." He looked at his hands.

"Stop feeling sorry for yourself. I know it hasn't been easy, but what has for us? Good things are worth waiting for. She'll come around eventually, if you can be patient and keep your pants zipped. I would bet money on it. Now, to Peter. His cancer is back."

"Oh God. Please, no." Casi dropped his head into his hands. He felt like he'd been punched in the gut, twice.

"He went for a check-up yesterday, and the doctor saw something he didn't like. We'll have to wait and see, but Gracie thinks he may require another round of therapy. He needs you to be positive and supportive."

"I'm here."

"Put your love woes aside for a minute and concentrate on the here and now."

"Hmm." Casi lifted his head and noticed Camila's hand on the desk. Her fingernails were polished bright red, and she was wearing a new ring.

"Are you wearing a diamond?" He stared incredulously at the sparkle on her ring finger.

"Yes. Isn't it beautiful? That is my other news. Last night Stefano proposed, and I accepted." She beamed at the brilliant flash centered on her outstretched hand. Casi leaned in to look closely at a cushion-shaped diamond, flanked by two equally brilliant trilliants, all set in a yellow gold band. She rocked her hand back and forth to catch the reflective light.

"What?" Casi looked shocked. "Is he really the one? Are you sure?"

"Yes, he's the one. Peter already gave me his blessing. Now I need yours." She waited while Casi swallowed and gathered his wits and words.

"You told Peter before me?" He ran his fingers through his hair, in disbelief.

"I'm sorry, but Gracie happened to call this morning, and Peter was next to her. If you had come to work on time, you would have been the first to know. I planned on telling you first."

"If he makes you happy, you have my blessing. Congratulations. I guess he's a nice man. Isn't this a little quick, though?"

"No. When you know, you know. There's more."

"More?" Casi gulped. "You're pregnant?"

"What? No! Stefano and I would like to move to Miami. I wanted to talk to you about opening my own restaurant there, a sister restaurant to the Sea Grape Garden."

"You want to move to Miami?" Casi repeated, a chill crawling up his spine. Bad news generally came in threes. First, Helena's confirmed movie role, then, his best friend has a cancer relapse, and now, his sister was getting married and moving off island. What was next? He hoped the news stopped here.

"Yes. We discussed it recently, but I didn't want to say anything until he actually proposed. Stefano owns a condo in Miami that is currently occupied. When the tenant leaves, we can move in. I'll keep my condo here so I can come back anytime. What do you think?"

"I need time to process this. Off the top of my head, I'll only help finance the restaurant in your name. What else have you got? Tell me while I'm still seated."

"Isn't this enough?"

"Totally. I don't think I can handle more. In fact, I don't think I can do all this here, without you, Camila."

"Of course, you can. You've handled far more and worse. I won't be leaving for a while, so take a deep breath and be strong for Peter. First things first."

"I don't want to be around when you tell Matias. The man will be crushed. He loves working with you."

"Nonsense. He and I are friends. He'll be happy for me."

As it turned out, Camila was dead wrong. Matias was equally shocked, and Casi heard angry pots and pans banging and clanging all day. Matias felt as blindsided as Casi. He had a serious soft spot for his girl, Camila, but he kept his true feelings hidden.

The next morning, Casi pulled into the Sea Grape Garden parking lot before anyone else arrived. He had gone to bed early and started his day at the crack of dawn with a vigorous work-out. Yesterday's news had overwhelmed him, but today was a new day. He sat in his truck with the windows rolled down, breathing deeply. The salty ocean air and sweet vegetation smelled so deliciously good. Ylang ylang hit his nostrils and soothed his tortured soul. He felt happy here, but once again, his endurance was being tested. Would he be this happy without Camila and Peter? What he was beginning to realize was, the more love you gave, the more vulnerable you were to hurt. For so many years, after his parents died, he had buried his childhood grief and functioned on pure adrenaline and cold calculations to get ahead. He had developed a hardened exterior, impervious to emotions. Now that he was emotionally invested, he felt powerless and vulnerable. Camila, Helena, and Peter's love and well-being mattered greatly to him and he wanted all of them in his daily life.

CHAPTER CV

Tying up Loose Ends for......New Beginnings

Cara was seated in her office alcove reading world news. El Chapo's wife, who faithfully sat through her husband's court proceedings without so much as a hug being granted *was* contemplating reality TV. A show entitled, 'Cartel Crew,' including 'offspring talent' from the Sinaloa Cartel was under consideration. "Move over the Kardashians," she muttered and laughed out loud.

Cara was captivated. Why would anyone in a cartel stray from a low-profile life? She was stumped. To add even more spice, El Chapo's son had allegedly instigated a shoot out on the streets of Culiacan, Mexico. The Mexican police briefly held him, then quickly released him to prevent further bloodshed, according to straight-faced government officials. The all powerful cartels ruled that country for sure, Cara surmised. Her final views on the matter involved Casi. If he ever returned to Mexico, he would be fodder for the pigs. All things considered, he had managed to eke out a nice existence for himself on a beautiful island. She hoped he was safe for Helena's and Summer's sake, her motivation for keeping her mouth shut, for now.

She moved on to her emails from Samson and Francois. Samson was fine, but still considering a location change. That boy had restless genes. Few would give up a plum position in Paris. Cara hoped he would find another girlfriend soon and told him so. It turned out Mimi was just a friend. As much as Cara wanted Samson to come home, she thought his job was wonderful and he would regret the change.

Francois's email was a little more complicated. She initially put off opening it, fearing a polite send-off, but actually, it turned out to be a heartfelt apology. He felt bad for his recent absence and his unavailability in Paris, but he was experiencing financial difficulties. The New York gallery had been a big gamble and an investment that wasn't paying off quickly enough. Hopefully that would change. He was concentrating on trying to make enough money in Paris to carry the expenses of the New York business until it did become more successful, but it was cramping his lifestyle. His immediate plan was to continue financing New York, but he needed to stay focused on Paris right now. Things were going well with Esme. He assured her he wasn't involved with anyone else. He was just super busy, trying to stay afloat. Cara sighed with relief. She wasn't ready to give up on him yet. She really did care for him. Perhaps she could help with the New York gallery? She decided to have dinner with Ted and see what his thoughts were. Her ringing phone jolted her.

"Hi, Sam."

"Hey, what are you up to?"

"Just reading an email from Francois. He's really busy in Paris and won't be back for a while. He's also worried about the New York gallery. He needs more clients to stay in business."

"Don't we all."

"I'm afraid he may have to close if things don't turn around soon. I was thinking about how I could help. I don't want to lose him."

"Well, that took balls to make an admission like that. He's being brutally honest. You have to respect that. Let me see if I can talk his gallery up to a couple of my clients."

"Thanks. I'm sure he would pay you a commission if you broker a sale."

"Yeah. Maybe we can help each other. I'll think of a campaign that includes all three of us. In the meantime, I'm happy to hear he isn't involved with someone else. He's trying, Cara. I do believe him."

"I want to."

"You two are good together. Go with it. Are you around? I wanted to come by and discuss some other business. I promise to bring a treat."

"I can be bribed if it's from Nero's. What kind of business are we talking about?"

"The best kind, a new job."

CHAPTER CVI

Helena's Dilemma

Helena left the doctor's office in a daze. After examination, he confirmed that her ongoing stomach problem was something entirely different--something she hadn't expected at all. She was pregnant. Approaching her fourth month. If she wanted to terminate her pregnancy, she would have to do so quickly. Helena was in shock. She had practiced safe sex, for the most part. Now she had a tough decision to make. Although not religious, she didn't want an abortion. She suspected her strong Catholic upbringing manifested itself. Wondering how Casi would feel about abortion given his own catholic background and view on the importance of family, she was fairly certain he wouldn't support it either. Would he want a child now? How long could she continue working before she started showing a baby bump? Another month or two? What would she do then? Did she want to be a single mother?

The movie dates Jasper had sent her wouldn't work with her pregnancy schedule either. They wanted to start filming in the Spring, when she would be in her last trimester. Helena doubted the filming dates would be revised for her. The studio could easily choose someone else this early in the game. Besides, what would she tell Jasper? Maybe that was her sign not to follow that path. She didn't like the secondary role she was offered, anyway. It was all so confusing. She needed to sleep on it and call Summer, when

"

her thoughts were more organized. Her trusted friend would help her sort through her options. When she got home, she collapsed in a heap and had a good cry.

Later that week, when she felt more at peace, she called Summer on the secure phone. She was feeling nauseous again, so she sat down on the toilet seat just in case.

"Hi, Helena. What have you decided? Are you going to do the movie?"

"There's a new development. Are you sitting down? This may be a long talk."

"What is it? I can talk." Summer sounded concerned.

"I'm pregnant." Helena sniffled but didn't cry.

"Oh my God. Well, that certainly puts a crimp in every plan. What are you thinking of doing?"

"Can we go over all my options?"

"Yes, let's. I have to ask this, so don't be mad. Is this Casi's baby?"

"Yes. I haven't been with anyone else."

She could hear relief in Summer's voice. "In that case, the first thing you should do is discuss this with Casi. He has a right to know. Let's talk this through, so you can go to him with a plan in mind, ok?"

"Yes. Thanks." Helena wedged a rolled towel behind her lower back and settled in for a long, cathartic chat on the throne.

CHAPTER CVII

Just When Things Couldn't get Worse….More Unexpected Surprises

asi sat across from Peter on Peter's terrace. His stomach roiled, and he wasn't sure what to say, so after his initial greeting, he let Peter take the lead.

"Thanks for coming, Casi. Congrats on Camila's engagement. She sounded so happy."

"Thanks, I think. How are you feeling?"

"I don't know. This relapse threw me. I thought I was done being ill. I guess that wasn't in the tea leaves for me. The doctor told me I'd have to do another round of therapy. He thinks that should take care of it. In fact, he's pretty confident, since I responded well first-time round. I start this week. I suppose I should feel more hopeful, but I'm not. I hate being sick. Fear of the unknown, I suppose."

"No one likes being sick, but it happens to all of us. Obviously, we can adjust your work schedule as needed, so don't worry about that. Just focus on getting better. I need you, Peter." Casi's eyes flooded.

"Don't get soft on me now, man. You're the rock in this operation."

"Funny. And here I thought it was you." Casi smiled warmly, patting Peter's hand.

"Guess we'll take turns as needed. So, what is Stefano going to do when they marry? Is he coming to take my place at the Sea Grape Garden?

"Hell no. Nobody can fill your shoes, Peter. There will be no job changes for either of them for a while. After they're married, Camila and I may open a second restaurant in Miami. Stefano is American, so when they're married, and she is legal in the U.S., we'll be able to open the business. They'll live there permanently, but Camila will keep her Bahamian residency. All this will take a while to organize, but that's the plan for now. Of course, this is not to be discussed with anyone."

"No worries. I got you."

"I'll have to adjust to the change. I had always hoped to open a second restaurant on the island or on a neighboring island."

"Well, Miami sounds like a good place."

"Yes and no. I really don't want Camila to leave. I liked having her here. I missed her when we were so far apart."

"I know what you mean."

"I'll need you more than you think. You and I will be alone again with that crazy Chilean in the kitchen."

"Oh, no! Don't tell me that. That will delay my convalescence by months. Camila was such a good buffer between Matias and me. She totally tamed the man." Peter laughed. It felt good to hear him laugh.

"And me. I hardly ever had to deal with him anymore. We might need to hire another party planner and go-between to keep our sanity. He was pretty upset when he saw Camila's ring. I heard clanging pots and cursing all day long."

Peter laughed heartily. "I'll start thinking. Damn, though. I'll miss your sister. She's a good lady."

Casi sighed. "Me too. I worry about her when she isn't around. I felt a void when she moved out and now she's thinking of leaving the country. Life is so complicated and out of my control. Why couldn't it stay the way it was? I was so happy with her here. We all were such a good team at the restaurant. Now look what happened."

"That's life, Casi. Just when things are going well, another curve ball whacks you from behind. At least you like Miami, and it's a short flight. You'll visit often."

"Yeah, but it won't be the same as having her here. You know that, Peter."

"I do. That's why you have to be thankful for every day." Peter looked at the terrace door, then down at his hands.

"You know, Casi. I've never told anyone about this, not even Gracie, because she would have tried to dissuade me from working for you, but I know more about your past than you think."

"What are you talking about?" Casi looked at Peter intently, raising one eyebrow.

"I figured out early on that you were Carlos Ortiz, the missing accountant from the Flores organization. I follow world news, not just island news, pretty closely. I recognized you from pictures in the media. I saw you when you first arrived on island. You had long hair in a pony tail and my friend Cyril drove you to the hotel from the airport. I drove you a few days later, post-haircut. When you came back to the island, after the surgeries in Brazil, I knew for sure. You were changing your appearance."

Casi swallowed and stared at Peter. He was frozen; couldn't move a single feature. His old poker face automatically resurfaced from muscle memory.

Peter paused. When Casi said nothing, he continued. "However, I feel that everyone deserves a second chance. Lord knows, I made a few bad mistakes in my younger life, so I get that sometimes, you have to try again to get things right. I'll tell you about my mistakes some other time, so we're even. Anyway, the more time I spent with you, the more I liked you and no matter what happens, I'll always feel that way. We're blood brothers now, Casi. Since I may die sooner than I thought, I had to get this off my chest."

"I don't know what to say other than thank you, Peter. Thank you for believing in me. Thank you for having my back and now, my family's back. Can we continue to keep this information between Camila, you, and I?"

"Yeah, man. I don't want Gracie to worry."

"And for the record, you're not dying. You'll make a full recovery. Gracie and I will make sure of that. Anything you need, I have you covered. If you want to go for a second opinion in Miami, we'll do that. I'll take you to the best doctors."

"Thanks, but I feel like I'm in pretty good hands here." Peter suddenly looked weary. Casi got up and put a hand on Peter's shoulder.

"I'm going to let you rest. One of these days, we'll have to swap war stories, but for now I'm going back to work. I love you, Peter. You're a blessing in my life. You came along when I needed you the most. Like a guardian angel."

"Same. See you tomorrow. I'll be in after the treatment." Peter turned his head, so Casi wouldn't see his tears.

"See how you feel in the morning," Casi said as he headed to the door with equally moist eyes.

Camila and Casi were having dinner together in his apartment. He had brought home two prepared meals from the restaurant and heated them. Over drinks, he filled her in on his shocking conversation with Peter.

"Oh my God, that's incredible. He knew all this time, and he didn't report you? Don't ever let that man go. He's a gem. I truly love him."

"I wouldn't dream of it. He's the best thing that's happened to me besides you, Felipe, and Helena. People like Peter don't come along often in life. I'm thankful for his friendship."

"Speaking of Helena. Have you heard from her? Called her since she told you about moving to L.A.?"

"No. It's been a busy week, and I wanted to give her a little time to miss me."

"Call her. This week end."

"Yes, boss."

For the rest of their dinner, they reminisced about Tampico, walking to Las Escolleras lighthouse and going to Playasco Beach. They remembered fishing with their father on the family boat and hearing the occasional gun battle in the street late at night. They hadn't talked about Tampico in a very long time. It was as if those memories had died with their old identities.

The next morning, Casi and Camila drove to work together. They sat in silence, each lost in their own thoughts. A lot had been discussed the previous night, and they were both still processing. Maria Alfaro's tireless help, Felipe's generosity of spirit, and Peter guarding their deepest secrets had touched both their hearts, and given them renewed faith in mankind, but it also stressed them a little. Secrets could never be fully contained, it seemed.

When Camila was out back, having lunch with Matias, Casi called Maria in Miami.

"Hi, Maria. How've you been? How's your family?"

"Hi, Casi. Nice to hear from you. All good here. The usual family drama. Nothing to worry about. Are you coming back to Miami?"

"No, but I have an important job for you. My sister got engaged to a man from Miami. I would like you to check him out for me. No need to rush, they aren't planning to marry until after the holidays."

"Congratulations? Or not yet?"

"Not yet. I'm not feeling it one-hundred percent; not sure why. I want a detailed report on him--his life, his family, all past relationships, any secret fetishes, what he has for breakfast and with whom. A thorough job on his adult life, you got me?"

"I got you. That bad, huh? You don't want her to choose the wrong guy again. What's his name?"

"Stefano Salas."

"I'm on it. Send me what you know about him. I'll do the rest."

CHAPTER CVIII

Memories are a Beautiful Thing......
Sometimes

It was a beautiful November day, and the restaurant was bustling with activity. The staff was cleaning and setting up for the first seating at noon. Casi was hiding in his office, not ready to face anyone. Camila's recent engagement still had him in a moody funk. On his desk were the decorative prints from Miami. Looking at his blank walls, he was thinking it was about time he hung some artwork.

Feeling nostalgic, he pulled up pictures of Helena in Miami on his phone. He longed to talk to her, hear her voice. He resolved to call her later today. Why wait until the weekend? Camila was right. A knock on the door interrupted his thoughts. Peter popped his head in.

"You busy? Can I come in?"

"Hey, Peter. Sure. How are you today?" Casi felt his day brightening in an instant.

"I'm here. Thankful for that." Peter walked over to view the prints lying on Casi 's desk. He studied them with interest.

"Miami? Are you going to hang them?"

Casi saw his eyes travel to Helena's portrait. "Yes. Have you ever been there? And… do you know a decent framing business on the island?"

"No, I haven't. Gracie has a cousin who does that kind of work. What are you thinking? Wood? Frameless glass?"

"I'm not sure. Frameless for the portrait and bleached wood for the other two?"

"Hey, isn't that the girl you were looking at online a while back?"

"Can't squeeze anything past you. Yes. We used to live together."

"Really?" Peter's eyes lit up. "What happened?"

"I had to run."

"Damn. Do you still care for her?"

"Very much."

"Sorry. That stinks. Does Camila know her?"

"Yes."

"But she doesn't know where you and Camila are now?"

"No." Casi shook his head grimly. "It's for her own safety. I don't want to talk about her here. I'll tell you about her another time, privately."

"Got it. Let me get you the framer's address. The Miami pictures are dope."

CHAPTER CIX

Love Can Make You Shine Like the North Star

The pre-Thanksgiving season kept Casi overly busy in the restaurant. Peter was looking forward to wrapping up his treatment. He wanted a break before the busy holiday season kicked in. Casi was pleased to see his friend's mood improving with the end of treatment in sight. Hopefully, he would feel better and less tired in the upcoming weeks. Casi prayed the doctor would give Peter a good report. *Santa Muerte* still sat on his desk for added protection and he glanced at it daily while muttering his thoughts.

Casi's recent phone calls to Helena were disappointing. She seemed distant, as if her mind was on other more important things. California, maybe? He was too busy to pull teeth so he let her be. If she didn't want to chat, he had plenty of work to keep his mind occupied. A few special events at the restaurant had him buzzing around the clock. He wanted Helena to make more of an effort and until she did, he would sit back and give her space. However, her silence hurt, a knife in the gut.

Casi didn't discuss any of this with Camila. She was consumed with special events and wedding planning. Her planning made him particularly nervous as he hadn't heard back from Maria. Should he have set a time limit for her research? Camila and Stefano were talking about a trip to Miami in the New Year. They wanted to get married at city hall, Stefano's idea. Their wedding reception would follow at the restaurant in the Bahamas, possibly in late February. Gracie was helping her plan the blessed event by sharing all her most trusted resources. It would be a small gathering, obviously. Casi was confident the result would be a visually stunning day, but that same confidence did not extend to his future brother-in-law.

The big move to Stefano's apartment in Miami was to take place March first, after his current tenants moved out. Casi was hazy on Stefano's work situation because whenever he asked Stefano if the hotel was allowing him to transfer to Miami, Stefano's answers were vague. Was Stefano counting on Camila to provide a job? He would have to discuss this with his sister at some point. He dreaded broaching the subject.

The thought of Camila leaving, evoked anxiety in Casi. Together with Peter, he determined not to tell Stefano about their checkered past. The fewer people who knew, the better. Casi was relieved Camila agreed with this decision. Some things were best kept buried in a mental crypt. Regarding Camila's departure, Casi didn't have time to wallow in self-pity. He was too busy at work. When he was alone in his apartment, he felt pangs of loneliness. Camila's presence had been sweet medicine for his sour side. She was the ice cream topping that balanced out a tasty, tart cherry pie.

A few days before Christmas, Casi was busy placing orders when Peter burst into the office, grinning shamelessly. His face was lit up like a holiday bulb.

"Casi, there's someone outside to see you."

"Can you handle it, Peter? I'm swamped."

"I think you'll want to handle this one yourself. Can I bring her back here?"

"Her? No, I'll come out. I don't want anyone in my office. Is it Rose?" Casi looked up at his screen, hopefully. He didn't see any familiar faces.

"No, not Rose, but I think you'll be happy to greet this client."

"I'll be out in a minute." Casi grimaced. Which woman could possibly make him happy besides Camila or Rose?

When Casi exited the office, he saw his sister standing on the beach. She was facing a woman seated on one of the beach benches looking out at the water. When Camila saw him, she waved him over. The expression on her face was beyond goofy. The woman stood up, and Casi studied her profile. From a distance, nothing registered as she was wearing sunglasses and had a baseball cap pulled low. When Camila gestured her to turn around for the big reveal, Casi gasped. His heart felt like a speeding metronome. Helena was standing next to Camila, fidgeting. He broke into a run. When he reached Helena, he swept her off her feet and swung her around. Camila stepped back, giving them air space. Joining Peter at the bar, she watched her brother's broadening smile.

"How did you find me? What are you doing here?" Casi didn't know if he should be cross or overjoyed, but he was so happy to see Helena, he couldn't muster anger.

"I suspected you were in the Bahamas, I just didn't know where."

"How?"

"I saw the area code on one of your phone calls when we were in Tobago. I looked it up."

"I worked hard to leave no trails. The only person who could possibly have told you where to find me is Summer." Casi was trying hard not to be annoyed.

"Don't be mad at Summer. I pushed her hard to tell me. I suspected she knew when she refused to search for you after I figured out the area code. She only gave me your location when

I told her, I intended to stay. Do you still want me to stay?" She smiled tentatively.

"Are you kidding? Of course, I want you here. You gave no indication in our phone calls that you had any interest. In fact, I feared the opposite was true. When you got the part in L.A., I gave up completely."

"I was conflicted, but I've decided against L.A. There's more I need to tell you, Casi. Sit down."

"More? Just tell me. What else is there?" His heart was skipping beats.

Helena took a deep breath and spoke softly. "We're having a baby, Casi." She was fidgeting again, and her hand traveled to her tummy as she waited for his reaction.

"What?" He searched her face. Was she serious? She looked so anxious.

She continued, "I didn't plan it, obviously. It was a total surprise. At first, I was upset because of the movie part, but when I thought about it, I knew I wanted this baby so much more than a minor film role. I needed to tell you this in person. That's why Summer shared where you were."

"A baby!" Casi was flabbergasted. "Oh my God. What a blessing!" He looked down and saw a small bump under her flowing white top. Gently folding her into his arms, he placed one hand on top of hers on her belly. "I'm so happy you came." He felt her melt against him in relief as he kissed the top of her head. Over Helena's shoulder, he winked at Camila and Peter, who were watching from the bar, pretending to be busy, but gaping like owls.

"When are we having our baby?" Casi looked into Helena's face, noticing its slightly rounder shape. He cupped both sides of her chin and kissed her. He could barely contain his joy.

"In early June." She was smiling now.

"What? Why didn't you tell me sooner?"

"I didn't know until a month ago, and at first, I wasn't in a very good place. I was in shock. I needed time to sulk. Then, I talked to Summer about my options for a few weeks. She was so patient and she helped me figure things out. She's a good, caring friend."

"Summer told you to come here?" Casi felt his heart softening toward her.

"No, she told me you had a right to know. I was considering abortion in the beginning because I got the film part and was confused about what I wanted. After talking to Summer, I realized I couldn't go through with an abortion. It just didn't feel right. I realized I didn't want the stupid part in L.A. anyway. I wanted to be with you and have our baby. I've always wanted to be with you. I guess the pregnancy made me realize it."

"And I was always praying you'd come, but lately, I wasn't very hopeful, especially after what happened in Brazil. I knew how scared you were."

Helena sighed. "I was, but Summer helped me arrive at my decision by listening and asking me all the right questions. She didn't push or influence me. I came to this decision myself under her guidance. I'm so glad you're happy because I put all my belongings in storage and rented out the apartment in Paris. I have no home to go back to now. I took a leave of absence from the agency as well."

"You have a home here, Helena. I would have tried to talk you into having our baby, even if you didn't want to join me. Camila and I would have wanted my child."

"I knew that in my heart. I guess that's why I waited to tell you. I just needed time to figure everything out for myself. I love you, Casi. Always have."

"Do we know what we're having?"

"Do we want to know or should it stay a surprise?"

"We can decide later. It doesn't matter. As long as the child and you are healthy, I don't care."

She put her arms around his waist and rested her head on his strong shoulder. Pulling her close, he felt her beating heart against his chest. He was having a hard time processing his unexpected windfall. Fate was a bitch, but now he believed it came in the form of bliss, too.

"You just made this Christmas very special," he whispered in her ear. My two favorite women in the world are here to celebrate the holidays with me and I'm going to be a father. I don't think it gets any better than this. Those are the joys of life."

Casi motioned to Peter and his sister.

"Get over here, you two." His smile was infectious.

Peter and Camila walked to the beach, grinning.

"Peter, this is the love of my life. I'm hoping she's here to stay." He turned to Helena.

"Meet my inner circle. Camila you know, and this is Peter, my best friend and restaurant manager. I'm happy you've finally met."

"Hello. So nice to meet you. The pictures of you, really don't do you justice." Peter flashed a welcoming smile. "Has anyone ever mentioned that you look like Dakota Johnson?"

"No, you're the first. Thank you for that. It's so nice to finally be here, in Casi's world. I never imagined it would be so beautiful and fragrant. It's paradise, really." She turned to Casi, "Are you going to show me around your restaurant? The location is spectacular!"

"Yes, and then we'll take the rest of the day off. Is that ok, Camila?"

"You just got to work! I guess I can give you the day off," Camila joked. "Go have fun, catch up. Peter and I will handle things here."

CHAPTER CX

Holiday Scheming

The first few days Helena spent in the Bahamas, she and Casi took long walks on the beach and talked about their future. Casi knew the change would be overwhelming for her. Coming from the fashion world of Paris and New York, the Bahamas was a momentous switch. Secretly, he hoped his world would be enough for her after the baby arrived. He intended to keep her very busy at his restaurant. His game plan was to take her on wonderful trips when the restaurant closed in the summer and for long weekend jaunts whenever they suffered from island fever. He hoped this would mitigate any feelings of missing out on the big world. For now, Helena was excited about the prospect of working at the Sea Grape Garden with Camila and him, but Casi had his doubts. Camila, always well-intentioned, promised to show Helena how to run all special events. When Camila moved to Miami in March, Helena could take over the party planning. It sounded good in theory, but how would Matias treat Helena after having a stellar working relationship with his sister? Helena wasn't tough or thick-skinned like Camila.

Once the baby arrived, they would have to reevaluate Helena's happiness at work. Casi didn't want to think too far into the future. One day at a time. From past experience, he knew how fickle life could be. For now, he was still trying to digest the idea of being responsible for a child. The mere thought made his eyes water and his heart race.

Helena's unexpected arrival during the restaurant's busy season was somewhat challenging. Casi still had to go into the office daily to handle orders and payroll, but he managed to do so early, leaving Helena to lounge in bed and pamper herself. They decided to hold off on having her work at the restaurant until certain intangibles were settled. She would be introduced to the staff in January. Occasionally, she came to the restaurant as Casi's nameless guest. Nobody questioned her presence in the holiday crowd. When Casi was busy, she sat at the outside bar with Camila or Peter, wearing a hat and sunglasses.

Prior to a Christmas get together, Helena's first coming out event, Casi and Helena strategized on how to fabricate Helena's background. They also needed to rename her. Asking her to change her appearance proved to be a touchy subject, since Helena was pretty close to perfection. Because she was pregnant, her hair was getting darker, her high lights disappearing, and her body filling out. For now, Casi let the subject of transformation rest. They could always address it later.

When Casi finally introduced Helena to Stefano and Gracie, he referred to her as Sarafina. Since Helena's middle name, Sara, also started with the letter S, they both settled on Summer's fictitious name. Sarafina wasn't such a stretch. Helena was tickled the name had biblical origins. Casi would have to work on getting her new documents. His old sources were no longer an option but a marriage license would help matters along, he thought. It would facilitate a name change. At the right moment, he planned on popping the question. First, he needed to get his hands on a spectacular ring. His heart quivered at the thought.

Christmas was a quiet event at home with Helena, Camila, and Stefano. Their holiday meal was catered by Matias and it was exquisite—apricot duck, mashed sweet potatoes and three different greens. Amelie added a classic French lemon tart and a Bahamian coconut mango cheesecake for dessert. Peter and Chrissy manned the restaurant which closed after brunch at 3pm. For Christmas, Casi treated Helena and himself to a high-speed blender and an electric fireplace. His purchases arrived just before December 24rth, so Christmas eve and day all his guests sipped spiked eggnog in front of a lukewarm, crackling fire. Helena's eggnog was of the virgin variety.

Gracie and Peter stopped by after the restaurant closed, to have dessert and a drink by the new fireplace. They came bearing gifts, a jar of Gracie's homemade sea grape jam and a beautiful sarong for Helena. Casi couldn't believe his luck—for the first time since childhood, all his favorite people assembled in his home for a major holiday. It was everything he hoped for, dreamed about for so long. He had to pinch himself to believe that Helena was here to stay and he had a growing family who cared about him and who he loved.

CHAPTER CXI

Holiday Bliss….Ends with a Bang

The arrangements for New Years' Eve were in the planning stages way before Christmas. Weeks before, Peter had asked Casi and Camila if they wanted to celebrate big on Dec 31st, and party with a popular Bahamian band.

"We can sing and dance our way into the new year. What do you think?" Peter's enthusiasm was contagious. "Let's start the year on a good vibration, man."

Casi was pleased to see his old spark back. "That sounds good to me, let me check with Camila."

His sister was excited and on board. "We deserve a fun night off. Let's do it. When was the last time we celebrated big? I can't even remember."

The next day they collectively decided to work out a prix fix lunch schedule for the holidays. Since Casi pretty much worked around the clock, he decided early on to close the restaurant midday over the Christmas and New Year holiday. They would host spectacular prix-fixe lunches only. These he could easily swing with just his regular staff, and they brought in good revenues without having to splurge on extra decorations, temporary hires and expensive entertainment all of which was risky and stressful. He decided to leave the big parties to the big hotels.

With Helena's surprise arrival, Casi was particularly glad he had made that decision. It gave him the opportunity to introduce his girlfriend slowly and in informal settings. For the people who didn't know Helena, she didn't look pregnant. With flowing clothes, she looked radiant. The debilitating nausea had subsided. Casi was looking forward to celebrating the arrival of a new and exciting year with those he loved.

On Friday, Dec 30th, Casi took Helena to his favorite restaurant on the island, the one he had modeled the Sea Grape Garden after, the Blue Sail Restaurant Beach Bar at stunning Sandyport Beach. It boasted a traditional white two-story building with spectacular water views, luscious vegetation and a white, casual chic interior. The menu was a mix of French fusion, infused with Bahamian touches. It also advertised a pizza oven which Casi had studied closely before building his own. He and Matias had gone for lunch one day and checked out the oven and the fare.

Tonight, Casi ordered for Helena and himself. They arrived well before sunset so Helena could admire the ethereal surroundings. Within minutes they were sipping strawberry margaritas, one with tequila, one without, in a fragrant bubble of love, at a picnic table overlooking hints of palm tree shadows in the sand. When the waitress interrupted their blissful moment, Casi put in an order of all his favorite finger foods—Bahamian conch fritters with calypso sauce, calamari with aioli dipping sauce, BBQ chicken and jalapenos tacos, and the pizza primavera. Life couldn't be much better than this he thought as the sun set in a fiery blaze.

Casi, Helena, Camila, and Stefano celebrated New Years' Eve with a festive dinner at Baha Mar's Fi'lia, a top-notch Italian restaurant. They enjoyed a sumptuous meal laden with fresh herbs, olive oil, accompanied by handmade artisanal breads. Clinking glasses with *aperol spritz,* they toasted the close of a tumultuous year and shared their heartfelt wishes for the new one. As they were leaving, Stefano stopped at the entrance of the hotel's casino.

"What do you think? Shall we stop in and see if we can start the new year off right? With a financial boost?"

"The only boost here will be for Baha Mar's coffers. Besides, I told Peter we would meet him by 10pm. If we don't show up on time, they'll give away our table." Casi nudged Helena toward the exit.

"Another night, Stefano." Camila linked her arm through his, pulling him along.

They arrived at the Atlantis in Casi's jeep. Peter and Gracie were already there, holding the table for six. As usual, Peter had negotiated a good spot, mid-room by the dance floor. Jalen and the Jamaican Diamonds were the opening act for the Baha Men, an international band that liked to come home to Nassau for the holidays and for the Junkanoo. Casi and Helena danced the night away and drank champagne until well into the morning hours. The atmosphere was festive and tropical, with exotic edible blooms decorating the tables. Colorful streamers hung from the ceiling and sparkling confetti was periodically shot into the air over the dancing crowd.

On the way home, Helena was the designated driver, a challenge since in the Bahamas they drive on the left side of the road. When they reached the Baha Mar, they said good night to Camila and Stefano, who were beyond tipsy, and walked around the hotel grounds admiring the rainbow lit fountains and the fire pit.

Helena reminisced, "This was even more fun than the New Year's Eve party in Paris. Do you remember that magical night?"

"I do. It was spectacular in a sophisticated way."

"I couldn't get you to dance back then. You were always so tense in public. You're a much better dancer than you think."

"Thanks! I guess not having to watch my back every second makes dancing all the more enjoyable," Casi reflected enjoying her closeness.

"What a nice feeling that must be. To finally let loose." Helena smiled and rested her head on his shoulder. "I love the new you even more, if that's possible." She wrapped her arms around his waist and leaned her forehead on his collarbone, nuzzling his neck.

"Woman, stop talking and kiss me."

Helena giggled as he tightened his embrace. The stars had never fully aligned for him until now and he was grateful. The holidays had been perfection. He reflected on his first full year in the Bahamas and recognized how far he had come from his difficult, humble beginnings in the underworld of Tampico. *Good karma is the best revenge.*

Casi was still humming to the Baha Men's hit song, *Night and Day*, when he awoke the next morning, his arms wrapped around his future wife, who gazed at him with adoration. From his nightstand, he pulled out a small, black velvet ring box with the gold inscription *cathleen helene b. jewelry*. Swinging his legs out of bed, he kneeled, opening the lid in suspense-evoking, slow motion. Carefully, he lifted the two-carat marquis-shaped, pink diamond perched on a delicate 18 kt white gold band set with micro pave' diamonds and asked, "Helena Sara Majewski, will you marry me and change your name to Sarafina Santos?"

"Yes!" Helena giggled as he slid the ring on her slender finger. "I will marry you, Casimir Santos." She marveled over the ring. "I love this stone. It's magnificent!"

Casi smiled. They sealed the moment with a passionate kiss and slid down under the covers, his hands exploring her curves. Casi's phone interrupted the tender moment and his rising heat. Thinking it would be Camila, he picked up without checking the caller ID.

"Happy New Year, Casi. Maria Alfaro here. We need to talk." Overseas static permeated the air waves. "I waited until after the holidays to contact you. I'm afraid I have some bad news. You're not going to like what I found out about Stefano Salas."

To be continued...

Island Allure and Black Magic is book three in the **Crenston Family Suspense Series** featuring the globe-trotting Crenston family and their extended inner circle.

The Santos siblings, who recently broke away from the dangerous Flores posse have built an idyllic life in the Bahamas. Cutting all ties to their Mexican cartel roots, they both found love and started a small empire. When Casi gets a phone call from Maria Alfaro, his Cuban private eye in Miami, the news surrounding his future brother-in-law shakes him to the core. He needs to shatter his sister's wedding bliss. To make matters worse his bored and vulnerable fiancée gets entangled with a dangerous psychic, inviting a new kind of danger into the fold.

The Crenston family seems to have an uncanny propensity for encountering trouble, especially when in the vicinity of Casimir Santos, but more often than not, they manage to bounce back with minor scuffs and bruises. An uncanny penchant for risk-taking always keeps one or more family members immersed in hot water, but in a pinch, the whole family rallies and comes through as a team. When Summer Crenston is hired to write a script following the contentious life of a dangerous gambler, she can't resist. Summer loves a challenge. The fact that the story is based on truth fuels her heated resolve. However, when things start going sideways, will her family and friends be able to protect her? Good Karma has occasional lapses.

Book One- The Rogue Tangerine Tablet

There is nothing Cara Crenston wants more than to have her three globe-trotting children home in New York for the holidays, however falling in love with a charming Frenchman on an impromptu trip to Paris and crossing paths with a Mexican smugglers' ring whose family kingpin shares her unbridled passion for quality ceramics, puts a crimp in her plans. Cara is unknowingly drawn into a complicated web that involves her unsuspecting children in a sinister string of events. Each family member has their own brush with the malevolent smugglers, who think nothing of leaving an inky trail of dead bodies across the globe. The only way Cara can keep track of her scattered life is with her trusted tangerine tablet, but when it goes missing all hell breaks loose.

Acknowledgement

571

I would like to thank:

Sandy Ebel at Personal Touch Editing for making my manuscript shine. Her eye for detail is appreciated.
Donna McGullam and the Westhampton Writers Group for their weekly criticisms and valuable input.
Lacegarden for digitally enhancing and formatting my illustrations.

About the Author

572

Bleue Rose lives and works in New York where she makes precious hand-crafted gold jewelry in a collaborative studio. She has studied art, art history, design, gemology, jewelry making and creative writing. She loves the balance of both worlds, splicing the artist's and the writer's crafts. Bleue was born and raised in central Europe and loves to travel to remote destinations worldwide. Her writing is a reflection of her travels. Her stories are strictly her imagination at work.